Forest Folk

Book Two of the Folklore Cycle

John Hood

Paperback ISBN:

eBook ISBN:

Published by Defiance Press and Publishing, LLC

Bulk orders of this book may be obtained by contacting Defiance Press and Publishing, LLC. www.defiancepress.com.

Defiance Press & Publishing, LLC

281-581-9300 info@defiancepress.com

In honor of my Warriors Three,
Who form our growing family tree,
To graceful Jerri, kick and cuff,
To mighty Andrew, trusted, tough,
To playful Alex, rapier wit,
With each your gallant team outfit.
Pray sink your roots in fertile ground,
Make strong your trunk, stand fast, confound,
And stretch your branches wide and high
To gather all, to fill the sky.
Adventure beckons — peril, too.
The story's end depends on you.

Prologue – The Bridge

It was the forked tail that did it.

Not the curved talon on its spindly foreleg. Not the sharp edge of a hoof on its massive hind leg. Not the jagged prongs of its enormous antlers. Not the daggerlike fangs that jutted incongruously from its cervine mouth.

No—it was the triangular blade on the end of its whiplike tail that had slashed him. Keen as a razor, it left a painful line across Samuel's forehead. He felt the blood trickle down his face. It covered his eyes, stinging and blinding them. He tasted the blood on his lips. When he parted them to scream in agony, the blood flooded into his mouth, choking and silencing him.

So it wasn't Samuel who emitted the bone-chilling shriek. Angling its bat-like wings to propel its fifteen-foot-long body into a tight turn, the creature bared its teeth, shrieked again, and dove straight at Samuel's helpless prostrate form.

"Wake up, Colonel!"

Samuel cracked open his eyes and saw the earnest face of John Chavis hovering over him. Moisture trickled down the black man's cheeks, as if he'd been weeping. But Samuel's face felt wet too. So did his arms and legs. Was he drenched in his own blood? Had the flying monster dealt him a mortal wound? Was it circling for another attack?

"Wake up, sir!" Chavis repeated, gripping Samuel's shoulders and shaking him. "You're having another nightmare!"

It was then that Samuel realized he wasn't in New Jersey. He wasn't a captain in Dan Morgan's rifle corps. He wasn't dawdling by a campfire while General Washington's army fought a pitched battle a few miles away at Monmouth Court House.

And it wasn't the year 1778. It was 1798.

No, he was *Colonel* Samuel Houston now, of the Rockbridge County militia. War veteran. Farmer. Scholar. Cofounder of Liberty Hall Academy. Father.

He saw another face. "Are you all right, Daddy?" asked Sam, his five-year-old son.

At that, Samuel Houston smiled. Young Sam's face was wet too. They were all wet, of course—a light rain was falling. Samuel could hear it drizzling the fallen leaves and drumming a rhythm in the shallow water of Cedar Creek. He could see a fine mist glistening in the soft morning light. Sitting up, Samuel glanced around the camp. Chavis had already pulled their supplies under a tent. The man must have been up for a while. Samuel could see a fishing pole jabbed into the soft mud, its line cast far into the flowing water.

He was a remarkable fellow, that John Chavis. He'd worked for many years as an indentured servant for an attorney with a huge library. A largely self-taught reader, John had spent much of his spare time in the library, eagerly devouring books on history, theology, philosophy, and ancient mythology.

Like Samuel, John Chavis had fought in a Virginia regiment during the war with Britain. Afterwards, as a free black, Chavis had married and worked as a tutor, then he'd relocated to Princeton to study with John Witherspoon to become a Presbyterian minister. After Witherspoon died, he'd come to Liberty Hall Academy in 1795, seeking to complete his studies. While some had expressed reservations about educating a black man, Samuel had insisted John Chavis be given the chance.

The other trustees agreed with him. After all, Samuel had cofounded the school. And he still served as its secretary.

It was in that capacity that Samuel had written a letter to Mount Vernon, thanking former President George Washington for the gift of canal company stock that had rescued Liberty Hall from financial ruin. It was Samuel who'd suggested honoring their new benefactor, and after the response letter from Mount Vernon expressed no objections, it was Samuel who'd suggested a formal ceremony to celebrate the newly renamed Washington Academy.

A ceremony that, Samuel just realized, would begin in a few short hours.

"I'm fine, son," he said as he rose unsteadily to his feet. "Thanks for waking me up, John."

"Was it the same dream you had before, Colonel Houston?"

"Yes." Samuel shook his head, still a bit groggy.

Nightmares didn't have to make sense, he knew, but this recurrent dream was particularly jarring because it mixed clear recollections of something that happened twenty years ago—Morgan's Rifles missing the biggest battle of the war because of a badly written order—with a ridiculous image of some flying devil of a monster swooping down on him.

It was the kind of image his precocious son Sam might conjure out of his vivid imagination and then put in a bedtime tale to scare his brothers and sisters. But Colonel Samuel Houston, a pillar of Rockbridge County society, ought not to be prone to such flights of fancy.

The rain had stopped. "Better get packed up," Samuel said, stooping to roll up his thin blanket. "Guess we'll have to settle for the trout we caught yesterday. Shouldn't be late for the ceremony."

Chavis looked longingly at his fishing pole and sighed. Shortly after, he bent over to get started. Young Sam wasn't so compliant.

"I don't want to go!" he insisted. "I want to play on the bridge!"

"You sound just like my son Anderson," said Chavis, chuckling as he slung the cookpots over the withers of their packhorse. "Come on, Sam, wrap your bedroll."

Uncharacteristically, the boy made no reply. Focused on their tasks, neither man thought to investigate the reason why. It was several minutes before they realized the boy was gone.

▲▲▲

It took no great feat of woodcraft to follow young Sam's trail. They knew precisely where he was headed. Samuel Houston and John Chavis soon reached a bend in the creek and looked up at the natural feature that gave Rockbridge County its name. Spanning ninety feet from cliff to cliff, the High Bridge of weathered limestone, dotted with thin lines of evergreen and bright bursts of autumn-colored leaves, towered some two hundred feet above Cedar Creek. It was as if some giant hand had punched an enormous hole in the hillside so the modest creek could make its way south to feed the James River.

The men soon found they weren't the only ones walking along the creek and gazing at the High Bridge. Several dozen paces ahead trotted young Sam and a taller youth. Sam was gesturing and chattering up a storm. The newcomer, clad in a hunting shirt and buckskin leggings, looked to be about thirteen. Where young Sam's hair was light brown and his eyes blue, the older boy's hair and eyes were both dark.

"Whoa there, where do you think you're going?" Samuel called out as he and Chavis hurried to catch up. "Who gave you permission to—"

But then he stopped short, for his eyes had followed young Sam's pointed finger and seen what the boys saw: a group of men walking out onto the High Bridge. Three wore the standard dress of gentlemen: suitcoat, waistcoat, breeches, shirt, cravat, and cocked hat. Two of the gentlemen were tall and thin, while the other was broad-shouldered and heavyset. The fourth man, who had been the first out on the bridge, was a bit shorter than the others and barrel-chested. He wore buckskins and a beaver hat with a flat brim.

The men were looking in the opposite direction as Samuel Houston and John Chavis caught up with the two boys.

"You're right — that's really somethin'!" said the taller boy to young Sam. "I saw an old rock bridge one time back home in Tennessee, over near Lost Creek. But this-un's twenty times higher."

Samuel Houston cleared his throat behind them. "Tennessee, eh?" he said as the startled boys whirled around. "You're a long way from home."

"He's my new friend!" young Sam interjected excitedly. "His name's David."

"Pleased to make your acquaintance, young man. I'm Colonel Samuel Houston, and this is John Chavis."

The youth nodded amiably. "To answer your question, sir, I was hired out to a friend of my pa's to help drive a cattle herd over the mountains. But I aim to get back to Tennessee right quick."

"Not much for traveling far from home, I take it?" Samuel asked.

"Oh, naw, that ain't it," said the youth, brushing off the suggestion with a languid wave of his hand. "I like seein' new sights and swimmin' new rivers and huntin' new forests. But all the best spots are in Tennessee."

The two adults guffawed loudly. "Why, now, how could you know that unless you went off and explored the other places?" Samuel asked. "You said yourself you've never seen the like of this High Bridge here."

"I'll give you that-un," said the young man with a nod. "But I figure the more west you go, the more adventure a man can see."

"So, it's *adventure* you want, Davy," Samuel mused. "Well, when my company first went off to war—"

"That's not my name!"

Samuel was taken aback by the youth's interruption.

"I'm near grown, not some little boy," the newcomer insisted. "I've already killed more bears than you can count! I'm half horse and half alligator, with a touch of earthquake. I've got the prettiest sister, the fastest horse, and the ugliest coon dog in the county. I can outrun, outjump, throw down, drag out, and whip any Virginian. I've got a man's name, a real man, a man of Tennessee. I'm David—David Crockett!"

Young Sam looked up in shock at his father, evidently expecting his new friend to get a severe scolding. But Samuel Houston found that he couldn't stop laughing; neither could Chavis. After a moment, David and young Sam joined in. Then the boys stomped over into Cedar Creek, splashing each other and John Chavis with water. Chavis responded by chasing the young Tennessean down the creek, howling like a wolf.

As Samuel watched the three giggle and play, his own thoughts took a serious turn—and, not for the first time, turned toward the very place that this bold youngster David Crockett had been bragging about. The Houston family had lived in Rockbridge County for generations. Samuel loved the place. But all his years of militia service, inspecting far western outposts at his own expense, had distracted him from tending to the farm. He was deeply in debt. Several neighbors in similarly dire circumstances had left Virginia and started over in Tennessee.

Perhaps the Houstons ought to do the same, Samuel thought.

With his mind elsewhere and the others still frolicking in the creek, it had escaped their notice that the four strangers were no longer atop the High Bridge. Samuel didn't realize it until he heard footsteps behind him. Turning, he saw the four men standing on the rocky bank of the creek beneath the arch. Three were looking intently at a spot in one rocky wall. The fourth, the one in buckskins, was looking directly at Samuel.

In an instant, they recognized each other. They'd met during one of Samuel's inspections of frontier outposts. The man was a militia colonel, just like Samuel.

He was Daniel Boone, the famous long hunter of Kentucky.

Samuel was astonished to see Boone in Rockbridge County. He was even more astonished as he flicked his eyes to Boone's companions and recognized two of them as well. The heavyset man was Isaac Shelby, the former governor of Kentucky—Samuel had once bought supplies from Shelby for the garrison at Fort Randolph—and the tall, thin man running his hands along on the rocky wall of the High Bridge, as if looking for something, was another former governor, this time of Samuel's own state of Virginia.

In theory, seeing the tall Virginian should have been no surprise. After all, the man owned the High Bridge and all the surrounding land. But he was an absentee owner. As far as Samuel knew, he hadn't seen his property in more than fifteen years.

Why visit now? Samuel asked himself. As the vice president of the United States, surely Thomas Jefferson had more pressing matters to attend to.

"What's the governor doing here?"

Samuel found David Crockett standing next to him. Young Sam and John Chavis were still splashing each other back in the creek.

"Neither is governor anymore, young man," Samuel corrected him. "And since you're from Tennessee, how is it that you recognize them, anyway?"

"He is *too* still governor!" David interjected.

"Who is?"

"John Sevier—that man right there," said the young Tennessean, pointing at the man Samuel hadn't recognized.

It was at that moment that Boone tugged the sleeve of Sevier, who then said something to Shelby and Jefferson. All four men looked back at Samuel. After what seemed like a long while, Boone turned and headed off along Cedar Creek at a leisurely pace. Sevier, Shelby, and Jefferson followed him.

An instant earlier, Colonel Samuel Houston had been wondering what could have brought those four famous men together. But now he suddenly realized there was nothing to be curious about; the men were just sightseeing, of course. Even before the sightseeing party was entirely out of his sight, Samuel had turned to the others.

"John, Sam, we best be getting over to Lexington or we'll be late," he said matter-of-factly. "Davy—I mean, David—nice to meet you. Staying around for a spell?"

Obviously confused, David stammered a reply. "My . . . my pa wanted me to work here for a while, but I don't . . ."

10

He stopped midsentence and looked over at Chavis and young Sam. Their puzzled expressions matched David's.

"Colonel, didn't you just see that?" Chavis wondered.

Now it was Samuel's turn to be confused. "See what?"

"They . . . they just walked into the wall!" David exclaimed.

"Who did?" Samuel still didn't understand.

"The strangers," Chavis replied. "Looked like they just up and vanished into the side of the hill—the whole lot of 'em."

Samuel felt puzzlement yield quickly to impatience. He had no time for games. He couldn't very well be late for the renaming ceremony. He didn't mind indulging his son Sam's fertile imagination from time to time, and the new boy from Tennessee was obviously fond of hijinks and tall tales. But Samuel had thought that John Chavis, at least, would have sense enough to know when it was time to stop playing around.

"Those are four busy men," he said as he began leading them back to camp. "They had to be on their way, just as we must."

The party walked in silence for several minutes. It was young Sam who broke it.

"Pa, where did the other ones go?"

Samuel didn't understand the question. "The *other* ones?"

"The little people standing with the big men. Where did they go? Are the little people busy, too?"

Chapter 1 – The King

The tunnel was thronged with colonists. Some were artisans and craftsmen hurrying from their residences on the edges of the settlement to their shops and forges in the central caverns, while others were heading home after a long day of work. Grizzled hunters walked by, bragging about their latest exploits, as tired warriors ambled on, grumbling about their latest duty shifts.

After twisting through several intersections, however, the corridor became much less crowded. Few colonists had a reason to journey in this direction, it seemed. So when Har the Tower reached his destination and bent low through the doorway, there were no other Dwarfs to witness him enter a room he'd never expected to see again.

A simple table and chairs stood at its center. Har remembered the time he had spread a map of North America over the table's surface to show his queen the position of the British and American forces. It had been crudely drawn; Har was no draftsman. Virginal had teased him incessantly about that map.

Walking to the table, Har brushed the edge of his dark-red cloak aside and placed a meaty hand on the back of one of the chairs. Pulling it out, he recalled the occasion his wide hips got stuck between the armrests. Virginal's taunts that day had been merciless.

Har would give anything to hear that voice once more, even if it expressed only the playful ridicule he had so often earned from her. But the queen's chamber was silent as the grave. And soon, it would no longer be a queen's chamber at all.

For those dwelling in the Dwarf colony of the Shenandoah Valley, nearly a year had passed since they lost their ruler. To those in the human world, in the Blur, it had been seventeen years. Queen Virginal's death at the battle of Yorktown had been a heroic end to a remarkable life—an end worthy of epic verse and fond remembrance. But to the Dwarfs of Grünerberg, the memory of Virginal's death at the point of a Pixie spear brought a bitter taste, not a bard's song, to their lips. Hailing from six often-contentious Dwarfish nations in Germany, the Grünerberg colonists had formed a coherent community in America due in large measure to Virginal's force of personality. Without her wise and decisive leadership, factional disputes now threatened to rend the colony apart.

Nor were the circumstances of Virginal's death without controversy. From the start, some Dwarfs had questioned her decision to intervene in America's war for independence in the first place. Many more Dwarfs questioned it after Yorktown. What had their intervention really accomplished? Did American independence really make Dwarfish Folk better off? Had it been worth sacrificing Virginal's life?

They blame me for getting her killed, Har knew. *Can I truly argue the point?*

He wondered if Grünerberg's new monarch would share their condemnation. Neither Har nor anyone else in the colony knew whom the Dwarfmoot had sent to America to replace Virginal. They knew only two things: The colony's new ruler was long overdue and male.

This will become a king's chamber, Har thought. *And given my reputation, I will likely be unwelcome in it.*

From behind him came a creak from the planked floor of the tunnel. Har turned and saw that his closest friend had, out of respect for his feelings, stayed just outside the door. Goran the Sylph—now widely known among the Folk of America as Goran Lonefeather— looked back at him with a knowing expression and shrugged his shoulders. The Dwarf motioned his friend inside.

Unlike Har, Goran didn't need to stoop to enter. Even the yellow-tinged tips of Goran's wings, stretching well above the feathered cap on his head, passed more than an inch below the door frame. Sylphs were, on average, shorter and slighter than Dwarfs. Standing more than four feet tall, Har had always towered over them all. Indeed, in his travels Har had met only a couple of Folk who nearly approximated his height: rangers from a Dryad colony in the woodlands of western New York. And even Dryads, while tall, tended to be willowy of build.

No one had ever called Har "willowy."

"Perhaps we should go back to the square," Goran suggested. "Whatever books the queen may have kept here, your mages seem to have returned them to their library."

The two friends had come to Grünerberg with many questions about magecraft—questions Folk mages had proved unwilling to answer. Har and Goran had hoped to find some answers in the library of the Dwarfs' Rangers Guild, only to discover that access to books on the detailed workings of magecraft was carefully controlled by the Mages Guild. Har suspected their ranger friends, Dela of the Gwragedd Annwn and Tana of the Nunnehi, would be equally frustrated in their efforts to wring secrets from the mages of their own villages.

Har, Goran, Dela, and Tana had all learned the troubling truth about magecraft during a meeting at Mount Vernon when an Oneida woman named Polly Cooper revealed herself to be a Thunderbird, a "monster" capable of assuming a human form. The Thunderbird told them she'd been penned within a Folk village and, along with other captive monsters, drained of vitality in order to fuel the village's protective Shimmer walls and other spells.

Har and his friends struggled with the implications of their discovery. Did Folk mages know that at least some of the monsters they milked for magical energy were intelligent creatures? Were the monsters drained until they died? Did their energy somehow power the spellsong that rangers employed as well?

And most importantly: Might there be some way to power magecraft other than capturing and draining monsters? If not, the very existence of Folk realms required a practice that Har and his friends found abominable—one that, they had to believe, many other Folk would find abominable as well if they knew about it.

"I suppose you are right, Goran," said Har, his hand still resting on Virginal's chair. "There is no enlightenment to be found in this room. Only shadows."

He looked around one last time, trying to burn every feature and furnishing into his memory. Wherever his search for the truth might take him, Har intended to take the best of Grünerberg with him—to take *her* with him, both the Virginal he knew and the Virginal he'd yearned to know.

The sound of raised voices and heavy feet pounding the floor of the tunnel interrupted Har's reminiscing. He shot a look at Goran, who was already heading to the door to discover the cause of the commotion.

"There was no transport spell!" a Dwarf shouted from down the corridor.

"He came all the way from Philadelphia . . . by foot?" asked a second voice in a skeptical tone.

"I will proudly serve under him again!" exclaimed a third.

14

Then the excited voices fell silent. Har could hear only the sound of a single pair of boots clicking and clacking as someone approached at a brisk pace. Even before the boots, and their owner, came into view, Har had guessed his identity.

Only one Dwarf lord could have arrived at Grünerberg by foot, without mage escort, without perishing in the Blur. And only one lord would have relished the theatricality of it.

Clad in a doublet and stockings of crimson and silver stripes, topped by a long crimson cloak, Lord Alberich stood in the doorway, dark eyes blazing, a dashing grin on his ruddy face.

No longer Lord Alberich, Har corrected himself. *He is* King *Alberich now.*

▲▲▲

"I had my doubts about this American adventure, I admit it, but my journey from the coast has confirmed its importance."

Alberich, onetime ranger and Dwarf lord of the Rhineland, scratched his short beard as he paced the floor of the Rangers' modest guildhall, a recently completed chamber built of chestnut and decorated with trophies and tapestries. The head of a massive Lindworm, its reptilian jaws yawning wide as if to strike, was mounted just above the entrance, while the head of a Bahkauv, with long fangs jutting incongruously from its bovine face, topped the opposite doorway leading into the library. Stopping to stare at a tapestry depicting an ancient Dwarf battle with a troop of Moss Folk, Alberich ground one fist into the other in what looked to Har like eager anticipation.

"America has game aplenty," said the new king of Grünerberg, "as well as thriving farms and towns offering an inexhaustible supply of humanwares. And there are other . . . opportunities."

Alberich turned to the three guildmasters in the room. Har had been surprised to find himself among the rangers called to an initial audience with their new king. Standing next to Har was Sudri, a squat, powerfully built ranger with a bushy reddish beard and a perpetual scowl on his plump face. Originally from Queen Virginal's realm in the Tyrolian Alps, Sudri had been stationed at Grünerberg during the American war.

Standing on the other side of Sudri was Lynd, a highly skilled spellsinger and the sister of Onar, who'd once been one of Har's closest companions. The bookish Onar's expertly chosen spellsongs

15

had more than once rescued an American army from defeat. Alas, like Virginal, Onar had been slain by Pixie warriors at Yorktown.

Har was the third Dwarf guildmaster in the hall, but Alberich had actually summoned *four* rangers to the meeting. Har looked over his shoulder at Goran, who leaned against the wall in conspicuous discomfort.

It was strange enough for King Alberich to insist on including Har, who'd been on a self-imposed exile from the colony for months. But Goran held no guildmaster rank among either the Sylphs or the Dwarfs; he was an outsider in more ways than one. *Why did Alberich want Goran here?*

"It is my intention not only to secure this stronghold but to prepare the way for more of our Folk to emigrate," began Alberich. "Conditions at home remain challenging. Shortages. Conflicts. A decline in the potency of spellsong. And the Elfish threat remains."

During his first encounter with Alberich at the Brocken Dwarfmoot so many years ago, Har had learned the man hated Elfish Folk with a deep passion. Alberich's Dwarfs of the Rhineland had repeatedly warred with the Elves of the Black Forest, and as a young ranger he'd reportedly carried out missions against other Elf nations.

"The Rangers Guild stands ready to serve you, Your Majesty," said Sudri stiffly.

"*Your Majesty.*" Alberich repeated the title with relish. "Has a nice ring, does it not?"

Sudri grimaced—or so it looked at first. *That may be his best attempt at a smile*, Har realized upon reflection.

"We are pleased to welcome you to the guildhall," Sudri added, "and we beg you to pardon its unfinished state. As a former ranger yourself, you no doubt can appreciate the challenges we faced in building a new colony during wartime."

Now it was Har's turn to grimace, though very intentionally. Sudri had advocated maintaining Dwarfish neutrality during the American rebellion and was now one of Har's harshest critics.

"I understand entirely—eh, *Sudri*, is it?" Alberich turned back to face the tapestry without waiting for Sudri's nod of acknowledgement. "The ranger's path is one of duty and action, not domesticity. Think nothing of your guildhall's unfinished state. The brave rangers of Grünerberg were out earning glory for themselves and all Dwarfkind, not staying home to paint walls and polish floors. It is what I would have done in their shoes."

16

Taken aback by the king's words, Har cast a sideways glance at Sudri, who seemed equally astonished but for a different reason; it was Sudri who had remained at Grünerberg while Har and the other rangers fought alongside the American Patriots. It was Sudri who was responsible for what meager furnishings the guildhall contained. Sudri had even polished its wooden floor.

To be sure, the colony had *needed* a ranger to stay home, to assist hunting parties and scout for threats. Har could hardly fault Sudri for doing so. Queen Virginal had assigned Sudri to the task—at Har's suggestion. But as Sudri returned Har's glance with a glower, it was clear the surly ranger had found yet another reason to fault him.

Har decided to change the subject. "Sire, you speak of the declining potency of spellsong back home. We have noted the same effect here—indeed, Americans seem more resistant to our spells than the average human. There are some questions . . ."

Alberich waved his hand and Har fell silent. "The lords discussed this extensively at our last Dwarfmoot," said the king, his back still turned as he admired the tapestry. "There is already a strategy underway to address the spellsong matter. Now, on a more pressing concern: What is your latest information on the Elves of America? How many colonies have you confirmed? What are their military capabilities?"

"The . . . the *Elves*, sire?" Har asked.

"Yes, yes, Elfish Folk—have you concocted some new dialect of Folktongue here in America?" the king snapped.

Lynd spoke up for the first time. "There is a troop of Elves in Georgia," she said. "They have battled periodically with indigenous Folk to their west, a Folk called the Nunnehi. During the war, the Elves joined the British side in hopes of gaining an advantage, but the Nunnehi soundly defeated them anyway. The Elves withdrew to their forest stronghold near the human settlement of Augusta."

"So, I presume we have formed a strong alliance with these Nunnehi," said the king, not bothering to frame it in the form of a question.

"Yes, sire, in a way," Har replied hesitantly.

Alberich whirled to face the rangers. "In a *way*? We are either allied or not. Which is it?"

"The Nunnehi were one of the few Folk to join us in supporting the American cause," Har explained. "Still, we took no part in their war with the Elves, nor did they ask us to."

The answer seemed to satisfy Alberich for the moment. "Nevertheless, in containing Elf aggression, they have done us a great service, and they have won an ally whether they know it or not. I would have them know it, by striking a formal alliance. I did not leave one Elf menace and journey across the sea only to see another take root here."

From behind them came a shuffling noise as Goran shifted his weight awkwardly from one foot to the other. The sound drew the Dwarfs' attention.

"Have you something to add, Sylph?" Alberich pressed, his eyes narrowing.

"I do, Your Majesty, if you will allow me."

"By all means," said the king, lacing his fingers together and thrusting them out to stretch his arms. "Why do you think I summoned you?"

Goran cocked his head at that and continued. "Thank you for raising that matter, King Alberich, because the truth is I do *not* know why you asked me here. I am only a guest in your realm and have no formal role in this hall. But if you seek my counsel, my knowledge of American affairs, I would advise a diplomatic mission not just to the Nunnehi but to the Elves themselves. Most Folk sided with the British cause, forming a Great Alliance. Many now regret it. The Elves may be among them. Their attack on the Nunnehi bought them nothing but death and destruction. They may welcome peace."

Alberich looked searchingly at the Sylph ranger. His gaze swept up from Goran's light-green stockings, leather jerkin, and forest-green cloak to his angular face. It seemed to Har that the king was not looking the Sylph directly in the eyes but past them, to the side of Goran's head.

"Is that what you would do in their place, Sylph?" asked Alberich. "Would you welcome peace overtures from your enemies, all the while clandestinely preparing your next strike?"

Goran looked perplexed. "I did not mean to imply that talk of peace from Elves would be a pretext. It may well be genuine."

The king arched an eyebrow. "You are either embarrassingly naïve or a talented liar. Your reputation suggests the former. But your heritage argues for the latter."

The Sylph seemed even more confused. "My *reputation*. My *heritage*? I do not—"

"I have not been in America long, but I have already heard tales of Goran Lonefeather and his idealistic crusades," Alberich interrupted with a smirk. "You turned against your own Folk when you discovered their plan to use monsters in battle, did you not?"

"Yes, that is so."

"Youthful naïveté, indeed," continued the king, "unless, of course, you had always planned to turn your cloak and merely expressed your so-called scruples as subterfuge."

Har the Tower could not stand by and watch Alberich insult his best friend. "Your Majesty, I must strongly object," he said, balling his hands into tight fists. "Goran is an honorable ranger who joined our cause at great personal sacrifice."

"Oh, I welcome the outcome of the affair, make no mistake," said the king, keeping his voice level even as his dark eyes flashed displeasure. "Generous rewards will always await all who serve Grünerberg."

Turning back to Goran, Alberich continued. "But let us understand each other plainly. I hold to the old ways and venerate the ancient lore. Although your Folk have played no known role in Dwarf history, your features reveal your natural allegiance. A Dwarf could no more fully trust a Sylph than he could an Elf."

Then the king brushed his hand up along his close-cropped beard and gave his rounded earlobe a flick. Goran's pointed ears flushed red as he caught Alberich's meaning.

"Surely you do not mean to suggest," Har cried, his exasperation impossible to contain, "that we should see as enemies any Folk whose *ears* resemble those of Elves!"

"I do not mean to *suggest* anything," said Alberich, now looking at Har with undisguised anger. "Long was I a lord. Now, I am a king. I do not suggest. I *command*."

Sensing the need for a tactical retreat, Har responded with a brief, curt bow.

The king smiled and let his hand drop to the hilt of the sword hanging from his richly embroidered belt. "You are young and rash, just like your friend. Experience will harden you. It will sharpen your edge. But just to be clear: I spoke only of trust, not of expedience. Over the course of the Eternal Contest between Dwarfkind and Elfkind, we have on occasion made common cause with other Folk—with Kobolds and other wretched Town Folk, with Goblins and other grotesqueries, even with pointy-eared Nixies of lake and stream who would be indistinguishable from Elves except for their blue skin. All were temporary arrangements, however. They served our interests at the time. Nothing more."

It was the first time Har had heard the phrase "the Eternal Contest" since his studies as an apprentice. Although individual nations had battled occasionally over territory and honor, it had been decades since the last continent-spanning war between Dwarfkind and Elfkind. The horrendous slaughter and devastation had finally led leaders of both sides to bring the long-running Eternal Contest to an anticlimactic end—or so Har had been taught.

I had no idea any Dwarf lord still thought in such terms, he reflected, then shivered.

King Alberich noticed Har's shiver but appeared to interpret it as a shrug of acceptance. He nodded approvingly.

"Consider this your first lesson in statecraft," he proclaimed. "I do not mean to speak ill of the dead, and Virginal was an admirable woman, but her inexperience has placed this colony in peril. That, we must rectify."

Har felt cold misery and hot fury war for supremacy within him. Staring stubbornly at the floor, he resolved to let neither show.

"Indeed, your Sylph friend has the right of it," Alberich said. "We *should* treat directly with our adversaries in America. I would know their capabilities and designs. Guildmaster Lynd, you will journey north to visit and investigate the Ellyllon and any other Elfish Folk you may find in Pennsylvania and beyond. Guildmaster Har, you will journey south to establish formal relations with both the Nunnehi and the Elves of Georgia."

Har glanced up in shock at the king, who reciprocated with an expression of mock surprise.

"Have your wartime exploits not prepared you for this task, Har the Tower?" Alberich remarked. "You may even take your friend along—that is, if Goran *Lonefeather* is willing to match words with deeds."

The Sylph met the Dwarf king's snide expression with one of resolve. "I will always be at your disposal to promote peaceful relations among the Folk of America."

"Peace has always been my goal," Alberich said. "Peace with honor, that is. Peace with security. Peace with access assured to the supplies we need to sustain and expand our colony."

Out of the corner of his eye, Har saw the knuckles of Sudri's large hand whiten as it tightened on the hilt of his curved alpine sword. No doubt the Tyrolean Dwarf feared he would once again be left at Grünerberg while others ranged far from home.

Perhaps Alberich had always intended to voice his next words. Or perhaps he, too, had noticed Sudri's dour disposition.

"Rangers of Grünerberg, why have you not yet gathered your membership together to elect a grandmaster for your guild?" the king asked.

"Your Majesty, with all that has happened since we arrived, we have not found the time," Sudri explained. "Besides, Queen Virginal preferred to deploy and consult individual rangers at her discretion, rather than rely on an elected grandmaster." At that, Sudri glanced sideways at Har.

Alberich smiled. "You should have *made* the time. Formalities matter. Guilds, no less than nations, require strong traditions and decisive leaders to thrive and grow. Do you not agree, Master Sudri?"

He did, indeed—or so Sudri's second grimacing attempt at a smile revealed.

▲▲▲

The steaming bowl of rabbit stewed in onions and greens should have brightened Har's spirits. He lifted his spoon half-heartedly, dunked a chunk of meat into the spicy broth, and looked across the table at Goran, who'd already slurped up half his stew since the two friends had sat down to lunch at one of Grünerberg's most popular eateries.

Har had eaten his last cooked meal at the village of an indigenous nation, the Yehasuri, some ninety miles southwest of Grünerberg. There, he and Goran had met with Thomas Jefferson, Daniel Boone, and several other friends. Then the rangers had remained for a few weeks with the Yehasuri. Magically concealed underneath a natural bridge of rock spanning a small creek, the village had well served their need for privacy.

Infrequently visited, the location also served well the needs of the Yehasuri, a reclusive Folk who preferred to live next to flowing water. It had surprised Har when John Sevier, the governor of Tennessee, had passed along the Yehasuri offer to host the meeting. Har knew Sevier and the Yehasuri had a lengthy history, although Sevier had steadfastly refused to share its details. Har also knew they'd been one of the few Folk to enter the war on the American side.

21

Only after the humans departed did the Yehasuri's aims become clear. They had little interest in the security of the new United States or satisfying Thomas Jefferson's insatiable curiosity about magical creatures; it was with Har, Goran, and Dela that the Yehasuri had really wanted to confer. Like the other Folk, they were puzzled by the declining potency of spellsong, the form of magic used to manipulate human perceptions and moods.

Alas, Har and his friends had no solid answers to offer on the subject. But something the Yehasuri said had whetted Har's curiosity. Asked to describe the founding of the village, the Yehasuri explained they'd chosen the natural rock bridge not just because of its remoteness and proximity to water but also because of its "magical bones."

"I have never heard that term," Dela the Water Maiden had said. "What do you mean?"

"Can you not feel it?" a Yehasuri had replied, his eyes widening with awe. "The rock, the very skeleton of the natural bridge, radiates elemental magic. It was expertly enchanted long before we arrived. Although abandoned, its Shimmer walls had not entirely faded. Its properties lessen the burden on our mages and make their magecraft more potent."

This revelation had still been the topic of conversation the day that Har, Goran, and Dela left the Yehasuri village, the first two headed for the Dwarf colony, the Water Maiden for her home in Tennessee.

"My father once told me the Sylphs had settled the Knob in part because it had been previously occupied by other Folk, but I did not understand the significance of that until now," Goran had said.

"I, too, was trained to look for sites with 'magical resonance,' " Dela had replied. "Now that I know what powers magecraft, I can see why."

The three friends had resolved to find out more—Dela from her Folk, Har and Goran from the records of the Dwarfs. But so far, Har's return to Grünerberg had brought only frustration, doubt, grief, and a new assignment from a new king whose fanaticism about "the Elf threat" struck Har as both baseless and ominous.

The Dwarf looked back at his friend, now dipping a piece of bread into his bowl to sop up the remaining broth. "Goran, I feel I must apologize for what Alberich said about you and your Folk. That kind of talk is no longer—"

"Why should you apologize for another man's words?" Goran mumbled, his mouth half full. "Besides, I am grateful for the opportunity he presented, whatever his intentions."

It took Har a moment to catch his friend's meaning. "Then you will go with me to Georgia?"

"Naturally," the Sylph affirmed. "The mission suits our needs. First, we can visit Tana's Folk at Blood Mountain and see what she has learned. Then we can use your diplomatic initiative to the Elves to gather more information. The more Folk we visit and question, the closer we will get to answers."

The prospect of a lengthy and potentially productive ranging with Goran at his side brightened Har's mood considerably. He dipped his spoon into the stew and drew out a hearty first swallow soon followed by many more.

There is nothing like home cooking, Har thought as he signaled a young attendant to refill their bowls. *Even if this place no longer truly feels like home.*

Chapter 2 – The Voyage

"Once past Spuyten Duyvil Creek, there'll be fewer boats in our path and we'll pick up speed."

The captain, a rotund young Dutchman, lounged against the rail of the sloop and pointed to a narrow channel off the starboard bow.

Dela the Water Maiden glanced briefly at the creek that led to the Harlem River and thus defined the northern tip of Manhattan Island. Then, shielding her eyes from the late morning sun, she looked up at the billowing white canvas of the mainsail that, along with the triangular topsail and the headsail, would propel the single-masted ship up the Hudson River from New York to Albany.

"Spuyten Duyvil, eh?" croaked an elderly man perched on a rum barrel, looking wistfully at the other passengers. "Did you folk ever hear the tale?"

Dela's eyes widened at the word "folk" but then relaxed. The old man hadn't meant "Folk," surely. He hadn't pierced her disguise.

To the humans on the ship, Dela's spellsong of illusion made her appear to be a middle-aged matron clad in the standard attire of the region: a light-blue gown worn over petticoats, dark stockings extending to stiff leather shoes, and a white lace cap on her head. In reality, Dela stood only two feet in height and wore a simple dark-blue shift cinched at the waist that closely matched the dark blue of her long flowing hair, contrasting sharply with her pale-blue skin. In her hand was her three-bladed trident that the humans saw as a simple walking cane.

"I would love to hear the story!" said an excited youth sitting next to another man on a long crate of citrus fruit. Both were finely attired young gentlemen, no doubt of some prominent merchant family.

"Then hear it you shall," replied the old man on the rum barrel, clearly happy to have at least an audience of one. He stood up, wiped his hands on the sides of his frayed knee-length breeches, and adjusted the neckcloth encircling his high collar. His surprisingly ornate cravat—woven of fine linen, fringed with lace, and tied in the American fashion with a small, tight knot—struck a sharp contrast with the old man's dingy shirt, which looked like it hadn't been washed in a very long time.

He looked around hopefully at the other humans on the deck, seeking a larger audience. There were eight other potential recruits. The sloop's crew consisted of the Dutch captain and three black mariners: an aged pilot with close-shaven gray hair, a wiry sailor with a pipe in his mouth, and a cabin boy wielding a mop.

As for the rest, in addition to Dela, the would-be storyteller, and the two gentlemen sitting on the crate, two other passengers lolled on the deck. Standing next to Dela and looking down at the river with a practiced eye was a massively built young man. Dressed in a blue-and-white checked linen shirt and long gray pantaloons, he had a broad, flat nose, short black whiskers on his cheeks and chin, and the largest biceps Dela had ever seen on a human. The other passenger—a small, barefooted man in raggedy clothes of mismatched colors and sizes—lay against a seed bag, apparently asleep. The little man's hat was folded in a distinctive fashion, at the back and on both sides, while its brim protruded long in the front. At the moment, the hat was pulled low, shading the sleeper's eyes from the sun.

My shipmates are quite the assortment, Dela reflected. *To observe humanity in its varied forms is, after all, why I am here.*

As a ranger of the Gwragedd Annwn, she'd have been more at home—and made faster time—swimming up the Hudson rather than sailing on its surface. But her mission wasn't urgent. Happening on the sloop being loaded with cargo, and hearing the captain call for any passengers interested in joining the voyage upriver, Dela opted for the sure-to-be-enlightening experience.

Assuring himself of a sufficient audience, the old man in the lace-fringed cravat cleared his throat. "This tale dates back more than a hundred and fifty years, to the early days of New Amsterdam. The gallant Peter Stuyvesant himself still led the colony and, through some mysterious means, seemed always to possess prior knowledge of future perils."

The young man on the citrus crate blew out an excited breath.

"That was how, before anyone else, Peter Stuyvesant learned one stormy night that the English were launching an invasion," the old man continued. "Determined to repel them, he sent for the stout, red-nosed trumpeter of the New Amsterdam garrison, Anthony Van Corlaer—who, it is said, could twang so potently on his bugle that it was as if a Scotsman were blowing his bagpipes under your nose. 'Go forth and rouse the militia!' the governor commanded. 'Let neither man nor beast nor vagary of fate hinder you!' "

The youth was hardly the only passenger hanging on the storyteller's every word. His older companion on the crate, the captain, the crew, the veritable giant of a man in checked shirt and pantaloons standing at the rail—all were engrossed in the tale. Even Dela found the storyteller's melodious voice and dramatic style compelling.

Only the small, raggedy man dozing on the deck seemed inattentive.

"Through pounding rain and howling winds, Anthony Van Corlaer rode forth to do his duty," the storyteller related, "traversing the whole of the isle of Manhattan. At every tavern, every warehouse, every farmhouse, every street corner, he stopped his horse but briefly to sound a blast from his horn. 'To arms,' the trumpeter cried, 'to arms all men of New Amsterdam! The English are coming!' "

It occurred to Dela that the tale's plot sounded vaguely familiar, as if she'd heard something like it before during her travels among the Americans.

The storyteller paused for effect. Then his eye widened. "When Van Corlaer reached the tip of the island and gazed over the Harlem River at the villages beyond, he could see no boats. 'I must have a ferry!' he shouted and blew his trumpet. But no ferryman could hear him over the raging storm, if indeed any were on the riverbank. So, his national pride and sense of duty overwhelming his caution and filling him with courage, Anthony Van Corlaer dismounted, gripped his trumpet tightly, and leapt into the fast-flowing water, intent on rousing the rest of the militia."

To her surprise, Dela felt her own breaths quicken, her heart beating faster. It was almost as if the storyteller were singing a powerful spellsong . . . but that couldn't be. Dela could readily see he was no Folk ranger behind some magical veil. He was human. Then she recalled something she once told her friend Isaac Shelby: *Words need not be infused with magic to exercise great power.*

"The trumpeter was halfway across the river when something brushed his side," the old man continued. " 'Neither man nor beast nor vagary of fate shall hinder me!' exclaimed Van Corlaer. Then a giant monster leapt from the surface, soared through the air, and dove back into the water, seizing the man's leg. 'Let go, foul demon of the deep!' shouted the hero, and he blew a thunderous blast. 'I will cross in spite of the devil!' But the thunder of the storm grew louder still. And there was no one on either shore to hear. Inexorably, the river devil pulled Anthony Van Corlaer below, until his bright-red nose was the only feature still visible above the surface. A moment later, it, too, was gone."

A sudden, stiff gust of wind hit Dela's face, breaking the trance of the storyteller's yarn.

"Yeow!" someone wailed.

Snapping to alert, her hand jerking instinctively to the shell necklace she used to amplify her spellsong, Dela turned to see the ship's sailor wincing in pain, one of the mainsail's halyards wrapped tightly around his calf. She quickly surmised that, distracted as he listened to the story, the sailor had absentmindedly wound the line around his leg. Then the sudden burst of wind had filled the sail, constricting the line.

The sloop captain jumped to the same conclusion and cut the line with his knife while letting loose a stream of expletives in his native Dutch at the sailor, the old storyteller, and anyone else in earshot. Dela know only a few words of the language, but it was enough to catch his meaning.

Then the gray-haired ship's pilot stepped forward, pointed a finger at the sailor's bleeding leg, and spoke rapidly in Dutch as he glared at the young captain. The two mariners argued back and forth for a while until the Dutchman grudgingly nodded and turned to the passengers.

"My sailor is badly injured, and Poppy insists we cannot sail the ship without him," said the frustrated captain. "We must return to the dock."

"Hold there," a new voice boomed. "I can handle her for ya."

All eyes turned to the huge passenger at the rail. His short black whiskers bristled, his flat nose snorted, and his mouth formed a determined grin. His dark eyes shone like polished obsidian.

"What's your name?" the captain snapped.

"Call me Bull," said the young man, his biceps bulging above his rolled-up sleeves as he pressed his fists together.

"You look strong enough," the captain said, "but sailing a sloop's no job for a beginner."

The young man's shining eyes met the Dutchman's. "I can handle her for ya," he said again.

The captain stared back for a few moments. "Show me," he replied.

And Bull did just that.

▲▲▲

Some time later, Dela sat with the other passengers and watched the newest—and by far the largest—crewmember skillfully trim the mainsail. As the sixty-foot-long sloop knifed through the water of the Hudson, Bull seemed to require direction from neither the captain nor the pilot to manage the sails. Before either could finish describing a task, Bull had already completed it.

"Any of you seen that one before?" the old storyteller asked.

"Not I," said the elder of the two men on the fruit crate. "But I'd be surprised if this is Bull's first time crewing a ship. My name's William, by the way."

"Mine's Deacon Peabody," the storyteller said, "but most just call me Old Deac. I work the Indian trade, so I've been up and down the river dozens of times. Never seen the likes of him, though."

"Sir, aren't you ever going to finish the tale of Anthony Van Corlaer and the Spuyten Duyvil?" the youth asked eagerly.

William looked apologetically at the Indian trader. "My little brother, Washington," he said, shaking his head. "Can't see what's right before his eyes."

Hurt and embarrassed, Washington shot William a dark look. Then, as if a dawn had come in an instant, the youth's face brightened. " 'In spite of the devil' the doomed trumpeter had cried. *Spuyten Duyvil*. Now I get it."

The boy's hearty laughter proved infectious. Dela joined in the merriment as well, although in truth she had, like young Washington, only just deciphered the wordplay of the tale.

The old Indian trader inclined his head in Dela's direction. "You laughter is most pleasant, and most welcome, ma'am. Is this your first voyage up the Hudson?"

The first one on the surface rather than beneath it, she thought. But aloud, she simply said, "No, I have traveled the river before, Mister Peabody. My name is Cordelia Lynn."

"Old Deac, if you please, ma'am," he insisted.

"I enjoyed your story immensely, Old Deac," Washington interjected. "Did you dream it up yourself?"

"Oh, heavens, no," the Indian trader replied. "Over years of travel by foot and wagon and sail, I've picked up many a tale. Some are light as a lark. Others are sad tales of sprites and goblins. Always used to just listen to 'em. Here lately, though, I feel like I ought to be telling 'em."

"I'd love to tell stories someday—and come up with new ones on my own," said Washington.

The young man's earnestness reminded Dela of a certain Sylph ranger, an image that brought an affectionate smile to her lips. "Why not go ahead and try your hand at it?" she asked Washington. "I once had occasion to hear the president of the United States, John Adams, make a speech in New York. 'Practice makes perfect,' he said. Sound advice, is not it?"

"The tongue is the only instrument that gets sharper with use."

The high-pitched, playful voice they heard seemed inconsistent with the gravity of the aphorism. But what really surprised the ship's complement was its source: the small, narrow-faced man whom they thought was still asleep on the deck.

Now the man was sitting up with his back against the seed bag, his too-large shirt hanging loosely on his thin frame and his cap pushed back to reveal straight black hair falling nearly to his shoulders.

"How, uh, how do you do, sir?" Washington stammered.

"I do as well as a servant of the Lord may expect, thank you. My name is John Chapman, but most folk call me Johnny." Then he winked one of his dark eyes at Old Deac.

"Your own tongue seems well-sharpened by frequent practice," Dela observed. "Are you a minister of the faith?"

"In a manner of speaking, ma'am," Johnny answered, scratching the scanty beard on his chin. "I lead no congregation. But as my teacher once said, 'All religion relates to life, and the life of religion is to do good.' I believe that a life lived in kindness is a ministry."

"Well said!" Old Deac exclaimed. "Bound for Albany?"

"To the wilds far west of that city, in truth," Johnny said.

"What about you two?" Deac asked the brothers. "What takes you up the river?"

"I've worked the Indian trade myself in the past, the Mohawk and Oneida mostly, but my brother's never been north of Tarrytown,"

William said, "Washington and I are headed to Johnstown to visit relatives."

Upon William's mention of the Oneida, Dela perked up. She had no intention of revealing her own travel plans, but to a Folk ranger, gathering information was always a priority.

"I have friends among the Oneida," she said. "A chief named Skenandoah and a woman named Polly Cooper. Might you be acquainted with them?"

William nodded. "Few visitors to the Oneida country would fail to be acquainted with Skenandoah. I once spent an afternoon with the chief and his friend Samuel Kirkland in Whitestown, a year or so before work began on the school there."

"The Hamilton-Oneida Academy, I think it is called," Dela suggested tentatively, although in fact she knew all about the school— and its namesake, Alexander Hamilton—intimately. But she also knew better than to let that show.

"Yes, that's it," William said. "But as to the other name you mentioned, 'Polly Cooper,' can't say I know it."

"Nor do I," Old Deac broke in, "and I've spent many a season among the Oneida."

"Ma'am, you mentioned President Adams," said William. "His predecessor once visited our family home in New York. In fact, my brother is named after that great man."

Dela saw young Washington beam with pride and suppressed a knowing smile. She was an even closer friend to the late George Washington than she was to Alexander Hamilton. As before, she chose to say nothing of it.

Johnny Chapman removed his distinctively cocked hat, ran his fingers through his long hair to sweep it out of his face, and then returned the hat to his head. "Washington, Adams, Hamilton—all fine men and servants to our new republic. Indeed, my father served under General Washington during the war and stood guard at his headquarters at Valley Forge. But it is John Jay whom I most respect."

Johnny's pronouncement left the two brothers, Washington and William, looking perplexed and Old Deac looking curious. "What makes you say that?" asked the Indian trader. "Wouldn't have taken you for one interested in foreign affairs."

"Oh, it's not for John Jay's treaty with Britain, although I cherish peace, or his service on the Supreme Court," Johnny explained. "Governor Jay has earned his reward on Earth and in Heaven for founding the Manumission Society, and for signing New York's new Emancipation Act. Though it will take many years, the slaves here will finally be free, praise be to God."

The last time Dela had seen Goran, which had been during their visit to the Yehasuri village, the Sylph had mentioned New York's new manumission law. Apparently all children born to slaves in New York after July 4, 1799, were considered free. However, they were still indentured to work as servants for their mothers' masters for some years. It was a limited measure. *Still, a welcome one.*

Turning away from the other passengers, Dela saw Bull rapidly pulling in a sheet while the old pilot, Poppy, watched with grudging admiration. Both were skilled sailors. Bull was white and free; Poppy was black and, Dela assumed, a slave belonging to the Dutch captain. That humans could put so much stock in such a meaningless difference as skin color frustrated and saddened her.

But we Folk have our own sins to atone for, she reminded herself, thinking of Polly Cooper.

▲▲▲

"The *New Moon* headed swiftly upriver, piloted by Captain Henry Hudson. Soon, a sailor spotted flickering lights and cried out in excitement. As the ship grew closer, he and his fellows saw bonfires on a plateau overlooking the river. What made the fires seem to flicker was neither wind nor fog but the strangely painted figures dancing around them."

Standing at the port rail, Old Deac was recounting another legendary tale and pointing to a place just south of a small creek. The brothers, William and Washington, were sitting nearby and hanging on his every word, as were the captain, the pilot, and the cabin boy.

Dela wasn't. She'd spent the last hour at the starboard rail, staring pensively into the river, wrestling with the problematic connection between monsters and magecraft. Rehearsing the questions she would pose about the matter to Chief Skenandoah—and to Polly Cooper, the shapeshifting Thunderbird. Wishing her travels were taking her not north to the Oneida country but south to Georgia, to visit her friend Tana of Blood Mountain and to meet the Nunnehi ranger's newborn daughter.

Her longing to visit Tana was, admittedly, tinged with feelings of envy about her friend's growing family. After the trauma Dela's Folk had experienced—a devastating war with Pukwudgies followed by a relocation to a new home under Long Island-on-the-Holston—they had finally begun to establish a new life. Many of Dela's surviving peers among the Gwragedd Annwn had started families of their own.

After Dela's brother died beneath of the points of Pukwudgie spears, their mother, Tesni, had become particularly insistent that her daughter settle down with one of the many unmarried men of the village. "You must make me a grandmother before you grow too old to accomplish it—and before I am too old to enjoy it," Tesni had insisted.

Dela certainly had no shortage of suitors. But as much as she wanted to please her mother, and as much as the prospect of children appealed to her, Dela found an even stronger attraction to the world outside her village.

To the Blur, and to those she had met there. She found herself missing Har the Tower with great affection. She found herself missing Goran with a mixture of unnerving emotions.

Standing on the deck, staring down at the river, Dela now experienced a more immediate longing—a reckless desire simply to cast aside her magical disguise and plunge into its welcoming, refreshing depths.

Dela heard Johnny Chapman walk up beside her, his bare feet making squishy sounds on the wet deck. "Why not?" he asked.

"Why not what?" she replied absentmindedly, still gazing down at the dark water.

"Why not dive in?"

Startled, the Water Maiden wheeled to face the raggedy man. Johnny's haggard look and reedy voice had made her assume he was middle-aged, if not older. Upon closer inspection, however, she judged him to be only in his mid-twenties.

"Sir, you forget yourself," Dela said, regaining her composure and affecting an air of offended stuffiness. "I have not the slightest intention of 'diving in,' as you suggest."

Johnny smiled. "It is written that 'Man looketh on the outward appearance, but the Lord looketh on the heart.' With the Lord's help, I see you plainly, Missus Lynn. Or is it Miss Lynn?"

Dela was about to reply when she realized that, unlike the other humans on the ship, Johnny was looking not at a spot above her head, not at the matronly human face projected by her illusion spell but downward, directly into the Water Maiden's blue-green eyes.

"Where his sailors saw only the leaping, undulating bodies of Indians dancing around the fires," spoke Old Deac from the other side of the ship, "Henry Hudson was sure he saw other figures: animals with the legs of men, men with the heads of animals, ghostly apparitions of gossamer white, shadows of forms still more outlandish."

The Water Maiden returned Johnny Chapman's gaze for a long while, then turned away, shrugging her shoulders.

"How long have you possessed the Sight?" she asked quietly.

Johnny looked down at the passing water. "If you mean how long have I glimpsed what others could not, little people and the like, then as long as I can recall. But only since I found my way to God have I truly been able to *see* anything, material or spiritual, for what it is."

Dela looked back at the strange human with his threadbare clothes and oddly cocked cap pulled down over stringy hair. She'd just met him. She had no sound reason to trust him. And yet his easy manner and kindly directness inspired trust.

"When you look at me, what do you see?" she inquired.

"I see one who would swim rather than walk. I see small size and big dreams. I see alabaster blue and battle red. I see riverweed and regret."

Caught unaware by his insights and resenting the intrusion, Dela drew her lips into a tight line. "Perhaps you see only what you imagine."

The human surprised her by kneeling on the deck and take one of her hands in his. "I can also tell you what I don't see—the beasts in a human form I've seen so many times before. Their hearts were false. Yours is not. Your heart is true. It is merely torn."

The tenderness in his eyes disarmed her. Rather than jerking her hand away, as was her first impulse, Dela squeezed his firmly before withdrawing her hand slowly to her side.

Behind them, the old man was continuing his tale. "It was at this same Danskammer Point, the 'Devil's Dance Chamber,' that much later a Dutch couple from Albany suffered their tragic fate. A spurned Indian suitor of the woman had provoked the jealous rage of the Dutchman, whose violence in turn earned him only merciless Indian vengeance . . ."

Johnny removed his cap and shuffled his bare feet. "You need not fear. In the presence of our Lord, I vow I will not reveal your secret to the others, Cordelia."

"I *know* you will not, Johnny," she whispered. "And my friends call me Dela."

▲▲▲

After a night spent anchored near the riverbank, the sloop resumed its course shortly after dawn. As Dela emerged from her sleeping berth and walked onto the deck, she could see distant peaks to the west draped in clouds lit by the morning sun.

"The Catskills," breathed young Washington, standing next to his brother.

"Not the tallest mountains you'll ever see, but they may be the prettiest," William said.

Yawning, Old Deac walked over to join them. "They aren't just pretty," he said, adjusting the cravat around his neck. "Look at how they lord over the surrounding country. Their magical hues and otherworldly shapes stir the imagination. They're fairy mountains, in truth, the home of wondrous tales and hobgoblin places."

Once again Dela studied the old Indian trader carefully, trying to figure out if he, like Chapman, might have pierced her disguise. But Deac was either entirely unaware he was in the presence of an actual fairy, or he was a gifted actor.

Washington was, of course, begging the storyteller to speak more about the "hobgoblin places" of the Catskills, and Deac happily complied. As Dela's attention was again fixed on her own ruminations about home, family, and duty, she caught only snatches of Deac's latest yarns. Some concerned magical beings who took the shape of animals to play pranks on the local Indians. Another was about an ancient spirit who lived on the highest mountain and used her magic to weave clouds out of cobwebs and chop the moon into stars once a month. Still another tale spoke of winged spirits whose eyes flashed lightning and voices boomed thunder.

"But such Thunderers are not to be found only in these fairy mountains," Old Deac clarified, his use of the name reclaiming Dela's attention. "There are also tales of winged spirits in the valleys and lakes to the west. I myself saw such a creature during my last trip across the narrow neck of land that separates Lake Erie and Lake Ontario. I witnessed it soar high into the sky and then dive into the great falls of the river."

Had he seen Polly Cooper herself? Dela had never journeyed to the famous Niagara Falls, but she knew the site was west of the Oneida country. She resolved to ask Polly about it when they met.

Presently the captain steered the ship to port and anchored at a small dock. "Esopus," he announced. "Delivering and loading. Feel free to go afoot, but be back in an hour, or you'll stay afoot."

Dela watched as the other passengers left to stretch their legs. The crew remained to manage the cargo, Bull inspiring gasps of astonishment from the others when he hefted two heavy crates of glassware, one on each brawny shoulder, and stepped with seeming ease over the ship's rail to the pier.

As the Water Maiden began to follow in Bull's footsteps, she saw two blacks approaching from a nearby road, where they had just left a horse and small wagon. The contrast between the two couldn't have been starker. One was a little girl, two years old or thereabouts, wearing a simple shift and a Dutch-style cap over tightly braided hair. The other, a middle-aged man in work shirt and trousers, was perhaps the tallest human Dela had ever seen.

That was saying a lot; her friend George Washington was a big man. The sloop's new sailor, Bull, was bigger still. Skenandoah was so tall that when Dela and her friends had first seen him at Valley Forge, they'd thought he was some sort of magical giant.

But the approaching black man must have been close to seven human feet in height. Though not as massively proportioned as Bull, he was still an imposing sight. His strong build, Dela realized, was likely the result of years of toil as the slave of some Dutch farmer. The newcomer and the sloop captain exchanged a few words, which Dela's limited knowledge of Dutch did not allow her to interpret. It soon became evident, however, that the black had come to accept a delivery of cargo. He turned and strode back toward the wagon, presumably to move it closer.

"James Baumfree!" the captain called after him, following that with another string of undecipherable Dutch words. As the two conversed some more, Dela looked across the walkway at the little girl, who was standing quite still and looking back at the Water Maiden with what looked like a mixture of wonder and glee.

Have I found another Sighted human on this voyage? Dela mused, smiling back at the girl while she sang in low tones to reinforce her illusion spell just in case. Then it occurred to her that she could, at least, translate the Dutch name the captain had shouted. *Baumfree. Free*

Tree. The man certainly stands as tall as one. Would that he and the little girl were as free.

▲▲▲

It was on the fourth day of the voyage that the sloop at last reached Albany. From here, Dela would go on without human companionship, first swimming further up the Hudson, then transferring to the Mohawk River to continue westward.

As she disembarked, Dela nodded to the captain and crew, observing that Bull was staying aboard rather than leaving with the other passengers. *Has the young man found his natural calling,* Dela wondered, *or just returned to it?*

The seemingly lazy Johnny Chapman had been the first passenger to pack up his belongings and make his way onto the docks. She found him waiting for her at the end of the walkway. "May you find the blessings of Heaven in your journey, Dela," he said, eyes twinkling.

"Your prayer is most welcome, although I do not intend to travel quite as far as Heaven," she replied with a chuckle.

"My teacher once wrote that Heaven is where the Lord is acknowledged, believed in, and loved," said Johnny. "In that way, a community of faith is a kind of Heaven. Are you headed to such a place?"

Dela nodded. "And you?"

The raggedy man lifted the strap of a sack over one shoulder and bowed. "I go, as the Prophet Hosea once advised, to sow in righteousness, reap in mercy, and break up the fallow ground." Then he tramped off down the road.

Next, the old Indian trader stepped off the sloop. "T'was a pleasure meeting you, ma'am," said Old Deac as he hurried off in the direction of the workmen unloading the sloop's cargo.

"Indeed it was," said the next departing passenger, William, tipping his hat. "May we be of service to you here in Albany?"

"No, thank you," she responded politely.

"Then we'll soon be off again, right, William?" said his brother, panting from either exertion or excitement. *Probably both*, Dela thought and favored Washington with a broad smile.

The youth returned it. "The next time you are in New York, my family would be honored if you would visit us at our home on William Street."

William aimed a scowl at his brother. "That was presumptuous, don't you think?"

"Clearly no offense was intended, and none was taken," said Dela, laughing playfully. "Perhaps we will, indeed, meet again."

"It will not be hard to find us on William Street!" the youth added as they walked away. "Just ask around for William or Washington Irving."

▲▲▲

Many days later, Chief Skenandoah bent his tall frame low and pointed toward the foundation of the modest building that housed the Hamilton-Oneida Academy. "That cornerstone was laid by someone you may remember from Valley Forge: Baron von Steuben, who served with General Washington's army."

And later as Peter's commanding officer in Virginia, Dela recalled. Von Steuben and her friend Peter Muhlenberg, the Lutheran minister turned general, had delayed the march of British forces on Richmond in 1781, thus allowing Thomas Jefferson and Virginia's government to relocate to safety, first to Charlottesville and then to Staunton.

Goran and Har had done their part, too, as had Dela's own rangers during the subsequent battle at Yorktown. As had Alexander Hamilton, one of the founding trustees of this very school.

It had been some time since Dela had last visited her friend, but Skenandoah looked as though he'd aged far more than the passing Blur years could explain. The Pine Tree Chief, as his people had once named him, looked more brittle and swayed less gracefully. Still, he clearly had a passion for the work he and his friend Samuel Kirkland were doing at the school.

Skenandoah led Dela to a high-backed chair next to a large, smooth rock and sat with evident relief. The Water Maiden climbed atop the boulder and looked down at his face.

There is a first time for everything. The thought made her smile.

"I know you have come with many questions," he said, "but I fear if you seek more knowledge of monsters and magic, I have few answers to share."

Dela tried not to let her disappointment show. "Anything more you can tell me of your time among the Jogah may prove useful. I have long known that for some of my questions, only Polly Cooper may be of help."

The Oneida chief shook his head gravely. "Polly cannot help you."

The Water Maiden paled and gasped. "Surely you do not mean that . . ."

Skenandoah held up a long-fingered hand. "No, she is not dead. Polly Cooper is very much alive and lives quite contently not far from here with her family."

"Her . . . family?"

"Polly married a fine man, a chief among the Oneida, and has children of her own," Skenandoah explained. "If you had grown up hearing the traditional tales of my people, you would not look so surprised. Many stories speak of a Thunderer and human falling in love and having children together. How this can be, I cannot say. But it is so, and I am glad for her."

Another friend now happily married and raising a family. Dela was lost in her own reflections for a few moments. Then she turned her attention back to the original issue. "Why do you say Polly can be of no help?"

"Because she no longer possesses a memory of her true past," Skenandoah replied, looking down in exasperation. "At first I noticed Polly no longer withdrew from the village periodically to soar among the clouds. Then she began to forget certain events and places. Within months, she remembered only life among the Oneida, and that I was her friend. For that, at least, I was grateful."

The two sat for a long while, he in his chair and she on the boulder. Then Skenandoah spoke again.

"A year ago, I made one more attempt to restore her memories. I took her west to the shores of the great lakes, where a friend told me he had seen Thunderers flying over the falls of the Niagara. I thought that if she could see one of her own kind, it might kindle a spark within her, a yearning to assume her true form and join her people in the clouds."

Dela saw a tear trickle from the Oneida chief's right eye.

"But you found no Thunderers there," she surmised.

Still fixed on a spot in the sparse grass, Skenandoah's eyes widened. "You leap too quickly, Dela. We *did* see winged creatures fly over the falls during our visit, on two separate occasions. The sight *did* bring to Polly's mind the tales of the Thunderers. But she recalled them only as creatures of legend, not as her true form. My plan failed."

Chapter 3 – The Spout

April 1801

Banking to the right, Goran circled twice above the thin, forested island while he studied the surrounding terrain in the late afternoon sun. His investigations confirmed it: The narrow river he and Har the Tower had been following bent only briefly to the northwest before resuming its southern course.

The Valley River had proved to be a welcome route to take through the Carolina mountains. Har was an avid fisherman, keen to start his mornings with a tranquil hour or two on a riverbank or lakeshore, resulting more often than not in a fresh catch for breakfast.

Goran appreciated Har's fresh-caught additions to their field rations. But the Sylph liked to follow rivers and creeks whenever possible for a different reason; they reminded him of Dela. Indeed, as Goran completed a third circle above the curved island, descending to land on its mossy tip, its shape reminded him of Long Island-on-the-Holston, the home of Dela and her Folk.

During their most recent time together in the Yehasuri village, Goran had seized every opportunity to make conversation with her. He'd asked after her mother, Tesni, and Dela's other surviving relatives and friends. He'd described in detail the flora and fauna he and Har had encountered during a ranging in Pennsylvania, including a saggy-skinned porcine monster that had managed to elude them in a thick forest of hemlocks and white pines. And Goran had spoken of human affairs, including the internal struggles of the new American nation, its conflicts with Britain and France over trade and maritime rights, and Daniel Boone's financial woes and plans to emigrate to Spanish Louisiana.

I talked and talked and still said nothing, Goran admitted to himself. *Why is it so hard to tell Dela how I feel about her?*

He wanted to blame the scars of war—not the physical scars, but the ones that cut deeper. The American war for independence had left him an exile and, in the eyes of many, a traitor to his Folk. Goran felt tremendous guilt for the pain his actions had inflicted not only on his own family but also on Har, his best friend. Goran had urged Queen Virginal to intervene personally at Yorktown, a decision that had cost the life of the woman Har loved. What could a homeless, widely despised ranger have to offer Dela other than a few hollow words of love and a lifetime of rootlessness and regret?

Goran also wanted to blame those around him. He and Har had never talked much about Virginal's death. Had Har forgiven him for his role in it? A few words of absolution from his friend would have lessened Goran's guilt. But Har had never volunteered such words, and Goran felt he had no right to request them.

As for Dela herself, whenever they talked, she routinely brought up the very subjects that magnified his shame and guilt. When she asked about his childhood, it only reminded Goran how much he'd hurt his father, Brae, and sister, Ailee, as well as the ruined lunatic who had once been his brother, Kaden. When Dela asked if he had finally decided to make his home with Har at Grünerberg, it only reminded Goran of how many Dwarfs resented his role in Virginal's demise. And when Dela invited Goran to find a home with the Gwragedd Annwn, it only reminded him how unrealistic it was to dream of becoming her mate. He had nothing to offer. In her village he would always be the Other, an outsider, a winged Sylph among wingless Water Folk, some of whom had lost loved ones in battle with Sylphs at Yorktown.

For his reticence with Dela, then, Goran wanted to blame the circumstances, what others said or did not say, or even what George Washington had so often called "Providence." But no matter how hard he tried, he couldn't fool himself. Goran knew the real truth of it.

In the end, I am just a coward.

"How far do you want to go?"

Har's question made Goran jerk. Then the Sylph realized his friend was only asking how much longer they should travel before camping for the night.

"Another hour, I'd say," Goran yelled. "It turns back to the south like we thought."

"As long as that gives me time to catch something for dinner before dark," said Har, his hands spinning the stout fishing pole he'd been using as a walking stick.

Goran leapt out over the water and quickly crossed the short distance. "Do you think Tana has made any headway with the mages of Blood Mountain?"

"We can only guess," Har replied as the two resumed their walk. "Mages seem intent on keeping their secrets from everyone but their rulers. Alberich said he and the other Dwarf lords knew all about monsters and magecraft. That must have been one of the reasons they chose to establish our American colony in the first place—because the stock of monsters in Europe could not sustain the growing population of Dwarfs needing Shimmer protection."

Goran nodded. "That was probably one of the motivations for my Folk as well, and for the other Folk of the British Isles—the Brownies, the Pixies, and the Folk of Scotland, Ireland, and Wales. They knew there would be more monster game in America. And growing settlements where they could obtain humanwares."

"The part about monsters still puzzles me," Har said. "If Folk came to America to hunt American game, why do we continue to encounter monsters from Europe? The beast that attacked us on our very first day at Grünerberg was a Tatzelwurm, a monster of Germany, not Virginia. How could it have arrived here before we did?"

Goran had been thinking a lot about this particular mystery. "Dwarfs are not the only Folk who emigrated from German-speaking lands," he pointed out. "For all we know, the Elf colony in Georgia is heavily populated by Elfkind from Germany. Perhaps the Tatzelwurm and other monsters stowed away on ships carrying Elf colonists to America, or were brought here in Elfish monster pens and then escaped into the wild. After we Sylphs arrived in America, we encountered Spriggans, Buccaboos, and other Cornish monsters we thought we'd left behind, never to see again. There must be some explanation."

Har laughed. "As there are surely explanations for all our other puzzles, Goran. So far, however, we have managed to collect no explanations but just more puzzles."

▲▲▲

Their remaining hour of travel was not yet spent when Har stopped, planted his fishing pole in the ground, and whooped with gusto.

"I refuse to walk another step, Goran!" he exclaimed.

The Sylph looked at him quizzically. "Could Har the Tower be tired so soon?"

"Not tired, my friend. Distracted. Look there!"

Har was pointing toward the water. The first thing Goran noticed was that, in the distance, the stream they were following ended in a confluence with a much wider river.

River junctions were, indeed, excellent places to rest and forage. That wasn't what Har had in mind, though, surely. Then Goran spotted what really captured his friend's attention. A couple dozen paces ahead of them, a ledge of rock stretched across the Valley River like a natural bridge. It was nothing like the High Bridge they'd visited in Virginia, however. The ledge jutted only slightly above the surface, glistening where the coursing water intermittently splashed over it.

"A perfect fishing spot," Har marveled. He dropped his gear, withdrew a line from his pack, and set about tying and baiting it. Goran placed his own pack next to Har's, followed by his bow and quiver of bronze-tipped arrows.

When Har was ready, he pushed his way through the weeds lining the stream and stepped carefully onto the rock ledge. "If I slip and you laugh at me, you will be stuck with hard venison and dried fruit for dinner," said the Dwarf. "Fair warning."

"Warning received," Goran replied, suppressing a chuckle.

After the first couple of steps, Har grew more confident. He scrambled to the middle of the natural footbridge, threw back his arm, and launched his baited hook into the rushing water.

"Should be a good trout stream," he commented. Then he pointed to a spot a few feet upriver. "I think I see some movement right there. Come and see—but watch out for that first step. Slippery."

In response, the Sylph flew into the air, soared over the rock ledge, and landed next to Har, who waved a dismissive hand. "Those wings make you lazy," the Dwarf joked.

Goran tried to find the spot his friend had indicated. "I see no trout yet, Har, but I will give you this: The river is far deeper here than I expected."

As he watched, there was a pronounced ripple followed by several more. Soon the water began to churn and bubble, like broth boiling over a cookfire. A white foam formed over the spot Har had originally indicated, growing so thick Goran could see nothing beneath it.

Then he heard a whooshing sound and saw an enormous plume of water rise from the foam, arching in their direction.

"Look out, Har!" Goran cried. "A waterspout is—"

But the Sylph never finished the sentence, because the waterspout struck him, not Har, directly in the face.

The waterspout was so wide that it also struck a large section of the rock ledge with an earsplitting crash. The sound registered only briefly in Goran's mind, however. The force of the spout was like the punch of a stone giant. It knocked him into the water, where he became instantly entangled in a patch of tall weeds and long vines.

As he struggled to regain his wits and free himself from leafy shackles, Goran caught only fleeting images of what was happening around him.

He saw Har dive into the water and reach out his beefy hands to grasp the vines encircling Goran's wings and arms. The Sylph's next sight was of something moving beneath the two fairy rangers, something long and bright red with white stripes stretching horizontally across a series of thin, snakelike segments. Then he glimpsed the flick of a stubby, bright-red tail. A moment later, the force of the powerful flick hit the Sylph like another giant's watery punch.

Goran twisted and turned, his lungs burning as he tried desperately to help Har free him. His next fleeting glimpse was of the other end of the monster coming right at them. Goran saw no face— there were no eyes, no nose, no ears. He saw only a mouth, a large and terrifying maw of dark gray. A maw that, as he watched in horror, shot out from the monster's head on a thick stalk, beyond what Goran had thought were its lips, to engulf the entire upper body of the Dwarf— head, shoulders, and upper arms—and yank Har into the depths of the river.

With a last burst of failing strength, Goran parted the weeds and vines that imprisoned him. Realizing he could render no assistance without refilling his lungs, the Sylph kicked himself to the surface and took a breath. As he did so, he heard a deep voice calling out in a language he recognized.

"Tlanusi!"

Even as Goran dove back into the abnormally deep water of the stream and yanked his knife from its sheath, he marveled at what he'd just learned. *Tlanusi* was the Cherokee word for "leech." So it was a monstrous leech that was dragging his friend to a watery grave. Against such a beast, a weak swimmer with a knife would be a pitiful rescuer. But Goran had to try.

The Giant Leech must have reversed direction, for as Goran swam he saw its red-and-white body passing swiftly below him. Thrusting his knife out in front of him, the Sylph kicked hard, trying to reach the monster before it slipped away. Out of the corner of his eye, Goran saw the Dwarf's legs thrashing at the front of the creature. He welcomed the slight comfort that his friend still clung to life.

Down Goran went, feeling as if he were darting through the water, yet also feeling there was no way he could catch the Giant Leech. Then, just as the thick tip of the creature's tail came into his immediate field of vision, Goran felt his knife strike home.

It was far from a deadly wound. Still, it pained the creature enough to draw its attention. Goran managed to keep his hold on the knife as the Giant Leech jerked away, so he thankfully retained his weapon and drew it back for a thrust into the creature's tail as it whipped quickly around to launch its own attack.

Only it was no tail.

Goran saw the same horrifying maw as before, projecting out from the body of the creature on a thick stalk. Projecting itself right at him.

The Sylph kicked his legs and swept his wings in tandem, managing to spin himself just as the second, posterior mouth of the Giant Leech attempted to swallow his upper body like its other mouth had already done to Har. Rather than envelope Goran's head, shoulders, and torso, the monster's proboscis managed only to seize his left shoulder. Nevertheless, the strength of its suction formed a viselike grip. Goran flailed and tried unsuccessfully to dislodge it with his knife. If he could not free himself quickly, he would surely drown. He feared it was already too late for Har.

Then Goran felt another wave of pressure hit him. The nearby water churned and bubbled as a body plunged into the depths. It was a large body, suntanned and lithe, the well-muscled body of a bare-chested man in a buckskin breechclout and leggings.

Without hesitation, the man thrust the point of a long spear between two segments near the center of the leech's hide. Even underwater, sparks flew briefly as the weapon sank deep into the monster. Just as it had when pierced by Goran's knife, the creature jerked and twisted in response to this new attack—only this time, when the monster freed itself, the offending spearpoint tore off a broad strip of flesh and muscle with it.

Instantly, Goran felt the suction on his shoulder disappear. Without waiting to see what would happen next between the Giant Leech and the human, he swam as fast as his injured shoulder allowed toward the other end of the beast, where he hoped the suction holding Har in its anterior mouth might also have dissipated.

He needn't have bothered; far faster in the water than the small Sylph was the large human. The man pushed past Goran and reached Har, who was falling lifelessly toward the bottom of the river. Wrapping one arm around the Dwarf and still holding his spear with the other, the human kicked himself upward. Goran did the same, gulping down air as soon as his head broke the surface.

Treading water, he watched their human rescuer swim to the riverbank and lay Har on the grass. Then, ignoring the pain in his shoulder, Goran kicked as hard as he could, propelling himself into the air and flapping his wings to gain altitude. As he flew, he was overjoyed to see the Dwarf turned on his side, coughing and spitting water.

Goran landed and crouched low, speaking words of encouragement and rubbing Har's back to induce more coughs. Then he looked up at the face of the human, now risen to his feet and leaning on his spear.

The Cherokee man's face was broad and handsome, framed by prominent cheekbones and a square jaw. His eyes, almond-shaped and set far apart, were wide with astonishment. His wide mouth was curved into a delighted smile.

That the Cherokee could see them was unsurprising, as neither Goran nor Har had sung a concealment spell. And surely the man wouldn't have dived into the river to battle the Giant Leech if he couldn't see those he intended to rescue. But what *did* surprise Goran was the Cherokee's congenial expression. Many humans reacted to their first glimpse of Folk with fear or antagonism.

"We friend," Goran began in his serviceable but far from eloquent Cherokee. "We come to place to—"

"You have the wings of the Tlanuwa yet you are no larger than a Yvwi Usdi," said the man. "Are there more of your kind?"

His English was better than Goran's Cherokee—another pleasant surprise. "There are no more of my kind in America, as far as I know," Goran replied. "My Folk are known as Sylphs. My name is

Goran. My friend, the man you saved, is a Dwarf named Har the Tower."

"We are well met, Goran the Sylph. I am called Gulkalaski."

Gulkalaski, Goran repeated in his head. *One who leans and falls.* "We are fortunate you happened to lean over and fall in the river when you did, sir."

Gulkalaski's mouth erupted into a hearty gale of laughter that the Sylph soon joined in.

"We are also fortunate you came *armed* as you did," Goran said, glancing at the human's spear. It more closely resembled the lance of a human cavalryman than the short stabbing spears he'd seen among the Indians. It was tipped with a long, jagged blade of bronze. Goran also noticed a well-worn hunting rifle discarded on the ground next to them.

"You were fortunate I came by, yes, but as to arming myself, I leave nothing to chance," Gulkalaski said. "When I travel these hunting grounds, I always bring my gift spear. There are more terrible dangers here than the Leech."

The Leech!

Snatching up his bow and quiver, Goran hurried to the river bank. The monster would likely be just as formidable on land as in the water. Although the Cherokee spear had dealt it a severe wound, it could not have been killed so quickly.

From behind him, Gulkalaski laughed again. "You will see no more of the beast this day. The Leech is a danger to those who foolishly stand too close. But once sated with blood, or stung by enchanted blade, it removes itself through an underground passage to its lair. This is known."

"Once . . . stung? Do you mean to say such a gigantic monster has been fought off before?"

"Twice that I know of," Gulkalaski answered. "I was present for one such battle."

The Sylph eyed the Cherokee with even greater respect. "And the other?"

"I . . . heard the tale from someone I trust," came the reply.

Har coughed again and sat up. "How came I here? Where is Goran?"

"Har!" the Sylph exclaimed, rushing to his side. "How do you feel? Did the Giant Leech wound you?"

"So *that* is what it was," breathed the Dwarf as he patted his head, shoulders, and chest. "No, I am neither bitten nor bruised too seriously."

Goran looked up at the human. "We have Gulkalaski to thank for that. He drove away the monster and rescued you. Take a look at that blade on the end of his lance."

The Dwarf did so, then met Goran's eyes for a moment. "You are no stranger to Folk, I take it, nor to magic or monsters," Har said as he rose unsteadily to his feet.

"I am not," the Cherokee man stated as he steadied Har with a helpful hand.

"You called your weapon a 'gift spear,'" Goran said. "Might we guess that you received it from Folk, from someone like us?"

Gulkalaski's eyes narrowed. The Sylph thought at first that he had said something to offend the human. Gulkalaski's face formed a wistful expression, however, not an angry one. The human appeared to be lost in thought. Goran deemed it best to change the subject. *As my friend Daniel Boone would do.*

"Har and I have a good friend among the Cherokee," Goran began, "a woman who, as a child, saw Folk like us and eventually befriended them. Did you have a similar experience growing up, Gulkalaski?"

The man nodded his head. "Yes, although those I saw in my childhood were the Yunwi Tsunsdi, not the Nunnehi."

Chuckling at Har and Goran's surprised reaction, Gulkalaski continued. "Yes, I know of whom you speak. Nanyehi, the Beloved Woman the whites called Nancy Ward. I saw her once on a trip with my grandmother to the healing springs at Citico. I watched Nanyehi from behind a tree as she talked with a Nunnehi woman no taller than my knee. It was then I realized the true meaning of her name. And it was then I realized I was not alone."

"Did you talk to her?" Har asked.

Gulkalaski shook his head. "I was only a child. It was enough for me to know my visions were not some form of madness. If the great Nanyehi could see the spirits, even talk to them, I had no reason to fear the shadow things when they came out to play. My visions could be a gift, not a curse."

"You used the word 'gift' again," Goran pointed out, seeking gracefully to get an answer to his initial question. "So, is that why you call your weapon a 'gift spear'? Did you observe some Folk craftsman at work and then make it yourself?"

Again he saw Gulkalaski's eyes narrow, but now it seemed he was less recalling a distant memory and more struggling with a decision.

With a shake of his head, the Cherokee appeared to make up his mind. "No, you were right the first time. I made the shaft myself, from the trunk of a hickory sapling. But the bronze point, originally the blade of a knife, was a gift from 'someone like you,' as you say."

Goran exchanged a furtive glance with Har, wondering if it would be impolite to ask for more. Gulkalaski, however, needed no prompting.

"I do not think my grandmother knew of my visions," the Cherokee began. "All she knew was that of all her grandchildren, I was the most eager to hear her wondrous tales of gods, spirits, monsters, and little people. Naturally, my favorites were about the Yunwi Tsunsdi, whose forms I had already seen climbing trees, swimming streams, and hiding in the canebrake. Through her tales, I came to know the very clans I would later see in the mound of the Yunwi Tsunsdi. The Rock Clan, fierce warriors with spear and shield; the Flame Clan, masters of magic; the Laurel Clan, masters of herbs and medicines; the Beaver Clan, workers of wood and enchanters of stone; and the Dogwood Clan, who scout for the Yunwi Tsunsdi in the human world beyond their mound, what I later learned they called the Land of Shadow."

Goran slowly nodded his head. "We Folk can vary considerably in appearance and other particulars. But when it comes to how we live and support ourselves, every new Folk nation we discover shows a remarkable similarity to the others."

Gulkalaski quickly grasped Goran's meaning. "So if I were to visit a Nunnehi nest on a mountaintop, or one of the villages of your people, I would find the same clans?"

"Different words and traditions, perhaps, but comparable functions," Goran explained. "Among Sylphs and Dwarfs, for example, the clans you mention would, in order, be called the Warriors Guild, the Mages Guild, the Greenweavers Guild, the Craftsmen Guild, and the Rangers Guild."

The Cherokee man was silent for a moment, considering Goran's words, then continued. "As I grew older, I grew more curious about the Yunwi Tsunsdi. Were they a threat to my people? Or could I, like the wise Nanyehi, befriend them? I resolved to find out. I hid myself in thickets. I dug pits next to rivers. I waited many hours, sometimes even days, to catch sight of them. I succeeded several times, only to lose their trail in the woods."

Seemingly recovered from his near-death experience only minutes before, Har was rocking back and forth, rubbing his hands excitedly. Goran could tell his friend was enjoying the Cherokee's tale of youthful exploits.

They remind him of the carefree exploits of a certain young Dwarf.

"It was on another trip over the mountains with my grandmother, to Tuskegee town, that I finally got my wish," Gulkalaski went on. "I spotted an Yvwi Usdi. He saw me, mumbled something under his breath, then ducked into a hole. He thought he had shaken me, for he soon resumed his uphill climb. I followed. When he reached another hole, he passed through a wall of light and disappeared into a broad, grass-covered mound. I ran up and tried to crawl through but was pushed back as if some invisible spirit had shoved me with fists of wind."

"A Shimmer wall, powered by magecraft," Har interjected.

"Well, I refused to let this 'Shimmer' defeat me," Gulkalaski said with a wry smile. "I pounded the unseen wall with my fists. I swung a heavy tree branch at it. I even collected a pile of stones and starting throwing them at it, hoping at least to make so much noise that the Yvwi Usdi would come out and face me. Imagine my surprise, then, when one of the stones I hurled at the magic wall passed right through it!"

Goran had not expected the story to take this turn. "A stone, you say?"

Gulkalaski shrugged. "I thought it was a stone at first. Then I looked more closely at the pile of stones at my feet. Among the ordinary rocks, there were extraordinary shapes. Some had perfectly flat surfaces on three or four sides, some had small points jutting out like expertly knapped flints. A few looked like what white missionaries call crosses: one four-sided slab thrust through another four-sided slab as if pushed by a very strong force."

Har sucked in a breath. "They were not natural rocks."

"They were not," Gulkalaski agreed. "Later, I learned that they were missiles enchanted by an enemy race, another race of little people, and hurled at the mound's defenders with slings. Although the Yunwi Tsunsdi thought they had collected all the missiles after the battle, they

49

had clearly missed some. By throwing enough of them at the same spot, I broke through."

"I take it you kept hurling sling bullets through the hole?" Goran asked.

"Long enough for an Yvwi Usdi to come out and confront me," Gulkalaski replied. "My grandmother always said I was headstrong. I kept talking to the little man and he kept responding with a strange song in a strange language. After a while, he greeted me in my own language and conducted me into his village."

Goran smiled and lifted off the ground, hovering a couple of feet before the Cherokee's face. "Next you will tell us that you stayed for several days, and that when they sent you back into the outside world your people said you had been missing for months."

Mouth agape, Gulkalaski looked first at Goran and then at Har. "My tale is not so special, after all," he said, appearing crestfallen.

"You are wrong," Har assured him. "Your tale *is* special, although not unique. Only a very few humans possess the mixture of imagination and insight that renders them immune to Folk spells."

"Was that your only direct encounter with Folk, then?" asked Goran.

"With the Yunwi Tsunsdi, yes," Gulkalaski allowed, then fell silent.

The Sylph thought for a moment, then pointed to the human's bronze-tipped lance. "They did not give you that blade, did they?"

Gulkalaski shook his head, then met Goran's gaze with a penetrating stare of his own. "That was a present from another—one who looked more like you."

"A Folk ranger with light skin, you mean, but without wings."

The Cherokee grunted his assent. "After I came back from the Yunwi Tsunsdi, I learned that my family and friends had thought me killed by a fall or wild animal. I lacked the heart to leave them again for a long while. It was a year later before I returned to the mound of the Yunwi Tsunsdi. They refused to allow me in. Before returning home, I collected all the sling stones I could find along the hillside. Since then, it has become a pastime of mine to search for other enchanted stones. It was on one such trip, just over the white man's border into what they call Georgia, that I met her."

"Met whom?" Goran asked.

"She was old and slow-moving, her skin wrinkled and spotted, her long hair white and falling past her shoulders like a cascade of thin moonbeams. Her large round eyes, the color of a mountain fir, her ears curved into points—they jogged a memory in my mind of one of my grandmother's stories, the tale of the Moon-Eyed People."

"*Moon-Eyed*, did you say?" Har pressed.

Again, the human grunted in confirmation. "Her tale was of a strange race of small white-skinned people and how we Cherokee forced them from their forest strongholds. Now I was facing one. Perhaps, based on Grandmother's story, I should have seen her as an enemy, but I saw only a frail, lonely old woman. I spoke to her gently. She spoke back just as gently."

"Did you learn the true history of her people?" Goran asked.

"I did," Gulkalaski replied, "but there is a reason I have been hesitant to speak of her. I gave her my oath I would never repeat what she told me."

The three spoke no words for a time. Then Goran sheathed the knife that he had, without realizing it, had still been holding firmly in his hand. "We would not dream of pressing you to betray a confidence. Given what you have already told us, however, we can guess it was the elderly Folk ranger who gave you the bronze blade."

Gulkalaski looked wistful once again. "I told her it was unnecessary, that I had guided her to the place without any promise of reward."

"What place was that?" Har asked, then seemed immediately to regret it when Goran glared reproachfully.

"The place where her people once lived," said the Cherokee. "The place where she wanted to die." His eyes flicked, however briefly, to the wider, westward-flowing river that lay a short distance ahead, and then to a spot somewhat to the left of the confluence.

Goran did not need to speak with Har, or even look in his direction, to know what the Dwarf was thinking. Goran had the same thought. *Any human a Folk ranger deemed trustworthy enough to keep her dying wish a secret is a human worthy of our trust as well.*

"Har and I are headed south to visit an old friend," Goran said. "Care to journey with us for a time? Your companionship would be most welcome."

Chapter 4 – The Smith

Har had never expected to become a ranger.

After all, rangers tended to be small and swift, while even as a youth Har had towered over everyone in his village. Rangers tended to be scholarly, able to memorize and categorize immense bodies of knowledge, while Har had managed to pass his exams only by a combination of late-night cramming, educated guesses, and blind luck. Rangers tended to be disciplined and serious-minded, while young Har had preferred to spend his mornings fishing, his afternoons hunting, and his evening laughing and cavorting. Rangers were spies and diplomats, keeping track of the latest political intrigues and skilled at employing words as weapons. Har, however, had always made friends easily and could, on occasion, come up with a persuasive plea or a humorous jest. But when faced with an adversary, his sharpest rejoinder was the blade of his battleaxe, not his wit, which bore no resemblance to a rapier.

With these facts in mind, young Har had always assumed he'd either grow up to be a craftsman, working a forge like his father, or deploy his size and strength as a warrior. Yet here he was, a slow-moving ox of a Dwarf. A mediocre student. An inveterate loafer. A blunt-spoken brawler. A wanderer haunted by the wartime deaths of close friends.

And now, however improbably, Dwarfkind's first emissary to the colony of the Elves—if he could ever manage to find the place.

▲▲▲

Weeks earlier, when Har and Goran had reached the Nunnehi village at Blood Mountain accompanied by their new human companion, Gulkalaski, Tana had greeted the news of the Dwarf's mission with a derisive snort. "Your king has sent you to treat with Elves? Har the Tower, Ambassador."

"Perhaps Alberich thinks it a fool's errand to make peace with Elves, so why not send a fool to do it?" the Dwarf had chimed in, laughing as gustily as his friends.

Later, however, after Gulkalaski left for home and Goran began interviewing the elderly scouts of the Azalea Clan to discover what they knew about magecraft, Har had talked more seriously with Tana about his assignment. Tana, now clan chief as well as a new mother, had more experience with the Elves of Georgia than anyone else he knew. After breaking the siege of Blood Mountain, the Nunnehi had retaliated by attacking the Elf's forest fortress near Augusta. Tana had helped broker the peace that followed.

"The Elf village is well guarded," Tana had told him. "While they are in many ways like the Kowi Anukasha, our forest-dwelling rivals to the south and west, the Elves are far more dangerous. They use strange devices and expertly enchanted weapons. Fortunately for us, though, they are short on mages and poorly led."

"Poorly led?"

"Prince Elbegast." Sitting on the floor of the Azalea Clan lodge, Tana had uncrossed and stretched her legs. "A more vain and avaricious man, I have never met. He wasted his warriors in pointless assaults. And even when suing for peace, he seemed concerned only with making demands and preparing for future wars."

Tana's words had made Har's stomach lurch. *This Elbegast is precisely the sort of Elf leader that Alberich rails against.*

▲▲▲

And now Har was here to meet him—wherever "here" might be.

Following Tana's instructions, Har had headed south from the human settlement of Augusta and entered the woods. At first the trees he passed—oak and river birch and green ash—were spaced far apart and separated by low grasses. As he continued into the forest, however, the way became increasingly difficult. Thick walls of elder, willow, and sycamore trunks deflected his course. High stands of elderberry, yellowroot, and giant cane blocked his path. More than once, he'd blundered into thickets of creeper, hempweed, and crossvine, entangling his arms or tripping his feet. Although he left Augusta right after breakfast and could not have been at it for more than a couple of hours, the dense forest canopy made it look as if it were twilight.

It was only when Har happened upon the creek Tana had spoken of, the one flowing east to the great Savannah River, that he could be sure he was still headed south. "I am lost," Har admitted aloud to no one in particular, "but not aimless. At least I know what direction I stumble."

"You are found," said someone particular.

"And yet still lost," said another.

At the first word, Har filled his hand with a throwing axe and bent into a crouch, scanning the nearby trees. "Show yourself!" he demanded.

The only response was a rustling of leaves.

Har saw a possible ford in the creek. Carefully, with each step followed by a lengthy pause to listen, Har walked to water's edge and then into the shallows.

From the trees in front of him came a voice. "I am spirit."

"I am spirit," said a voice from behind.

Har kept going until he was across the creek. Then he halted and let his hands drop to his sides. "I come to parlay with Prince Elbegast, not play games with the likes of you."

This time he was answered neither by rustling leaves nor hostile threats but by chuckles.

Har felt his patience disappearing. "Take me to the Prince of Elves, or begone!"

"Spirit is deadly," warned a voice from Har's left.

"Spirit never dies," proclaimed someone from his right.

"If you will not take me to Elbegast, I will find him myself," the Dwarf muttered, provoking another round of chortling.

Then, barely visible in the dim light of the ancient forest, a face appeared between two tree trunks, followed a second later by the bronze tip of an arrow. "I will gladly send you on your way," said the Elf emerging from the forest, her thin hand squeezed tightly around her bow grip of ornately carved bitternut hickory, her gray eyes narrowed menacingly.

"Not if I do it first," said a second, darker-eyed Elf, aiming his own orange-fletched arrow at Har's chest. Both newcomers were clad in belted tunics, trousers, and cloaks of muted greens and browns. Supple leather turnshoes rather than sturdy boots covered their feet, sacrificing durability in the service of stealth.

My diplomatic mission has gotten off to a promising start.

"I come not as an invader but as an emissary," said Har in a level voice. "I range for the Dwarf colony of Virginia."

The female Elf eyed him skeptically. "You are too stupid and heavy of foot to be a ranger. Yet here you are in the Blur, neither dead nor mad. So, are all Dwarf rangers stupid and clumsy?"

Remembering the Elves' earlier snickering, Har decided to try levity. "No other Dwarf rangers are like me. I am in a class by myself."

The Elves didn't laugh. Instead, they walked toward Har, their drawn arrows still pointed at him.

Time to throw my best-weighted dice.

Transferring his axe to his left hand, the Dwarf reached into his pack, removed a small object, and held it up. "You recognize this device, do you not?"

The male Elf sneered and continued his approach. But the female sucked in a breath and gestured for him to halt. "An Irminsul!" she exclaimed. "How came you by that?"

Har paused for a moment, lifting the statuette higher. Carved of sourwood and mounted on a stone base, it depicted a tree trunk leaning at a 45-degree angle with a longsword thrust through its center at the opposite angle. The crossed shapes were expertly enchanted, emitting a soft green glow from the tree and a coppery glow from the sword.

"I have come here not only as the emissary of the Dwarf King Alberich but also as a duly appointed representative of the Nunnehi of Blood Mountain, with whom your Folk have a peace treaty," Har explained. "By the terms of that treaty, you are obligated to receive any such representative bearing the Irminsul as an official token."

Neither Elf looked convinced, but they seemed loath to reject his claim outright. "We will conduct you to the prince," said the female Elf, removing a square cloth from her belt and fashioning it into a blindfold. "But you will remain lost."

▲▲▲

Although he walked in darkness for half an hour, Har suspected he hadn't gone far. It felt like the rangers were marching him in circles in an attempt to confuse him. Through it all, the sound of water flowing over the stony bed of the creek stayed constant. When he felt the telltale tingling sensation of passing through Shimmer, Har supposed the need for secrecy was at an end. He reached up and removed the blindfold.

What he beheld was unlike any other Folk village he'd visited. Most Dwarfkind lived in underground complexes of caverns and tunnels. Town Folk such as Kobolds and Brownies lived in elongated, Shimmer-shielded cellars beneath human structures such as halls, houses, streets, cisterns, and sewers. Atop Blood Mountain, the Nunnehi village consisted of a precisely ordered set of lodges, halls, barns, and pens laid out within a single spacious cave. And according to Gulkalaski, the Yunwi Tsunsdi lived in similar settlements within hollow mounds of earth and stone.

But the Elf village sprawled before him under an open sky, albeit one discolored by Shimmer and lit by a filtered sun that hurtled so quickly above him that the shadows it cast through the trees seemed to crawl, slowly but inexorably, across the leafy ground.

What also set the Elf village apart was its sheer size. Indeed, Har was seeing Elf *villages*, plural—not just one. To his left, over a hill, Har could see two distinct clusters of huts, one only a few hundred paces away and the other more distant. Three clusters of tents were visible to his right.

Directly ahead, the Dwarf was surprised to see a high wooden stockade. It strongly resembled the frontier forts he'd seen humans construct. About two hundred paces across, the wall consisted of a row of pine logs buried deep in the ground, sharpened at the top and bound together with two horizontal lines of rope. Behind it, Har guessed, was a second row of logs, arranged obliquely to cover the gaps between the logs of the front row. The space between the two rows was filled with rammed earth. At each end of the wall was a bulky three-story blockhouse and at its center was a gatehouse, similarly constructed and manned by a line of guards standing on a parapet above its double doors of oak.

Har's surprise at seeing the stockade turned quickly into grave concern. Most Folk used Shimmer walls and other magical means to defend their villages against external attack; they saw no need to build additional physical fortifications *inside* the Shimmer. The Elf stockade, then, was either evidence of the settlement's inherently military character or a sign that the Elves felt constantly in danger.

Neither bodes well for my mission, Har realized. *Either Alberich is right to fear the hostile intentions of the Elves, or they harbor the same deep-seated fears about us.*

At a shout from the female Elf ranger, the great double doors opened. Once Har entered, he could see additional walls extending from the blockhouses. In those blockhouses, and along the walls in pairs and trios, were many Elf sentries. Most stood with weapons in hand, talking and laughing. A few practiced their skill with bow or sling, pointing to targets among the surrounding trees and either praising or ridiculing their competitors' shots as deserved.

The grounds enclosed by the log fort were extensive—and almost entirely occupied by buildings of various shapes and sizes. Unlike the Nunnehi's orderly grid of lodges or the chambered caverns of Grünerberg, there was no apparent rhyme or reason to the layout of the Elf village. The structures appeared to have been built hastily, and in some cases haphazardly, wherever additional space could be found.

The rangers conducted Har along a zigzag route of narrow streets, then along the market square. It was packed with booths, stalls, carts, and groups of Elfkind buying, selling, eating, and arguing.

Elf*kind* was the right description. Among the throng, Har could readily spot the familiar features of the Black Forest troop and other Elves he had encountered back in Germany. Like the female Elf ranger who'd first accosted him, they typically had long, narrow faces, nut-brown or straw-colored hair, and eyes of gray.

But the Dwarf spotted other varieties of Elfkind too. There were broad faces, freckled and pink, with rust-colored hair and large green eyes. *Ellyllon from the British Isles*, Har recalled from his ranger lessons. There were small, dark-featured faces so pale as to be nearly the color of snow. *Alven Folk from the frozen north.* Some were greenish faces, almost perfectly circular, surrounded by wildly unkempt hair embedded with moss and leaves. *Moss Folk from the Wetter valley.* Others were ruddy-cheeked faces with periwinkle eyes and wavy hair. *Sanziene from Transylvania.* Others still were sallow, triangular faces with white hair and gold-flecked eyes. *Psotniki from Pomerania.* And then there were faces rising far above the others, perched on long straight necks surrounded by long, straight hair. *Samodiva from Thrace.* And there were many other faces still whose national origins Har could not identify.

His escorts ushered him onto another narrow street that wound its way past ramshackle houses and sheds. Although the street was far less crowded than the square, they passed several pedestrians. Nearly all stopped to stare at the Dwarf ranger. The exception was a Samodiva mage nearly as tall as Har, her long, blonde hair shaking from side to side as she struggled to control the stag-like creature she was leading down the street by a rope. She seemed not even to notice Har and his escorts.

From a modest dwelling, the Dwarf spotted twelve Elfling faces looking back at him. Ranging in age from toddlers to teens, the children looked thin and haggard. In front of another overcrowded hovel an Ellyllon greenweaver was kneeling in an herb garden, running an enchanted glove over a newly planted patch of ground. He looked up at Har, scowled, and muttered something under his breath.

Har couldn't quite make out what the greenweaver said, and he decided that was his good fortune.

The next building was long and multistoried with four separate chimneys belching smoke and soot. Even before Har saw the sign over the door, depicting a hammer striking an anvil in a shower of sparks, he guessed the structure housed the colony's Craftsmen Guild.

The male Elf ranger pointed to the door. "You will find the prince within. We will wait here to escort you out."

Feeling awkward about proceeding alone but disinclined to insist they come along, Har walked to the door and knocked gently. There was no answer.

Another round of laughter erupted from the rangers behind him. "The craftsmen are too hard at work to hear your child's tap," sneered the female Elf. "As tall as you stand, are you truly so weak?"

Har grimaced and rapped on the door more loudly. Still, no answer.

"He has nothing anyone wants to buy, Roza," said the male Elf to his female companion, who held out her arms in a mocking shrug.

"Move along, peddler man," Roza jeered.

Trying the door and finding it latched, Har felt impatience welling inside him. He clenched his firsts in frustration. His first diplomatic assignment as a ranger, inviting the Lutki to the Dwarfmoot so many years ago, had ended as soon as it began in failure. Now, his mission to the Elves seemed just as ill-fated. *I have no talent for fancy words and first impressions. An ox will never be a fox.*

His accidental rhyme made Har smile. Then he looked down at his still-clenched fists, chuckled, and recalled what Polly Cooper had told him during their first meeting: *We all hate to be mistaken for something we are not.* Perhaps it was time to embrace his true self rather than seeing it as a disadvantage.

Backing up a dozen paces, Har the Tower let out a whoop, ran at the door, and knocked it completely off its brass hinges with a kick of his heavy-booted foot. Splinters flew in all directions. The door landed on the stone floor of the hall with a loud crash.

Standing in the now open doorway, Har found several Elf craftsmen staring at him in stunned silence from an anteroom. Over his shoulder, Har heard Roza and the male ranger shout curses and rush forward. He also heard running feet from an adjoining room. Two more craftsmen soon appeared, one armed with a mallet and the other, a crude sword with an unfinished handle and no pommel.

"Hold!" ordered a new voice, low-pitched and even. It was authoritative but contained no hint of anger or panic. Then a third figure emerged from the adjoining room. He was dressed like the others, in simple work clothes and an apron stained by frequent use. His bare arms were impressively muscled and shining with sweat. On his hands were leather gloves banded with enchanted metal studs that glowed faintly orange in the low light of the guildhall anteroom.

The newcomer's lean, expressionless face was also shiny from perspiration. The points of his long, upswept ears nearly touched the small fringe of gray hair encircling his otherwise bald head. Har felt the craftsman's dark eyes bore into him.

My course is set. I might as well follow it to its end. "I seek the Prince of Elves. I am Har, emissary for King Alberich of Grünerberg."

"What have you come from your green mountain to acquire in our green forest?" pressed the Elf, whom Har guessed might be the grandmaster of the Craftsmen Guild.

"Only a new acquaintance and the promise of peace, sir," said the Dwarf, saying what he imagined his friend Goran might have said in his place.

"Which you have chosen to secure by violent means." The Elf put his gloved hands on his hips, looked down at the broken door, and then back up at Har scornfully. The Dwarf returned the look with as much bravado as he could muster under the circumstances—circumstances which included the grim reality that the other Elves, armed and seething, had formed a circle around him.

Then the guildmaster did the last thing Har expected. He threw back his head and laughed heartily.

"You cut your leather quick and deep, Dwarf," he said. "Although I know you must be a ranger, you strike me as a craftsman at heart."

Har relaxed only slightly. "My father works a bronze forge back home," he said tentatively. "I had always thought to follow in his footsteps, but fate had other plans for me."

The Elf's eyes widened at that. "We craft our own fates, or so I had always believed until recently. You certainly saw fit to craft an opening for yourself to our guildhall."

Har decided an explanation was in order. "I knocked several times on the door, you see, and—"

"And decided that indiscretion was the better part of valor," interrupted the Elf with a playful lilt to his voice. "Still, I find that I like you, emissary. Dwarfish boldness is a trait I have long thought my own Folk should emulate."

Relief washed over Har. "Might I, then, be permitted to meet the Prince of Elves? My escorts told me Elbegast was here."

"I doubt they said any such thing, except in jest," said the Elf. "Elbegast has been dead for months. His body lies buried in a distant hillside. As for your request, however, consider it granted."

"Sir, I do not—"

"I am Veelund, now called Prince of Elves."

Trying to disguise his astonishment, Har bowed low. "And I am called Har the Tower."

"Well of course you are," quipped the prince. "Welcome, Har the Tower, to Spirit Forest."

▲▲▲

An hour later, having changed into a clean set of clothes more suited to Veelund's current station—amber-colored breeches and stockings, a long robe of forest green cinched at the waist by a finely wrought belt of leather and gemstones, and a yellow-green surcoat bearing the sigil of the Craftsmen Guild embroidered in silver thread—the prince looked over the table at Har and held up his hands. "So, Har, what do you think of our Royal Hall?"

Although the building was rather small, its ceiling just a couple of inches higher than the top of Har's head, it was well furnished and comfortable, its corridors, bedchamber, and great room brightened considerably by an extensive collection of colorful tapestries, sculptures, and other works of art. Dwarf craftsmen were justly proud of their own skills at forge, anvil, table, and loom, but there was no denying the exquisite craftsmanship of their longtime rivals.

"Impressive," Har said. Then he inclined his head to the corner and added, "I think my father would have a special fascination with that device."

What stood in the corner was an elaborate contraption of tubes, vessels, and moving parts stretching from the floor nearly to the ceiling. From a small pipe embedded in the wall came a constant stream of water that flowed into a chamber at the top of the apparatus. Har couldn't tell precisely where the water went from there, but he could see a trickle turning a brass wheel in the center as well as another smaller wheel to the side.

"You have seen a water clock before, I assume," Veelund said. "This is a model of my own design. As you can see, there are two faces. The one on the left measures time passing here within the Shimmer. The other face, the one with the rapidly spinning disc, measures time as humans experience it in the Blur—at a pace twenty times faster than ours. Both are geared to brass bells. One sounds a deep, rich tone at the beginning of every Shimmer hour. The other chime is differently constructed and marks . . . ah, well, you are about to witness it."

From somewhere within the clock came a brief, high-pitched trilling sound, as if a child's hand had shaken a toy bell.

"It marks the end of a Blur day," Veelund explained. "As I have to hear that chime twenty times a day, I decided to make it short and pleasing."

Although he admired the workmanship, Har was mystified as to its object. "If I may ask, Prince Veelund, why must you hear the chime at all? What purpose does such a clock serve?"

The Elf leader idly traced a pattern on the tabletop with a fingernail. "There are many applications, Har. Accurate timekeeping is useful for scheduling hunts into the Blur, for instance, and aids our scholars in keeping historical records. As for me, I have always nursed a fascination with the regular circuits of the Sun, the Moon, and the other heavenly bodies above this world."

At that, Veelund looked up at the ceiling. Har followed his gaze and saw something he hadn't noticed before: a round aperture, paned with glass, through which the sky was clearly visible. He could see it was nearly dusk, although the ample lamplight of the otherwise windowless room had kept him from noticing. Possibly before their conversation was over, he knew, the sun rising swiftly in the sky would once again illuminate the little window in the ceiling.

Pulling a volume from a shelf, Veelund ran his finger along its thick spine. "My clock aids me in my astronomical studies."

"Is it powered by magecraft?" Har wondered.

The Elf prince replaced the book and shook his head. "Its workings are entirely hydraulic and mechanical. I will not deny I used some enchanted parts during its construction, but magic is too scarce a commodity to use for its ongoing operations."

Veelund's explanation reminded Har of something Tana had mentioned several times—that the Elf colony seemed to be weak in

61

magecraft. It was one reason the Nunnehi had been able to win their war. Har decided to test the prince's willingness to trade information.

"Magic has become scarcer," Har agreed. "When the Dwarf lords founded our colony here, they assumed would be abundant game. Our monster hunts were, indeed, very successful—at first. That has begun to change."

The Elf prince nodded somberly. "It is a challenge for all the Folk of America, no doubt, but the paucity of game presents a far graver threat to our colony."

"Why is that?" Har asked.

"Tell me, Har the Tower, when you beheld our settlement for the first time, what struck you as its most distinctive feature?"

Several images flashed through the Dwarf's mind. Extensive fortifications. Fierce sentries. Winding streets. Rickety structures. Dirty children. The surly greenweaver. But saying anything to suggest Veelund's Folk had warlike intentions, bad city planning, poor hygiene, or atrocious manners struck Har as not especially diplomatic.

"The, uh, the people," he finally said, deeming a vague reply less likely to offend.

"Precisely," said Veelund, rising from his chair and walking over to the water clock. "We are teeming with people. Crowded, like a swollen river spilling over its banks. Elfkind came over the water from the Schwarzwald, the Spreewald, the Zauberwald, from the troops of Haguenau and Teutoburg and Rügen Isle and so many others. We came looking for more space, more game, larger harvests. And many were fleeing the ravages of incessant war—war with the Goblinkind of Europe, with the Folk of the towns and ports, and with your kind most of all."

Har felt his mouth grow dry. *I must choose my words carefully.*

"From my own home in the Gespensterwald, on the Baltic Sea, Elves came in large numbers, nearly half the entire population of my village," Veelund went on. "And yet shortly after we arrived here and began building our settlement, the first wave of refugees found us."

"Refugees?"

"Ours was the largest expedition to the New World, Har, but it was hardly the earliest one. Elfkind, in its many varieties, had previously emigrated in smaller groups: adventurers, dissenters, outcasts. At first they found a paradise. Then they found new enemies, as well as old ones who had followed them to these shores. The first refugees arrived at Spirit Forest from the west, remnants of an audacious troop of Ellyllon who had sailed with some of the first European travelers to America and then settled far inland, living atop high mountains. Subsequently dispossessed by fierce Folk, the surviving Ellyllon found their way here, forming the first camp of refugees on the outskirts of our village. You saw the camps on the way in, did you not?"

Har nodded. He tried to imagine what would happen at Grünerberg if waves of Dwarf refugees began to arrive from war-ravaged colonies. *At first, we would be hospitable. Then, once our halls and caverns grew crowded, there would be frustration, resentment, even desperation.*

"Soon enough, what had seemed like plentiful harvests of humanwares became pitifully inadequate, as did the hauls from our larder hunts," Veelund continued. "We could no longer feed and clothe our Folk. So, my predecessor, Elbegast, devised a plan."

The prince returned to his chair and sat down, looking intensely at Har. "I know why you have come, Emissary of Grünerberg. Your Folk and mine were on opposite sides of the late war. You would know our intentions and assess our military strength. Your leader would be ready to win the next war. I would rather not wage it at all."

Veelund admires boldness. "It was *your* Folk who launched a war of conquest," Har pointed out. "You attacked the Nunnehi in alliance with the English king and unscrupulous Folk such as your cousins, the Ellyllon of Pennsylvania."

"Yes, and it was a colossal blunder," Veelund admitted. "Elbegast's plan was simple: We would seize the Nunnehi's village and resources, harvesting game and humanwares in the quantities we required. Once better clothed, fed, and armed, we would next march on the other Folk of the region, conquering a large enough empire to sustain Elfkind for generations."

Not for the first time, Har felt thankful Tana's Folk had proved to be such formidable allies. If the Elves had prevailed, their dreams of larger conquests might have been realized.

"Elbegast's plan was simple—and utterly foolish," Veelund continued. "It is only by prudence, wisdom, and dexterity that great ends are attained and obstacles overcome. Despite our superior numbers, we lacked the military and magical capacity to defeat the Nunnehi in their mountain stronghold, much less to subdue and rule a vast territory. As grandmaster of the Craftsmen Guild, I had long advised Elbegast and the Council that brute force was *not* the solution. It took defeat on the battlefield to convince the Council. One hothead, his identity still unrevealed, decided to end Elbegast's misrule by murdering him as he slept in these very chambers. I would have preferred he be deposed without violence, of course. Still, when the Council turned to me to rule in this time of crisis, I felt I could not refuse."

Veelund's words sounded persuasive and conciliatory to Har's ears. Despite this, he found he could not fully dismiss King Alberich's strongly voiced suspicions, nor could he fully dismiss the image of the walled stockade, the ready warriors, and the hungry, desperate look of the Elfish throngs.

"If force of arms offers no remedy for your woes, what does?" asked the Dwarf.

A broad smile came to Veelund's lips as he reached into a pouch at his waist and produced the rough work gloves Har had seen him wearing earlier. Tossing them before Har, their enchanted metal studs producing a shower of sparks as they struck the table, the prince rose again to his feet.

"Elbegast leaned too heavily on the promises of warriors and mages," Veelund said. "I prefer to listen to the voices of humbler Folk, to greenweavers and craftsmen. Their time—*our* time—has come. We must grow, weave, craft, and forge. We must rely more on our own ingenuity, on the fruits of our own labors, rather than waste lives in fruitless sieges or forage for scraps among the humans. I would have my Folk be bold, to be sure, but bold in the employment of our brains, not just our brawn."

It was the answer Har had longed to hear—and not just from the Prince of Elves. Veelund's words sounded much like Virginal's in the early days of the Dwarf colony. She, too, had envisioned a future for her Folk that elevated the values of hard work, cooperation, and mutual respect above expediency, confrontation, and hatred.

"If this be your policy, Prince Veelund, then it could build the foundation of a lasting peace between us," Har said, inclining his head respectfully.

Veelund acknowledged Har's gesture. Then he twisted his broad smile into a skeptical smirk. "Will your King Alberich be as open to a new understanding between Elfkind and Dwarfkind?"

Not at first, the Dwarf admitted to himself. *But Alberich would not be the first monarch of Grünerberg to yield to my persistence.*

Chapter 5 – The Fliers

July 1806

Goran thought he spotted wings in the trees, but he couldn't be sure. Being in no particular hurry as he headed northward from Spirit Forest to Long Island-on-the-Holston, the Sylph ranger halted his flight and hovered over a cluster of oak and black locust trees next to a gently flowing brook. Spending a few minutes bird-watching, or perhaps even taking a short rest, was greatly appealing after staying aloft for hours.

The setting prompted him to think of Daniel Boone, now in his seventies and living with his family in the Missouri territory. In his youth, Daniel had spent as much time as he could ranging through remote forests like this one, hunting and trapping and reveling in the freedom of the frontier. As that frontier receded westward, pursued by the steady advance of human settlement, Daniel had chosen to recede with it.

The Elf leader Har had brought Goran to meet at Spirit Forest, Prince Veelund, reminded him of Daniel in some ways. Although Veelund was a craftsman, not a hunter, and had thus spent little time outside the protection of the Shimmer, he had Daniel's easygoing manner and talent for making new friends, traits Goran wished he possessed. As a child, he'd spent little time befriending other young Sylphs. He preferred to read, listen to his father Brae's colorful tales, or assist his mother, Wenna, in the greenweaver fields. Then Goran had spent his apprenticeship in the Rangers Guild studying in the library and training in the armory rather than cavorting with his fellow apprentices.

And look where that got me, he thought. *I would have been better off making friends. Perhaps more Sylphs would have listened to me when war came. Perhaps I would have saved lives. Perhaps I would not be such a pariah.*

During his last conversation with Veelund, Goran had shared these self-recriminations. The Elf prince was sympathetic. "I myself questioned the wisdom of joining the Great Alliance. I did not champion the American cause, to be honest; I just did not think we were ready to launch the attacks Prince Elbegast had promised our allies. Over time, my Folk came to recognize the wisdom of what was then my unpopular opinion. Yours may well do the same."

Goran had shaken his head sadly. "You did not take up arms against your own kind. I did. And your Folk were not forced to abandon their home. Mine were."

Veelund had rubbed his chin. "We did not have to flee, true, but it was a close-run thing. The Nunnehi assault was ferocious. Without our high wall of thaumaturgic pine and cypress, Spirit Forest would surely have fallen."

The Elf's reference to the wooden stockade had distracted Goran from his melancholy thoughts. "I have never heard the full story of that siege. I had no idea the height of your wall had been critical to your salvation."

"It was not the height of the wall that made the difference, Goran. It was the composition. Only some select varieties of evergreen trunks have the thaumaturgic properties needed to form a defensive shield."

"That is the second time you have used the term 'thaumaturgic.' Is it a craftsman's word?"

Veelund had smiled. "It is a mage's word, actually, although some craftsmen and greenweavers train for years in thaumaturgy. It is the study of how different plants, rocks, and metals store and structure the flow of elemental magic. Thaumaturgy has long been one of my passions."

Goran's eyes had widened as he realized the import of Veelund's words. "Is it thaumaturgy that aids ranger guildmasters in their selection of sites for Folk settlements?"

While the Sylph's eyes had widened in excitement, the Elf leader's eyes had narrowed, apparently in concentration. He'd looked as though he were about to respond when an Elf warrior rushed into the Royal Hall, reminding Veelund of his next appointment. The prince's explanation, although cut short, offered Goran critical new information about magical resonance.

Now I know why Har has spoken so highly of Veelund, Goran reflected as he looked down at the small mountain brook. Unlike the arrogant and closed-minded King Alberich of Grünerberg, the Elf leader seemed open to new ideas rather than only entertaining his own. Veelund also seemed to recognize that responding to the challenges facing his Folk would require ingenuity and change, not just blind adherence to tradition.

What was that?

The upper branches of a tree on the other side of the creek suddenly swayed. Then a form, bright but indistinct, streaked into the air. As it rose into the sky, moonlight threw its silhouette into stark relief. It was, indeed, a winged creature. But despite the distance separating them, Goran knew in an instant that it was no songbird or gamebird. The wingspan was too large.

Curious to see what bird of prey he'd flushed out, Goran darted after it, his fatigue forgotten in the thrill of the chase. Within a few minutes, he had drawn close enough to the flier to see a clearer outline against the sky. The sight made his heart skip a beat. The flier didn't just have large wings; it had two arms, two legs, and what appeared to be light-colored clothes hanging from its limbs.

A Sylph? How could that be?

When Goran had journeyed to the Knob after the war, hoping to make his apologies and find some way to reconnect with his family, he had found the site completely abandoned. Later on, rumor had it that the Sylphs had relocated to British Canada, just as many human Tories had done rather than remain in the newly independent United States.

But ahead of him, unmistakably, was a winged humanoid like himself. It was a mystery Goran felt compelled to solve.

Ignoring the protest from his tired limbs, he sped over tree-covered hills with a determined expression on his windblown face. If there were Sylphs still in America, he had to know. Perhaps they would want nothing to do with him. Perhaps they would even despise him as a traitor. Nevertheless, Goran had to know.

Presently he saw an object shining in the moonlight straight ahead. Rising hundreds of feet above the surrounding hills was a narrow outcropping of light-colored rock, possibly granite. The other flier headed right for the top of the rock formation, which somewhat resembled an enormous chimney.

Having thrown caution to the wind during the chase, Goran now realized it might be wise to approach with care. If what he wanted was knowledge, it would not do for the flier to see Goran as desperate or threatening. As the other figure landed gracefully on the outcropping, Goran banked to his right and glided behind a stand of poplars, using the cover to get closer.

When he emerged and regained a clear line of sight to the chimney-like rock, Goran was startled to see not one fairy standing on its surface but three. All wore clothes of white, yellow, and light tan. He was still too far away to see their faces.

Suppressing his anxiety about the welcome he might receive, Goran ascended toward the trio of rangers—only, as he climbed higher, he realized it was no trio. There were additional figures standing on the rocky cliff and still more hovering about it. A dozen? Fifteen? He couldn't be sure. Certainly more than he could handle if they proved hostile.

Goran stopped short, hovering and reconsidering his original plan. Then he watched, fascinated, as one of the figures stepped to the edge of the rock, hesitated for a moment, and then stepped out into the open air. Rather than flapping its wings to rise above the ledge or stretching them wide to soar over the trees, the figure shot downward, twisting and turning, toward the rocky ground below.

Goran gasped. Was this fairy just learning to fly for the first time? In his experience, all Sylphs except the lame gained at least basic hovering and gliding skills at the same time they learned to walk. The struggling figure was too big to be a toddler. Goran was puzzled and horrified at the same time.

Seconds before the flightless fairy would have crashed into the ground, another winged figure rose from behind a clump of greenery and grabbed the falling one beneath both arms, arresting its momentum. Then the two rose slowly, the newcomer seeming to do all the work, until they regained the top of the chimney rock. Mesmerized by the scene, Goran had paid no attention to what the rest of the winged fairies were doing. Not all watched the rescue of the flightless one. Two were looking in a different direction.

Goran's direction.

With shouts of alarm, they announced his presence to the others on the cliff. A moment later, all had launched themselves into the air, even the recently rescued one, whose arm was around its rescuer as the two joined the rest of the fliers.

Instantly regretting his course of action, Goran grabbed for the bow slung across his back. He was about to sweep it over his shoulder and nock an arrow when he realized that none of the fairies was heading in his direction. Instead, they were rising higher above the chimney rock.

Now more fearful of learning nothing than of facing attack, Goran beat his wings to pick up speed. It soon became evident, however, that he was in no condition to catch up with them. Hours of steady travel followed by a long chase had left him drained, his wings and lungs aching.

Dejected, Goran watched as they flew out of sight, then retraced his path to the chimney rock, hoping at least to find some clues there about the identity of the rangers who'd so recently occupied it.

After nearly half an hour of searching, Goran was forced to conclude with great reluctance that he would get no answers this night. He landed in a small clearing at the base of the rock formation and sat on a fallen log, his chin resting uncomfortably against two clenched fists. He thought of home. Of his father, his sister, Ailee, and his brother, Kaden, driven to lunacy from exposure to the Blur. Of his family, who surely lived far from this place.

His family? They were his *victims*, really, staying as far away as they could from a notorious traitor.

"It's this way, Elizabeth, you can't see the top from over there!"

From behind Goran came a human voice, one belonging to a young male.

"No, I first saw him over here," insisted another human voice, a girl.

Realizing he'd again allowed his emotions to compromise his vigilance, Goran leapt from the log and rose into the air just as the two humans entered the clearing.

The girl, Elizabeth, was giggling and running on bare feet, her long dress billowing out behind her. The older male, presumably her brother, had managed to slip on some shoes and was striding deliberately after her.

The fairy sang a concealment spell, cursing his lack of caution. To his surprise, however, the two children paid Goran no attention. Instead, Elizabeth stood on the very fallen log where the Sylph had been sitting moments earlier and pointed up at the outcropping. "I saw him right there, Morgan. Don't you believe me?"

"Of course I do, sister, that's why I came," came the reply. "I saw him, too—and then I saw a lot more of them. So did Ma. We didn't believe you at first, but there they were. A host of flying little people. Even little Polly and the neighbors saw them soaring up there like birds."

Elizabeth stopped giggling. "What do you think they were, Morgan?"

"Ma says angels ascending into Heaven," her brother replied. "She and the others fell to their knees and starting praying. Reckon we ought to do the same."

Goran had heard enough. The children couldn't see through his magical disguise. But evidently they, and other humans, had seen the winged host just as clearly as Goran had. Why had the fliers not shielded their movements from human eyes with spellsong?

With a groan of exasperation, the weary ranger resumed his northward course toward the Holston River and Dela's village. His adventure at the chimney rock had answered none of the questions he and his friends had been trying mightily to answer. Instead, it had only added another volume to their expanding library of mysteries.

Chapter 6 – The Lodgers

March 1807

It was pitch-black when Bell opened her eyes, but that told her nothing. It was always close to pitch-black, even on a sunny day, unless someone lit a lantern. The cellar had no proper windows. Only narrow slits and cracks in the floorboards let in thin beams of natural light.

It was her ears, not her eyes, that told Bell she could stay wrapped in her thin, frayed blanket a while longer. One of the tells was something she did not hear. If dawn had been approaching, the rooster would be crowing. But the bird, perched somewhere across the dark cellar from Bell, was silent.

The other tell was something Bell *did* hear. It was the sound of whispered words mixed with plaintive sobs, the prayers of the woman lying next to her on the straw. If it *had* been time for Bell to go to the kitchen to help with breakfast, her mother would already be up there.

"Mau-Mau?" Bell asked quietly. "What's wrong? Why you cryin'?"

She felt fingers on her arm, then the strong arms of her mother drawing Bell into a warm embrace. "Oh, my child, it's your brothers and sisters sold away from me," Mau-Mau replied. "Back to sleep, now."

"Tell me," Bell insisted. "I want to hear their tales."

"You have, many times," said her mother wearily. "Now, close your eyes."

Bell shook her head determinedly. "Can't sleep, Mau-Mau. Rooster's gonna crow."

It was some time before her mother spoke again. "How 'bout a different tale?"

"Tasks of Anansi?" The girl took an excited breath. Of all the adventures of Anansi the Spider, the one about the four tasks had always been her favorite.

71

"Yes, child," Mau-Mau said soothingly. "Now, let's see, where'd I leave off?"

"Anansi spun a high web and climbed up to Heaven to ask God for the gift of story," Bell recalled eagerly. "God gave him four tasks to do first. So Anansi tied up Omini the python, trapped Osebo the leopard in a pit, and caught the Moboro hornets in a gourd."

"Next is Mmoatia," Mau-Mau said with a gentle chuckle. "Anansi's fourth task was to take that prideful forest fairy up to Heaven. Anansi knew it would be hard; Mmoatia was small as a mongoose but strong as an elephant. Her feet pointed backwards but she could run fast. Still, Mmoatia had a weakness. And Anansi knew what it was."

"Yams!" Bell exclaimed.

Her mother hushed her with a cluck. "Are you the storyteller and I the quiet child?"

"No, Mau-Mau."

"Well, then," the woman huffed, pretending to be cross. "Yes, Anansi knew the fairy loved the taste of sweet yams. So he made a baby doll from the wood of a gum tree, smeared sap on it, and put it the forest with a bowl of yam paste at its feet. Anansi spun a web to the head of the doll and hid nearby. Before long, the yam smell drew out Mmoatia. 'May I have a taste?' the fairy asked. Anansi used his web to make the doll nod, so Mmoatia ate. 'Delicious,' said the fairy, smacking her lips. 'May I have more?' Again the doll nodded, thanks to tricky Anansi."

Bell sighed. No matter how many times she heard the tale, it entranced her.

"After Mmoatia licked the bowl clean," Mau-Mau continued, "she turned back to the doll. 'Thank you,' said the fairy. But the doll didn't move. 'Thank you,' she said again. No nod. Insulted by the gum doll's bad manners, Mmoatia slapped its head—and her hand stuck. Then the fairy hit the doll with its other hand. Also stuck. Now mighty angry, Mmoatia attacked the doll with both legs and got trapped."

"So Anansi took her to Heaven?" Bell asked.

"So he did," her mother agreed, "and brought back the gift of story to us all."

The girl snuggled up to her mother more closely. "Now, Mau-Mau, tell the one about . . ."

The next tale came not from her mother, however, but from the rooster. It told them, very loudly, to arise.

▲▲▲

"Make sure the mush pot is full, Betsy," Mister Hardenbergh said as he hurried into the kitchen. "Had a full house of lodgers last night."

Charles Hardenbergh, master of the household, rarely made an appearance before breakfast. Actually, Bell couldn't recall the last time she'd seen the master in the kitchen at any time of day. As she tended a small stewpot of pork and vegetables left over from last night's dinner, the Dutchman wiped his hands nervously on his breeches and peered over Mau-Mau's shoulder at the cornmeal mush she was stirring.

"We will serve molasses and milk at table," Hardenberg said.

Mau-Mau's head whipped around. "We low on molasses, sir."

"If we run out, we run out," the Dutchman insisted. "We have a special guest today. A war hero! That he and his brothers chose to lodge here is a great honor."

Bell wasn't sure what war Mister Hardenbergh was talking about. She knew as much about such things as any nine-year-old slave girl could pick up around an inn, which is to say she knew rather a lot, or at least she thought she did. The American war against the British had ended long before she was born. She'd heard gray-haired lodgers from New York, Albany, and other points along the Hudson talk about fighting in that war when they were young. But there was also that time, a couple of years ago, when an old trader visiting the inn had mentioned an Indian battle out west at a place called the Timbers.

"Where'd the soldier fight?" Bell blurted out.

Mister Hardenbergh wasn't a cruel man. He wasn't like masters Bell had heard about from other slaves, masters who'd beat you if you did something wrong. Nevertheless, ever since "Old Colonel" Hardenbergh died and Bell, her parents, and her brother, Peter, had moved into the house of the colonel's son, Charles had made it clear that slave children were to be seen, not heard. "Old Colonel" may have been fond of Mau-Mau Bett and "Faithful Baumfree." He'd even given them land where they could grow corn, flax, and tobacco to use or sell. But Charles had also made it clear that, to him, slaves were worth only what work they could do for his household.

Which was, in this moment, making breakfast for his guests, not asking questions. Mister Hardenbergh glared at Bell, who quickly lowered her head and turned back to her pot.

"He's a sailor, not a soldier," he snapped.

"She meant no harm, sir," Mau-Mau said apologetically.

Hardenbergh cleared his throat and headed for the door. "The lieutenant and his brothers are hungry. You will not keep them waiting."

When he was gone, the girl felt another glare replace that of her master. "Mind your wanderin' tongue, child, 'fore you will bring down sufferin' on us."

Bell felt a flash of anger. "We already suffer, Mau-Mau! You cry for all your lost babies. It was Old Colonel who sold 'em! He wasn't a good master. His son ain't, either."

Her mother's expression softened slightly. "Could be worse."

"Couldn't it be better?" the girl demanded.

Mau-Mau sighed. "Deliverance is comin', Bell, but not from rash words. It's comin' from God."

"We pray to God every night," the girl pointed out.

"And we will pray again tonight," said her mother. "Now, finish spicin' that stew."

▲▲▲

The inn was indeed full. When Bell followed her mother into the dining room, carrying a jar of milk, she saw Charles and five other members of the Hardenbergh family sitting around one table and another half dozen guests crowded around another. There was a middle-aged couple in traditional Dutch dress, probably farmers from somewhere upriver of Ulster County. An old man in hunting shirt and cloth breeches sat next to them, lighting his pipe, and on the far side of the table sat three young men chatting in English. One of them was obviously the "war hero" Mister Hardenbergh had mentioned. He wore a fancy uniform while the other two were dressed like the merchants who sometimes visited from New York.

Bell spoke Dutch, like everyone else in the Hardenbergh household, so she couldn't follow the young men's conversation. Still, she was able to pick out three words as she walked toward their table. "Ship" and "pistol" sounded like Dutch. The other one, however, was unfamiliar: "bar-bar-y."

I don't know what that means, Bell thought, *but it sure is a funny word.*

The uniformed man—Mister Hardenbergh had called him "lieutenant"—was tall and broad-shouldered with big green eyes and curly black hair. His cravat, waistcoat, breeches, and stockings were all white. His dark-blue uniform coat had gold stripes and shiny buttons.

His brothers shared the uniformed man's large green eyes but otherwise looked quite different. One was short and stout, with short hair and a round face. The third brother was as tall as the lieutenant but much slighter in build. His ear lobes were floppy, his nose prominent, his hair stringy, his shoulders narrow, and his arms too long for his sleeves. His spindly legs were folded uncomfortably beneath the table.

It was that brother, the lanky one, who first noticed Bell standing at the table and looking intently at them. He met her eyes and smiled, inclining his head. Startled by the gesture, the girl nearly spilled the milk as she quickly placed the jar on the table and backed away.

From across the room, Mister Hardenbergh fixed her with yet another stern stare. "You be careful!" he warned her before bowing and saying something in English to the three brothers. The lieutenant responded by holding up his hand and shaking his head. Then the lanky brother spoke up, calling the uniformed man "Will" and the other brother "Joe." When Will answered him, Bell learned that the lanky brother was named "Ben."

"Go get the molasses," said Mau-Mau, looking anxious. As Bell hurried to do so, she heard Mister Hardenbergh speak a few more hurried English words to the brothers.

Wish I knew what they were saying, she thought. *Tonight, when my mother prays to God for deliverance, I'll pray to know English.*

In the time it took her to walk to the kitchen and back with the molasses jar, Will had begun to tell a story. Everyone else in the room was watching the lieutenant with rapt attention as he stood behind the table, waving his arms excitedly. Two more familiar words stuck out to the otherwise mystified Bell: a "skipper," she knew, was in charge of a ship, and a "schooner" was a kind of ship with sails.

The words conjured up a nearly forgotten memory: the first time Bell had ever seen a sailing ship. She recalled a small version of herself, maybe two years old, riding in a wagon from the Old Colonel's house to the river landing at Esopus. She recalled a skipper walking over from a docked sailboat and talking to her father, calling him "James Free Tree." And she recalled something else, too—a cloudy image of a tiny woman standing on the deck of the boat, holding some kind of pitchfork and looking back at Bell with a strange expression on her face. It was a face not dark brown like Bell's, nor ruddy pink like the skipper's, but the color of a ripe blueberry.

Perhaps it was because Bell kept trying to bring that cloudy memory into sharper focus. Perhaps it was because Will's storytelling had become even more animated and distracting as she approached. Or perhaps it was simply because Will's gangly brother Ben was wearing light-brown trousers, making it hard to see his long, thin leg stretched awkwardly across the maple planking of the floor.

Whatever the cause, the effect was dramatic.

Bell tripped over Ben's leg. The jar flew from her hands and crashed into the tabletop, exploding into many pieces as a dark, thick clump of molasses splashed up onto the navy-blue uniform coat, white cravat, and shocked face of the lieutenant.

The subsequent explosions were verbal—Ben shouted, Will cursed, Joe guffawed, Mister Hardenbergh bellowed, Mau-Mau pleaded. And the rest of the lodgers and diners gasped, shrieked, scolded, and laughed, forming such a cacophony that it was impossible to sort out which was which and who said what.

Bell didn't try, nor did she wait to hear her censure or learn her punishment. Instead, she ran.

She ran into the kitchen. She ran out the back door. She ran across the meadow behind the Hardenbergh house and into the forest. She ran past trees and berry bushes and thickets and nests. She ran out of shame. She ran out of fear. She ran because she couldn't think of anything else to do.

Presently, Bell emerged from the woods to find herself at a crossing between two dirt trails. One led, by a more-circuitous route, back to the settlement and the Hardenbergh House. The other, she guessed, led to a point further up the river.

Exhausted, her face streaked with sweat and tears, the girl stopped running and bent over, trying to catch her breath and pondering her next move. *The longer I stay away, the more trouble I'll be in*, she knew. But the sun was up, the sky was clear, and birds were singing merrily. Still bent over, she peered through the gap between her legs and watched a butterfly land daintily among a patch of wildflowers behind her. Of course, her head being upside down, it looked to Bell as if the brilliantly hued butterfly had floated up, not down, to drink from the yellow flowers.

Everything is all topsy-turvy, she reflected. *What a beautiful world this would be if we saw everything right side up.*

Then she glimpsed something behind the butterfly, something else moving in her topsy-turvy world. Bell groaned, straightened, and wheeled around when she realized it was a pair of dark leather shoes.

Thrust into the shoes were a pair of feet sheathed in stockings of coarsely knitted wool. At the knee, the stockings gave way to tan breeches, then a red work shirt open at the neck, then a brown cloth coat. The man standing before her at the crossroads—standing not much taller than Bell, though she was only nine years old—wore a cloth sack over his shoulder and a floppy cloth hat on his head, each a shade of brown different from his coat.

As was the shade of his skin, which nearly matched her own.

Bell didn't recognize the man, whose short black hair was speckled with dots of gray. He wasn't one of the slaves of the valley who occasionally came calling at the Hardenbergh House. She wondered if he might be a sailor from a river sloop or a traveler from some faraway town. *At least he didn't come to fetch me home.*

"How d'you do?" Bell asked as meekly as she could, given the morning's excitement and her irrepressible curiosity.

In response, the man smiled, shook his head, and spat on the grass.

Bell wasn't at all offended by the gesture. She'd seen many a man—and more than a few women—chewing tobacco as they worked, walked, and talked. But she had a hard time believing any slave of Ulster County couldn't understand Dutch, so she tried again.

"Name's Bell," she said, bowing her head slightly.

The man seemed to understand. "John," he said, pointing to himself.

"You from Esopus, or Poughkeepsie?" she asked.

Once more the man shook his head and smiled, still working his jaws vigorously on his chaw. But Bell didn't smile back; now she was put out. How could this John understand what she said sometimes but not other times? Did he just not want to talk to a girl?

Of course, Bell was also tired and upset and fearful of what awaited her back home. But in her mind, that wasn't why she felt so ornery. The man was just rude.

"Go, then, and leave me alone!" said the frustrated girl, turning away and sinking dejectedly to the ground.

As she sat with her chin in her hands and mulled her fate, fresh teardrops trickling from the corners of tightly shut eyes, Bell heard the man shuffling behind her. It wasn't the shuffle of a worn-out field hand coming in sundown or an old woman trying to move her stiff limbs across a slippery floor without falling. No, what she heard was the sound of feet brushing and striking the hard ground in a regular pattern. It reminded her of the way Mau-Mau sometimes clapped her hands or tapped her chair while singing a hymn. And it reminded Bell of the music and dancing she saw every year at Pinkster celebrations in the valley.

The man kept up his rhythmic shuffling while circling to her right. Despite her frustration, she couldn't help opening her eye a crack. John's back was turned to her at that moment, the tail of his coat sticking out almost flat as he twirled his body. When his grinning face reappeared and he caught her eye, Bell closed it—but not before she caught a glimpse of John's floppy hat floating improbably high above his head.

Once the strangeness of the image registered in her head, Bell opened her eyes wide to take another look. John's hat was no longer floating above his head but was now spinning around the index finger of his left hand. Lifting his right hand high in the air and pressing his fingers together to form the shape of a beak, John used it to snap at the hat's brim like a bird trying to grab a worm off a spinning wheel.

Bell laughed. No child, no matter how forlorn, could have resisted the impulse. And John laughed back.

Then the man made a few flourishes with his right hand and placed it inside the crown of the hat. Digging a heel into the dirt and executing a sudden turn all the way around, he removed his right hand to reveal a long stem ending in a whorl of three narrow green leaves and a beautiful blossom of broad white petals and tiny yellow stamens.

Her mouth forming a perfect circle, Bell marveled at the flower John had mysteriously produced from the hat. Then she sucked in a breath of pleasure when John danced over and presented the lovely flower to her.

"Thank you," said Bell, daring to take a sniff.

The man spun on one heel again, using the momentum to launch a wad of spittle all the way over the dirt road and into the trees. Bell giggled and clapped. Looking down at her, his kindly expression not quite concealing a hint of mischief, John reached into his sack and pulled out a handful of odd-looking roots. They were bulbous, red-orange, and contorted into twisty shapes. John tossed them into Bell's lap, spun once more, and leapt into a handspring.

Puzzled, the girl looked down at the roots. When she returned her gaze to John, now standing on the dirt road, he gave her a wink and removed another red-orange root from the bag. He lifted it to his mouth and bit off a large chunk. Even from a distance, Bell caught a whiff of strong aromas—of mornings at a cookpot, of afternoons by the river, of evenings in a pine forest. Watching her closely, John sat down on the ground and chewed, fattening and hollowing his cheeks as he swirled the pulp around his mouth. Then he parted his lips and shot out a stream of juice between gritted teeth.

Delighted, Bell clapped again and brought one of the roots up to her own mouth. Gingerly she bit off the tip, only to wince as the powerful flavor made her eyes water and her mouth feel numb. Her reaction made John laugh his loudest laugh yet.

The two sat for what seemed like hours, although it may only have been a few minutes, watching each other chew and competing to see who could spit the farthest. Then John glanced up at the sky, shaded his eyes from the sun, and let out a low whistle. Rising to his feet, he placed his brown floppy hat on his head, tucked his red shirttail into his breeches, and started walking toward the forest, nodding amiably at Bell and saying something in English.

She'd pocketed the roots and now held up the pretty white flower appreciatively. John shot her a sly grin and strode toward a low bush. As he passed behind it, the top half of the man suddenly disappeared from Bell's sight. She gasped as she watched the branches stir as if something were crawling through the bush, then gasped again when John's head, chest, and arms reappeared, along with the rest of him, on the other side. With a final wave, the man shuffled off into the woods.

Well, I guess that's that. Time to go back and get what's coming to me. As Bell got to her feet, however, she realized she didn't feel scared anymore.

Chapter 7 – The Raven

There were many places closer to Gulkalaski's farm where he could sell pelts, buy trade goods, and swap stories. But none held the attraction of the summer house he could see ahead of him, its chestnut-bark roof painted with yellow streaks by the sun peeking through the trees.

On the porch, in front of the red clay walls of the house that was also a store, there was a table stacked with horseshoes, hoe blades, and other metal objects for sale. But Gulkalaski hadn't left his wife, Yona, and their home in the deep gap of the mountains—following Alarka Creek north to the Tuckasegee River, then travelling westward more than a hundred miles to the banks of the Little Tennessee—merely to buy horseshoes or hoe blades.

No. He'd come all this way, to Tuskegee Town, to see the owner of the store, his close friend. He's come to see Sequoyah.

They'd met as boys in Citico. Orphaned as an infant when his father was killed at the Battle of Boyd's Creek and his mother died from the pox, Gulkalaski had been raised by his kindhearted but sickly grandmother. Her frequent trips to the healing springs of Citico had eased her suffering only a little. Indeed, the visits had aided Gulkalaski more by introducing him to Sequoyah—and later, through a glimpse of the famous Nanyehi, to a wondrous world of myth and magic.

As Gulkalaski climbed the steps to Sequoyah's porch, he heard someone speaking rapidly, though somewhat indistinctly, in Cherokee. The voice was loud, youthful, and bore the unmistakable accent of a white man. Gulkalaski crossed the porch and paused outside the door to listen, pressing his necklace against his shirt to keep its cat claws from jangling. The voice from inside was now talking in English, not Cherokee, although the man's words still sounded slurred. Upon reflection, Gulkalaski realized that "talking" wasn't the right description; it was more like the white man was reciting the words of a song. Because Gulkalaski had learned English in his youth, he found he could understand a fair amount of the strange recitation:

Then Jove to Themis gives command, to call
The gods to council in the starry hall:
Swift over Olympus's hundred hills, she flies,
And summons all the senate of the skies.
These shining on, in long procession come
To Jove's eternal adamantine dome.
Not one was absent, not a rural power
That haunts the verdant gloom, or rosy bower;
Each fair-haired dryad of the shady wood,
Each azure sister of the silver flood;
All but old Ocean, hoary sire! Who keeps
His ancient seat beneath the sacred deeps.
On marble thrones, with lucid columns crowned,
The work of Vulcan, sat the powers around.
Even he whose trident sways the watery reign
Heard the loud summons, and forsook the main,
Assumed his throne amid the bright abodes,
And questioned thus the sire of men and gods . . .

The speaker showed no signs of taking a break, so Gulkalaski pushed open the door.

Seated next to a window, its reed shutter open to let in fresh air, was his friend Sequoyah. On the other side of the room, between a rack of trade goods and the stone hearth of the summer house, was the young white man, his mouth agape in surprise.

The white was tall and well-built with long brown hair swept back over his ears and patches of brown stubble not quite obscuring the pronounced cleft in his chin. Like the other two, the white youth was dressed in Cherokee fashion, a trade shirt of cloth belted at the waist over buckskin leggings. In his hand was a bundle of paper bound in leather like the books Gulkalaski had seen white missionaries carry.

"Sorry for interrupting," said Gulkalaski pleasantly, noting that the stranger was swaying awkwardly.

The unsteady youth blinked blue eyes. "I am not interrupted, sir," he said, looking offended. "I merely pause for dramatic effect."

Gulkalaski glanced at Sequoyah, who seemed mystified in more ways than one. His friend spoke only Cherokee, Gulkalaski knew, so the white man's recitation must have sounded like gibberish to him. And now the youth's haughty expression was heightening Sequoyah's confusion.

Was it truly haughty, though?

Gulkalaski could see the youth's eyebrows twitching and the corners of his mouth quivering. *Your game needs two players.* "Will you leave us in suspense, boy," Gulkalaski demanded, "or tell us what this watery god with his fish spear demanded of the one called Jove?"

Whooping with delight, the young man bent into an exaggerated bow, nearly losing his footing as he did so.

Sequoyah, visibly relieved, smiled and greeted Gulkalaski. "Your face is a welcome sight after so long, my friend," he said in their mother tongue. "This young man is on his way back to Cayuga Town from his mother's house in Maryville. He is called Kolana."

Gulkalaski gave the youth a searching look. "So you go by 'The Raven', eh?" he asked in English. "Are you such a wanderer? Or are you an imposter out to steal our souls?"

Kolana straightened and met Gulkalaski's gaze, still looking delighted. "Neither," he replied in his own tongue, flourishing a hand in front of his flushed face. "My ancestors' coat of arms bore three ravens. It's a good name for me. But I know the legend you speak of, the soul-stealing Raven Mocker. I heard it from Oolooteka."

Sequoyah rose with difficulty from his chair, rubbing his lame knee with a pained expression. "Is it too much to ask that you speak words I can understand? The only one I caught there was the name of my uncle Oolooteka of Cayuga Town, the chief the whites call John Jolly."

"My apologies, Sequoyah," Gulkalaski said. "Your new friend here was just telling me he knows the tale of the Raven Mocker."

"The evil spirit who can turn itself invisible and ride its fiery wings on the wind as it stalks the souls of its prey," Kolana agreed, swaying from side to side. "A dream tale to frighten Cherokee children, no doubt."

Then he hiccupped loudly, confirming Gulkalaski's suspicions. Kolana was drunk.

Gulkalaski shot a questioning glance at Sequoyah, who gave a quick nod. The young man certainly had not gotten drunk in this house. Years ago, shortly after taking over the Tuskegee store from his deceased mother, Sequoyah had taken to consuming too much of his own stock, becoming a widely ridiculed drunkard. At the urging of his

82

remaining friends, Gulkalaski included, Sequoyah had finally found the courage to quit. Since then, he had neither consumed nor sold a drop of liquor.

Now Gulkalaski understood why Sequoyah was willing to sit inside and listen to Kolana ramble on unintelligibly in English. He was giving the young man shelter to sober up.

"You do not believe in evil spirits, Kolana?" Gulkalaski asked, filling a vacant chair in hopes of encouraging the youth to do the same.

"What grown man would?" Kolana responded, seeing Sequoyah resume his own seat. Taking the hint, the white boy sat precariously on the edge of a barrel, resting his elbows on his knees.

His retort made Gulkalaski think of the marvelous discoveries of his own youth and early adulthood. Witnessing the Beloved Woman Nanyehi speaking with a Nunnehi scout. Finding the village of the Yunwi Tsunsdi. Meeting the elderly ranger of the Moon-Eyed People and helping her find her final rest. Battling the Giant Leech and other magical beasts with his gift spear. And befriending the fairy rangers Tana, Goran, and Har the Tower.

"When I came in, you were telling a fantastic tale," Gulkalaski pointed out. "It spoke of otherworldly creatures. A children's story, too?

Kolana ran a finger lovingly along the cover of his book. "Not at all, although I first read *The Iliad* as a child in the library of my father. It is a long, bloody tale of heroic deeds and moral struggles. One of the great works of any age, in any language."

Gulkalaski pointed to the book. "And yet your talking leaves speak of sky gods, water gods, and if I recall rightly, 'fair-headed dryads of the shady wood' and 'azure sisters of the silver flood.' What are these but spirits?"

Smiling as much from sheepishness as from the effects of drink, Kolana nodded. "A Dryad is an Elfin spirit of the forest, yes, and the 'azure sister' is a Naiad, a spirit of river and lake, although I do not know if her skin is always blue."

"But all the Naiads you have ever seen have blue skin," joked Sequoyah.

"I've only seen one!" the white youth exclaimed.

Gulkalaski watched Sequoyah's expression of joviality shift to one of surprise, then of pity. *He thinks the liquor is talking, not the boy.* Gulkalaski wasn't so sure. He had often seen strong drink free a tongue to speak a truth the drinker might otherwise conceal.

If I am right, however, it might be best to keep that truth concealed for now.

"Kolana, you promised to tell us what happens next in the tale," he observed. "Does Jove's council assemble?"

The youth seemed confused at first by the question. He looked not at Gulkalaski but at the wall, his eyes flitting back and forth as if he were watching some invisible warrior leaping and dancing around a ceremonial fire.

"The sky god," Gulkalaski prodded further. "What does he say to the water god with the fish spear?"

The young white man turned his eyes to meet those of Gulkalaski. "Jove orders Poseidon and the others to watch the final, furious assault of the Greek hero Achilles on the city of the Trojans. Without divine intervention, Jove says, Troy will surely perish before its appointed time."

Pleased by the turn in the conversation, Gulkalaski encouraged it. "Do the other spirits intervene to help the city?"

"Some do," Kolana affirmed, "while others favor the side of the Greeks. But the sea god, Poseidon, does the most surprising thing of all. Although he is on the Greek side, Poseidon intervenes to save a Trojan hero, Aeneas, from the sword of Achilles. Aeneas goes on to found a city more glorious than Troy or any in Greece: the great nation of Rome."

Although he had asked about it merely as a distraction, the tale gave Gulkalaski much to consider. "The ways of spirit creatures can be mysterious," he observed. "Their motivations are often unclear, perhaps even to themselves."

The three sat silently for a while in Sequoyah's store, lost in their respective thoughts. Gulkalaski was recalling his encounters with Tana and Har over the eight years he'd known them. He ran his fingers along his necklace, feeling the claws of the Wampus Cat and remembering when Tana had presented her gift after one of his visits to Blood Mountain. He also recalled the times Har the Dwarf had stopped by Gulkalaski's farm on the way back from his missions to the Elf colony. During their conversations, Gulkalaski had learned a great deal about the magical forces that played a hand in America's struggle for independence, as well as the long war Dragging Canoe and his Chickamauga faction of Cherokees had waged against white settlers. Like the spirits in Kolana's story, the Folk of America had gone from simply watching human conflicts to intervening in them.

And the results weren't what they expected, either.

Gulkalaski was also thinking about how much his own life had changed. He had taken his beautiful Yona to wife and built his farm on Alarka Creek. While continuing to hunt for meat and pelts, and to sharpen his skills with rifle and spear, Gulkalaski had also sharpened his skills at building fences, herding livestock, and breaking horses. Sometimes he'd even taken his turn tending the corn, squash, and bean fields with Yona and her two little sisters who had come to live with them after their mother died. It was hard but rewarding life in their creek-side home, marred only by the fact that he and Yona had not yet produced children of their own.

He looked over at Sequoyah, nine years his senior but also childless and, indeed, as yet unmarried. His friend had shaken his reputation as a drunkard, but most still saw Sequoyah as eccentric. Because of his lame knee, the man would never be a mighty warrior or hunter. He had instead become a talented worker of silver and iron, and his tools, cookpots, knives, and jewelry were prized goods. Nevertheless, they had not earned Sequoyah the respect he sought.

His friend met Gulkalaski's gaze and smiled. Sequoyah rose stiffly and strode to the open door. "I have been drinking honey locust tea all afternoon," he offered in explanation, looking meaningfully at Kolana, who was still sitting uncomfortably on the edge of the barrel.

When they were alone, the white youth rubbed his eyes and turned to Gulkalaski. "Why do you call a trident a 'fish spear'? How do you even recognize the word?"

"I have a . . . friend who once described a trident to me," Gulkalaski replied, remembering the time he'd challenged Tana to a shooting contest with blowguns and then listened patiently as the victor lectured him on the different weapons of Folk nations. "I assume its three blades are as good for spearing fish as anything else."

Kolana again looked misty-eyed. "The Naiad I saw was carrying a trident. I don't think she catches fish with it."

Glancing warily at the door, Gulkalaski decided to risk satisfying his curiosity. "Tell me of her."

The youth stood up quickly—too quickly, for he wobbled and sat back down on the barrel. "It was along ago, back in Virginia, before my father died."

"Were you very young?" Gulkalaski asked.

"The Naiad was far away, but I see her clearly in my dreams," said Kolana, seeming not to hear Gulkalaski's question. "She was small and slender, standing no taller than this." He held out his hand out flat next to his knee. The hand was shaking.

"And her skin was blue?"

"Yes, a very light blue, although her hair was a darker shade. She carried a trident in her hand and a net over the opposite shoulder. The others were armed differently."

"The others?" Gulkalaski was puzzled. "I thought you said you saw only one."

"Only one *Naiad*," Kolana answered. "But she wasn't alone. There were several people with her, regular people like you and me, and two others. A little winged creature with a bow slung over his back. And a bigger one, wingless, holding an axe."

Goran and Har, Gulkalaski realized. *So this "Naiad" the white youth speaks of must be the friend they told me about, the Water Maiden named Dela.*

Kolana burped and groaned. "I feel awful."

"I am not surprised," Gulkalaski said.

"After that day, I never saw them again," said the boy, rubbing his temples. "But in the years since, and especially since my mother moved us to Tennessee, I've seen other mysterious things. I saw one of those Dryads from *The Iliad*. She was sleeping in the crook of a sycamore tree. Then there was a bird too large to be, well, a bird. I even saw a jackrabbit with horns! At first I thought I was sick in the head. As I got older, though, it got to be like a game. I'd rather look for magic folk in the woods than farm or mind a store."

"This is why you ran off, right?" Gulkalaski guessed.

"One of the reasons. My mother and brothers were constantly after me. Called me wild. 'There's no hope for Sam,' they'd say."

"Your white name is Sam, then."

"Yep—Sam Houston," the boy said. "Cayuga Town is the first place that's truly felt like home. Oolooteka lets me live as I choose. And Cherokee girls are mighty pretty."

At that last remark, he managed a weak smile. Then he groaned again. "I know you don't believe me. You think it's the drink making me see such things."

No, Gulkalaski mused, *I think seeing such things throughout your childhood may have driven you to drink.* But as much as he might want to ease the white youth's troubled mind, he knew better than to entrust secrets to one with a liquor-loosened tongue.

"I believe you speak the truth as you know it," Gulkalaski said gently. "And now, Sam Houston, you'd best follow Sequoyah's example and go water a tree."

▲▲▲

"Oolooteka and his brother may be my kin, but that does not mean I agree with them."

It was hours later, the blazing heat of the late afternoon sun replaced by the cool light of the crescent moon. Something was still blazing, however: the eyes of Sequoyah. The three sat on his porch, looking west toward the river glistening in the moonlight, watching pines sway in the breeze and discussing Cherokee politics. Given Sequoyah's strong feelings about recent events, Gulkalaski thought he was being remarkably restrained as he contested the claims of the white youth, who was calmer but paler after retching a couple of times in the woods.

The latest blow to Cherokee unity had a long arc. In the years since the Treaty of Tellico had ended war on the frontier, some of the leaders who'd once fought alongside Dragging Canoe had modified their lifestyles significantly. They'd adopted white styles of dress, sent their children to learn English in mission schools, and established large-scale plantations, employing tenant farmers and, in some cases, enslaved blacks to work their fields.

The similarities of their new agrarian lifestyles masked deep disagreements among the Cherokee leaders about how best to respond to American expansion. Some believed it wise to sell lands to whites in exchange for trade goods and guarantees that their remaining towns and farms would be secure, while others thought that land sales would beget only more land sales, inevitably endangering Cherokee sovereignty.

When two well-off chiefs of the Lower Towns in Tennessee and northern Georgia—Doublehead and Tahlonteeskee, the half-brother of Oolooteka—signed treaties selling prime hunting lands to whites, the infuriated chiefs of the Upper Towns accused them of treachery and corruption. They assassinated Doublehead and threatened Tahlonteeskee. After protesting his innocence for years, Tahlonteeskee decided to relocate to the Arkansas Territory with more than a thousand followers.

"They only want what's best," Sam Houston insisted. "They aren't saying *everyone* should move west. After all, when Tahlonteeskee was chief, he didn't try to make everyone in Cayuga leave with him for Arkansas. His own brother Oolooteka stayed behind and became chief. Those who would live as friends and neighbors with Americans can stay; those who would rather live on their own can go west."

Sequoyah threw up his hands in exasperation. "Why are those the only choices? This is the land of *our* ancestors, not yours. We should not have to adopt the white man's ways to live freely on our own land."

Gulkalaski cleared his throat. "Did you not work your *iron* forge today, my friend?" he asked dryly.

Sitting back in his chair and straightening his lame leg with difficulty, Sequoyah affected a half smile. "I have no objection to learning useful things, Gulkalaski. But a forge is just a tool. A cotton shirt from a trading post is just a garment. I can buy them with the products of my fields or my workshop. What the chiefs buy, however, is dishonor. And what they sell is our land. Without it, we will no longer be a nation."

"On that, we are agreed," said Gulkalaski, willing himself to keep his temper in check despite his own strong feelings. Although he had grown up in a town like generations of his ancestors before him, he'd carved his own farm out of the mountainside with his own two hands and those of his family. *We fence it. We tend the animals. We sow and reap.*

Although the old men in town called it "the white man's way" to grow crops for sale or to herd cows and pigs for milk and meat, Gulkalaski was proud of the home he had built. It was his. Neither the guns of his enemies nor the blunders of foolish chiefs would make him give it up.

"Oolooteka believes as you do," Sam Houston insisted. "The people of Cayuga Town combine the best of both worlds. They live in peace. They want no part of the intrigues of Cherokees or the schemes of whites."

"I fear intrigues and schemes will find them anyway," Sequoyah replied. "If Cherokees do not present a united front, we will be swept away."

"That is the purpose of the meeting later this summer," Gulkalaski pointed out. Many chiefs had agreed to convene at Willstown, in the shadow of Lookout Mountain, to negotiate a pact to forbid the selling of land without the approval of national councils.

Houston was staring at the planks of the porch, looking chagrined. "I talk too much about things I shouldn't," he muttered in a subdued voice that, Gulkalaski suspected, was more comfortable being loud and boisterous. "I do appreciate your hospitality, Sequoyah."

Gulkalaski watched his friend turn a sympathetic face to the youth. "You are welcome, Kolana of Cayuga Town," said Sequoyah. "Now, if you will be so kind, show me this treasure of yours again. The leather pouch with the talking leaves."

Chapter 8 – The Weepers

April 1810

"Stupid girl!"

It was one of the few Dutch phrases Mistress Nealy had mastered—from constant practice.

No matter how hard Bell tried to please the mistress, the wall between them proved to be too high for even an exceptionally tall twelve-year-old girl to scale. Bell knew little English; the Englishwoman knew even less of Dutch. John Nealy, her husband, could at least understand what Bell was saying some of the time, but he spent most days in the fields and most nights at the tavern in Kingston, drinking too much and winning too few of the fights he picked. Mister Nealy wasn't around the house enough to translate for the two women even if he had cared to.

Bell never thought she'd miss Master Hardenbergh and the dark, dirty cellar under his inn. But when he had died unexpectedly and Bell was sold away from Mau-Mau Bet and James Baumfree, she came to recall her earlier life with fondness. Yes, it had been filled with discomfort and toil. Still, she hadn't been so scared all the time, and so alone.

Mistress Nealy was speaking rapidly in English, nodding at the trammel hook in Bell's hands and pointing meaningfully at the hearth. She wanted the frying pan, Bell realized, not the hook for hanging it over the fire. She tried apologizing in Dutch, but as usual, this only annoyed the Englishwoman. Bell turned and ran quickly to where the pots were stored, her strong arms lifting the cast-iron pan with ease.

When Bell returned, Mistress Nealy accepted the pan without another word, secured it over the hearth, and placed bread inside to be toasted for breakfast. Bell assumed her mistress would want her to stir the corn mush in the other cookpot but when she knelt and reached for the spoon, the Englishwoman slapped her hand and muttered,

"Stupid girl!" Then she jabbed a bony finger toward the barn visible through the window.

Unsure if she was being sent on another errand or simply being banished, Bell merely nodded and walked out. There was no point in asking for more instructions. She wouldn't have understood them, anyway.

As she approached the barn, Bell heard no rustling or mooing. She guessed Mister Nealy had already led the cows into the pasture. That meant she could start cleaning the stalls. It was a task she understood without instructions, and it meant an hour free of prying eyes or listening ears—an hour Bell could use speaking her prayers as Mau-Mau had taught her.

God won't hear me unless I pray out loud. Mau-Mau had taught me that, too.

Bell longed to be wrapped in her mother's arms like that day in front of the Hardenbergh House—the day Mister Nealy had yanked her from Mau-Mau's grasp and taken her away.

The death of Charles Hardenbergh had led to Bell's parents being emancipated. It was not out of kindness, though. None of Hardenbergh's relatives wanted two old slaves. James Baumfree had lost much of his eyesight and strength. And whether the cause was years of unending toil or the trauma of having her children stripped away from her and sold, Mau-Mau Bet had become slow, forgetful, and sickly. To honor the Old Colonel's wishes, the Hardenbergh relatives had freed both slaves on the condition that they support themselves. That Bell's parents had, living as hired hands in the cellar of what had been the inn and was now the home of a Dutch couple newly arrived from upriver.

The Hardenbergh House wasn't far away from the Nealys. Bell could walk there and back in just hours, but the Nealys didn't trust her. And even though they expressed nothing but scorn for her work, they didn't seem to want to do without her for a single day.

As she neared the barn, Bell relished the feeling of young grass on her bare feet. With the winter chill giving way to hints of spring, the soles of her feet were no longer hardened, blistered, and aching from frostbite. Patches of snow still lay on the ground, but its effect was more to create muddy spots rather than icy ones between the patches of resurgent grass. Even the mud felt good on her feet.

When she reached the barn, Bell spotted the pitchfork leaning against a post. Sighing, she reached for it.

"Stupid girl!" barked a voice. A man's voice.

Before she could reply, before she even could turn her head, Bell felt hands seize the back of her dress and spin her around. While Mistress Nealy was slender, wiry, and crone-faced, John Nealy was round, husky, and red-faced. He grabbed her wrists with one beefy hand and produced a long, thin strap with the other.

Bell felt a terror she'd never known before as Nealy tied her hands together, his face contorted in a malicious sneer. He had beaten her in the past, and Mistress Nealy had slapped her, but Bell's hands had never been bound. She'd never felt entirely defenseless.

Not wanting to provoke him further, she averted her eyes to the straw-strewn floor. That also spared her from having to see his mocking face—but only for a brief moment.

"Look!" Mister Nealy demanded. Bell looked up and saw several sticks tied together in his shaking hand. Their tips were glowing orange as if they were embers from the hearth.

Nealy spun Bell around and pushed her against the post. Then she gasped as, with rough hands, he yanked the top of her dress down enough to bare her shoulders and the top half of her back. The first blow from the bundle against her skin stung worse than any whipping she'd ever gotten. The second blow delivered more than just a sting— it felt like the kick of a bull. The third blow was like a long, sharp knife slicing her bare flesh. The fourth felt as if she'd been tossed, back first, onto a roaring fire.

After that, Bell lost count of the blows. Clinging hopelessly to the post, she knew only pain, shame, and flame. Through her tears, she could see her own blood painting the floor with drops and splashes. Her thoughts became a silent scream of anguish. *Oh, my God, how can any human being treat another this way?!* Then the screaming stopped.

▲▲▲

She woke up on the blood-painted floor, her dress still loose at the neck, her limbs stiff, her back burning. It was only after struggling to her feet, adjusting her dress, and stumbling outside did Bell discover it was no longer morning. It was midafternoon. When Mister Nealy had finished scourging her, he'd simply left her in a lifeless heap.

Like that time at the inn, years earlier, when she'd spilled molasses on the blue-coated lieutenant, Bell began to run without a destination in mind. She ran across the pasture, past the grazing cows, into the woods. As she ran, Bell thrust a hand into the pocket of her apron and felt the familiar, stubby shape of the red-orange root. It was her last one. She'd guarded it jealously for months, taking only nibbles, chewing the pungent pulp for hours until the numbing effect wore off and all that was left was the discolored saliva she spat on the ground.

Chewing it had made her think of the day she met the strange little man named John and of other happier days. It had made her life bearable—that, and speaking the prayers Mau-Mau taught her. She planned to do both, chew and pray, as soon as she felt safe enough to try.

After a while, Bell slowed to a trot. She found herself in an unfamiliar part of the forest. The trees were larger and more colorful. Most were evergreens or hardwoods dotted with fresh green leaves. What most caught Bell's attention, however, was a lone willow tree, about fifty feet high, in a clearing next to a small creek. It was draped with curtains of long, wispy blossoms dabbed in golden yellow.

The curtains of spring blossoms caught the attention of the sad, suffering girl, to be sure. But that wasn't all. The willow was swaying in the breeze, the gentle motion beckoning to Bell like the wave of a friendly hand. And as she looked more closely, another motion caught her eye. Above halfway up the forked trunk, through the curtain of blossoms and leaves, Bell could see something rising and falling even as the rest of the tree rocked side to side. It was too small to see clearly, but it didn't look like a willow branch. Its yellow-brown color stood out from the dark-brown trunk of the tree.

Her pain and anxiety momentarily forgotten, Bell spotted some small oaks that had grown together to form a bower of leafy branches. She walked to it, slowly and carefully, keeping her eye on the object in the willow tree, which she guessed was some kind of forest animal or large bird. Pleased her actions hadn't chased it away, Bell slipped underneath the bower and sat. Her hand found its way to her pocket. Then the corner of her last remaining chewing root found its way to her mouth.

Bell sat there a long time, moving the root pulp around her mouth with her tongue and savoring the sharp, lemony flavor. She also watched whatever was perched in the willow. Its up-and-down movement ceased for a time, then resumed. It was no bird, she decided. It had arms and legs. It looked to be well over two feet long, maybe three. She'd have guessed it was a big raccoon gnawing on a nut or fruit, but raccoons had dark fur, and this creature was a very light brown.

It was only after the arrival of the second stranger that Bell got a clearer look at the first.

She heard the man long before she saw him. From across the creek came a song. Although she couldn't understand the words, it sounded like the hymns Mau-Mau used to sing. In the tree, the creature suddenly stopped moving. Then a white man came into sight and waded into the creek. He was one of the strangest-looking people Bell had ever seen: His tattered red shirt was much too large for his skinny frame, his faded blue trousers were too tight, and on his head was a hat with its brim cocked up on three sides and thrust forward in the front.

The man's face was lit with a bright smile. It wasn't meant for Bell, still hidden under the oak branches. The stranger walked to the willow and called up to whatever was sitting up there. The figure dropped to the ground—and Bell found herself startled by the form of a tiny woman clad in a simple brown shift cinched at the waist with a yellow belt, her long wavy hair intricately braided and encircled by a wreath of leaves and flowers. Similar bands of leaves and flowers adorned her wrists, her ankles. From her bare feet to the tips of her pointed ears, the woman looked remarkably like the tiny creature Bell had glimpsed on the river sloop so many years before, except this woman was taller and her skin was yellow-brown, not pale blue.

The odd white man and the little tree woman spoke rapidly in English. Not for the first time, Bell wished she spoke that tongue. Whatever they said, the conversation evidently upset the woman. She bent over and started to sob, the man patting her affectionately. Then Bell realized what the up-and-down movement in the willow had been: the head and shoulders of the tree woman rising and falling as she wept.

Bell wanted to run out and ask what was wrong. Her face was still streaked with the paths of her own tears shed during her flight from the Nealy house. But Bell's sad plight was obvious: a slave girl, separated from her parents and cruelly treated. Why would the tree woman, surrounded by natural beauty and free to roam the forest, have cause to weep?

Fear of exposure warred with Bell's curiosity, however. What happened next did little to resolve the conflict. The raggedy man knelt beside the tree woman, bowed his head, and began to speak so reverently that it was unnecessary for Bell to understand the words. She knew he was praying. The sight conjured up pleasant memories of lying next to Mau-Mau, offering heartfelt prayers to God.

Bell wanted to know more. But she was loath to interrupt anyone in prayer; she knew better. Instead, she kept chewing the remnants of John's root and watched.

After a time, the man rose, took the tree woman's hand, and led her over the creek. Just to make sure, Bell waited for a few minutes after they disappeared into the forest. Then she crawled out from the bower and walked to the willow, looking up at its twisted trunk and running her fingers over a long strand of yellow blossoms.

She thought of her parents. She thought of what had happened since she'd been sold to the Nealys. She thought of what she'd just witnessed. Then Bell knelt on the same spot the white man had, closed her eyes, and lifted her head toward the heavens.

"Is it right, God?" she pleaded, new tears welling. "Is it right for any of your children to live like this? I ask you to protect me. Help me. Please, God, I pray like Mau-Mau taught me. Deliver me from this evil."

Bell stood up. Breaking off a blossomed stem from the willow, she held it in front of her, like a spear-wielding hero from one of her mother's stories, and headed back in the direction she thought the Nealy house would be.

She soon realized that she was following a different path than the one she'd taken. The going was harder. After passing through a particularly treacherous patch of bramble, Bell found herself in another clearing. What awaited her, though, wasn't another lovely willow beckoning in the breeze. It wasn't a mysterious tree woman or a singing man. It was a mound of fur, flesh, and blood.

A beast lay dead on the ground. Shaped like a dog but impossibly large, it had dark, curly fur and a long, fat tail with a ragged edge that reminded Bell of a broom. Most terrifying of all was the creature's head. Its massive jaws lay open, revealing discolored teeth the size of dinner knives. Its eyes were open as well but had no whites or irises. They were solid red orbs.

If Bell hadn't been sure the dog creature was dead, she'd have run away as fast as her legs could carry her. What told her she could stay put were the three arrows protruding from the breast of the lifeless animal.

Is this why the tree woman was crying? she wondered. *I'd be scared, too, if this monster attacked me. Did the singing man kill it to save her?*

Then Bell sighed.

I have my own monster to face back home. Who will save me?

▲▲▲

What was waiting at the Nealy house was not some singing man in mismatched clothes—it was only more scorn and abuse. Nor did some heroic warrior out of a story come to rescue her. The person who did show up, about a week later, was the slow-moving figure of James Baumfree.

Given the high standing of the Hardenberghs in Ulster County, few residents would have the courage to refuse the Old Colonel's favorite slave the chance to visit his daughter. As mean as the Nealys could be to a twelve-year-old slave, they had no acquaintance with real courage.

James and Bell sat and talked in the house. She saw him wince when she bent to offer him cider. After an hour, her aged father rose with difficulty from the chair and nodded to the Nealys sitting in the adjoining room. "Walk me to the gate, Bell?" he asked. Casting her own glance to her master and mistress, who looked annoyed but permissive, she nodded.

Once outside, words tumbled out of Bell like the contents of a kicked-over stewpot. She told James of her struggles with the Nealys and showed him the stripes on her back, the tops of which he had already glimpsed in the house. However, she chose not to reveal what she'd seen near the willow. She didn't think her father would believe it anyway.

"Do what I can," he promised her. "Ain't much, but it's all I got to give."

It was a slim hope, but still Bell clung to it desperately. She prayed to God to help her father work a miracle. She retraced the steps she and James had taken from the house to the gate, relishing the sight of her father's large footprints preserved in the melted snow. She imagined those large feet bringing him back to carry her away.

However, that was not what happened. Instead, one day a Dutchman named Schryver came to the door and asked to see Bell. She remembered seeing him at Hardenbergh's inn. "Would you like to come live with me?" he asked.

"Yes," Bell replied instantly.

The price Schryver offered Mister Nealy must have be enough, because within the hour Bell was following the Dutchman down the road to the Schryver farm five miles away. Like Charles Hardenbergh, Mister Schryver also maintained a tavern. It catered to a poorer set of diners, though, and his farm was paltry and ill kept. Bell's work there proved to be difficult and solely needed. She didn't mind; she was away from the Nealys. And the Schryvers were kind.

Within a few months, Bell found herself sold to another master, John Dumont. His family was large and prosperous and Bell was soon put to work in the kitchens, where the cooking skills she'd learned from Mau-Mau were put to good use. From the start Master Dumont was pleasant, if distant, and his two young children warmly welcomed a new slave just a few years older than they were. The master's wife, Elizabeth, was less welcoming. Both aunt and stepmother to the children—after John's first wife died, he'd married her sister—Elizabeth was often critical. But at least she didn't scream at Bell in a foreign language. No one beat her. And better still, she was given free rein to wander through the woods.

It was during one of those wanderings, after she'd finished her chores early, that Bell found a small stream running northeast to the Hudson River and a small island in the middle of the stream where a clump of low willows grew next to the nourishing water. Delighted at seeing what had become her favorite kind of tree, Bell waded through the shallow stream and lay in the shade of the willow shrubs, listening to the sounds of singing birds and flowing water.

"I can pray to you here," she told God. "If I had some of John's chew left, it'd be a perfect day." But Bell had consumed the very last morsel of the root before coming to the Dumont farm.

Then, without warning, and without any conscious intent to do so, Bell began to weep.

Her body shook as tears, and years, poured out of her. She wept with sorrow at being so long separated from her mother, wept at the physical toll a lifetime of field work had taken on her father's once vigorous body. She wept with longing for the brothers and sisters she'd never known, and the brother she might never see again. She wept with rage at the scars still plainly and painfully covering her back. She wept with relief at being away from the Nealys. She wept with gratitude at what God, through her father, had done on her behalf.

And she wept with joy at having found a private sanctuary on the island. It would be her weeping place. Her willow place.

Chapter 9 – The Gap

September 1811

He awoke in darkness. Groggy and disoriented, at first he thought he was back at his own house on Alarka Creek. Then he heard snoring. It wasn't the light, breathy sound of his wife sleeping beside him; it was the heavy, raspy sound of the man asleep on the other side of the room.

Gulkalaski sat up. The moonless sky refused him illumination. Defiant clouds ensured no beams of starlight came through the window. Their aid was not required, however. His mind soon remembered what his eyes could not see. He was at Tuskegee, staying in the house of his friend Sequoyah.

He'd expected a long, deep sleep, as his journey to Tuskegee had been exhausting. And his hearty meal of rabbit stew, corn cakes, and vegetables fried in venison grease had filled his stomach heartily. His limbs tingled. His eyelids sagged.

Perhaps it was a bad dream that woke me.

Then, as clear as if Sequoyah were calling to him, Gulkalaski heard a voice say his name. Loud snoring confirmed that his friend was still asleep.

"Gulkalaski," the voice repeated. "I bear a message."

The voice came from outside. Softly, so as not to wake Sequoyah, Gulkalaski rose and walked to the window, pushing open the reed shutters. Contrary to his expectations, no man or woman of Tuskegee stood there.

What was that?

About fifty paces away, something long and shaggy ducked behind an oak tree. Against the darkness of the cloudy night, the figure gave off a soft white glow. No longer concerned about waking Sequoyah, Gulkalaski leapt toward the door, thrust it open, grabbed his gift spear leaning against the wall, and ran toward the oak.

As he approached, the strange figure darted out from cover and scampered deeper into the forest. This time Gulkalaski got a clearer look at it. That's why his hands closed more tightly around the hickory shaft of his spear.

For what retreated into the forest was a wolf, the largest Gulkalaski had ever seen. As it disappeared from view, he marveled at its swiftness and the light emanating from its shaggy hide. This was no ordinary wolf poking around town for discarded scraps or a tasty rodent—it looked more like one of the spirit animals that populated his grandmother's bedtime tales. Some of those tales, he knew, had been based on events and creatures that were all too real.

Gulkalaski dashed into the woods, catching enough glimpses of glowing fur to stay in pursuit. As he passed the thickening lines of trees and brush, he heard the sound of his own moccasins striking the forest floor. But he heard no sounds from the beast ahead. No howls or growls. No footfalls. Not even the sound of leaves and limbs bowled aside as it fled.

After taking two sharp turns to bypass a thicket of holly bushes, Gulkalaski stopped and scanned the trees. He saw no sign of his quarry.

"I have a message, Gulkalaski," said the voice.

So the wolf has a master! "Show yourself, messenger, and I will listen."

"Turn your weapon not against me but against your true enemies," came the reply.

Gulkalaski gripped his spear tightly and smiled. "He who commands a great wolf to prowl around another man's house is no friend."

"I do not command the Great Wolf," the voice said. "I *am* the Great Wolf."

"Face me, then!" Gulkalaski replied, his Wampus claw necklace rattling as he spun in frustration.

Then he saw the eyes. They glowed a dark blue, the color of a mountain lake. The rest of the creature's face, thin and savage as it shone in the dark, emerged from shadow.

"My message is for you and for all Cherokee, Gulkalaski," said the Great Wolf.

"How do you know my name?"

Its fur gleamed brighter. "Long have I watched you become a leader of your people, though none yet calls you chief. Long was your journey from your mountain home. I saw you there. I followed. Now it is time for you to follow."

If he'd been some other man, he might have been struck with fear. But over his thirty-two years of life, Gulkalaski had seen many strange sights, some even stranger than the sight of a glowing wolf's head speaking from the shadows. What intrigued him more than the face of the mysterious canine were the words it spoke.

"Follow?" he asked. "I see no chief to follow. I see only a spirit."

"Your people have followed your chiefs to ruin. You have followed your chiefs by adopting the evil ways of your enemies, the whites, who have seized your lands and made women of your warriors."

Chuckling softly, Gulkalaski thought of his wife, Yona, and her sisters back home, working the fields and bravely guarding their home in his absence. *If I had a band of warriors as fierce as they, I would be invincible.*

"I did not leave my bed to suffer insults in the forest," he said, waving the point of his spear. "Be off with you."

The Great Wolf seemed unimpressed and stepped out farther from the shadows, revealing a massive chest and two long, powerful-looking forelegs. "Across the lands of the red men, the blood of too many fathers and brothers runs like water on the ground. The whites are like poisonous serpents: When chilled, they are feeble and harmless, but invigorate them with warmth, and they sting their benefactors to death. From their graves, your fathers reproach you as slaves and cowards for nurturing these white snakes and trying to wear the white skins they shed. But soon, one will come to you. He will come with the vision and power to make all red men strong and proud again, united as one in a common cause. I am his messenger."

"You make this visionary of yours sound less like a leader and more like a scolding grandmother," Gulkalaski replied dismissively. "The grandmother who raised me would laugh and send you both away."

"He who is coming brings neither switch nor swaddling clothes," the Great Wolf continued. "He is a man who brings truth. He is a warrior who brings the tomahawk. He is a chief who brings deliverance."

As he tried to discern the meaning of the Great Wolf's words, Gulkalaski stared into its solid-blue eyes—then started in surprise as the eyes wavered for a moment, like grass rippling in the breeze, and disappeared altogether. Through what were now holes in its head, Gulkalaski could see the boughs of the tree behind it. Then the blue-glowing eyes reappeared.

Have I been dreaming all this time?

Gulkalaski still felt groggy. He remembered waking up in Sequoyah's house, seeing the glowing figure, and running off after it. But he sometimes had such vivid dreams that they left startlingly realistic memories in their wake.

He shook his head vigorously. He waved his hand back and forth, as if to fan smoke away from his face. Both actions made the claws of his necklace jangle loudly once again. Then Gulkalaski looked back in the direction of the Great Wolf.

And found no beast at all.

Instead, he saw the outline of a lithe figure the size of a raccoon. And instead of the otherworldly voice of the Great Wolf, he heard singing. He'd heard such songs before, within a riverside mound. Remembering that first encounter so long ago, the warrior smiled triumphantly.

"Your kind never fooled me, Yvwi Usdi!" Gulkalaski cried.

The singing stopped. The small, shadowy form beneath the oak made no move and uttered no sound.

Gulkalaski spun his gift spear in his hands. "Your words do not deceive me. I see your true form."

The gasp from the little man in the shadows gratified Gulkalaski. He was unsurprised when, an instant later, the figure turned and fled. Gulkalaski had already started running in the same direction.

"Now that I know what mischief you seek to spread, I will not let you escape!" Gulkalaski called after the little man. "Even fleet-footed Tana of the Nunnehi has never bested me in a footrace!"

In pursuit, Gulkalaski heard the sound of rushing water. A river! Unless the little man was one of the blue-skinned Water Folk that Goran and Sam Houston had told him about, Gulkalaski was sure the fairy couldn't cross the stream fast enough to escape him.

Just as he emerged from the trees, the dense cloud cover parted, allowing the first rays of dawn to paint the scene in reds and yellows. There was no sign his quarry. But the fairy was still nearby. It was Gulkalaski's ears, not his eyes, that told him so.

The song seemed to come from no particular direction. The voice was strong, powerful, suffocating, the drumbeat accompanying it steady, pounding, insistent. The song surrounded Gulkalaski like a thick mantle of bearskin. It covered his eyes like a mask. It filled his lungs like smoke from a raging fire. It wrapped around his throat like the hands of a desperate killer. It stung his chest like some giant bee.

Infuriated, Gulkalaski made his own drumming sound on the ground with the butt of his gift spear. "You will not prevail with evil medicine and magic tricks, Yvwi Usdi! You are no match for me!"

The fairy spoke no reply. But his song changed. Gulkalaski felt the pressure against his body recede. While retaining its power, the song now seemed to travel *inside* him. It conjured an image in Gulkalaski's mind. He saw himself swimming in deep water and plunging into soft mud. He felt his blood turn cold and his arms and legs draw tightly together. And he found he could hear no sound other than the fairy's drum battering his defenses, the fairy's voice burrowing into his mind.

Gulkalaski resisted. His will battled that of the fairy for a moment—and then, abruptly, the weird images were gone. Gulkalaski's perceptions were again his own.

His smile of triumph faded as he saw a huge reptilian snout, covered in metallic scales, break the surface of the river. Each time the nose exhaled, it projected drops of liquid that sizzled when they struck the water.

As the unseen fairy continued his spellsong, Gulkalaski watched the snout rise higher and higher, revealing the rest of the face. Its bronze scales glowed like the embers of a campfire. Its jaws yawned wide, unsheathing yellowed teeth as large as hunting knives. On either side protruded horns shaped like those of a young buck, only larger, glowing faintly orange.

The monster fixed its eyes, black as obsidian, on Gulkalaski. Higher up on its head was another object—not a third eye, as Gulkalaski had initially imagined, but something like a small mirror or precious stone embedded directly into the scaly head. It was transparent except for a streak running from top to bottom.

A streak colored bloodred.

"Uktena!" Gulkalaski exclaimed aloud.

As if in response, the monster hissed loudly as its head shot up high above the river to reveal ten feet of serpentine body the width of an ancient bole. At regular intervals, its bronze scales were striped with darker rings of reddish brown. Still more of the Uktena's great length remained, appearing coiled beneath the surface.

Gulkalaski was afraid; any sane man would have been at the sight of a massive horned serpent rising from the water. But Gulkalaski's fear was mixed with other emotions: Resentment at the fairy's insults. Frustration at the prospect of the fairy's escape. Regret at not having brought his other weapons, especially his rifle. And, in truth, *exhilaration* at the prospect of battling one of the most fearsome beasts of Cherokee legend.

The Uktena showed no signs of conflicting emotions. It merely radiated fury.

The great snake hissed again, long and hoarse. Its black eyes narrowed into slits. Then its head swooped rapidly toward Gulkalaski, its left horn aimed at the warrior's unprotected breast.

The horn found no target. Gulkalaski leapt to one side, rolling along the riverbank and regaining his footing.

The glittering gem in the monster's forehead prodded Gulkalaski's memory. He recalled his grandmother's tales, the one detailing how the Yunwi Tsunsdi had magically transformed a human into the first Uktena and used it as a monstrous weapon in their war against the Sun. How that first Uktena's horned descendants liked to lurk in remote mountain streams and pounce on unsuspecting prey. How the Uktena had long fought its hereditary enemy, the winged Tlanuwa. And how the great medicine man Aganunitsi, a captive Shawnee, had once slain the great Uktena by shooting an arrow into its putrid heart, located seven rings down from its head.

Gulkalaski could clearly see a similar spot on the belly of the monster raging before him. Once again he rued having left both his rifle and Sequoyah's bow back at the house. The only missile he could launch at the spot was the gift spear in his hand. *If I throw and miss, I will face the monster unarmed.*

A second time, the Uktena narrowed its eyes and tried to impale Gulkalaski. Again the warrior was able to evade its horn by leaping aside at the last moment.

Its eyes give me warning before each strike. But I cannot win by dodging.

Over many years of hunting game, Gulkalaski had honed his skills and sharpened his reflexes. For him, to think was to act. So, even as the Uktena began its next attack, Gulkalaski was ready with his own.

The hideous head swung at him, teeth bared. Rather than dodging or running away, Gulkalaski sprinted *toward* the Uktena, his necklace jangling at his throat. After a few strides, he planted the butt of his spear on the ground and used its length to propel himself high into the air.

The snake's eyes widened in surprise as its horn thrust into empty space. Keeping a firm hold on his spear, Gulkalaski vaulted onto the rough metallic scales between the Uktena's horns, then pushed off again to hop further up the thick trunk of the beast.

The warrior's hop turned into a semicontrolled fall as the Uktena reared its head and turned around. Tumbling through the air, Gulkalaski kept his eyes trained on the spot where the seventh ring of the beast crossed its back. He kept the bronze tip of his spear trained on the same spot, praying that its enchanted blade would be strong enough to penetrate the scaly armor.

And it was.

His weapon plunged into the flesh of the Uktena, showering sparks on the water. But Gulkalaski's elation turned to despair as his momentum carried him beyond the point of impact. He'd kept a firm grip on his spear, hoping to wrench it free for a later strike. Instead, Gulkalaski felt its long hickory shaft break. Then he fell, twisting, into the river, clutching the lower half of his broken spear.

His back hit the surface with a bracing blow, dislodging most of the lungful of air he'd managed to take in before impact. He sank into the stream, stunned and dismayed, only to revive as the water wrapped its cold hands around him and tried to expel his remaining air. Kicking mightily, Gulkalaski fought to the surface. He filled his lungs with air. A second later, however, the cold water of the river again wrapped itself around him and yanked him below.

No, not the water, he realized—it was the massive trunk of the Uktena coiled around his legs that drew him downward.

Gulkalaski flailed at the monster with the butt of his broken spear to no avail. The water slowed his blows too much, and the snake likely wouldn't have felt them anyway. His hands longed to draw his knife from its sheath, or his tomahawk from his belt. He had neither. He had nothing.

As the Uktena's coils pulled his body through the water as easily as a child playing with a cornhusk doll, Gulkalaski thought of his friend, Sequoyah, still sleeping blissfully. He thought of it his other friends, his long-dead grandmother, and, most of all, his beloved Yona and her sisters. What had his impetuous pursuit of the fairy and his reckless attack on the Uktena brought? Only grief and loss for those he loved. Only a lonely, unwitnessed death at the bottom of a distant river.

Even as his left hand clung stubbornly to the remains of his spear, his right hand had continued to roam, searching without conscious direction for some weapon to use. It found only Gulkalaski's necklace.

There his fingers lingered, gripping a Wampus claw and remembering the occasion the Nunnehi had presented the necklace to him. Gulkalaski closed his eyes and prayed, his lungs about to burst.

In an instant, the icy grip of the river was replaced by a cool wind pressed against his face and body. Gulkalaski was traveling through air, not water. He seized a breath and opened his eyes. What he saw was terrible. The Uktena's approaching head was thrust back, its maw wide open. From its curved yellow fangs dripped a dark liquid he knew must be deadly poison.

The tableau came into sharp focus. The great snake had lifted its prey out of the water so its head could deliver a killing blow.

Then Gulkalaski saw something else—the shard of his gift spear embedded in the Uktena. In lifting its prey from the water, the monster had twisted its body to the side. Instead of sticking straight up, the broken spear was now parallel with the surface of the river. He was about to pass by it on his way to his doom.

For Gulkalaski, to think was to act.

His right hand yanked hard, parting the leather thong of his necklace. As Gulkalaski flew past the broken spear, he whipped the necklace at it. The thong and its Wampus claws wrapped around the shaft. Then Gulkalaski winced in pain as the line jerked tight and wrenched his arm.

It only jerked tight for an instant, though. Then the pain vanished.

Gulkalaski looked down with satisfaction at the shard of the spear, its bronze blade intact, dangling from the tangle of leather and claws. Then the warrior looked up, just in time, to see the fangs of the Uktena closing around his head.

With his left arm, Gulkalaski swung the bottom half of the broken spear above his head, thrusting it between the closing jaws. Whether it was just surprised or now beginning to suffer the effects of the magically enhanced wound Gulkalaski had already delivered to its midsection, the Uktena jerked its head in confusion, its mouth held apart by the hickory stick embedded in its soft gums.

Using his brief respite wisely, Gulkalaski spun his wrist around and around, rolling up the necklace and bringing the top of the spear close enough to grasp with his free hand. A surge of renewed hope sharpened his senses and strengthened his limbs.

Crack!

The Uktena's jaws broke the hickory stick. A moment later, Gulkalaski felt burning sensations as drops of poison fell onto his unprotected face and arms. Willing himself to blot out the pain, he transferred his weapon to his right hand, his necklace still wrapped around his right wrist, and braced himself.

The monster's head shot down to strike. Gulkalaski struck first— but not at the head.

Instead, he stabbed the scaly coil pinning his legs together. Thrice he stabbed with the enchanted bronze blade, and at the third blow he felt the Uktena's hold slacken. Placing his left arm underneath the coil, Gulkalaski pushed upward. His reward was to shoot downward, arms and legs akimbo, and strike the water at an odd angle, producing another jolt of pain as his left shoulder popped out of its socket.

Gulkalaski's other reward, the more satisfactory one, was to hear the agonized hiss of the Uktena as it yanked its fangs free from its own scaly skin. Unable to arrest the momentum of its strike, the monster had bitten the coil that had, an instant before, held its prey. Even if it was immune from its own poison, the self-inflicted wound would further weaken the beast.

Or so Gulkalaski hoped.

Treading water, the warrior looked up at the dark blood oozing from the bite marks on the Uktena's side as well as the spear wound on his back. The monster began to withdraw its body, slowly and with evident pain, into the river.

His skin still burning from the poison spray, his dislocated shoulder hampering his efforts, Gulkalaski was nevertheless determined to strike again. But he was unable to swim at normal speed. By the time he reached the side of the monster, its vulnerable midsection was already submerged. Only the serpent's head remained above the surface, thrashing back and forth as it hissed.

Gulkalaski held his spear shard over his head as he kicked his legs furiously to keep himself afloat. Whether because of its proximity to the beast or some other feature of its enchantment, the bronze blade was emitting a bright orange glow.

Seemingly attracted by the glowing blade, the Uktena turned its head toward him. The orange light of the spearhead was reflected in its obsidian orbs. He saw no more fury in its face. He saw no menace. There was only agony.

And suddenly he heard . . . nothing. For the first time since the battle began, Gulkalaski realized the fairy's song had ended.

Then he remembered what Goran and Har had told him, their horrified discovery that some magical monsters possess a self-awareness, an intelligence, completely at odds with their external appearance. Could this Uktena be one such monster? A moment earlier, Gulkalaski could think of nothing more glorious than to end its life. Now, face-to-face with the creature, he hesitated.

Whether the Uktena *did* possess intelligence or was simply reeling from multiple wounds, it did what an intelligent creature would do in that moment. It fled.

Gulkalaski did not follow.

▲▲▲

"You fell into the river and dislocated your shoulder? How is that even possible?"

Bowl and cloth in hand, Sequoyah walked to where his friend sat wincing in pain. Roused from his sleep when Gulkalaski stumbled into the house, Sequoyah initially thought Tuskegee was under attack. Gulkalaski insisted, however, that his injuries were merely the result of his clumsy attempts to swim in the dark.

"How do you explain those lesions on your face and arms, then?" Sequoyah demanded as he held up the warrior's limp left arm.

"On the way to the river, I stumbled on a nest of yellow jackets," Gulkalaski offered, hoping Sequoyah's sleepiness would improve the story's plausibility. "I thought a swim would make the stings hurt less, but I slipped and . . . yee-ow!"

There was a loud crack as his shoulder popped back into its socket. Sequoyah rubbed it for a moment, then dipped the cloth into a thick paste and began dabbing the "stings" on Gulkalaski's face.

"Some 'expert hunter' you are," Sequoyah chuckled. "Maybe you should let me do the tracking and killing while you stay home and make anklets for pretty young girls."

"What, on your pitiful excuse for a leg?" Gulkalaski retorted with a chuckle of his own. "A pregnant possum could run circles around you."

He saw Sequoyah's hand drop from his face and clench into a fist. "If war comes, I can do my duty, Gulkalaski. I can be brave. I can fight. You think I cannot?"

I have struck a nerve I did not know was there.

Gulkalaski stood, slowly rotating his left arm. "I do not doubt your courage, Sequoyah. But why talk of war? We have been at peace for years."

The older man shook his head. "We have an *illusion* of peace, even as our enemies wage war on us. They seize our lands. They disrupt the balance between our two peoples, a balance between fire and water, sky and earth, light and darkness. The spirits who range those lands cry out to restore the balance. The spirits of our mighty dead cry out for vengeance. Brush the sleep from your eyes, my friend, as I have—with their help."

"With *whose* help?"

Sequoyah sighed. "Please do not laugh at me, but I have had . . . visions. The spirits come to me in the night, as if I am dreaming yet also wide awake. They assume the form of animals yet speak our tongue. They speak truths we have forgotten."

The poison wounds on Gulkalaski's face were still stinging, but not as painfully as his friend's words. Either the same fairy or another like him had been visiting Sequoyah. And Sequoyah lacked the Sight to discover who was truly speaking to him.

"How do you know you are not dreaming?" Gulkalaski asked.

"Even after my second vision, I was unsure," Sequoyah allowed. "But I *know* I was awake for the third. I was up late working when a voice called from the window."

Troubled, Gulkalaski gazed out the same window. The sun was now fully risen, illuminating the surrounding trees.

"I know it is hard, my friend, but there is an even better reason to believe me," Sequoyah added. "I am not alone."

Gulkalaski felt a dull pain in his stomach. "What do you mean?"

Sequoyah's words, initially slow and plaintive, now became rushed and excited. "Many others report similar visions. Even some chiefs have seen them. They say the spirits urged our chiefs to take up arms, that the spirits called them to Tuckabatchie."

The pain in Gulkalaski's stomach sharpened. "The Creek town? Why Tuckabatchie?"

"The chiefs of the Creeks went there to talk about the new road the Americans are building through their territory. They have invited Choctaw, Chickasaw, and Cherokee delegations. Several Overhill chiefs left for Tuckabatchie weeks ago."

"I did not know of this," Gulkalaski said, alarmed. "I have been hard at work at the farm, and I only agreed to take a break and visit you at Yona's insistence."

Sequoyah paused for a moment, then scowled. "Of course, this comes from rumors and travelers' tales. Our people suffer because we do not inform ourselves more reliably the way the whites do, by the printed word. Have I told you my latest ideas about—"

"Some other time, my friend," Gulkalaski cut in. "Now I must know: What does the meeting at Tuckabatchie have to do with the spirit visions?"

"It is said," Sequoyah began, still frowning, "that the true purpose of the Tuckabatchie conference is to meet with representatives of the Northern tribes—the Kickapoo, the Potawatomi, the Lenape, and the Shawnee, among others. Their leader is a Shawnee named Tecumseh, said to be organizing a great confederacy to resist the Americans."

Gulkalaski felt his stomach lurch. He had his answer. Disguised as the Great Wolf, the fairy had claimed to be a messenger. The visionary he spoke of must be this Tecumseh.

"Would our chiefs truly lead us into another all-out war against the whites?" Gulkalaski wondered aloud.

Sequoyah answered his question with his own. "If the spirits of our ancestors will us to defend ourselves, how can we refuse?"

What I saw was no ancestral spirit or herald of the Creator, Gulkalaski replied, but only in his mind. *We are being manipulated by magical Folk, just as our fathers were during the American rebellion. We are being used for their purposes, not ours.*

"When is the meeting at Tuckabatchie set to begin?" Gulkalaski said, a plan already forming in his mind.

"It has already begun. Indeed, it may well be over by now."

"So the chance to head off this madness has passed?" Gulkalaski asked.

"Only some chiefs made the journey to Tuckabatchie, Gulkalaski, not nearly enough to form a consensus. You know this, surely."

"I am sure of very little," Gulkalaski said quietly, "other than following the lead of this Shawnee visitor will bring us nothing but death and ruin."

"If you had the visions I had, you would not be so sure," Sequoyah said, placing a reassuring hand on Gulkalaski's injured left shoulder. "But if you feel so strongly about it, you may be able to hear the words from Tecumseh himself."

Gulkalaski whirled. "How would I do that? This is very important."

"Again, this was a traveler's tale, but it bears the ring of truth. It is said that after the meeting at Tuckabatchie, Tecumseh plans to visit Creek towns along the Coosa River and then journey north and east into Cherokee territory."

"Where he will try to convince our chiefs to join his confederacy."

"That may well be," Sequoyah agreed. "Still, you are no chief. You may attend such a meeting, but you will not get the chance to speak."

Gulkalaski smiled. *That may well be. So, I will arrange of meeting of my own.*

▲▲▲

The cool leaves of summer now burned with the fires of autumn. Lying flat on a rocky ledge, Gulkalaski looked out over the trees that blanketed Soco Gap, the blazing yellows of ash and birch in the valley interspersed with the impervious greens of fir and spruce.

It was an apt location for his vigil. Soco Gap was a well-trod path, long the site of momentous journeys and encounters. In the time of his grandfathers' fathers, an invading party of Shawnee had traveled south to raid the mountain towns. It was at Soco Gap that Cherokee warriors had taken the Shawnee by surprise, killing all but the single raider they sent back north with his ears cut off as a warning. Among the Cherokee, the gap was called *Ahalunun-yi*, the "Ambush Place."

Gulkalaski glanced over at the bronze blade of his gift spear, newly mounted on a long hickory pole. Because Soco Gap was east of his farm on Alarka Creek, he'd been able to stop by home on the way back from Tuskegee, spending a few days with Yona and repairing his spear, before setting off to track Tecumseh.

Another ambush will occur here. I will use words if I can, a deadlier weapon if I must.

It was many hours later when he finally spotted the signs. A flock of birds rose abruptly from their perch. Boughs of yellow and green shook as a small party of figures pushed through the gap. Gulkalaski crawled from the ledge and began to descend past the evergreens that dominated the higher elevations, heading for the point where the strangers' trek would take them through a small clearing.

He reached it only minutes ahead of them. Opting for clarity over surprise, he stood at the edge of the clearing, his spear planted blade first in the ground, his hunting rifle in his hands.

The first stranger to appear was not Tecumseh, said to be middle-aged and robust. The Shawnee who entered the clearing was a much older man. His hair, secured by a dark-green bandana, was more gray than black. He was short and rail thin; his buckskin mantle, tunic, and leggings hung loosely on his frame, as did the copper gorget around his neck.

When the man spied Gulkalaski, his eyes widened. He cried out and touched the handle of his tomahawk before a hand reached out and touched the shoulder of the old man. A moment later, a powerfully built Shawnee wearing a bright-red turban stepped into view. Like the other, he wore only native clothing—deerskins and native weaves, no cloth shirts or blankets obtained in trade. Behind him came two more men, both similarly dressed except for their hair, which was cut in the Mohawk fashion.

Those two carried rifles. All four had tomahawks and knives. But none drew a weapon. Instead, the man Gulkalaski guessed was Tecumseh strode forward and held up his hand in greeting.

"Have you come to guide us to the meeting place?" he asked in reasonably good Cherokee.

"There will be no meeting, Shawnee," Gulkalaski replied.

Tecumseh's sharp eyes widened. "I learned your tongue years ago, when I fought alongside your great chief Dragging Canoe. Perhaps I did not learn it well. Has the meeting been delayed?" .

Gulkalaski eyed the other three men of the party warily. "You know my tongue well enough to understand my words. There will be no meeting with the chiefs of our people, Tecumseh. I will see to that."

The Shawnee chief's nostrils flared. "*You* will see to that? Does one chief now speak for all your towns?"

"I am no chief," Gulkalaski said. "I own a farm not far from where we stand. But I, Gulkalaski, know your true errand—and your true masters. I will not allow you to spread your poison among us."

The anger on Tecumseh's face made Gulkalaski move his finger closer to the trigger of his rifle. If they attacked, he would likely get off only a single shot before the others trained their weapons on him. He would make that shot count.

But the Shawnee chief ordered no attack. He matched Gulkalaski's grim smile with one of his own and took another step forward. "You have been corrupted by the ways of whites yourself. The proper calling of a man is to hunt and make war. Instead, you admit you work in fields like a woman. And yet you speak such bold words to me? My only errand is to speak true words to your chiefs. And my only master is the Great Spirit, for whom my brother Tenskwatawa speaks as the Prophet."

"You would speak only half truths, Tecumseh," challenged Gulkalaski. "You would speak of the misdeeds of Americans, yes, but also of an alliance that will bring misery, not victory."

"What we build from the Great Lakes to the Great Gulf is no temporary alliance. It is a lasting confederation. We are one people. We must unite to become one nation."

Gulkalaski waved at the nearby trees. "You stand in the Ambush Place where my forefathers once defeated an invasion by your forefathers. We have always been separate nations. My people will never accept the rule of a Shawnee."

"But we are of the same blood, Gulkalaski—it is the whites who keep us apart. It is they who have destroyed many nations because we were not united. They have tempted the weak among us to wear the white man's clothes and take up the white man's ways. They make us enemies to each other so they can sweep over and desolate our hunting grounds, like devastating winds or rushing waters."

Gulkalaski snorted. "If the Americans truly move against us like devastating winds and rushing waters like you say, what weapons can you offer to turn them back? Airy words and slippery promises offered around a council fire?"

Tecumseh fingered a bundle of long, odd-looking sticks thrust in his belt. They were painted crimson along most of their length except for their knobby heads, which were inlaid with small stones.

"The Great Father over the great waters is angry with the Americans," the Shawnee said. "He will send his brave warriors against them. He will send us guns, and whatever else we want, if we stand together with them against our common enemies."

"You talk of others tempted by white man's ways," Gulkalaski sneered. "Yet you also talk of the white king of England as your 'Great Father' and would use his guns to fight the Americans. You speak half-truths, Tecumseh, just as I said."

The Shawnee chief pointed to the rifle in Gulkalaski's hands. "You carry the white man's tool yourself. We will use whatever we must to resist the invaders. But our most powerful tools do not come from the forges of our white enemies. They are the gifts of the Great Spirit."

"Delivered to your door by the Great Spirit's animal messengers, no doubt," Gulkalaski said, seeing confirmation in Tecumseh's shocked expression. "A messenger came to me as well, but I was not so easily fooled."

"The spirits commune with my brother Tenskwatawa, not with me, though he speaks often of his visions," Tecumseh said, sounding hesitant for the first time. "There is no doubting the miracles they have brought, however, and the prophecies already fulfilled. The white governor William Henry Harrison spoke as you did. He called my brother a trickster. So, Tenskwatawa prophesied that the moon would come and blot out the sun. Harrison laughed. His laughter stopped when the moon covered the sun and turned day to night."

The three other visitors grunted in affirmation.

"Now the Prophet offers new warnings," the Shawnee chief went on. "Soon, the Great Spirit will speak in thunder and throw a fiery spear across the sky. His voice will make the very ground beneath our feet rumble and shake. With the help of the Great Spirit, we will destroy our enemies and cause the rivers to stain the great oceans with their blood."

Gulkalaski stood impassively as Tecumseh spoke. Then he held up his rifle. "I have seen magic tricks before, Shawnee. They are not enough for your few followers to defeat the many guns of the Americans."

"I spoke of tools, not tricks," Tecumseh said. "A man who digs in the dirt should understand the difference. But, yes, today my followers are few. Once the campfires of the Shawnee twinkled at night like the stars of a fallen sky. Then the white man came. Our campfires dwindled. Everywhere, our people dwindled like snow in May. But the gifts of the spirit messengers will unleash a new and terrible winter on our enemies. They will protect us from the weapons and even the eyes of the whites. So have the spirits told Tenskwatawa. So have I seen myself."

With that, Tecumseh removed one of the long red sticks from his belt and pointed its tip at Gulkalaski with a dramatic flourish.

The Cherokee and the Shawnee stood in the clearing, staring into each other's eyes for a long while as the other three men looked on in wonder. At first Tecumseh's expression was one of triumph. As the seconds passed, however, his triumph was replaced by surprise, then puzzlement, and finally frustration.

Unsure what Tecumseh was trying to accomplish, but deeming it prudent to pretend otherwise, Gulkalaski simply returned the Shawnee's glare. After a while, when Tecumseh lowered the red-painted club, Gulkalaski saw a chance to rattle the chief still further. As loudly as he could manage, he yawned.

Tecumseh scowled, but only for an instant. Then the Shawnee changed his approach.

"You are a strange and interesting man, Gulkalaski," he deflected with a chuckle. "Back in our community at Prophetstown, though, others would not see you as a man at all."

"Because I do not live as you do?" Gulkalaski pressed. "I *own* the land we farm. I *own* the livestock we tend. Whatever we produce but do not use, I own and can sell as I wish. What do you own, Shawnee? The clothes on your back?"

Tecumseh grinned indulgently, as if lecturing a small child. "Only the Great Spirit can truly *own* land. We all live within his creation and may take from it only what we need. At Prophetstown, we are returning to the old ways. We claim a common and equal right to the land, as it was at the first and should be now. None of us may sell any portion of it to the whites without the consent of all."

"I agree our chiefs have often sold land they had no right to sell, at prices made too low by drunkenness and bribery," said Gulkalaski. "But I will never recognize the right of a Shawnee, or any other foreign chief, to decide what I or my family may do with what we have claimed for ourselves with toil and sweat. And I will never stand by and watch as hot-headed men launch pointless wars against the Americans. My father died in such a war. I will not suffer the same fate, nor will my sons after me."

Tecumseh closed his eyes. "I, too, lost my father to the guns of whites. Puckshinwa was his name—a mighty warrior. As a boy, I witnessed another bloody battle at Piqua Town, just north of the Mad River. I saw white men gun down Shawnee while I stood by, powerless to help. I swore that when I grew to manhood, I would never feel powerless again."

I understand his determination, even his rage, Gulkalaski realized. *But he does not truly understand the power he has been given. Nor does he truly control it.*

"Of course I wish for peace," Tecumseh continued. "All our people wish for peace. But where the white people are, there can be no peace. They have built their homes where our hunting grounds once were. Now they are coming into your mountain glens. Soon there will be no place for you to hunt the deer and the bear. The tomahawk of the Shawnee is ready. Will the Cherokee raise the tomahawk? Will the Cherokee join their brothers the Shawnee?"

Gulkalaski gulped. He knew his next words might determine not only the fates of four men at Soco Gap but possibly the fates of a far greater number.

"It has been many years since the Cherokee have drawn the tomahawk," he said. "We have forgotten how to use the scalping knife. We have learned with sorrow that it is better not to war against our white brothers. They have come to stay. They are like the leaves in this forest, they are so many."

With a nod, Gulkalaski gestured at the firs and birches that enclosed the clearing.

"I have found both good and bad among the whites, and I take them as they come," he continued. "For the most part, they no longer molest our lands. Our crops grow in peace. I will not raise my arm against them. And if the Cherokee do decide to raise the tomahawk again, it will be because *we* decide it—not you, not other foreign chiefs, not a white king from over the sea, and not some hidden Spirit Folk who speak in riddles and manipulate us for their own ends."

Tecumseh sighed deeply. "The farmer who is not a chief certainly gives speeches like one. I return to my original question: Who are you to keep me from my meeting with your chiefs?"

In answer, Gulkalaski lifted his rifle to his shoulder with one quick motion. "This farmer has never stopped being a hunter. No Cherokee can best me with gun or spear. You would be wise not to test my skill."

The other two riflemen raised their own weapons, and the short elderly man was moving his tomahawk from one palm to the other with a practiced hand. But Tecumseh held up a restraining hand.

"We did not come here to shed our brother's blood," he told them. "If we did so, their chiefs would not hear our plea. And my experience in Tuckabatchie tells me that bringing the Cherokee into the confederacy at this moment is unlikely, anyway. Duty calls us northward. We can always return later to talk to the real men of the Cherokee, at a time when their *women* are too busy digging in the dirt to interfere."

If the insult was meant to provoke Gulkalaski, it failed. He felt relief, not resentment, and said nothing as Tecumseh and his companions turned to leave. Then, at a respectful distance, he followed to make sure they were truly headed out of the lands of the Cherokee. All the while, he pondered the words of Tecumseh and absentmindedly ran his fingers along the claws of his necklace.

The gifts of the spirit messengers will unleash a new and terrible winter on our enemies, Tecumseh had said. Gulkalaski felt a chill run up his spine.

Chapter 10 – The Soldier

She was never alone for long.

Holding court near the door, her lilac-colored dress flowing gracefully from hip to ankle as she turned back and forth, Eliza King greeted the guests entering the drawing room. Each seemed inclined to say a few words to the young woman, who returned their pleasantries in kind while fingering the ends of the blue ribbon encircling her dress.

Ben Crane stood in the corner, his black *chapeau de bras* under his left arm and his right hand resting on the hilt of his cutlass. It seemed to the impatient lieutenant that each conversation Eliza had with a guest was longer than the previous one.

Will I get another chance? Ben wondered. *Or must I again return to the ship a defeated man?*

He felt like a fool for hurrying out of the dining room so abruptly after Eliza when the meal was over. Norfolk's leading citizens were in attendance, along with his own commanding officer. Ben's clumsy exit surely struck them as undignified, but he'd hoped to have Eliza to himself for a while. Instead, he'd managed only to mumble a couple of words to her before other guests pressed in behind him and forced his retreat.

How was Ben to know the other guests would treat Eliza King as the hostess of the party? She was a guest herself, although her longtime friendship with Susan Wheeler had made her a familiar face in the Wheeler home.

Ben scratched the side of his bulbous nose, the motion making the too-short sleeve of his coat droop far below his bony wrist. Still itching for another chance with Eliza, the lieutenant glanced to the other corner of the drawing room where Luke Wheeler, the former mayor of Norfolk, stood talking to Eliza's father Miles King.

A hearty laugh came from the hallway.

"I do not recall 'begging' you to go along, Will," chuckled Ben's commanding officer, Captain Stephen Decatur of the *USS United States*.

"Perhaps not in so many words, sir, but your meaning was clear enough," insisted the man who followed Decatur into the room, Lieutenant William Crane. "I was honored to join you in your recapture of the *Philadelphia*."

Ben groaned. He'd heard the story from his brother Will many times. During the war with the Barbary States of North Africa, pirates had captured one of the largest vessels in the American fleet, the frigate *Philadelphia*, and Decatur volunteered to lead sixty men in a daring raid. Dressed as Arab mariners and wielding only swords and pikes, Decatur's force recaptured and destroyed the ship without losing a single man. Will Crane had joined Decatur's raid and earned praise for his valor during the brief but bloody battle on the deck of the *Philadelphia*.

As Will has never failed to remind me on a regular basis, Ben thought gloomily.

Behind Decatur and Will, the final two members of the dinner party entered arm in arm. Susan Wheeler Decatur, the captain's wife, wore a Grecian gown of periwinkle blue that accentuated her lovely face and shapely shoulders. Walking beside her was her mother, Ginny. Also dressed according the latest fashion from Napoleonic France—a sleek gown, in her case light green, fitted close at the torso and hanging loosely below—Mrs. Wheeler made at least as striking an entrance as her daughter.

Or so Ben might have concluded, had his eyes rested for more than an instant on Susan Decatur and Ginny Wheeler. Instead, they immediately flitted back to Eliza King, Susan's childhood friend, now conversing with the other two women.

And with Will.

Ben's curly-headed brother bowed dramatically, eyes flashing, mouth forming an impish grin. Eliza laughed. Ben seethed.

"It's good to see you here, Lieutenant Crane."

Ben was staring at his brother, now holding Eliza's hand and whispering something only she could hear.

"I *said*, it's good to see you here, Lieutenant Crane. It's good to see you mingling with the fine people of Norfolk rather than staying on the ship to read a book."

Only then did Ben realize it was *he* who was being addressed, not his brother. Captain Decatur, imposing as usual in a well-tailored blue coat with bright gold epaulettes, now stood next to his junior officer.

Ben's ill-fitting coat was buttoned up to his throat, which felt suddenly dry. "Well, sir, the *United States* is a fine ship, the finest in the fleet, sir," he stammered. "That is to say, I was pleased to receive the invitation from the honorable Mayor Wheeler, sir, but I also enjoy my studies on the ship as well. Not that—"

"Oh, *do* be at ease, Lieutenant Crane. You act like a midshipman at inspection," Captain Decatur scolded, albeit genially.

"My apologies, sir," Ben replied, his eyes returning to the object of his fascination, Eliza King, still speaking in low tones with Will.

Decatur followed the younger man's gaze and nodded in understanding. "You seem to have gotten into the spirit of the proceedings even more than I hoped, lieutenant. But heed your lessons in tactics. If you cede the initiative to your opponent, you usually cede victory."

Ben felt his face flush red. "Sir, I am not certain of the subject to which—"

"I have eyes and ears, mister." The captain shot him a disdainful look. "And I have had two Lieutenant Cranes serve under me. Though you may share the same parents, two more different men I have never met."

"You should meet our brother Joseph Crane, sir. He's nothing like us. He's an attorney in Ohio. Even got elected to the legislature there. He doesn't like water at all. Won't even cross a pond in a rowboat."

The words had tumbled out of Ben before he quite knew what he was doing. Always keen to make a good impression, he'd rarely spoken of his private life to others, and certainly not his commanding officer. *Even my own brothers don't know my greatest secret.*

Ben grimaced. "My apologies, sir. You did not ask—"

"That is the second time you have offered an apology, and neither was required," Decatur interrupted, shaking his head. "I have seen you on deck with your marines, Mister Crane. You instruct them. You ask about them and see to their needs. You sing along with their chanties. When you ease into command, lieutenant, you perform well. But when I or other officers come near, you are either awkward as a schoolboy or prim as a schoolmarm. Why is that?"

From the burning sensation in his floppy earlobes, Ben guessed his face had again turned beet red. The captain expected an answer, but Ben was loathe to give it. He glanced back to where Will was waving his arms, no doubt telling Eliza of his heroic exploits on the high seas.

Once again Decatur followed his lieutenant's gaze and nodded. "You hesitate to speak ill of a brother, Mister Crane. I understand. I had a brother in the service as well—James. He'd always felt obligated to follow our father and me into the navy. James did so. And it cost him his life."

"I recall, sir," Ben replied gravely, "and may I offer—"

"Yes, yes," Decatur said, waving a hand to silence him. "James was the victim of a cowardly trick by a Barbary captain who feigned surrender only to attack my brother. I sought out the coward—a giant of a man, to be sure—and gunned him down with his own pistol."

Ben swallowed hard. *I am surrounded by heroes worthy of epic verse.*

"Thus, I know what it is like to import sibling rivalry into the service," Decatur continued. "Your brother Will is an able seaman and a fierce warrior. He has risen to the rank of commanding lieutenant of a brig."

My brother and I are, indeed, very different Lieutenant Cranes.

"You and I both know that affairs with Britain are driving our two nations toward war," the captain said. "Diplomatic attempts to end British impoundment of our trading vessels and British impressment of our seamen have failed. They continue to supply hostile Indian tribes threatening our frontiers, even after the defeat of Tecumseh's confederation at Tippecanoe four months ago."

Decatur paused and looked searchingly at his lieutenant. "When war with Britain comes, Mister Crane, you question whether you will prove to be your brother's equal. I pose this question back to you: Why must you try? You are your own man, with your own talents. Why not use them to chart your own course?"

His words rang with truth. Yet Ben couldn't help but feel the embedded sting. *I will never be Will's equal. My own captain admits it.*

"May we intrude, or will that interrupt some important navy business?"

Susan Decatur's eyes gleamed mischievously as she took her husband's arm. Her mother took the captain's other arm and smiled graciously at Ben. The handsome face of Ginny Wheeler was only faintly creased by the lines of middle age, yet there was something in her eyes, a misty, faraway look that would seem more at home on the face of a woman far older than this matron of Norfolk could possibly be.

Ben was reminded of the voyage he, Will, and Joe had taken up the Hudson River five years earlier. During their journey, they'd met elderly Dutch women with similarly distant-looking expressions, particularly at the humble inn where the nervous slave girl had spilled molasses all over Will's uniform. Ben had felt so guilty about that accident afterward, begging the innkeeper not to punish the girl for a mishap caused by Ben's own ungainly leg.

Ginny interrupted his reminiscences. "I haven't seen you here before, lieutenant. Are you newly posted to Norfolk?"

"Mister Crane has served for two years aboard the *United States*, although it's telling you never met him," Captain Decatur interjected. "When at port, most of my men seize every opportunity to disembark and enjoy the comforts of this modest town of yours. But Crane would rather fill his hand with a book than a drink."

"There's nothing wrong with that," Susan Decatur said playfully. "No nations are made, nor even wars won, solely by the heroic acts of rash young men. Words have their own power, too, as do those who wield them effectively."

Uncomfortable being the center of attention, and again feeling slighted by faint praise, Ben tried to change the subject. "Your home is beautiful, Mrs. Wheeler. Such a picturesque view of Chesapeake Bay."

"Thank you, lieutenant." Ginny Wheeler walked to Ben's side. "Sometimes I spend hours gazing out over the water and thinking of home."

"Were you not born here?" Captain Decatur asked in surprise. "I always assumed my mother-in-law was a local, like Mister Wheeler."

For an instant, Ginny Wheeler seemed startled. Then she smiled, though Ben thought he once again saw a faraway look in her eyes. "I was born in North Carolina, where I spent my early years in a home by the sea. I arrived in Norfolk later, as a young woman."

"Mother doesn't speak much about her childhood, Stephen, you know that," said Susan Decatur, this time more scolding than playful. "Mother lost her parents at a young age, Lieutenant Crane, and has no relations other than the family into which she married."

"Into which I married *happily*, of course," added Ginny Wheeler as she looked across the room at Luke Wheeler talking animatedly with Miles King.

Although Ben had succeeded at changing the subject, he felt no better than before. He'd only managed to stumble from one uncomfortable topic into another.

"I grew up next to a bay myself, ma'am, in New Jersey," he offered.

"Oh?" Ginny Wheeler seemed just as anxious to change the subject. "Was your father a naval officer, too?"

"No, he wasn't a seagoing man, although he sometimes worked in the shipping trade," Ben replied. "During the war, he was a captain in the New Jersey regiment and joined Richard Montgomery's assault on Canada in 1777. He was the original William Crane, in truth, although when my parents named my older brother, they christened him William *Montgomery* Crane. His middle name honors my father's old commander."

"So *you* are the brother of Lieutenant Will Crane, commander of the *Nautilus*!" Susan Decatur exclaimed. "What an impressive man. I feel certain he will add the name *Nautilus* to the annals of legendary vessels."

Ben's attempt to keep his face still as a mask failed miserably. His eyes grew wide as saucers. He ground his teeth, making his cheeks ripple. And when Captain Decatur pressed hard on his wife's arm and glared at her, the gesture only intensified Ben's resurgent shame.

"I . . . I need a breath of fresh air, if you will excuse me," he croaked, dashing unceremoniously for the door. A giggle from Eliza King—and a self-satisfied smirk from Will as Ben passed by—seemed designed by Providence to give his exit a special indignity.

▲▲▲

The evening was calm and peaceful. The approaching spring had removed much of the chill from the breeze blowing across Chesapeake Bay. Ben stood on a low bluff and looked out over the water, watching the moonlight dance along the tops of the waves and wondering if he would see those signs again.

Signs both wondrous and terrifying. Signs no one else could see. Two enormous fins, blue tinged with gold, knifing across the bay. Two reptilian eyes peering from the water, glowing blue with evil energy. A long, forked tongue protruding above the waves.

Ben had seen many strange sights since his boyhood. Giant things in the woods. Little people in the town, pixies out of some bedtime story yet real enough to talk to villagers and make off with clothes, shoes, and pies.

For years, Ben had chalked it up to an overactive imagination. He'd so loved tales of ghosts and goblins, haunted fields, haunted brooks, haunted bridges. They'd often frightened him, to be sure. On more than one sleepless night, young Ben had mouthed a prayer or bit of verse to guide him safely to daybreak.

A favorite poem had been John Milton's *L'Allegro*, with its light take on the magical folk and fauna that populated the boy's nightmares. When Milton's poem spoke of "Fairy Mab" and "the drudging goblin" and "horrid shapes, and shrieks, and sights unholy," young Ben had clung to the promise of "heart-easing mirth." And when the poem spoke of leaping heroes winning the hearts of fair maidens, Ben's own heart leapt with anticipation:

> *Where throngs of knights and barons bold,*
> *In weeds of peace high triumphs hold,*
> *With store of ladies, whose bright eyes*
> *Rain influence, and judge the prize*
> *Of wit, or arms, while both contend*
> *To win her grace, whom all commend.*

But as he grew to manhood, Ben was surprised to find that those magical creatures of his boyhood imagination didn't fade away. With his grown-up eyes, in a wider grown-up world, he saw still more strange things. He saw tiny hunters stalking through groves and thickets. He saw figures too long and thick to be birds circling the tops of mountains. He saw figures too enormous and undulating to be fish cavorting in lakes and streams.

And, since his posting to Norfolk, he'd repeatedly seen an impossibly large reptile breaking the surface of Chesapeake Bay.

"No wonder I can never be my brother's equal!" Ben exclaimed aloud, punching one shaking fist into the palm of the other. "One who sees monsters in the waves cannot be a great seaman!"

At just that moment, the miserable young lieutenant spotted movement to his right. Had the sea monster returned to mock him in his misery?

No—the motion was clearly along the shoreline, not out in the water. It was too small to be a giant serpent. And while the shape had started off moving along the ground, it had soon lifted off into the night sky.

As Ben watched, mesmerized, he spotted more than one moving figure. The first one was flying toward Ben's position on the bluff. Another, also aloft, was about a hundred feet behind the first. A third figure was still aground, apparently running along the shoreline.

Although the crescent moon was bright, it didn't provide Ben a clear enough look at the two fliers to discover their identities. He knew only that they were no seagulls; their dangling legs told him that much as they flew overhead.

Thus distracted, Ben didn't sense the approach of the other until it was too late. "Another Sighted human, no doubt," said a female voice in apparent resignation, but with a lilt so charming that Ben forgot to be afraid.

The tiny, blue-skinned woman was dripping wet and clutching a three-pronged spear. Ben had spent the evening surrounded by some of the comeliest women he had ever seen—Susan Decatur, the matriarch Ginny Wheeler, the divine Eliza King—but the fairy, her blue-green eyes peering up from a heart-shaped face, gave the others a robust competition for the title.

"I . . . I do not . . . of course I am sighted, uh, ma'am," mumbled the lieutenant.

The blue-skinned woman sighed. "Sighted, yes, but as yet unmet by Folk, I take it. My name is Dela. I range for the Gwragedd Annwn, as we are known back home in Wales. The English call us Water Folk."

With great effort, Ben turned his face away and pointed at the flying creatures rapidly becoming specks in the sky. "And . . . are they, uh, some of your Folk as well?"

"They are Folk, naturally, but not of *my* Folk, strictly speaking," Dela replied. "One is a friend of mine, Goran Lonefeather. As to the identity of the other, we have only guesses."

"Hadn't you better go after your friend?" Ben asked excitedly, although he found that he was in no hurry for her to depart.

"Goran can take care of himself," Dela said with a chuckle, "though had I thought otherwise, I could not have kept up with them on foot. This high ground seems as good a place as any to await the result of the chase."

Over the course of their ensuing conversation, which could not have spanned more than a half an hour, a multitude of dreams and confusions and doubts came tumbling out of Ben's mind, forming themselves into words and questions that, for the first time, he could not only ask but answer. The experience reminded Ben of that time years ago in a coffee house in New York when he'd seen an Englishman place a puzzle called a "dissection" on the table. Beginning as merely a stack of carved wooden pieces with colored images on one side, it had quickly assumed the shape of a map as the Englishmen skillfully arranged the pieces in their proper positions.

Hearing Dela talk of fairy realms, spellsongs, and magical monsters made Ben feel as though a lifetime of puzzle pieces were finally, thrillingly, arranging themselves into a coherent picture.

I have not *been hallucinating,* he realized, relief washing over him like a warm bath. *I am neither a madman nor a fool. I am Sighted. I have a Gift.*

Then his relief turned to triumph.

I have a Gift that Will does not.

After a few moments spent savoring that thought, Ben realized he was no longer listening to the Water Maiden's story of how she and Goran came to Chesapeake Bay. He shook his head as if to wipe the image of his brother off a schoolboy's slate.

"No, I suppose I did not explain that very well," said Dela in response, misinterpreting Ben's headshake. "You see, we believe if we investigate abandoned Folk villages, we will better understand the thaumaturgical properties of wood and stone. When we learned that the Pixie colony had abandoned Norfolk for points unknown, we journeyed here to find answers. "

"And instead found yourself being spied upon by another Sylph."

"We do not know for certain the spy is one of Goran's Folk, although it seems the likeliest explanation," she said.

Human and fairy looked to the sky, in the direction the two fliers had taken. Both saw, simultaneously, the flying figure returning from the same direction. Dela lifted her trident while Ben reached to unsheathe his cutlass. He did not finish the action, however, for Dela smiled and placed her hand over his.

"It is Goran," she assured him.

The Sylph flew straight for the bluff and landed. Winded from the exertion, he spent a couple of minutes catching his breath and looking back and forth from Dela to Ben before speaking.

"I see you have made a new friend, Dela—a lieutenant of American marines, if I am reading your uniform correctly," said Goran.

"You are, sir," Ben confirmed, his usual awkwardness at meeting a stranger entirely absent for reasons he couldn't explain. "Have you prior experience with officers?"

"Prior experience with American officers, indeed, but not those in naval service," Goran responded with a genial glance at the Water Maiden. "I suppose that is more Dela's inclination."

"The ranger trailing us has escaped again?" she asked.

Goran nodded, his face suddenly glum. Dela touched the Sylph's arm tenderly. Ben was surprised to see Goran jerk slightly, as if her hand felt burning hot against his skin.

"Well, Dela, I think we best be on our way to find that village." Goran's words came out in a jumble.

The female fairy looked just as surprised as Ben felt. Then she smiled and glanced up at the human. "I was pleased to make your acquaintance, Lieutenant Crane. Perhaps our paths will cross again, be it on land or sea."

"I would welcome that," Ben said, and he meant it.

Goran stepped back and flapped his wings, rising a foot off the ground. "As our old friend of ours would have put it, may the unerring hand of Providence guide your steps."

"And may you both find the answers you seek," Ben offered as Dela turned and slid her way down the soft bank of the bluff.

He stood and watched the two departing fairies until they faded from view. At first his thoughts were as jumbled as Goran's words had been moments before. Ben had desperately wanted the two to remain for a while longer so he could learn more about the magical world, but he'd resisted the urge to cajole them into staying. Their mission was evidently important. He wouldn't impose.

Besides, Ben already had a great deal of new information to interpret and ponder—more than he could make sense of in a week of late-night musings. Or a month.

Then from behind him came an incongruous noise—the sound of a woman clearing her throat.

Ben wheeled, wondering if somehow Dela had managed to return by another route. But the lady standing in the shadow of a loblolly pine was neither blue-skinned nor two feet in height. It was Ginny Wheeler.

"I had no intention of startling you, Lieutenant Crane," Ginny said. "I could tell those two had given you a great deal to think about."

Ben stared at her, mouth agape. "You saw them? You saw the fairies?"

"Why, yes. I not only saw Dela and Goran as clearly as you but also heard them," Ginny replied. "I have been standing here for some time, Mister Crane—ever since your exasperated exclamation about glimpsing the Sea Serpent in the bay. It is a sight I, too, have seen. I was about to tell you that, and to apologize for the slight my daughter may unintentionally have done you, when your new friends made their appearance. I thought it best not to reveal myself. So here I stayed, in the shadows, listening."

Brushing off the woman's apology about an event that now felt like it had happened days earlier, Ben stepped eagerly toward her. "But that must mean . . . am I to understand that you also possess this 'Sight' they spoke of?"

"I do," the matron agreed. "I have always seen Them."

"Back where you were born? Back in Carolina?"

Ginny Wheeler's eyes dropped to the ground. Ben guessed that she was remembering events of bygone days.

"It is . . . a subject that brings me great pain," the woman began. "One day I may feel inclined to speak of them. But today is not that day."

Ben straightened and bowed stiffly. "I do understand, madam," he said with as much solicitude as he could muster. "May I escort you back to your house?"

"You may," she said, taking his arm. "I expect my family and guests have by now begun a search for two missing persons."

▲▲▲

Ginny Wheeler was not entirely correct. While Susan Decatur had, indeed, suspended her impromptu harp concert to look for the missing pair, none of the guests had followed. They were clustered around Captain Decatur when Ben, Ginny, and Susan reentered the drawing room together.

"As I heard the tale, Tecumseh's warriors attacked General Harrison's army on the Tippecanoe River without direct orders," Decatur was explaining. "It was Tecumseh's brother Tenskwatawa who urged an attack while Tecumseh was away visiting the southern tribes. According to a prisoner taken after the battle, Tenskwatawa told the warriors to infiltrate the camp and murder General Harrison in his sleep. That rascal had also told them he'd cast magic spells on the arms and armor they wore, spells that would sow confusion among our soldiers and repel our bullets."

"It serves them right for believing such rubbish," Luke Wheeler said.

For the first time he could recall, Ben had the firm conviction he knew something that the notable men around him didn't—something that neither the celebrated Captain Decatur nor the captivating Will Crane had the slightest inkling of. It brought a satisfied smile to Ben's face.

"Decided to come back to the party, did you, brother?" asked Will, standing arm in arm with Eliza King. "I thought you'd yielded to the irresistible charms of a book."

Whether the jibe was meant playfully or not, Ben chose to treat it so. "I did enjoy some marvelous tales tonight, Will, that much is true," he said, and nothing more.

Later, after Susan Wheeler had played her final song and the party began to break up, Ben finally saw his chance and, uncharacteristically, seized it without delay. "Pardon me, sir, may I have a word?" he queried Decatur when the captain found himself momentarily alone.

"By all means, Mister Crane. Care to solve the mystery of where you and my mother-in-law went so abruptly?"

Ben shook his head. "No great mystery, sir. She and I just happened to choose the same spot for some stargazing. No, what I would say is a belated response to something you advised earlier, about charting my own course."

The captain looked satisfied. "I suppose I *did* say something like that. Had a chance to think on it, then?"

"I have, sir," Ben said, "and I have come to a decision. With your permission, I would like to request a change in the terms of my military service."

Decatur looked aghast. "By God, man, do you mean to resign your commission? Don't be impetuous. That is not at all the meaning I intended you to draw."

"No, sir, I believe I understood you. Remember you also said our country and Britain appear to be heading toward another war. I have no design to shirk my duty in such a circumstance. Rather, my design is to serve my country to the best of my ability."

"So, then, what change of term do you have in mind?"

"I can best serve as a member of the army, sir, not the navy. As you say, my brother Will is an excellent seaman and commander of sailors. I believe my calling is to be a commander of soldiers."

Captain Decatur studied Ben's face carefully. Then he sighed. "I will write to a general I know with the highest recommendation that you be offered a commission suited to your experience and aspirations."

"My heartfelt thanks, sir," replied Ben. "Your generosity prompts me to ask another boon."

Decatur grimaced. "What, man? Do you demand to be commissioned a full colonel forthwith?"

Ben shook his head. "It is a simple request. You see, ever since a child I have gone by the name Ben, short for my middle name of Bennet. My first name is rather . . . uncommon, and I had long preferred a short nickname like my brothers Will and Joe enjoyed."

The captain seemed puzzled. "And?"

"When I am commissioned an officer in the army, sir, I would like the official order to state my given name. A name that, in Hebrew, describes precisely my present condition—the condition my transfer is designed to rectify."

Ben paused, glancing at the retreating back of his brother.

"Must you keep me in suspense?" pressed Captain Decatur.

"In Hebrew, my first name means '*without glory*,' sir," said the lieutenant. "From now on, I'd prefer to be called Ichabod Crane."

Chapter 11 – The Poplar

June 1812

It was hardly the perfect circle he'd been led to expect. But the patch of ground before Goran, some forty feet in diameter, was certainly distinctive. No wonder the local humans thought it was haunted. The "Devil's Tramping Ground," they called it.

For although it lay in the center of a grassy meadow, the rough circle was entirely barren. Not a single stalk or blade of vegetation was visible within its brown confines.

"Anything you plant in the Devil's ground withers and dies," the old widow back in Raleigh had told one of her neighbors while Goran and Dela rested, magically concealed, beneath the spacious porch.

The neighbor had replied in hushed tones. "Once two young men camped there for the night to 'catch' the Devil, or so I heard the tale. One ran away screaming. The other one stayed. Ever since, he hasn't been right in the head."

Goran and Dela had quickly guessed the two humans were talking about the very site the fairy rangers had journeyed into North Carolina to find. After their frustrating trip to Norfolk—the abandoned Pixie village had yielded little new information, and Goran failed to catch the flier pursuing them—Dela had suggested they return to her home in Tennessee by a more southerly route so they could investigate rumors of an indigenous Folk called the Mialuka.

Goran welcomed her suggestion. For one thing, taking the longer way home—first traveling up the James River from Norfolk to Petersburg, then following a well-worn trading path southwest along the fall line into the Carolina Piedmont—meant spending more time on the trail with the Water Maiden. Furthermore, according to the rumors they'd heard, the Mialuka were a rarity in North America: a winged Folk.

Could these Mialuka be the fliers of the chimney rock? Goran wondered. *Why would they be pursuing me?*

"If this circle conceals the entrance to a Folk village, it does its job well," Dela said in frustration, poking a clump of light-brown dirt with the butt of her trident. "All I see is dead earth."

"It could just be a natural salt lick or something," Goran observed. "It would hardly be the first time humans concocted a fanciful explanation for something they did not understand."

The Water Maiden said nothing in reply. Instead, she touched the shell necklace at her throat and began to sing.

It was a courage spell, one she'd sung many times to strengthen human morale. It was a particular favorite of their mutual friend Isaac Shelby. Even the Sylph, presumably immune from its magic, always found that his head grew lighter and his heart beat faster whenever she performed it.

Only this time, something was off. The song didn't sound right. From Dela's puzzled expression, it was evident she shared his perception.

"Whether by design or accident, this 'tramping ground' is more than a salt lick," she said. "Somehow it weakens the enchantment of my necklace. It smothers the spell, like a wet blanket thrown over a campfire."

"So there *is* magecraft here!" Goran exclaimed. "Perhaps it is the Mialuka's way of bolstering their Shimmer walls."

"Or there may be natural features of the soil that interfere with magic, much as iron disrupts enchantments," Dela pointed out.

Goran shrugged. "Either way, it is the first important clue we have run across in quite a while. Now we must find out what it means."

▲▲▲

The two fairies spent much of the following day at the so-called Devil's Tramping Ground. They walked its circumference. They dug pits and examined the dirt and rocks. They sang spells. Reluctantly, they concluded they'd learned nothing more. If the Mialuka lived underground, they chose not to reveal themselves. Pocketing some of the dirt for future study, the two rangers resumed their journey back to Dela's home, following a trail that took them first north and then west.

Having once ranged widely across the Carolina backcountry, Goran marveled at the changes the humans had wrought. What were once forested hills and plains had been cleared for farms and houses. What were once remote frontier settlements were now bustling towns.

Not yet bustling, but certainly new and vibrant, was the next settlement they reached just after nightfall, a place called Greensborough. There Goran and Dela stopped, at a gated fence beneath a grove of trees, to rest and eat.

"I have no wish to hurt you, Goran, but I still think you are mistaken," said the Water Maiden as she nibbled on dried venison. "After all, we *are* passing so close by."

Why will she not let this go?

"The Knob is the one place we need not study," Goran insisted. "It was my home. I know it well."

"I know, Goran, but . . ."

"The main formation is quartzite," the Sylph continued stubbornly. "And there are rich veins of beryls. Golden beryl. Emerald. Aquamarine. We already know what that means. Emeralds are used to craft enchanted objects. Your own trident has an aquamarine inset. No doubt all beryl crystals have thaumaturgical properties. That is why my Folk settled on the Knob."

The Water Maiden only stared at Goran as she ate. Feeling her eyes boring past his defenses, he sank back against a fencepost. "Go ahead. Though I know what you would say."

Dela inclined her head. "If you know what I would say, why must I say it? Should we not seek answers wherever we may find them?"

"You do not mean answers to our questions about magecraft," Goran observed. "You think my Folk have returned. You think the rangers spying on us are Sylphs."

"And you do not?"

"So what if I do?" Goran couldn't mask his exasperation. "They clearly have no desire to speak to me! When I first encountered the fliers above the chimney rock, they saw me and fled. And sending rangers to track us is hardly the act of those who would welcome back a traitor."

Dela flinched as if she'd been stung by a bee. "Every time you call yourself a traitor, you impugn yourself and your family."

Now it was Goran's turn to be stung. "My . . . family?"

"We both know you are no traitor. You chose the way of honor. You chose to honor your Folk's cherished traditions over your leaders' monstrous schemes. Calling yourself a traitor, whether in jest or bitterness, is unforgiveable."

Goran could only stare open-mouthed at Dela, her words somehow providing offense and succor at the same time.

"Why do you assume your sister and the others have no capacity for forgiveness?" she continued. "I think you do them a disservice."

Before he could reply, the pointed ears of both rangers detected the sound of approaching feet. Goran picked up their gear and sprang into the air while Dela climbed over the fence, singing a concealment spell.

Two black men soon came into view, speaking in hushed tones. One was young and tall, his too-short dark trousers revealing not only his ankles but most of his shins. The other man was shorter and older, the black of his close-cropped hair dappled with tufts of gray.

"You can trust 'em, Stephen" said the older man. "Ain't gonna betray us."

"Heard that before, Tom," Stephen replied. "If whites hadn't betrayed me, I wouldn't be here."

The older man stopped and put both hands on Stephen's shoulders. "They's no diff'rent than us. Some good. Some bad. This one, and his father—they's good ones."

"S'pose it can't get no worse anyhow," said the younger man dejectedly.

"Come on, New Garden woods is just ahead," Tom assured him. Then the two humans continued down the trail.

Goran glanced at Dela. Her blue-green eyes were shining in the moonlight. Or were they glistening for some other reason? She clambered over the fence and began following the humans. Goran was right behind her. Presently, the black men diverged from the trail and ascended a small rise toward a tree with a straight trunk and bright-green leaves. A tulip poplar, Goran guessed, recalling his mother's lessons in tree lore.

Standing beneath the poplar was a white youth, fourteen or fifteen years of age, dressed in homespun shirt and trousers. He held up a welcoming hand to Stephen and Tom. Goran and Dela missed the first few words of the resulting conversation as they moved cautiously forward. When they were close enough to the poplar, they could hear Stephen telling his tale.

The young man had been born free in the North and was later hired to help drive a flock of sheep to Baltimore for sale. After his arrival, Stephen was abducted and carried over the border to Virginia to be sold to a slave merchant.

"If they take me south, I never see my ma again," Stephen wailed. "I got to run back to my family!"

The white youth shook his head. "That's not the way. They're sure to catch you."

"Listen to young Levi, and be wise," Tom said as Stephen sank to his knees, groaning. "The Coffins'll help you."

"God will help you, yes, and we are his vessels," Levi Coffin agreed. "I'll take you to my father."

Levi helped Stephen back to his feet and threw an arm around him, guiding him down the path. Tom remained behind and watched them thread through the trees toward a nearby farmhouse. Then the black man reached into a sack hanging at his waist, fumbled around for a few seconds, and removed something long and reddish.

Crunch!

It was the last sound Goran had expected to hear, given the gravity of the meeting they'd just witnessed. Tom just stood there, beneath the poplar tree, working his jaw energetically as Levi Coffin and Stephen disappeared from sight. Then he took another bite, placed the object back in his sack, and spat a large stream of reddish juice onto the ground. Singing a few bars of a lively song Goran didn't recognize, Tom started off after the other two. Motioning to Dela, Goran rose to follow.

Suddenly, the old man spun on one heel to face the two fairies. Looking first at the Water Maiden, then at Goran, Tom smiled slyly and winked.

Dela started. Goran froze. And then, as if by reflex, Goran found himself winking back. Tom laughed heartily and picked up his pace to close the gap with the departing humans.

Goran did not move. Dela, puzzled, touched his arm. "Should we not pursue?"

I got to run back to my family, Stephen had said, with great passion.

"No, their errand is now clear to us," Goran told Dela. "And our own errand beckons."

"So it is back to Long Island-on-the-Holston, then."

"Yes," Goran agreed. "By way of the Knob."

▲▲▲

There had been no Sylph resettlement here. That much was immediately obvious.

Goran pushed past the familiar rhododendron bush, ascended the gray stone cliff, and hummed the spellsong that had once allowed

Sylphs to pass undisturbed through the Shimmer. It did the same for Goran and Dela.

The grassy plain of the Knob, impossibly large within the seemingly tight confines of the mountain's rocky summit, contained many signs of its previous habitation. The trail to the village proper was still clearly visible. The greenweaver fields were still furrowed, though now overrun by weeds. Nearby stood the ramshackle greenweavers' hut, not valuable enough to be magically transported to the Sylph's new home, and when Goran and Dela reached the village, the ground still bore the imprint of stone-and-timber buildings that once housed guildhalls, public houses, and personal dwellings.

"No Sylph rangers flew from here to the chimney rock, or to chase us in the Blur," Goran muttered, his voice sounding as hollow as he felt.

"Your Folk may have deemed it too dangerous to return here," Dela offered, "or too painful. Do not give up hope, Goran. We may yet find their new settlement on some nearby peak."

"We may," Goran answered.

But I doubt it.

Chapter 12 – The Gifts

Every time Har returned to Grünerberg, he found the sprawling Dwarf colony had sprawled further into the depths of the mountain overlooking the Shenandoah River. He found new tunnels led to new living quarters and newly enlarged caverns contained new shops, larders, and storehouses. Given the time difference between fairy realms and the Blur, the fact that Har always found something new upon his return was a testament to King Alberich's dynamic style of leadership.

Although a "frantic" style of leadership would also be an apt description.

"War with Elfkind is coming, whether you like it or not!" Alberich had said on more than one occasion. "We must be ready. We must have more arms, more supplies, more warriors. We must prevail."

Although it was only Har the Tower, not King Alberich, who'd met with Prince Veelund since the two nations established formal relations, Alberich was adamant that only *he* understood the Elf leader's true intentions.

"That this upstart prince rose from the ranks of craftsmen, rather than warriors or mages or rangers, does not make him a pacifist," Alberich had told Har dismissively during their last audience. "Next time, bring me reports of the Elves' armies and defenses, not transcriptions of Veelund's pretty words."

Despite his disagreements with the king's views about Elfkind, which Har attributed in no small measure to bigotry and paranoia, the Dwarf ranger felt duty bound to fulfill his king's commands. And so, Har had come back to Grünerberg with reports about the walls, warriors, and weaknesses of Spirit Forest. *If Alberich truly understood the desperate conditions Veelund and his people faced*, Har thought, *the king might stop forecasting imminent attack and open his mind to a different path.*

"Har the Tower!"

The Dwarf turned with difficulty in the crowded corridor to discover the face of Goran Lonefeather smiling back at him. The Dwarf roared with delight. "I did not know you would be here!" he said as his clasped the Sylph's arm in his own.

"Have you no greeting for me?" demanded Dela, now emerging from behind Goran's extended wings and holding out her own arms.

Har yielded happily to her invitation, clinging to the Water Maiden tightly as he whooped. As he did so, he saw Goran's face redden and not for the first time marveled at how easily his friend was embarrassed.

Har released Dela and slapped the Sylph on the back. "I had planned to send you a spellsong message as soon as I concluded my report to King Alberich. Walk with me to the king's chamber?"

"We are already headed to the same destination, Har," Dela said.

"You mean . . ."

"A message arrived at Long Island-on-the-Holston this morning summoning us to an audience," Goran explained as the three resumed their walk. "Alberich's costly offer of magical transport to Grünerberg convinced us the matter was urgent. We assumed it concerned the official declaration of war between the United States and Britain."

"Though, to be honest, we also feared Alberich's tidings might be more personal," the Water Maiden added. "We feared something might have happened to Grünerberg's distinguished emissary to the Elves."

Har struck his stomach with a brawny fist. "Thus far, the only risk I face during my diplomatic career is exercising so little and eating so much that I become Har the Tub."

The three laughed as they entered the tunnel leading to Alberich's chamber. Then they heard a voice booming from the door that was just opening to the chamber—a voice speaking Folktongue fluently but with an accent Har didn't recognize.

"Your words bite, Your Majesty, though they snap at us from a smiling face," the voice declared. "So why are you so quick to let your eyes shape your judgment of us?"

"Because I have encountered your kind before, Betua—in chambers *and* on the battlefield," King Alberich bellowed from inside the room. "Although, in my experience, your kind *always* stalk a battlefield, whether war be declared or not. All that varies is your choice of weapon."

"My teachers said the same of Dwarfs," came the acrid response. Then Har got his first glimpse of the respondent.

Betua stood in the doorway, glowering at the floor and evidently trying to regain her composure. She was short, shorter even than Dela, but stoutly built and dressed in a dark-blue shift cinched at the waist by a sword belt. The shift extended part of the way over baggy, light-brown leggings tucked into boots of boiled leather. A long, fur-lined cloak of light blue covered her wide shoulders.

When Har and the others stopped, unsure how to proceed, Betua sensed their presence and turned her head.

Two incongruous images sprung to Har's mind: fire and ice.

Betua glared at him with scarlet eyes only a few shades lighter than the crimson skin of her cheeks, neck, and long, floppy ears. Despite the blazing colors in her face, Har felt as though her glare was freezing him, not burning him. And when Betua opened her broad mouth to speak, her long white teeth, tapered into points like icicles, completed the chilly effect.

"Another stubborn Dwarf, by the look of you," Betua snapped at Har. Then her cold red eyes widened as she glimpsed the blue-skinned Water Maiden and the winged Sylph.

"Is Grünerberg hosting some secret conference?" Betua asked, more scornfully than inquisitively.

"Ah, I see you wasted no time," King Alberich said as he strode to the doorway and looked over Betua's shoulder. "Dela and Goran, your promptness is appreciated. As for you, Har, your report is long overdue."

"Please allow me to introduce myself," stated Betua, snarling resentfully at the king's obvious snub. "I am Betua of Detroit, grandmaster of the Rangers Guild and emissary of Goblinkind."

"Har, ranger of Grünerberg," said the Dwarf. "My companions are Dela, ranger of the Gwragedd Annwn, and Goran, ranger of the Sylph."

"Betua was just leaving," Alberich snapped.

"I was, indeed," said the Goblin, fastening her cloak more securely around her neck and staring with undisguised fascination at the golden-tipped wings stretched high above the single kingfisher feather in Goran's cap. "Not that I would mind a word or two with the winged one. He interests me."

"I have urgent matters to discuss with all three rangers," Alberich insisted. "*Private* matters."

Betua caught the meaning. "Goblins never overstay our welcome, Your Majesty. But pray share what I have said with these newcomers. They look more intelligent than your other servants."

Perhaps hoping to get the last word, Betua hurried off down the corridor, waddling more than striding on her widely spaced legs.

The king wouldn't permit her even that much. "Your talk of neutrality fools no one!" he called after her. "Where there is the prospect of bloodshed and booty, there will ever be Goblins."

Alberich whirled and strode back into his chamber, followed by Har, Goran, and Dela. Standing along the west wall were two familiar faces. Guildmaster Lynd, her narrow features reminding Har so much of Lynd's deceased brother, Onar, was staring off into space. Next to her, tugging nervously at the end of his bushy red beard, was Sudri, the burly ranger who'd been elected grandmaster of the Rangers Guild upon King Alberich's strong recommendation.

As Har took his place beside the others, he noticed an item propped up on a small table. Unlike the scrolls that filled the shelves behind it, the item was obviously of human manufacture—a large, rectangular book, machine-printed and freshly bound.

His curiosity piqued, Har walked over and lifted its leather cover to reveal the first page. *Kinder- und Haus-Märchen* stated the title page in an ornate German script. "Children's and Household Tales?" he translated aloud. "Your Majesty, have you been holding court with Dwarflings?"

The king laughed and waved a gloved hand at the book. "It is a humanware, meant for human eyes. This is one of the first copies printed, although it will soon be distributed widely throughout the German-speaking lands."

Har was puzzled. "Sire, I do not—"

"I must give him credit," Alberich interrupted. "I know Goldemar to be a vain, pretentious, grasping lord. But he is also clever. Very, very clever. Who else could have developed so ingenuous a solution?"

This time it was Goran who voiced his puzzlement. "A solution to what problem, Your Majesty?"

"The spellsong problem, of course," Alberich replied impatiently. "Of course, if those Grimm brothers had themselves been resistant to spellsong, Goldemar's plan would have failed at the start."

Har took one more look at the title page. "The Brothers Grimm," he read. "The authors?"

"In a way, yes," answered the king. "But, now, on to the matter at hand. The American king, James Madison, has formally notified his council of his declaration of war against Britain. Already facing the might of Emperor Napoleon's armies in Europe, the British now face the very real prospect of losing all their possessions here in America. Lynd, if you would be so kind."

The slender spellsinger stepped forward.

"I have just returned from a conference with our primary contact in Washington, Albert Gallatin, secretary of the treasury," she said. "*President* Madison and the *Congress*"—her emphasis on the correct titles was not lost on Har—"believe their forces will quickly overrun the British defenders and their Indian allies. The Americans have already ordered the governor of the Michigan territory to march from Fort Detroit into Upper Canada, where they expect a rapid capitulation by the local population."

"But what of Tecumseh and his confederacy of Indian tribes?" Dela asked. "Do the Americans expect their rapid capitulation as well?"

Lynd nodded. "Their rapid capitulation—or their rapid defeat."

The mention of the fort's name jogged Har's memory. "The Goblin who just left—she said she was from Detroit."

"That is where Goblinkind established its largest American colony, back when Detroit was a French outpost," Goran said.

"Betua just finished assuring us her Folk remain neutral," Sudri said dubiously. "The Goblins of Detroit joined the Great Alliance during the first war between the British and Americans only reluctantly, she claimed, and are loathe to enter another war."

The king snorted. "Which is clearly a deception. Throughout the history of the Eternal Contest, Goblinkind has rarely been other than the lackeys of Elfkind."

Har felt a vein in his forehead begin to throb. *Eternal Contest? This again?* "Sire, after all my visits to Spirit Forest, I see no indication the Elves are plotting against the Americans, with or without Goblin aid," he said. "Their colony is overcrowded and undersupplied. The plains outside their walls are crowded with refugee camps. Veelund is struggling just to feed his Folk."

King Alberich favored Har with a sneer. "Study your history, boy. Desperation often leads to violence—particularly when Elves are involved. They breed like rabbits, then find they can support the resulting multitudes in no other way but conquest."

Har cast a furtive glance at Dela and Goran, who still stood near the door. The Water Maiden looked astonished. The Sylph looked offended.

The glance wasn't furtive enough.

"Have you something to say, *Lonefeather*?" Alberich demanded.

"I do," Goran said, stepping closer. "First, I believe introductions are in order. King Alberich of Grünerberg, please allow me to introduce Dela of the Gwragedd Annwn."

The king acknowledged Dela's curt bow. "You are welcome as a representative of our brave wartime allies. Your bravery will soon be put to the test again."

"Indeed?" replied the Water Maiden. "Do you warn of a coming attack?"

Alberich drummed his fingers on the armrest of his chair. "It will come. The United States have resumed warfare against Britain. Folk nations who aided Britain the first time will surely do so again, hoping for a better outcome. Grünerberg will do our part to thwart their aim in support of our American allies. Will your Folk not do the same?"

"With respect, sire, we cannot be certain the Great Alliance will take the field again," Goran said. "Their operations during the first war brought them little but frustration and disrepute."

"Disrepute that Prince Veelund, at least, appears to be trying to overcome," added Har.

The fingers drumming Alberich's armrest formed a shaking fist as the king shot up from his chair. He opened his mouth to speak, then seemed to think twice about it. After a moment, Alberich visibly relaxed, the hard line of his clenched jaw relaxing into a wry smile.

"You three question my judgment," the king accused. "You have the optimism and naïveté of youth. You have yet to see your abstract ideas founder on the shoals of reality. You want to think the best of others. This is a luxury a lord cannot afford. I learned that painful lesson long ago."

Har and his friends made no answer. Alberich seemed to interpret the silence as affirmation.

"To rule is to act with certainty in an uncertain world," he continued. "The easy path is to do otherwise. Dither. Or pander. Dela, surely you do not always swim with the current. And you, Sylph—surely your Folk would fly into a raging storm if your survival were at stake."

Goran nodded. "But we do not yet know that this new human war threatens the survival of any Folk nation, including your own. Can you not withhold judgment?"

Once again, Alberich looked like he was about to explode. Once again, he quickly regained his composure.

He truly desires that we trust his judgment on this matter, Har realized. *Why?*

"You speak as though you assume I am about to order our rangers and warriors headlong into battle," Alberich said. "That is not my plan."

From Har's left came the sound of Sudri clearing his throat. "Your rangers stand ready to carry out your plan, sire."

The king turned and smiled at the red-bearded grandmaster. But there was something in Alberich's eyes that struck Har as less congenial than contemptuous. *Does the king think Sudri is just flattering him?*

"Your devotion to duty is commendable," Alberich replied as he resumed his seat. "While I have little doubt the Elves and Goblins will renew their conspiracy, the intentions of other Folk remain murky. It is also possible that with the British distracted in Europe, the Americans may bring their war to a successful close by the end of the Blur year they call 1812—before a reconstituted Great Alliance could make any difference."

Dela and Goran visibly relaxed. As for Sudri, the grandmaster appeared to be scowling at the suggestion Grünerberg might not play a decisive role in the new war. Of course, given Sudri's usually sour disposition, it was hard to tell for sure.

The king raised an unwieldy-looking bundle. "Har, take this and spread its contents out on the table."

The Dwarf ranger did so, unrolling a long piece of cloth to reveal two powder horns. Set into the thick end of each horn was a light-blue gemstone with symbols intricately carved in a circle around it. Har picked one up to study the carvings and gasped in surprise. The symbols were words, but not in English or some other human language. They were Folktongue words, forming phrases Har knew well.

Forming the first few lines of a standard confusion spell.

"These are enchanted talismans!" Har exclaimed. "Where did they come from?"

"I brought them back from Washington," Lynd said. "Secretary Gallatin thought they would be of interest to us. He got them from one of the officers who fought at Tippecanoe. Spoils of battle."

Alberich pointed at the table. "Have a look at what they were wrapped in."

Har grasped one end of the long cloth, striped in brown and black, and raised it above the table. For the first time, he noticed a hole cut into its center, a hole large enough for a human head to pass through. The cloth was fringed on all sides by a braided rope of golden threads.

This was no wrapping cloth. It was a mantle, the kind of garment Indians wore over their upper bodies during cold weather. But the braided rope was not of Indian design.

Goran pinched the mantle's material between two fingers and looked back at Lynd. "Do these items represent human efforts to mimic Folk artifacts?"

"That is a possible interpretation, yes," Lynd answered. "According to Gallatin, the battle of Tippecanoe may have started by accident, not intent. Indian prisoners say Tecumseh had instructed his brother not to launch a full-out attack, it seems, so instead Tenskwatawa recruited a select group of elite warriors and bade them infiltrate the enemy camp, killing Harrison and the other officers in their sleep and thus disrupt and demoralize the Americans. He also offered the warriors 'gifts of power' that would confuse the American sentries and make the Indians invulnerable."

Dela held up one of the powder horns. "A talisman for casting spellsongs of confusion?"

Sudri nodded gruffly. "Engraved on the tusk of an elephantine monster the Shawnee call a Yakwawi, we think."

Goran touched the mantle's golden fringe. "I have seen an enchanted rope like this before. A Pukwudgie scout named Atta used it to cast a magic barrier over the mouth of a cave."

"In this case," Lynd explained, "the magecraft was apparently intended to repel rather than contain."

Har was struggling with the implications. "If this Tenskwatawa was able to equip his assassins with enchanted 'gifts,' why did they not succeed? As I understand it, the Americans prevailed at Tippecanoe."

Alberich, who'd been uncharacteristically reserved during Lynd's explanations, now sat up excitedly. "Precisely the question at hand. The Americans *did* capture the Indian village, although it was a victory dearly bought, with nearly a fifth of their army killed or wounded. At first, we thought Tenskwatawa's 'gifts' must, indeed, be nothing more than ineffectual humanwares copied from magecrafted originals. But tests by our mages have revealed that those horns can cast effectual, if temporary, confusion spells. And while the enchanted fringe of the mantle appears somewhat depleted, it continues to soften blows directed at it."

Har held up the mantle and swung one of his handaxes at it. When the weapon got within an inch of the cloth, he felt it touch an invisible barrier, slowing considerably, as if Har were pushing an open palm against a strong wind. The bronze axe blade did strike the cloth, but only lightly.

"Humans so equipped would be formidable," Goran observed, "but hardly invincible. Their foes' initial confusion would turn to resolve when the spell wore off. And as we all know, iron disrupts magic. Every time an Indian's mantle was struck by a sword or bayonet, its enchantment would weaken."

For a time, no one spoke. Alberich resumed drumming his fingers. "It could still be that Tenskwatawa or some other human crafted them," Har ventured.

"Infusing them with magical power? Nonsense!" the king retorted. "Folk crafted them and supplied them to the Shawnee prophet. And we already know the likely culprits."

"The Elves of Spirit Forest?" Har's frustration proved uncontainable. "What would Prince Veelund and his Folk have to gain?"

Goran turned from the table to face the king head-on. "Many other Folk could have done this. The Sprites of Boston. The Gnomes of New York. The Brownies of Philadelphia. The Pixies who departed Norfolk for points unknown. Or indigenous Folk such as the Pukwudgies, who have long harvested humanwares from the Shawnee and Lenape."

Alberich shrugged. "I agree we need more information. At my direction, Sudri has sent rangers to the Brownies and other City Folk to assess their intentions. We must also discover if other Indian tribes have received similar 'gifts of power' as an inducement to attack the Americans. Goran Lonefeather, I know of your previous experience in Kentucky and the Ohio country. Will you journey there on our behalf to look for any 'gifts of power' and gather any other intelligence that may be helpful?"

"I will," the Sylph said. "I had hoped Britain and United States could find a peaceful resolution of their differences. But now that war has returned to America, I will not stand aside."

The king stood and swept his dark-red cloak aside, placing a hand on the hilt of his sword. "And if the Pukwudgies, the Goblins of Detroit, or other Folk take the field against our allies?"

Goran looked more pained than impressed by the Dwarf king's bravado. "I have fought alongside Americans before to defend principles I hold dear. I will do so again, if it comes to that."

"You think your American friends fight the British for *principle?*" Alberich balked with a sneer. "What principle has convinced them they should annex the broad expanse of Canada? The humans' ends are little different from our own: material gain and position."

The Sylph's pained expression turned to indignation. "The British have committed a series of hostile acts. American sailors have been impressed, American ships seized. The British use their secure base in Canada to supply and encourage vicious Indian attacks that spare neither age nor sex. The American cause is just."

Alberich raised his hands in mock surrender. "Our human allies are free to talk of just causes, and you are free to listen. As for me, I concern myself only with interests. I have given the command. You have accepted it. No more words are required."

With greater tact than Har could have managed, Goran merely inclined his head.

Then Dela took a step forward. "Sire, I have contacts among the Iroquois and other tribes of the north. I can undertake a similar mission in that direction if it would be a service."

"You have correctly guessed my purpose in summoning you here," said the king. "That will be your task."

Then Alberich fixed his gaze on Har. "And can I trust you, too? Or have you become too besotted with the Prince of Elves to do your duty?"

His face reddening, Har dug his fingernails into his palms, using the pain as a distraction so his temper would not get the better of him. "I am a ranger of Grünerberg. I perform every mission to the best of my ability."

"Glad to hear it," Alberich said. "Har, I want you to range southward again, investigating any attempts to instigate attacks along the southern frontier. And go back to Spirit Forest. Ask Veelund himself about these 'gifts.' Perhaps we can provoke him into showing his hand."

Rather than offering any more words of protest about Alberich's closed-mindedness, Har followed Goran's lead and merely nodded.

Veelund might have valuable insights, at that, he thought. *I will find the real origin of these gifts of power, for his Folk's sake as well as my own.*

Chapter 13 – The Fireball

April 1813

A strong easterly wind had propelled the American squadron rapidly across Lake Ontario from its base at Sackets Harbor, New York, to within sight of York, the capital of Upper Canada. But the wind had suddenly shifted to the northeast, delaying the American landing.

Captain Ichabod Crane stood on the deck of his transport, bracing himself against the stiff breeze and peering through the early morning mist. His regiment, the blue-coated regulars of the Third US Artillery, would not be going ashore with the first wave. The honor of leading the assault had fallen to Major Benjamin Forsyth's riflemen, their green uniforms only intermittently visible through the fog as they climbed down ropes from their schooners to their landing boats.

Although he shared his men's disappointment at being left out of the initial assault, Ichabod could see the wisdom behind General Zebulon Pike's decision.

It had been nearly a year since the United States declared war against Great Britain. The war had brought the Americans little but embarrassment. All of America's attempts to invade Canada had failed, and in August, American General William Hull had surrendered his entire 2,500-man command at Detroit.

Amidst such disappointments, Major Forsyth's regiment had been one of the few American units to win renown during the fall and winter of 1812, conducting successful raids into Canada. Now, with the April thaw making large-scale operations possible again, Forsyth's riflemen had been attached to the American Army of the North.

Commanded by Major General Henry Dearborn, the army's original invasion target was to be Kingston, on the eastern shore of Lake Ontario. But "Granny" Dearborn, as he was called behind his back, had heard rumors of a large British garrison at Kingston, so he chose to attack the lightly defended town of York instead.

When the American convoy arrived, Dearborn stayed aboard his flagship and appointed Zebulon Pike to command the assault. The men were delighted, including Ichabod. He liked Pike very much, even though the thirty-four-year-old brigadier general's national prominence served to remind Ichabod of his own lack of distinction. Zebulon Pike was no war hero—at least not yet. He'd earned his considerable prewar fame as an explorer, leading expeditions into the Rocky Mountains. Now Pike was keen to prove himself on the field on battle.

As was Ichabod.

"How can they hope to make landing against this wind?" asked Ichabod's first lieutenant, a heavyset man named Sylvester Churchill. "Those are flat-bottomed boats—they can't tack against the breeze. They'll have to lower sails and row to shore."

Ichabod chuckled as he accepted the spyglass the lieutenant handed him. It wasn't the first time Churchill, who'd grown up on a river in Vermont, had felt compelled to share his "expertise" on all things nautical with his commanding officer.

But Captain Crane of the United States Army had once been Lieutenant Crane of the United States Navy. "Forsyth may not reach his original landing spot, Lieutenant Churchill, but he'll get ashore soon enough."

Peering through the spyglass, Ichabod watched the landing boats drift further and further west, past two makeshift British artillery batteries and the ruins of an old fort. When the riflemen finally reached the lakeshore, a gray-clad officer leapt from the lead boat and splashed through shallow water to the beach. Several green-colored shapes followed Major Forsyth's lead and began scrambling up a slope.

"They look to be under intense fire!" Churchill exclaimed.

It was true. Flashes of fire came from the trees beyond the shore. As the resulting clouds of smoke slowly cleared, Ichabod could see faces in the forest. They belonged neither to British troops nor Canadian militia; the faces were painted in patterns of red, white, and black. Instead of shakos on their heads, they wore their long, dark hair in braids, Mohawk-style stripes, and other elaborate configurations. Ichabod had been told to expect warriors of the Ojibwe and other tribes among the defenders of York. Now he was getting his first look.

Boom! Boom!

The American squadron began shelling the shore batteries. The British guns returned fire, albeit sporadically and ineffectually. The

Indians kept firing their muskets and rifles at Forsyth's men, who struggled to make their way up the embankment. Just as Ichabod was about to pass the spyglass to Churchill, another flash of light from the trees caught his eye because it was so unlike the others.

It wasn't a fiery burst from a gun muzzle—it was a long, thin beam of light, as if the sun had found only a single path to shine through a dense canopy of clouds. But the beam Ichabod spotted didn't extend from the sky to the ground. It began among the trees and then lanced *up* to the clouds above Lake Ontario.

He traced the beam to its original source just before it disappeared. The beam had come from some kind of carved wooden object pointed at the sky by a copper-colored arm. Then Ichabod felt the schooner pitch hard to port.

"A storm is coming, Captain Crane!" Churchill cried out, raising his normally calm voice to make himself heard over whistling wind and crashing waves.

Returning his attention to the squadron, Ichabod saw several more flat-bottomed boats, filled with Americans, rocking precariously in the choppy water. He also saw Zebulon Pike climbing into a landing craft of his own. Ichabod turned, brushing aside a long strand of hair the wind had yanked from beneath his hat. "Gale or not, General Pike would have us join the fight. Prepare the men."

The schooner pitched again, this time to the right, throwing Lieutenant Churchill against the rail. He quickly recovered his balance and rushed off.

Looking again to shore, Ichabod tried to find the Indian with the strange stick. He saw only warriors firing from the trees and Forsyth's riflemen firing back. Then the next wave of American boats reached the shore, unloading scores of regulars who'd fixed bayonets to their muskets. Amidst the boom of naval guns and the staccato of small arms, Ichabod could hear the war cries of Indians and the yells and bugle calls of Americans. Then the sound of more shouting voices came from a new direction, followed by the sight of troops in red coats and tall black hats charging down the slope.

Grenadiers, Ichabod realized. The British garrison had finally found its way to the battle.

Impatiently, he watched mariners struggle mightily to bring the landing boats back from the shore. As soon as the first came alongside his schooner, Ichabod swung a long leg over the side and grabbed the rope. The breeze blowing against his uniform served to outline his lanky frame as he began an ungainly descent.

Soon the boat was full and headed for land. Adjusting his hat and checking the flint on his pistol, Ichabod thought of the years of officer training that had brought him to this moment. He would soon be in the thick of the fighting, responsible for many lives other than his own.

In his youth, roaming the pine woods of New Jersey, Ichabod had been easily startled by loud noises. He'd been easily frightened by shadowy images of snow-covered shrubs or branches waving in the breeze, images his wild imagination had easily transformed into specters or ghouls.

A wild imagination has no place on a battlefield.

Through the smoke and fog, Ichabod watched the furious struggle between British grenadiers and American regulars, both firing muskets and wielding bayonets to deadly effect. At first, the Americans were pushed back to the waterline. By the time Ichabod's boat reached the shallows, however, the tide of battle had turned, thanks in part to Forsyth's riflemen, now firing at the British instead of at the rapidly diminishing number of Ojibwe warriors visible among the trees.

Forming his men into ranks, Ichabod looked for an enemy to charge. All he could see, however, were the retreating backs of redcoats running past the rickety old fort toward the British artillery batteries, still lobbing occasional shells at the American squadron on the lake.

Countless bugles and whistles blew in chorus. "To me, men!" shouted Zebulon Pike, clearly visible on a patch of pebbly ground. Lieutenant Churchill urged the men of their company forward to join the larger force assembling around General Pike. Ichabod—who felt not only disappointed at missing the savage melee on the shore but also shame at being disappointed—glanced back at the water. The wind had died down as suddenly as it had whipped up, making it easier for their boats to disembark additional Americans.

We will have to prove our mettle during the assault on the town, Ichabod told himself.

He looked into the trees from which the Ojibwe had first fired on the Americans. Had they all fled too? Ichabod took a few steps into the forest, expecting at least to see a few dead or wounded warriors, but he saw none. Either Forsyth's riflemen had found no targets or, more likely, the Indians had removed their fallen companions as they withdrew.

Ichabod turned to rejoin his men—then stopped short.

What was that?

There was a rustling in the leaves behind him followed by a noise like a child's rattle.

Ichabod spun around and saw an Ojibwe standing next to a tree a dozen paces away. Yellow paint striped his weathered face. Long gray and yellow feathers stuck out in all directions from his headdress, marking him as a chief. In the Ojibwe's outstretched hand was the strange stick Ichabod had seen earlier, a small gourd hung from its upturned end. From the tip, carved in the shape of a bird's head, shone an unearthly light, the beam angling up toward the clouds that had once again begun to swirl over the lake.

"No!" shouted Ichabod as he drew his pistol and cocked it.

Surprised by the American's exclamation, the Ojibwe chief stumbled backward, his arm striking the tree trunk. The impact jarred the rattle from his grasp, but the man was able to grab it again higher up on the handle before it fell to the ground.

Then a sharp report, like a crack of thunder, startled both men. Ichabod looked at the smoking pistol in his own hand and realized, for the first time, that he'd fired it. But the Ojibwe chief wasn't looking at the pistol. He was looking at the stick that had nearly slipped from his grasp when he collided with the tree.

The rattle was smoking too.

Even as both men stared in confusion at its bird-head tip, now partly obscured by smoke, they heard an enormous roar from east of the woods.

The Ojibwe whirled and ran. Ichabod took off after him, struggling to draw his saber from its scabbard. He needn't have bothered; by the time Ichabod reached the tree, there was no sign of the chief with the strange rattle.

Then came another chorus of American bugles and whistles. As Ichabod ran to rejoin his company, he marveled at what he'd just seen. That the Ojibwe man had been using some kind of magic, there could be no doubt. Nothing else could have projected a beam of light into the sky, a beam that apparently could control the force and direction of the wind. But what had made Ichabod's pistol shot sound like a crack of thunder? Why had the magic rattle been smoking? And why had its wielder seemed just as surprised by that as Ichabod?

When Ichabod reached his unit, Lieutenant Churchill hurried over. "Sir, where did you go? Are you wounded?"

Ichabod shook his head. "I spied an Indian in the woods and chased him, but he got away."

"We exchanged fire with redcoats and militia," Churchill explained. "After a couple of volleys, they retreated toward the battery. Then we heard an explosion."

"As did I," Ichabod said. "Perhaps our naval guns set off their ammunition stores."

As Pike's army marched to within in sight of the enemy battery, Ichabod's theory appeared to be confirmed. Several British cannons had been blown completely off their mounts and now lay in jumbled heaps of blackened iron, timber, and corpses.

Pike's army surged forward, past abandoned British batteries and a shorefront house that looked as if it might have been a headquarters. The Americans' own artillery began preparations to fire on York. As he glanced over at the lake, Ichabod could see the American squadron drawing closer to the town, soon to add their own guns to the bombardment.

"I require assistance, Captain," said a voice from behind him.

Ichabod wheeled and discovered Zebulon Pike's sharp eyes taking his measure.

"Crane, isn't it?" the general asked.

"Yes, sir."

Pike yanked a short man forward. The prisoner wore the uniform of a British sergeant. "This fellow says the garrison has abandoned all the ground between here and the walls of York. But he claims not to know the exact size of the garrison, or its composition."

"Yes, sir?" Ichabod repeated in confusion.

"God, man, I have no need of another interrogator," Pike said quickly. "I need you to take some men ahead to confirm his story."

"Aye, aye, sir," Ichabod said, momentarily forgetting his reassignment from naval to army service.

Motioning for two soldiers to join him, Ichabod strode deliberately forward, scanning the scrub brush between the shore and the trees. At first the three Americans saw nothing. Then one of the men tugged Ichabod's sleeve and pointed to a low wall. There was movement—flashes of gray, red, and black.

A moment later the colors took clearer shape: Gray trousers. Red coat. Black shako.

Impulsively, the other soldier lifted his musket to his shoulder and fired. At such a distance, only a lucky shot could have struck its target.

The shot was unlucky. Bolting upright, the untouched redcoat dashed toward the town, followed shortly afterward by another regular and a British officer. "After them!" Ichabod cried—and then remembered he'd neglected to reload his pistol. Tending to the task, he heard grunts and shouts as his two men ran after the fleeing Brit. When Ichabod was finally ready, he rose and headed in the same direction.

Then stopped instantly.

He saw something ahead of him, but it wasn't bodies in motion. It was smoke.

Was it the Ojibwe's wind weapon again? No, this was only a small, wispy line of smoke. It seemed to be moving toward him.

Then the realization hit Ichabod hard, as if he'd been swatted by a bear.

His eyes flitted nervously over the broken ground. It took only seconds to find it—a thin line of powder. Stumbling as fast as his spindly legs could carry him, Ichabod reached it just as he saw sparks flying. With a desperate lunge, he dove into the dirt and brushed away two feet of powder line before the fire reached it.

Glancing over his shoulder, Ichabod could see that the powder line led to a low building of stone and timber. Countless blue-uniformed American soldiers and officers were standing near it or milling around in a nearby clearing. He could even see the high bicorne chapeau of Zebulon Pike moving among the men. No doubt the general was still interrogating his evasive prisoner.

Had Ichabod Crane just kept an enormous ammunition magazine from being surreptitiously detonated? Had he just saved General Pike and his army from catastrophe?

I wanted the chance to prove myself. Now it has come.

Then came the lightning.

Then came the earthquake.

The entire stone and timber outbuilding rose into the air, as if lifted by a giant hand, and disintegrated.

Then came the fireball.

It was like a flaming missile from some great and terrible dragon. It consumed the shattered pieces of the ammunition magazine. It blasted everything else in the vicinity either high into the air or flat against the ground. All was charred black—mineral, animal, vegetable.

The fireball might have consumed Ichabod Crane as well had he not stumbled back in horror and fallen into a muddy ditch. Flame lanced through the air above him. Moments later, he heard splashes all around as chunks of iron, stone, and timber fell from the sky.

Ichabod ducked into a crevasse just as an enormous boulder struck the ditch where he'd lain only a second before. It produced a shower of mud, caking the American captain from shaking head to trembling toe. From all around him came panicked shouts and agonized cries.

As he stayed under the crevasse, praying for an end of the deadly rain of debris, Ichabod looked over at the trees and saw a familiar face, painted yellow and crowned with yellow-and-gray feathers. The face was gleaming in triumph.

The lightning!

It had been the magic rattle, not British sabotage, that caused the magazine to explode.

And I'm the "hero" who let its wielder escape me earlier in the woods.

Ichabod's body shook more violently than before—but not in fright. Enraged, he leapt from cover and ran along the ditch, his heavy footsteps throwing up large splashes of mud.

The Ojibwe chief saw him coming. Still looking triumphant, the Indian pointed his rattle at Ichabod's chest. There was a loud report, only this time it sounded nothing like thunder.

Ichabod's pistol had jerked in his hand. He saw a portion of the Ojibwe's jaw disappear. He heard the man scream.

It wasn't enough. Ichabod wanted to silence the Indian enchanter's voice forever. He kept running. Then he felt something strike the back of his head, and all went dark.

▲▲▲

A lifetime later, Ichabod came to. He lay next to several Americans on the floor of what looked to be a drawing room. He sat up quickly, then instantly regretted it, his head throbbing with pain.

"Captain Crane, you're awake!" exclaimed a soldier in the doorway.

Ichabod recognized him as a private in his own company. "What—what has happened?" he stammered.

"The British set off a mine or something, sir. It was a messy business. We lost a couple hundred men, dead or like to become so. One of them was General Pike, sir. His ribs and spine got stove in by a big rock. He's back aboard the flagship."

"Who's in command now?"

"It was Colonel Pearce of the Sixteenth Infantry who led our assault on York—not that it was much of a fight. Most of the British fled the town before we got here, setting fire to the shipyard on the way. Later on, Granny Dearborn—"

Ichabod narrowed his eyes at the young man, who coughed.

". . . I mean, *General* Dearborn came ashore to take possession of York. But Forsyth's riflemen and many others pay little attention to Dearborn. They're looting the town. Some even burned the parliament building to the ground."

Groaning, Ichabod made to stand up.

"Don't worry, Captain, the men of the Third Artillery didn't join the ruckus," the soldier said. "Lieutenant Churchill made sure of that. He sent me here to look in on you."

Ichabod swayed unsteadily for a moment, then felt his dizziness subside. Looking around the floor unsuccessfully for his hat, saber, and pistol, he saw only wounded men. "Let's get back to the company," he muttered.

This is all my fault.

It looked to be early afternoon when Ichabod emerged from the house, so at first he thought he hadn't been unconscious for long. He was shocked when the private said an entire day had passed since the capture of York.

Ichabod soon found his company's camp. Sylvester Churchill stood against a tree, his round face forming a slight smile. "Good to see you on your feet, sir."

"How many did we lose?" Ichabod demanded.

"A dozen wounded, though only four seriously," Churchill replied. "Not so heavy a toll to pay for such a great victory."

I never knew a "great victory" could feel so much like defeat.

▲▲▲

He wasn't the only American officer who thought so.

The capture of York strengthened the flagging morale of the Americans, whose previous invasions of Canada had failed so disastrously. But the popular Zebulon Pike had died of his wounds, as had many others injured by the exploding ammunition depot. Instead of capitalizing on their momentum with new attacks, Dearborn and his army had found themselves trapped in York by endless storms.

If magic was behind the adverse weather, Ichabod at least knew it wasn't same hand wielding the same weapon. Before returning to the schooner, Ichabod walked back to the site of his confrontation with the Ojibwe chief. There, he found the shards of the magic rattle. Ichabod collected the pieces, hoping later to solve the mystery they presented.

It wasn't until two weeks after they captured York that the Americans were able to leave for their next destination: the Niagara Peninsula, on the southern shore of the lake. At the mouth of the Niagara River, which flowed northward from Lake Erie into Lake Ontario, the United States already had a stronghold on the east bank, Fort Niagara. The British had their own base, Fort George, on the west bank. Taking the latter would give the Americans full control of the position.

When the Americans arrived at Fort Niagara, however, they found it ill prepared to quarter a large army. After many days of discomfort and tedium, a messenger arrived in Ichabod's crowded camp. All company commanders were to report to the new adjutant general for a conference. When he arrived, he saw not one but two unfamiliar faces. The larger of the two newcomers wore an army colonel's uniform. Ichabod immediately recognized the uniform worn by the smaller man: that of a master commandant of the navy.

The colonel rose from his seat, giving the tail of his coat a precise jerk to smooth out any wrinkles. He was a magnificent specimen of a soldier, taller even that Ichabod, perhaps six and a half feet in height with a deep chest and graceful carriage. His narrow, penetrating eyes and prominent nose gave the man the visage of a predatory bird.

"I am Colonel Winfield Scott," he began. "You may have heard of me. You may have heard I insist on firm discipline. You may also have heard we have no time for that in our present circumstances. Only that last statement is false. We will attack Fort George presently. Until then, gentlemen, the soldiers of this army will conduct themselves according to the duty and honor their country demands of them. And while the enemy may think us capable only of engaging them by long shot, not cold iron, regular drill with a bayonet will soon permit you to disabuse them of that notion."

The officers exchanged puzzled expressions, often supplemented by mouthed words and hushed whispers.

"I will brook no interruption," Scott said, his voice commanding an instantaneous silence.

Except from one cleared throat. The colonel turned and found the naval officer shooting him a questioning look. Scott replied with a curt nod.

"Good morning, gentlemen," said the naval officer, who was shorter and slighter than Scott but made at least as strong an impression with his energetic bearing and dashing smile. "I am Oliver Hazard Perry, commander of naval forces on Lake Erie. I came downriver in search of men and materiel and was asked to scout landing sites for your assault on Fort George. Colonel Scott and I are acquainted, and he has asked me to help prepare you for the tasks to come."

As Scott and Perry continued their discourse, Ichabod found his mind wandering. The more he thought about it, the more he was convinced the Ojibwe chief at York hadn't known his magic rattle could cast bolts of lightning until Ichabod had surprised him in the woods. That meant the chief hadn't made the rattle himself. Perhaps no Ojibwe had made it. So where did it come from? Had one of the indigenous Folk Dela had spoken of, some hidden nation of two-foot-tall red men, supplied it to the Ojibwe? Would the Americans again face foes with magic weapons during the coming attack on Fort George?

"Have you something to add, Captain?"

Winfield Scott's stentorian voice chopped through Ichabod's reverie of suppositions like a knife through an apple. His slack limbs and shaking head must have betrayed his lack of attention. Feeling all eyes upon him, Ichabod straightened and took an anxious gulp.

"No, sir," he croaked.

When the conference was finally over, Ichabod tried to hurry away without being accosted. He wasn't quite fast enough. "Hold there, Captain," Master Commandant Perry called. With a sigh, Ichabod complied.

"Have we met before?" Perry asked. "Your face looks familiar. May I ask your name?"

"Crane, sir. Captain Ichabod Crane of the Third Artillery."

"Crane, eh?" Perry's face turned thoughtful for a moment. "Might you be any relation to Master Commandant Will Crane, the former skipper of the *USS Nautilus*?"

Ichabod grimaced. "Yes, sir. He's my brother."

"I have known Will for years!" Perry exclaimed. "First met him during the war with the Barbary pirates. An excellent seaman. Few blame him for the loss of the *Nautilus* to the British last summer. She's a fine ship—I once served as its first lieutenant, you know."

It was a lot of information to take in. Ichabod's mind reeling, he merely offered a brief nod.

"Now I remember where we met!" Perry continued. "It was a year or two ago, down in Norfolk. But that couldn't be correct—the Crane brother I met was a fellow naval officer."

"No, sir, you have it right. When war came, I sought an army commission. I, uh, I thought I could best serve my country on land."

Ichabod feared his admission might annoy the master commandant, who was clearly a proud naval officer. Perry was silent, his face adopting a dubious expression. He seemed to be studying Ichabod like a pilot might study a map.

"You know, Captain Crane," Perry said after a while, "I have three brothers in the service: Raymond, Matthew, and James. Young Jimmy serves with me in the Lake Erie squadron. Raymond is with Commandant Macdonough. And Matthew's currently aboard the *USS United States*, under the command of Captain Decatur."

"I met Stephen Decatur once," Ichabod blurted out. "He's a fine officer and gentlemen."

"I am glad you think so," the other replied drily. "If I may continue, though. Knowing something of such matters, I believe I understand you, sir. You would stand in the sun, not the shade."

Not knowing what else to do, Ichabod shrugged.

"And if it will not give grave offense, I must say that while I like and admire your brother, he does tend to go on and on about himself. I am pleased to know a Crane with a different, uh, disposition, shall we say?"

Commandant Perry's strategy worked like a charm. Ichabod found it impossible not to burst out laughing. A moment later, the other joined him.

"My assignment requires I scout along the shore and mark the channels," Perry continued. "I could use the assistance of an army man with naval experience. Might I speak to your commanding officer?"

This time, Ichabod's nod was an eager one. He'd gone from heavyhearted and crestfallen to lighthearted and hopeful in the space of minutes.

It's a new chance to prove my worth. And, perhaps, to make a new friend.

Chapter 14 – The Falls

June 1813

Dela lay on the steaming deck of the schooner and watched Poughkeepsie pass by. The town was far more populous that the little community she'd seen on her first cruise up the Hudson River more than a dozen Blur years before. On that occasion, Dela had used spellsong to pose as a Dutch matron so she could interact with the passengers and crew. This time, however, she'd simply sung a concealment spell to make herself invisible.

She was only resting on the deck after several days of strenuous hiking and swimming across Maryland and Pennsylvania. Soon, she'd slip back into the waters of the Hudson, where she could set a faster pace than the old Dutch schooner could manage sailing upriver. Her mission was an urgent one: to see if Iroquois nations had been offered magical "gifts of power" to join the war on the British side.

Her solo ranging had also given Dela the opportunity to think about her recent travels at Goran's side. They'd been shadowed by flying rangers, identities unknown. The sight had finally prompted Goran to speak at length, however painfully, about the family and friends he had lost when the Sylph abandoned the Knob. Alas, their conversations had left Dela no closer than before to learning his true feelings about finding his Folk.

And no closer to learning his true feelings about me.

A flush came to Dela's pale-blue cheeks. It *was* a hot afternoon, after all.

A strong breeze had filled the sails of the schooner since Poughkeepsie, speeding its way up the Hudson. The pace still felt frustratingly slow. She had needed the rest, but necessity had not fully conquered her impatience.

As the schooner passed the landing at Esopus, where Dela had gone ashore during her first Hudson cruise, she spotted movement in the trees. She rose and walked to the port rail. The tree branches continued to shake. At first Dela thought it was a single human pushing through the foliage. Then she heard merry laughter, followed by a deeper voice answering playfully.

Two figures emerged, both wearing ill-fitting clothes with frayed seams and faded hues. The man and woman were both tall, well-built humans. Both had dark skin.

Enslaved Africans belonging to some Hudson Valley farmer, Dela guessed.

During her first visit to Esopus, a little black girl had stared in wonder at the Water Maiden, evidently piercing her disguise with the Sight. Now, as the schooner sped past the two slaves standing there hand in hand, Dela thought she saw a similar expression on the face of the female. It was an expressive face, to be sure. A high forehead. Prominent cheek bones. Square chin. Lips full and drawn back unevenly in a mischievous smirk. Large, deep-set eyes.

Eyes that looked directly into Dela's own.

There was surprise written on those dark eyes, perhaps, but no shock. The tall girl's lips drew further back into a delighted smile. Then, as the schooner sailed on, Dela watched the retreating image of the girl as she glanced at her companion, threw her head back in apparent laughter, and pulled the young man back into the trees.

It was a free and easy gesture, the action of a young woman in love. It seemed incongruous to watch the action performed by a human in bondage. And yet the scene also filled the Water Maiden with longing and regret. She, too, was a young woman—perhaps even a young woman in love. Might Goran one day seize her hand as eagerly and lead her to some romantic hideaway?

Or must it fall to me to make the first move?

With a single fluid motion, Dela climbed the rail and dove into the Hudson, sighing in relief as cool water doused the flush that had returned, hotter than ever, to her cheeks.

▲▲▲

"My eyes no longer see, Dela, but your visit brings a flood of lovely memories."

The long, thin frame of Skenandoah stretched across two pallets of straw pressed together lengthwise. His people thought him well over a century old. They knew roughly when Skenandoah had been born, in a village of the Iroquois-speaking Susquehannock people. They also knew the date, decades later, when he'd been formally adopted into the

Oneida. What they didn't know about was the period a young Skenandoah had lived behind Shimmer walls with a Folk nation, the Jogah, a period that had felt like only a year to him but was actually twenty years of Blur time.

Whether a hundred years old or only eighty, Skenandoah was clearly suffering the maladies of advanced age. Blind, gravelly voiced, and no longer the robustly built giant of a human he'd once been, Skenandoah nonetheless could command the attention of a roomful of quarrelsome chiefs with merely a dissatisfied grunt or a whispered word.

Dela looked at him in sadness, now realizing her old friend might be unable to supply the information she sought. Such sadness was an inescapable experience for rangers when they formed attachments in the Blur. With every visit, the gap between ranger and human grew. Inevitably, death would render the gap unbridgeable.

It was why many rangers chose not to form such attachments. They did their work. They used subterfuge and spellsong to obtain humanwares. They conducted missions. They met humans. They charmed humans. They manipulated humans. But they did not befriend humans.

Which is why so many Folk have never understood humanity.

"I am sorry," Dela said. "I should have returned long ago,"

The chief waved a bony hand. "Nonsense. You had your duties. A life lived without responsibility is no life at all."

Dela nodded in appreciation, then remembered her friend's blindness and touched his arm. "You are kind to say so, my Pine Tree Chief."

Skenandoah inhaled deeply, coughed, and let out a long, wheezing breath. "My people no longer see a Pine Tree Chief, Dela. To them I am an aged hemlock, the winds of a hundred years whistling through my branches."

Then he ran a shaking finger across his closed eyelid.

"I am dead at the top," he continued. "Why I yet live, only the Great Spirit knows. I pray to Jesus that I may await with patience my time to die."

The Water Maiden felt a tear trickle down her cheek, resolving to change the subject. "Skenandoah, war has come again between Britain and America. I have come to learn the stance of the Iroquois."

The old man grimaced. "Even a hemlock dead at the top may still draw water from its roots. The words of the chiefs still find themselves to my ears. I know much of this war. What I know, I will say. What I do not know, others will say if I ask it of them."

"Then your people have already been asked to intervene?"

"Of course," he replied. "At the start, the chiefs of our six nations agreed to keep our confederacy neutral, to prevent Iroquois from meeting Iroquois again on the battlefield. But warriors follow their own consciences. Some Iroquois fight beside the British. Others of our people joined the American side."

The Water Maiden's eyes widened. "Skenandoah, this is very important. About those fighting with the British—have you heard anything, uh, out of the ordinary?"

"About magic, you mean?" The old man coughed and shook his head. "I have heard nothing of monsters taking the field, as they did during the last war."

"It might be something else entirely," Dela explained. "Unexplained incidents. Warriors demonstrating abilities beyond the reach of normal humans. A sudden loss of nerve by the Americans. Anything out of the ordinary."

The old chief lay his head back on the pallet of straw, lost in thought. After some time, he licked his parched lips. "That the American surrendered their fort at Detroit so quickly last summer has never made sense to me. But only a few of our warriors were there."

Then Skenandoah arched his eyebrows, as if his unseeing eyes had just spotted something important. "The tale of Teyoninhokarawen at Queenston Heights may interest you."

"What is 'Teyoninhokarawen at Queenston Heights?' " Dela asked.

"Teyoninhokarawen is a man, a chief of the Mohawk," Skenandoah replied. "His English name is John Norton. He joined the British cause. At a place called Queenston Heights, just downriver from the Great Falls of the Niagara, Norton and a few Mohawk warriors kept an American army occupied for hours, giving the British time to counterattack and win a great victory."

"How did they manage it?"

"It is said Norton used trickery to make the Americans think the Mohawk were present in great numbers, when it fact the Americans greatly outnumbered them. Perhaps Folk were present to accomplish this?"

Or Norton and his people possess powerful gifts.

▲▲▲

Despite the urgency of her mission—and the tantalizing information Skenandoah provided—Dela lingered by his side for the better part of a day, tending to his needs and listening to the tales of his youthful exploits, his decades as chief, his work with his friend Samuel Kirkland, and his friendship with Polly Cooper, the Thunderer who had taken human form and later forgotten her monstrous past.

The Water Maiden owed her friend that much. Even stories she'd heard many times before took on new shades of meaning when told by one facing imminent death. Skenandoah's humanity gave him a perspective Dela did not have, one she found fascinating as well as troubling. She even shared with him her mixed feelings about Goran.

"The very traits you admire most, his honesty and responsibility, are also barriers," the old chief whispered between coughing fits. "He is a man without a country, without a home—without anything to offer you."

"What of feelings? Companionship? They are not enough?"

Skenandoah's ancient face showed a few more wrinkles as he smiled. "Folk or human, it is the same. A man's deepest desire is to *earn* a woman's love, through feats of daring, strength, or endurance."

"Goran has nothing to prove to me," Dela said. "I have already said as much."

Skenandoah cleared his throat with a sputter. "You may *say* he need not prove himself. But what he *hears* is doubt, not reassurance. He wonders if you need anything at all from him. Everyone wants to be needed."

She groaned in exasperation, bringing another smile to the old chief's face. Then the face went slack as he fell asleep.

"May your dreams bring your comfort, my friend," Dela whispered.

Even as your words fail to bring me the same.

▲▲▲

It was nearly two hundred miles from the Oneida village to the Niagara River. During her journey, Dela couldn't help dwelling on what Skenandoah had said about her relationship with Goran. What if the Sylphs were never found? Could he ever feel at home among her people?

For that matter, even if he did, how might Dela's mother and the other Gwragedd Annwn react? While romantic relationships with outsiders were far from rare—Water Maidens had even been known to dally with human men from time to time—Dela was not interested in just a dalliance, be it with Goran or anyone else. Most Folk disapproved of mixed marriages. Dwarfs and some Town Folk were especially adamant, sometimes going so far as to imprison or exile those who married outside their own kind. The likely reaction of the Gwragedd Annwn wouldn't be as extreme—although no one had tested that proposition in generations.

When my mother talks of becoming a grandmother, a grandchild with feathers is not what she has in mind.

Something Skenandoah said had also darkened Dela's mood. What if Goran truly felt he must "earn" her affection with dangerous heroics? If so, his recklessness could keep them apart just as surely as his reticence.

As Dela emerged from the woods to stand on the bank of the Niagara River, she forced herself to concentrate on the task at hand. From snatches of human conversation, Dela learned that the Americans had taken Fort George and now controlled both banks of the river. But many British defenders had escaped into the countryside. In early June, an American foray from the fort had resulted in disaster at a place called Stoney Creek. Around the same time, the British fleet sailed across Lake Ontario and attacked the main American base at Sacket's Harbor, further demoralizing the Americans at Fort George.

Welcoming the chance to escape the blazing heat, Dela slipped into the Niagara. She swam with the current for a while, embracing the feeling of cool water on her skin. When her head broke the surface to take a breath, Dela heard thunder. She glanced up at the sky, seeing no clouds. Then she realized the thundering sound was continuous, not periodic.

The Great Falls lay ahead. Beyond them were Fort George and Fort Niagara. Once Dela reached them, she could range westward, looking for answers among the British-allied Iroquois who were raiding and harassing the Americans.

Dela submerged and swam with broad, powerful strokes and kicks, racing downriver with the accelerating current. The next time she rose for air, the rumble was almost deafening. She spotted a small, forested island. On either side of it, she could see the white caps of rapids. There were two large waterfalls there, she realized, one on each side of the island.

And above the island, framed by a brilliant rainbow arching through the bright blue sky, was a winged figure.

A Thunderer?

Dela's heartbeat quickened. She recalled Skenandoah's long-ago trip to the falls with Polly Cooper. Following rumors of Thunderers in the area, he'd hoped to restore Polly's awareness of her true self. They had, indeed, seen winged creatures, but Polly's memories never returned.

Dela's mission was about enchanted objects, not monsters. Nevertheless, she couldn't pass up the opportunity to find out if Thunderers lived nearby. Then another thought sent a chill up her spine. Could this instead be one of the Folk rangers who'd previously spied on her and Goran?

Seeing the figure fly west, Dela headed in the same direction. That meant swimming perpendicular to the Niagara's strong current, however, which took time. When she finally reached the shore and looked skyward, the flier was gone. Frustrated, she spun and looked out over the river. The westernmost set of falls was now clearly visible, forming a half circle, as if something had broken a gigantic bowl in half and thrust it forcefully against the raging river. The sheer volume of water pouring over its curved lip to crash on the surface below staggered her. She couldn't see the bottom but guessed the drop was well over a hundred feet.

"De . . . Dela?"

The man's stammering was barely audible above the angry roar of the falls. At first, the Water Maiden couldn't place the voice. Then recognition came. It was the last sound Dela expected to hear on the remote frontier between New York and Upper Canada.

She whirled and looked up into the great glassy, green eyes of Ichabod Crane.

"Lieutenant Crane? What are you doing here?"

The human snatched the bicorne hat from his head and managed an awkward bow. "It's *Captain* Crane now, ma'am, of the Third Artillery. My men and I were part of a force sent from Fort George to attack the British at a place called Beaver Dams. But we, well, we got separated from the main column during the battle."

As soon as Ichabod uttered the phrase "my men," Dela had begun singing a concealment spell. The captain was startled at first, then pointed to the woods. "No need to worry. My men are quite a distance away, looking for the trail of the Mohawks we were chasing."

"There were Mohawks in the battle?" Dela demanded, setting aside the mystery of the flier for the moment.

"It was mostly Mohawks we were fighting, actually. Only a few British soldiers showed up at the end, to accept our surrender."

Dela raised an eyebrow. "You do not look like a prisoner."

Ichabod shrugged his narrow shoulders. "My men and I weren't at the surrender. I should explain that . . ."

A series of crunching sounds made the captain halt in midsentence. As the noise grew louder, Dela ran to a fallen tree and crouched down, exposing only a sliver of her face so she could see what was happening. A moment later, a private wearing white trousers, a blue coat crisscrossed by white pack straps, and a black shako on his head came into view. Three more soldiers followed closely behind.

"Went south 'bout half a mile, sir," said the first man. "No sign of 'em."

"Yes, well, that's ill news," Ichabod replied, glancing nervously in Dela's direction. "I think they escaped us. Perhaps we should follow the river back to—"

"Look out, sir!" yelled another soldier.

Then Dela heard a gunshot. A second later, she heard something strike a tree trunk behind her. Trusting her concealment spell had been effective, the Water Maiden tightened her grip on her trident and leapt from cover.

The American soldiers responded just as quickly. Two were aiming their muskets in a northerly direction. One was reloading his weapon. The final was affixing his bayonet. Ichabod, saber drawn, was scanning the surrounding woods.

"Here they come!" shouted one of the aimers.

"So many this time!" shouted the other, who then fired his musket.

But Dela saw no one else.

"No need to panic, men!" Ichabod said, waving his saber as if trying to get their attention.

Neither his voice nor his waving sword did the trick. All four soldiers charged, brandishing their bayonets enthusiastically as they ran into the trees lining the river.

Ichabod glanced over his shoulder at Dela. "They see Mohawk warriors who aren't really there. But more than phantoms of the mind haunt these woods. There *is* a real enemy!"

Not waiting for a reply, the artillery captain dashed into the trees—but in a different direction than his men. They went north; Ichabod went west. Dela followed him but couldn't match the speed of his long-legged gait. Ichabod was almost out of sight when she heard him call out, "I see you! And I shall have you!"

A more distant male voice answered. As she sprinted forward, Dela heard the ring of metal striking wood, followed by grunts and groans.

She soon found Ichabod grappling with an Indian nearly as tall as he, and far wider. The officer's saber was embedded in the Mohawk's war club. The club was about two feet long, made of maple that was rounded on one end and carved into the shape of a bird's claw on the other. Clutched in its "claw" was a green-tinted ball about three inches in diameter.

Dela's eyes took in these details even as she hurtled forward, thrusting her trident before her. One of its three blades struck the leg of the Mohawk, who yelped as it sank into his thigh.

But the Indian was far from finished. Wrenching his war club free from the sword, the man punched Ichabod hard in the face with a clenched fist, knocking the artillery captain to his knees.

"Ichabod!" cried the Water Maiden. She lunged in front of him and swung her trident, meeting and deflecting the blow the Mohawk aimed at the American's skull.

Shocked, the Indian stumbled back a few paces, eyes darting from side to side. From the human's perspective, Dela realized, something unheard and unseen had first stabbed him in the thigh and then blocked the blow he'd aimed at Ichabod. The Indian must have been close enough when she sang her concealment spell to have been affected by it.

Uttering a word the Water Maiden didn't recognize, the Mohawk made a chopping motion in the air with his ball-head club. There was a flash of green light and a brief burst of sound like voices singing at an impossible speed. Emitting a satisfied grunt, the Mohawk looked contemptuously at the American, who was struggling to regain his feet.

Ichabod looked back with a steady glare. "Summon as many specters as you like," he said in a determined voice. "It won't help you."

Whether the Mohawk spoke English or not, he took Ichabod's meaning. Raising his war club over his head, he launched another attack.

"Let me, Ichabod!" Dela shouted. With a sweep of her arm, the Water Maiden yanked her enchanted net from her shoulder and threw it into the air. The net wrapped itself around the club, the shells and stones woven into its fringe providing enough momentum to wrench the weapon from the Mohawk's grasp.

Now it was the Indian's turn to cry out. Drawing a knife, the warrior bent his knees in a wary crouch, then backed away. When Ichabod made to follow, the Mohawk gave up all pretense of menace, turned, and raced into the trees.

▲▲▲

As they headed back toward the river, Ichabod completed the explanation that the arrival of his soldiers had interrupted. The previous day, his commanding officer had led the American column toward the last known headquarters of the enemy. Somehow guessing their intentions, or perhaps warned by a spy, the British and their Indian allies were ready. Warriors had ambushed the Americans from all sides, producing a bloody hand-to-hand battle in a thick forest.

"There were hundreds of Mohawks there, to be sure, but I came to realize that the rest of the army, including my own commander, saw even more attackers than that. My men aimed our field guns at Mohawk reinforcements that were never really there. Our shots ended up shaving the tops of trees rather than striking our enemies. I tried to redirect their fire. But my men wouldn't listen."

Dela saw his glum expression and heard the shame in his quivering voice. "It sounds like Folk rangers intervened with spellsong, Ichabod. There was little you could have done."

"That's just it—I should have guessed what was happening," he insisted. "I'd seen it before. Only I was expecting gales or lightning or driving rain, not phantom warriors."

"Saw *what* before, Ichabod? Folk rangers aiding the British?"

"I never saw any Little People," Ichabod clarified. "But when we took York, I saw an Indian chief use a magic rattle against us. He blew our boats off course. He killed General Pike and many soldiers by setting off an explosion."

Dela ran a finger along the polished maple of the ball-head club. It found the notch Ichabod's sword had cut. Then her finger found other notches, indentations carved methodically into the wood.

An illusion spell! "This enchanted weapon emits spellsong to make humans see more enemies than they truly face," she told Ichabod. "An effective way to demoralize an army."

Ichabod nodded. "During the battle, I saw a Mohawk sitting in a tree, casting his club at our men like it was a fishing pole. I took off after him. Some of my men followed, thinking I was running headlong into an entire band of Indians. The Mohawk ran, and I chased him for the better part of an hour. I never caught up—well, not until just now."

"And your men followed you all that way?"

"They're good soldiers, Dela—brave and loyal. They probably thought I'd lost my head, or my nerve. They wouldn't abandon me."

"Then you actually ended up saving your men from captivity!"

Ichabod shook his head sadly. "Only by accident."

This human sees only sunsets, never sunrises, Dela realized.

Chapter 15 – The Marathon

August 1813

As the site came into view, Goran gasped. It was far larger than his conversations with the local humans had led him to expect.

The Sylph's search for gifts of power had taken him into the Ohio country, where his friend Daniel Boone had once lived in Shawnee captivity and then faced off with their mutual Pukwudgie enemy Atta Yellow Jacket—although it had been Goran, not Daniel, who'd finally ended Atta's reign of terror at the place North Carolinians later named Tory's Den.

Now another war between the United States and Britain had brought a new wave of death and destruction to the northwestern frontier.

And unless I miss my guess, there are again Pukwudgie hands at work, Goran fumed. *Hands again drenched in human blood.*

Not knowing the precise location of the Pukwudgies, and inspired by his Cherokee friend Gulkalaski's description of a Folk village within an earthen mound, the Sylph ranger had decided to investigate similar sites along the branches of Ohio's Mohican River. Magically disguised as a peddler, Goran had entered the small settlement of Mansfield. The local settlers had directed him to a small creek north of town.

Goran was looking at an Indian "mound" here, yes, but it wasn't the low, grassy hill he'd expected. Rather, it rose dozens of feet above the ground. Across the top of the mound, spanning several acres in size, was a line of oaks so massive they must have been centuries old.

With a powerful sweep of his wings, the Sylph soared over a flower-dotted meadow and landed at the base of the mound. He ran his fingers along the steep side of the embankment, feeling wet grass, damp stones, and muddy dirt. It had recently rained.

Taking off again, the Sylph flew close to the ground, following the contour of the mound as it stretched hundreds of feet to the east.

170

Then Goran stopped short. There was a notch dug about four feet into the top of the embankment. Hovering in front of it, Goran felt the indentation with his hand. Whether dug by hand or water, it was no recent addition to the landscape. He felt moss and grass inside it.

There were similar indentations along the ridgeline. Some were shallow; others were deeper and wider. Moreover, the notches weren't randomly placed. There was a regular pattern, although its precise nature was hard to discern.

"A curious arrangement, would you not agree?"

The low, guttural voice made Goran spin quickly in the air, silently cursing himself for getting distracted. It would not do for an experienced ranger to be so easily surprised.

Particularly by a Folk not exactly known for stealth.

Betua regarded Goran with cold, scarlet eyes. The Goblin ranger was dressed the same way she'd been when the Sylph first met her at Grünerberg—a dark-blue shift of cloth, belted at the waist, hung over light-brown leggings. Betua's gloves and boots were made of boiled leather, as were her bronze-studded helmet and the breastplate now visible under the loose neckline of the shift. Both a broadsword and a short, wicked-looking mace hung from her belt.

"Yes, a curious arrangement," Goran agreed warily. "But not as curious as finding you here. An arrangement of your own doing, no doubt."

The Goblin shook her broad head, her huge red ears flopping back and forth, and showed her pointed white teeth in an apparent attempt at a reassuring smile. "A coincidence, I assure you. I have long been fascinated by ancient ruins. This is a star and planet calendar of some kind, I suspect. Standing stones back home in France served a similar function for the local humans."

I am not so easily fooled.

"You have been following me since I left Virginia," Goran accused, although with more confidence than he actually felt.

"I thought only Dwarfs capable of such arrogance," Betua replied drily. "Do you truly think yourself so important, Sylph, that I would track you over such great spans of space and time?"

"That is no denial." Goran allowed himself to drift to the ground. Betua did not flinch a muscle, so the Sylph resisted the temptation to reach for a weapon of his own.

The Goblin ranger stopped smiling. "Your accusation is worthy only of contempt, not rebuttal. Why should it not be *I* accusing *you* of following *me?*"

Although Goran had no experience with her Folk, he remembered well the lessons he learned as an apprentice ranger. Goblins were, as a rule, argumentative and aggressive. They enjoyed sparring with words as much as with blades. And in the so-called Eternal Contest between Elfish and Dwarfish Folk, Goblinkind had frequently played one side off the other and profited accordingly—in game, humanwares, and other valuable commodities.

Were the Goblins of Detroit playing the same game in America, seeking to profit by tipping the balance of a human war? If *they* were the Folk supplying enchanted weapons to the Indian tribes, that would explain much.

Including Betua's presence. *And that would mean she knows why I have come.*

"I am on no sightseeing trip," said Goran, deciding to test his theory. "I came here looking for Pukwudgies. Perhaps you did not follow me. Perhaps you are simply here to visit your allies."

Betua gave Goran a long, searching look with her dark-red eyes. Then she turned away and sighed. "I have come looking for Pukwudgies myself, Sylph. I have certain questions to ask them, questions that their cousins, the Paissa, have refused to answer."

"The Paissa?"

"A Folk of hill and valley," Betua explained. "An offshoot of the Pukwudgies, I suspect, although the Paissa would have me believe the reverse. Ever since we Goblins accompanied our human subjects to America and founded colonies on the shores of the Great Lakes, we have periodically encountered Paissa and other Folk like them. They have generally learned to stay out of our way. When they do not, we instruct them—with blade and ball."

Goran glanced at the ball-shaped head of her mace, bristling with spikes, and suppressed a shudder.

"I have my own questions," he said. "As I have yet to see a Pukwudgie, I will ask them of you. Have your Folk entered the new war? Are you assisting the Americans' enemies?"

Betua glared contemptuously. "Which Americans do you mean? The upstart bluecoats and land-hungry settlers whose cause you champion? The French- and English-speaking Canadians who have lived in North America for generations? Or the Indians who have occupied these lands for far longer than that? Are they not all Americans?"

Now we are getting somewhere, Goran thought, but he decided not to signal that she'd let something important slip.

"I do not expect self-righteous words from a Goblin," chuckled the Sylph.

"And I do not expect righteous deeds from a servant of the Dwarf king," snarled the Goblin.

Goran's eyes narrowed. "I am *not* Alberich's servant. I freely offer my services as a ranger in the interest of peace, and of defending the new American republic."

Betua's own eyes became little more than slits. "And what if the interests of peace and of their new 'republic' are at odds? Where, then, would your loyalties lie?"

It was no easy question to answer, even if Goran were inclined to try. But he had no intention of baring his soul to some random Goblin. Besides, Betua's belligerent responses seemed to advance him closer to his own goal. He resolved to keep her talking.

"You are a skilled warrior, Betua, trying to parry my question with one of your own. But this is far from my first duel, by word or weapon. I am not so easily defeated."

The Goblin's toothy grin returned. "Nor am I. We have reached an impasse. Shall we dispense with words and try something else?"

Betua's right hand stroked the head of her mace. In response, Goran ran a finger down the bowstring slung diagonally across his chest. It would take only an instant for the Sylph to lift off the ground, pull his bow over his head, and nock a bronze-tipped arrow. How long would it take for the Goblin to draw and hurl her heavy, spike-studded mace?

Given the relatively short distance that separated them, Goran thought it best not to find out.

Betua threw back her broad head and heaved, her large shoulders rising and falling. The resulting sound was clearly a form of laughter, though to Goran's ears it sounded more like the gasping and wheezing of someone afflicted with a serious malady of the lungs.

"You have pretty wings, Sylph, but you are too slow and skinny to provide me much sport," she said. "And I doubt either of us will meet any Pukwudgies today. Although the bones of this mound feel strong, they have held no magic for a long while."

Can she sense the thaumaturgical properties of wood and stone directly, without the aid of mage or instrument? Goran wondered. *Or is she just trying to bait me?*

Betua turned away. "I will seek my quarry elsewhere. Until we meet again, Goran Lonefeather."

She knows me by name, the Sylph realized as the Goblin ambled into the woods on short, squat legs. *Perhaps my first guess was right after all. Perhaps our meeting here was no coincidence.*

Goran flapped his wings and rose above the old trees dotting the top of the abandoned Indian mound. The action made him think of something else. Several times, he'd been tracked by flying rangers he'd failed to identify. Betua's belligerent words and seeming interest in his activities could offer an answer to that riddle.

If Goblins had wings, that is.

Goran sighed, heading back the way he came.

▲▲▲

The sun had nearly set when the Sylph reached the creek's junction with the rocky fork of the Mohican. He hovered and looked northward toward the settlement of Mansfield. In the fading light, he could see only the shadowy outline of the blockhouse the humans had built on the public square.

So it was Goran's ears, not his eyes, that alerted him to the presence of someone walking below him. A male voice was singing in a strong, clear voice:

> *Oh, the Lord's been good to me.*
> *And so I thank the Lord*
> *For giving me the things I need:*
> *The sun, the rain, and the apple seed;*
> *Oh, the Lord's been good to me.*

The Sylph murmured a concealment spell and banked to the right, craning his neck to catch a glimpse of the singer. He saw a slightly built man walking briskly along the river, leading a packhorse. Although the waning light made it hard to pick out details, it was obvious the man's trousers were ill fitting; Goran could see not just bare feet but bare legs almost to the knee. On the other hand, the man's shirt was far too large. Where his belt was drawn tight, a blousy fold of the shirt hung over the man's waist like a craftsman's pouch. Atop his head was an oddly shaped hat folded up on the sides and back but sticking out like a duck's bill over his face.

While the Sylph ranger hovered, watching with a mixture of curiosity and delight, the jauntily striding man continued to sing:

Oh, here I am 'neath the blue, blue sky
Doing as I please.
Singing with my feathered friends
Humming with the bees.

Then the singer looked over his shoulder at Goran and waved a hand in greeting.

First, a Goblin ranger. Now a Sighted human. My search has produced no Pukwudgies . . . but it has been far from fruitless.

▲▲▲

It took Goran only a few minutes of conversation to draw two conclusions about the singer. First, this was the same raggedy man, Johnny Chapman, that Dela had told him about long ago, the one she'd met during her cruise up the Hudson. He had the same odd clothing, the same intense eyes, the same easy manner. Like Goran's longtime friend Peter Muhlenberg, Johnny Chapman often quoted the Bible to make a point, or to lighten the mood.

The second conclusion Goran drew was that despite Johnny's curious appearance and incurious demeanor, he possessed much information relevant to Goran's mission.

The human certainly knew a great deal about Folk and the magical world. Over the years, Johnny had met rangers from a half dozen different Folk nations and seen a variety of monsters, which he'd always given a wide berth. Johnny spoke fondly of Dela, although their one encounter had been brief. "Any friend of hers is a friend of mine," he'd assured Goran.

Johnny also clearly knew the Mohican region well. While he'd been born in Massachusetts and traveled extensively in New York and Pennsylvania, he'd lately spent most of his time in central Ohio communities such as Mansfield.

"I find it fertile ground for what I want to plant," Johnny explained as he caressed the flank of the packhorse.

Goran smiled. "My mother, Wenna, was a grower herself, what Folk call a greenweaver. I spent a lot of time in her gardens when I was young. What do you plant?"

"Whatever will yield the fruits of the spirit," Johnny said. "By day, I build and tend my apple nurseries. The rest of the time, I plant the seeds of truth. Kindness. Gentleness. Peace. Love of God and love of neighbor."

The Sylph pointed to the sacks slung over the horse. "Appleseed?"

The human nodded. "Also fennel. Wintergreen. Catnip. And books to deliver fresh news straight from Heaven."

After some prodding from Johnny, Goran explained the mission that had brought him to the Ohio country.

"Those little people you're looking for, you won't find them around here," said Johnny as he slipped a finger underneath the cloth sash he was using as a suspender for his pants. "I have it on good authority the Puks up and left for a new home up north."

"On whose good authority?"

"That, I cannot say," Johnny replied good-naturedly.

A puzzled frown came to Goran's face. "I know we just met, Johnny Chapman, but you say we are friends. So I am at a loss to—"

"That, I *cannot* say," the human repeated with emphasis, still smiling. "As the Proverb goes, 'A froward man soweth strife: and a whisperer separateth chief friends.' "

Then Goran remembered the occasion he and Har had met Gulkalaski. The Cherokee man's refusal to betray a confidence had made them trust him all the more. Goran decided this Johnny Chapman was showing the same good character and decided not to press the matter.

Instead, he shifted to another subject. "What can you tell me of the local Indians?"

The human's smile disappeared as he visibly slumped. "There was a time when the Lenape and Shawnee and Wyandot were at peace with the settlers. The Indians lived just southeast of here at a place called Greentown, on the Black Fork of the Mohican. But last year, when the new war broke out, the authorities feared the Greentown Indians might run off to join Tecumseh's confederacy, or launch their own attacks. So they drove the Indians away."

"You mean, at the point of a gun?"

"It was more in the nature of a trick," Johnny replied. "The soldiers promised the Indians that if they'd relocate for a time, they'd be treated well and allowed to come back to Greentown when the danger of British invasion was past. Even got a minister friendly to the Indians to swear the soldiers were telling the truth. But after the Indians left, some soldiers burned Greentown to the ground. The Indians took revenge by killing the minister, three soldiers, and some settler friends of mine, the Zimmers. It's been tense around here ever since."

Goran scowled. As much as he held the British and their Folk allies responsible for fomenting unrest and violence along the frontier, Americans had often committed their own outrages. For a people so strident in their talk about "the blessings of liberty" and "all men are created equal," the Americans could truly be as hypocritical and cruel as any nation.

Human or Folk, Goran reminded himself. Then he thought of another question. "How many of the Indians are still . . ."

A gunshot rang out.

Then another.

"That came from north of town!" Johnny exclaimed. "I pray to God that—"

But Goran never heard the rest of Chapman's prayer; he was already streaking through the sky. Night had fallen. Although the moon had not yet risen, there was enough starlight for the Sylph to pick out figures moving over the fields and trees beneath him.

They were settlers, no doubt, running north from town. But Goran was flying, so he got to their shared destination first.

The sight sickened him. A group of Lenape warriors stood in a rough circle around a settler lying on the ground. The man's body was twisted unnaturally, bent just above the waist into an L shape. The legs were moving back and forth, but not at the dead man's direction. They moved because one of the warriors was kneeling on the ground, rocking the corpse as he scalped it with a knife.

Then Goran and the Indians simultaneously heard the sounds of running feet. The warrior with the scalping knife stood up quickly, his grisly prize in hand, while his fellows turned in the direction of town.

Are they about to ambush the approaching settlers?

Goran opened his mouth to cast a confusion spell, then closed it when a loud voice barked at the warriors from behind a tree. It was no attack order. The Indians took off in the opposite direction.

Goran flapped his wings to gain more altitude as the first settler came into view. "Over here!" shouted the man, holding his hunting rifle with trembling hands. "They've run off!"

Two more settlers appeared, similarly armed and anxious. "Levi!" wailed the first as he knelt beside the mutilated body. "It's Levi Jones, the shopkeeper. They killed and scalped him!"

The others removed their wide-brimmed hats and bowed their heads.

Goran had seen enough. The settlers didn't know which way the Indians had fled. The Sylph did. He'd make sure this Levi Jones was the raiders' only victim.

It took only minutes to find them. The Indians had reached a river and were looking for a shallow place to cross as Goran spotted a Lenape chief. He standing on a stump, clad in a finely beaded mantle, a cloth turban, and a shiny metal gorget.

While Goran halted to consider his options, the Lenape made the decision for him. At the first word the chief spoke, the Sylph recognized the same commanding voice that had ordered the Indian warriors to flee from the scene of their crime. What happened next, though, took Goran by complete surprise. The Lenape's voice changed.

Well, not exactly—it was more like a second voice, higher in tone and louder in volume, overwhelmed the first, which became barely audible. The new voice wasn't speaking in an unfamiliar human language. It was singing, in Folktongue, a summoning spell:

> *From dank, from deep, from earthen pool,*
> *To surface and to stalk the prey,*
> *A darkened sky, air still and cool,*
> *No blinding sun that burns in day,*
> *By river's edge, or still lagoon,*
> *The morsel waits beneath the moon.*

Goran could sense the spell's power spreading over the river, its banks, and the muddy ground beyond. But where was it coming from? The Lenape chief was, of course, incapable of wielding spellsong. What Goran heard could *not* be a human mouthing words the human did not understand. It was a real, magically potent spellsong, and yet it appeared to be coming from where the chief stood on the stump.

Or perhaps, Goran thought, *from behind! Is a ranger hidden behind the stump?*

The Sylph swooped lower, fitting an arrow to his bow. He circled the chief—and then stared in disbelief. There was no ranger behind the stump. He could see no Folk anywhere. Yet the spellsong continued.

By this time, the warriors had crossed the river. As Goran glanced back at them, he saw something moving downriver. At first there were only ripples. Then, two rounded objects broke the surface. Two large, bulbous, glowing eyes cast an eerie green luminescence on the dark water.

Instantly, Goran recalled the tale of the Giant Salamander that Atta had sent to attack Daniel Boone years earlier. That attack had happened in the Ohio territory as well. Could this be the same type of monster, responding to the summoning spell? The Sylph ranger clutched his bow more firmly. The arrows filling his quiver were a gift from Dela, expertly enchanted by a Gwragedd Annwn mage. He hoped they'd be enough to weaken and, ultimately, render unconscious the twelve-foot-long fire-spitting monster Daniel had described.

Only, on second thought, Goran realized the approaching beast *couldn't* be the same as what Daniel had fought. This creature was swimming rapidly, while the Giant Salamander had been seared when it fell into the Mad River. And Goran saw only the two glowing green eyes coming toward him. There was no long, scaly body undulating behind those eyes.

It was also at that moment the Sylph noticed the Lenape chief was no longer standing on the stump. While Goran hovered, watching the monster come closer, the chief had run up the riverbank, crossed, and followed the other Indians into the forest.

With the human gone, Goran drifted down and landed on the stump. That would conserve his strength while he tried to figure out what manner of monster he faced.

As if on cue, the two luminous eyes halted their motion through the water. Then, slowly, they rose from the surface, revealing an earless head and a sinewy, mud-covered body ending in two densely muscled legs. At first Goran thought the creature was armless. Then it moved its upper limbs, which proved to be short, thin stalks connecting the torso to a set of broad, taloned hands.

Where its body wasn't covered in thick mud, Goran could see dark-green skin dappled with patches of brown. The skin shone in the starlight as if coated with a translucent oil.

During his studies, Goran had read about a rare amphibian called a Mud Beast. This monster fit the description well. Goran judged it to be about the height of a small human—but then revised his estimate as the creature suddenly leapt from the river, soared over the water in a high arc, and landed on the riverbank. Its legs were far longer than he originally thought, ending in webbed feet.

The monster stood at least seven feet tall. Its bright-green eyes stared at the Sylph ranger for several seconds. Twice it opened its ragged, toothless mouth. Twice a red ribbon of tongue flicked out at blazing speed, extending nearly three feet from its gaping maw like a narrow plume of flame.

Then the Mud Beast pounced.

Goran was ready. He loosed his first arrow and jumped sideways off the stump, sweeping his wings back to gain momentum. Banking left, he skimmed the surface of the river and turned back toward the stump as he drew another arrow.

The Mud Beast was watching him, motionless except for the occasional flick of its long red tongue. The first shot must have missed, for there was no shaft protruding from the monster's shiny chest. The Sylph let his second arrow fly, then groaned as the Mud Beast leapt high in the air, allowing the missile to pass below it.

Goran had fought larger, more fearsome-looking monsters before—the Catawampyrie. The Stoneclad. The Jersey Devils. But none before had been so quick or agile.

It may not be as dangerous, he thought. *But I will have a hard time subduing it.*

Choosing a different strategy, Goran nocked a third arrow and, with two powerful wing strokes, hurled himself at the Mud Beast. As expected, the monster leapt to the side. Once airborne, however, it could not alter its trajectory. Goran turned and followed the arc with the tip of his arrow, leading the target as he shot. The missile struck home, driving deep into the flesh of the creature just above its right hip.

The Mud Beast opened its mouth as if to cry out, but there was no sound. There was only the sight of its red tongue streaking out like a dancing flame.

Hoping to repeat his success, Goran rose high into the air, reloaded, and dove at the monster. Even as the distance between them rapidly closed, the Mud Beast stayed completely still.

For an instant, the Sylph felt panicked. Then he willed himself to finish the attack run.

At such close range, I can take it down for good.

Then he saw its massive thigh muscles tense. It jumped.

Directly at Goran.

He shot.

But the Mud Beast was turning a reverse somersault. Goran's arrow passed harmlessly over the creature's backward-rotating head. A second later, he felt searing pain as the wide, webbed feet of the monster struck him full in the chest. There was a sickening crack.

Desperately, Goran spun and flapped his wings to gain speed, wincing as the motion confirmed multiple ribs were broken. At every stroke, it felt as if he were being stabbed with fiery lances. But he couldn't know quickly the second attack would come, or how high the monster could leap. Altitude was his best defense.

When he felt safe enough to do so, Goran stopped to hover and look down. The Mud Beast stood motionless in shallow water, its head tilted slightly. The sleep arrow still sticking out from its body had not rendered it unconscious—at least not yet.

The pain from Goran's cracked ribs made it hard to concentrate. He recalled the image of a few minutes earlier, the body of the human shopkeeper twisted into an unnatural L-shaped position, as if something had punched him so hard it severed his spine.

The Lenape didn't kill Levi Jones, he realized.

Goran felt an old fury. It washed across his body, easing his discomfort and filling him with a singular purpose. Folk rangers had again wielded a monster as a weapon against humans. He could think of no other explanation.

I will not let their crime go unpunished. And I will not let them claim another human victim.

Wings outstretched, Goran fell into a graceful dive. When his altitude had fallen to a dozen feet, the Mud Beast leapt. Goran's bowstring twanged. Without waiting to see if it hit its target, he changed direction, banking left in a tight circle as he reloaded and shot another arrow at the monster passing just inches from the tip of his wing. Then he changed direction again, his wings propelling him upward several feet and then retracting as Goran performed his own half somersault and shot yet another arrow straight down at the monster's broad back.

His ribs punished Goran mercilessly for every twist and turn. He knew his strength would soon flag. Again, he drew an arrow. Again he turned to his right, aimed at the Mud Beast just as its feet touched the riverbed, and released.

In an instant the monster was airborne again, hurtling up at what seemed an impossible speed. Goran aimed his next arrow right between the creature's glowing green eyes and watched it go slightly above the mark, carving a bloody groove along the skull instead of plunging into it.

Watching the arrow's path came with a cost. The Mud Beast's head slammed into the Sylph's legs, creating a fresh source of pain.

With a grunt, Goran plunged for a few feet, then managed to flatten his trajectory and glided over a patch of ground. His legs didn't feel broken, only bruised. Thankful, he landed and looked for his adversary.

The Mud Beast was on the riverbank. It was squatting, not standing. As Goran watched, panting from exhaustion and grimacing with each painful breath, the monster keeled over, its long ribbon of a tongue hanging lifelessly from its open mouth.

Goran felt relief wash over him. This wave of emotion wasn't as effective as his previous wave of fury had been at numbing his pain. Still, the sensation was welcome.

"Did you take its life?"

Johnny Chapman walked from the trees to stand next to Goran. He'd removed his oddly shaped cap and held it over his heart. Johnny's eyes were downcast, but Goran thought he saw something more than relief or sadness in their expression.

Reproach?

"It merely sleeps," the Sylph answered. "My arrows are enchanted to render them unconscious. It took several shots, but they did their work."

"Thank God." The raggedy man approached the prone form of the Mud Beast. Most humans would have been terrified, Goran knew. But this man showed no fear. Instead, he knelt next to the creature and laid a hand against its slimy, dark-green throat.

"Its blood still flows," he said. Then he turned to face the Sylph. "We should leave before it wakes up. Are you badly hurt?"

Goran stared at Johnny, struggling to understand the man and to come up with the words to help *him* understand. "I am Goran Lonefeather. I have no Folk to call. There are no rangers or hunters to take possession of the monster. It has already killed one of your kind. When it wakes, it may kill another."

"So you would kill it in its sleep," Johnny said with surprising vehemence. "A *monster*, you say? I see only a fellow creature. All things in the world exist from a Divine Origin—clothed with such forms in nature as enable them to exist there. I've run from wild animals many times, yes, and sometimes from hostile men. I didn't believe it was God's will for them to harm me. I *know* it is God's will that I not harm them."

Goran could see the man's convictions were deeply felt. They were also impractical. "When innocent lives are stake and we can save them, do we not have a duty to act?"

"To act, yes," Johnny insisted. "But our actions need not be violent."

"This monster—this 'fellow creature,' as you put it—was sent to attack your friends," Goran pointed out in frustration. "If we leave it alive, it may yet carry out its design."

"Then we should make sure my friends are safe inside their homes, or in the blockhouse," answered Johnny in a determined voice.

The Sylph sighed, exasperated. The human saw and smiled.

"Is this not a creature of the night, Goran Lonefeather? When dawn comes, will it not return to its home in some muddy hole or murky depth? As you say, it didn't arise by accident. Someone summoned it. We got to make sure no one's around for it to harm. When dawn comes, the danger will be over."

Sending humans into hiding was no certain way to end their peril. Goran was about to argue the point when a flash of motion from downriver caught his eye. Then the import of what he'd seen registered in his mind—and produced a shudder of fear.

"You are right, Johnny," Goran said, thinking quickly. "We must save your people. You can tell them one settler is already dead. You can tell them more Indians could be on their way. It would all be true. And it may convince them to seek shelter."

We just cannot tell them Levi Jones was killed by monster. Or that more than one such monster prowls the night.

Goran was in no condition to subdue the second Mud Beast he'd just seen headed downriver. And worse still, he couldn't know how many more had been summoned by the mysterious spellsinger.

Taken aback by Goran's sudden change of heart, Johnny Chapman stared at him for a moment. Then his face relaxed into a kindly smile. "The way of the Lord is not an easy one," he began. "With prayer and study—"

"Johnny!" shouted one of the Mansfield men emerging from the trees. "When you wandered off, we feared the Indians might get you, too."

Still shielded by his concealment spell, Goran walked to the river's edge, scooped up a handful of water, and splashed his face. While the humans conversed, the Sylph removed a cloak from his pack and, with great and painful difficulty, wrapped it around his ribcage, tying the ends in a knot and hoping the tight binding would keep him functional until he could get proper treatment.

"We'll take our families into the blockhouses," said one of the men. "But what about the farms on the Clear Fork? Or the Black Fork? Or folks down Fredericktown way? They'll be defenseless. We've got to warn them, and we've got to send word to the militia in Mount Vernon. If the Indians return in force, we can't hold out alone."

"It's more than twenty-six miles to Mount Vernon!" exclaimed another. "It'll be hard going and dangerous in the dead of night."

The men stole furtive glances at each other. They knew the trip had to be made. But they were all hoping someone else would volunteer.

"I'll go," said Johnny Chapman. His eyes seem to gleam in the darkness, much as the eyes of the Mud Beast had gleamed. There was no menace in his eyes, however. No fury. No vengeance. No fear. The man's face was lit by something more powerful.

I will go, too, Goran resolved, gritting his teeth. *But not because he would be alone without me. A man of such faith is never alone.*

The Sylph rose into the air and reached a hand back to count the arrows left in his quiver.

I will go because my bow may be needed again before the sun rises.

▲▲▲

The raggedy man ran on and on through the still, damp air of the dark night, over broken fields and rocky creeks and brush-strewn forest floors, on bare feet, and with no visible or audible signs of discomfort.

The runner was far from silent, though; Johnny Chapman spoke fervent prayers. He sang joyful hymns. And when he took breaks, it was only so to shout his warning into cabins and farmhouses. "Fly! Fly for your lives! The Indians are murdering and scalping at Mansfield!"

Flying overhead, Goran marveled at the nurserymen's endurance and determination. But he knew fatigue was not the only obstacle to Johnny finishing his marathon. As fleet as the human was, he couldn't outrun the leaps of a Mud Beast.

So Goran continuously scanned the ground in front of the running man like a predatory bird looking for prey. Twice, he'd seen a moving figure and swooped down to investigate. One had turned out to be a doe and her fawn. The other proved to be an old spotted dog. Both times, the Sylph had breathed a painful sigh of relief.

It was when Johnny reached the bank of another river that Goran saw motion for the third time. On the opposite riverbank, something was moving among the high branches of a tree. For a split second, the image of the phantom flier crossed Goran's mind. Then he realized the creature was too small. He glided over the river and saw a mother owl land on a branch. There were two owlets there, nearly full-grown. Each took an unsteady practice flight under the watchful eye of the mother. Goran welcomed the brief distraction, and the reminder that risk was an inescapable fact of life.

Thump! Thump!

The Sylph looked down and saw the carcass of a freshly killed deer. It wasn't just dead—it was crushed flat. As he watched in horrified fascination, its killer, a Mud Beast, bent over the carcass and dismembered the pulverized deer with rapid strokes of its sharp talons. After each section was sliced from the body, a red ribbon of tongue shot out and drew it quickly into the ragged maw to be swallowed whole.

Splash! Splash!

When Johnny waded into the river, the Mud Beast jerked upright, seven feet of muscle and menace covered in slimy green-and-brown skin. It stared at the approaching human with its big, bulbous, green-glowing eyes. Then it sprang.

The Sylph's arrow took the monster in the back. Even as it continued its high arc into the river, the Mud Beast turned its head and saw the Sylph swooping down at it from the trees.

"Goran!" cried Johnny, backing quickly out of the water.

"Get away from here!" Goran insisted.

The Mud Beast landed in the river, spraying water in all directions. Judging its winged foe a higher priority, the monster spun around and tensed, ready to make another jump.

Hoping to evade it, Goran withdrew his wings, letting himself fall almost to the water before swooping along its surface. He also loosed another arrow in an upward-sloping trajectory. When the monster jumped, it would be struck in the chest while the Sylph flew underneath it.

But the Mud Beast didn't jump. It did the last thing Goran was expecting: It dodged, and it extended one of its short, thin arms as the Sylph flew rapidly past.

Goran felt a new blaze of agony. The monster's talons tore two bloody gashes in his side. Then his entire body screamed in protest as something grabbed his ankle and jerked him to a sudden halt.

He tried to yank free. Then he felt the water of the river close around him.

Somehow, Goran had the presence of mind to hold his breath. Somehow, he didn't faint right away from pain and fatigue. Instead, drew his knife. Even as he felt himself being dragged across the river, Goran twisted to his back and bent at the waist, ignoring the new stabs of pain from his battered body.

His head broke the surface. The Mud Beast was backing out of the river, its long tongue still gripping his ankle. Goran brought the blade of his knife down as hard as he could. The first blow cut a deep notch in the tongue. The second blow severed it completely.

The Mud Beast staggered back, the stump of its tongue hanging from its open mouth. With a new burst of energy, Goran pushed off the riverbed with his feet and leapt at the retreating monster, his knife thrust forward.

It plunged into the beast's chest, just left of where the point of Goran's arrow protruded from its tough green skin. Again and again the Sylph stabbed—wildly, desperately—until his arm felt numb.

Now it was Goran's turn to stagger backward. He nearly fell into the water. Then he felt two hands pushing on his back. He found his footing and turned his head. Johnny Chapman was looking down with kindly eyes.

"Looked like fire was coming from its mouth," Johnny said. "Yet still I grieve the death of another of God's creatures."

Then Goran's eyes widened. Panic squeezed his heart. Johnny looked up and saw it, too—another Mud Beast approaching, its green eyes glowing bright in the night.

"We must flee!" said the human. "You are in no position to—"

"Run *now!*" Goran agreed. "Run as fast as you can. Run all the way to Mount Vernon! Get your people inside! Get help!"

Johnny shook his head. "I won't leave you."

"Run, or more lives will be lost." Goran lifted his bow and winced as he drew another arrow.

"The Lord will protect us," the nurserymen insisted.

Goran managed a grim smile. "A remarkable human I once met in my travels said, 'The Lord helps those who help themselves.' Battle is my mission. Yours is to run. With His help, both missions will end in success."

Johnny swallowed hard. "Prayer will be my companion." Then, as the Mud Beast came closer, Johnny took off in the opposite direction.

Goran gritted his teeth and rose slowly into the air. He aimed his arrow at the green glowing eyes moving along the ground. Then, abruptly, the eyes changed direction. The Sylph released his bowstring. He banked left. Then he spun in the air as the leaping Mud Beast, its features blurry and shrouded in shadow, brushed past him.

Goran heard another crack. He felt a jolt of pain greater than anything he'd felt that night, and then he saw the jagged edge of his radius bone jutting from his broken, useless right wing.

The Sylph fell like a stone and hit the river's surface hard. Kicking frantically, he tried to keep his head above water. He could see the dark form of the Mud Beast silhouetted against the starlit sky as it waded in after him.

Then, just before he blacked out, Goran saw something moving behind the monster. A flash of blue. And a pair of cold, red eyes.

Chapter 16 – The Envelope

August 1813

Clutching the reins with a white-knuckled grip, Ichabod Crane chanced a brief glimpse down at the rust-colored back of the mount carrying him along the sandy shore of Lake Erie. It was an old horse, gaunt and unsteady, clearly more accustomed to the plow than the trail. It was sufficiently obedient to gallop at Ichabod's command and sufficiently ornery to resent it.

The horse's owner, a farmer, was much shorter than Ichabod, who'd neglected to adjust the borrowed saddle and stirrups accordingly. So as Ichabod galloped along, desperate to keep up with the officer ahead of him, his knobby knees collided repeatedly with his scrawny forearms, which stuck out from his sides like a pair of bony wings.

Panicked by a particularly hard bounce, Ichabod reached inside his coat to make sure the envelope was still there.

"Don't worry, Ichabod," said the Water Maiden seated behind him. "If it is jarred loose, I will see it fall."

He blew out a breath and returned his hand to the reins. The officer ahead of him, Midshipman John Montgomery, rode his own borrowed horse with grace and skill. Montgomery had an important envelope stuffed in his coat as well. It held a letter for Oliver Hazard Perry from Lieutenant Jesse Elliott, the officer in command of the hundred sailors Montgomery and Ichabod had left walking along the lake a few hours earlier.

As for Ichabod's envelope, it contained only a blank sheet of paper.

And I'd be lost without it.

▲▲▲

After Ichabod had returned to Fort George with the survivors of the disaster at Beaver Dams—along with the magically concealed

188

Dela—the American commander forbade any further sorties into the Canadian countryside. Then Ichabod learned his regiment and most others were to be withdrawn to their original base at Sackets Harbor, as the British had attacked the base while they were away taking York and Fort George. Keen to protect Sackets Harbor, the American army hurried back to it, leaving only a few militiamen to defend Fort George.

The news left Ichabod Crane first disbelieving, then frustrated, then angry. After all their pains and losses, the 1813 campaign would essentially end in retreat.

And he couldn't help but feel responsible. He'd failed to keep the enchanted Ojibwe war rattle from setting off the devastating fireball that killed Zebulon Pike and so many others at York. He'd also failed to keep the enchanted Mohawk war club from bringing ruin on the American column at Beaver Dams.

Those failures left him frustrated. His anger came from what his commanders were doing to his friend Oliver Hazard Perry, commander of the naval squadron on Lake Erie. Perry had ships. More were being built. But he had far too few sailors to crew his ships and take the fight to the British.

For months, Perry had begged for more men. Also for months, the War Department had insisted that General William Henry Harrison, commander of the Army of the Northwest, drive British and Indian forces from Detroit—but Harrison, in turn, had insisted on naval support from Perry.

So Perry continued to beg for more men. At first, there had been only a trickle, many inexperienced or unfit for duty altogether. Then Ichabod had heard that a hundred sailors, led by Lieutenant Elliott, would be marching down the coast to Perry's position. Some, at least, were experienced seamen.

As was Ichabod.

"I thought I'd be more valuable to the army," he complained to Dela one night at Fort George. "But here I sit, useless, while my friend has need of navy men."

"Can you not request to reenter naval service?" the Water Maiden asked.

He shook his head. "It doesn't work that way, Dela. And I have hardly earned enough of a military reputation to merit special consideration."

But Ichabod hadn't counted on the ingenuity of his fairy friend. Indeed, he hadn't fully appreciated the implications of *having* a fairy friend.

So it was that when he reported a few days later to his commanding officer, the colonel opened the envelope Ichabod handed him and read an order assigning Captain Crane temporarily to the army of the Northwest.

And so it was that when Ichabod handed the same envelope to Jesse Elliott, the naval officer charge of Perry's reinforcements, the lieutenant read an order assigning Captain Crane to the Lake Erie squadron as an army observer.

It was all a deception, of course, and Ichabod felt guilty about it. But if guilty feelings were the price for placing himself in direct service to his country, the price for rectifying his mistakes and for aiding his friend Oliver Perry, Ichabod would pay it.

Elliott's column had marched toward Presque Isle for several days. Then, despite his inexperience in the saddle, Ichabod was assigned to ride ahead with another courier to let Perry know reinforcements were on their way. As far as Ichabod knew, no magic was involved in the assignment. But Dela had insisted on accompanying him.

"Look there, Ichabod," she said excitedly, standing up in the saddle. "The top of a mast. We are close."

She was right. Ichabod looked across the water and counted ten sets of sails: three brigs, five smaller schooners, and a single-masted sloop. The squadron's anchorage was far out in the lake, to the east of a small, curved peninsula Ichabod took to be Presque Isle. The nearby village of Erie was a modest one, no more than a few dozen houses. Soon the riders were dismounting in front of one of them. The sun had set, and the moon had yet to rise, so at first Ichabod didn't notice the sailor sitting in the dim light.

As he and Montgomery approached the house, however, a figure bolted up quickly from a chair next to the door and barred their way. The sailor was a powerfully built man of average height, dressed in white trousers and shirt, a short blue jacket, a red waistcoat, and a round-brimmed black hat. His dark-skinned face wore a wary expression.

"What business have ya with Mister Perry?" he demanded.

"I am Midshipmen John B. Montgomery, seaman," snapped Ichabod's irritated companion, "and I bring an important dispatch."

The sailor seemed unimpressed. "Most dispatches are bad news. Like dat one a few weeks back 'bout the death of Mister Perry's friend Captain Lawrence of the *Chesapeake.*"

"Our news is good, I assure you," Ichabod chimed in. "We had a hard ride bringing it."

"The commandant's tired," the sailor insisted. "Been provisioning ships all day."

Montgomery jabbed an angry finger. "Stand aside, man, or you will pay dearly."

The sailor merely crossed his arms. The potential price of his stubbornness was never revealed, however; the door of the house suddenly flew open. Oliver Hazard Perry himself stood in the doorway. He did indeed look exhausted—slumped, haggard, his normally sharp eyes half-closed and glassy.

Ichabod saw those tired eyes widen in shock as he read the note Montgomery handed him. Perry shouted an exaltation to someone inside. Then he caught sight of who was standing behind Montgomery. His eyes widened even more.

"Captain Crane!" Perry exclaimed. "Fortune indeed smiles on us."

"They sent us a *captain?*" bellowed the slender, light-haired man who appeared next to Perry in the doorway. Ichabod recognized the uniform of a warrant officer.

"No, Sam, not a ship's captain," Perry said with a chuckle. "This is the fellow I told you about, Ichabod Crane, the army captain who assisted me before the assault on Fort George."

The purser merely shrugged in confusion.

"You remember, Sam," Perry pressed. "Will Crane's brother?"

"Oh, that one," came the bemused reply. "A pleasure to make your acquaintance, Captain Crane. I am Samuel Hambleton."

"And I yours, sir," said Ichabod.

Even here, on the remote shore of a distant lake, I am known only as Will's relation.

Perry jerked his head toward the sailor, who'd stepped aside when the door burst open. "Seaman Cyrus Tiffany, gentlemen. Known each other a long time. He's a mite protective—and tough as a goat. Handy man to have around. Just try not to butt heads with him."

Tiffany nodded silently. His square jaw and forbidding look still spoke loudly.

"Sam and I were having our supper," Perry added. "You're welcome to join us. Cyrus, see to their horses."

Montgomery smiled eagerly and approached the door. Ichabod was about to follow when he saw Cyrus Tiffany jerk. The sailor was looking past the messengers to their mounts. Ichabod followed his gaze. Dela still sat on the back of the borrowed plow horse.

"Thank you, sir, but first I'll help with the horses," Ichabod stammered.

Perry looked puzzled. "Suit yourself," he said as he and the other two naval officers entered the house.

Tiffany seemed not to notice. He strode quickly to the plow horse and removed his hat, revealing he was older than Ichabod had guessed. His close-cropped hair was sparse and nearly white. When Ichabod came up beside him, he could see deep wrinkles on Tiffany's dark face.

The sailor paid the artillery captain no mind. "Never thought I'd see ya again," he breathed, looking directly into Dela's blue-green eyes.

"You have me at a disadvantage," said the astonished Water Maiden.

"Valley Forge," Tiffany replied. "I's in the First Rhode Island Regiment. Saw you, the little winged man, and the little bearded man around camp. Thought I's going mad. Forgot all 'bout it after dat. Till tonight."

Dela smiled. "Another human gifted with the Sight, Ichabod."

"The *Sight?*" Tiffany asked. "What's dat?"

Ichabod clapped the sailor on the back. "We're surrounded by magical creatures, Mister Tiffany, but they're only visible if they wish to be. Except to men like us. We can see through their disguises."

The old man looked confused. "Never seen any but the three at Valley Forge."

"Oh?" Ichabod found that surprising. "You didn't discover your ability as a child?"

The seaman looked embarrassed. "Don't recall much about my young days. Mister Perry says I must've got hit on the head real hard sometime. Get addled easy."

Dela placed a hand on his forearm. "I am sorry, Cyrus Tiffany. We Folk have healing arts that humans lack. Perhaps we can help you."

The man flashed a grin as he stroked the flank of her tired mount. "Don't matter now, lady. Figure I's nearin' the end of my days, anyhow. Must get the horses watered and rubbed down."

▲▲▲

Perry sent a ship that very night to pick up Lieutenant Elliott and the rest of the reinforcements. Although a scant hundred men couldn't wipe away his manpower shortage, his ten vessels would now have at least skeleton crews.

The crew assignments got complicated a couple of days later when another courier arrived bearing new officer commissions. Among other promotions, Jesse Elliott had been made master commandant, the same rank Perry held.

The two couldn't have been more different, though. Elliott was a slovenly, swaggering officer who clearly thought *he* should be in charge of the squadron. He claimed one of the two large brigs, the *Niagara*, as well as the best of the reinforcements he'd brought.

To his credit, Ichabod thought, Perry chose not to put Elliott in his place. He'd planned to make the other big brig his flagship anyway, naming it in honor of his fallen comrade Captain Lawrence, who'd died a few weeks earlier. "Don't give up the ship!" Lawrence had reportedly cried before succumbing to his wounds. Sam Hambleton persuaded Perry to get the slogan embroidered on a strip of blue cloth. Standing with Perry and Hambleton on the deck of the *Lawrence*, Ichabod felt his heart skip a beat as Hambleton unfurled the flag and let the wind show its full length to Perry for the first time.

"Now you just have to raise a crew worthy of it," Ichabod told Perry as he eyed the few hands on the deck. Unsteady hands they were, for the most part.

Perry smiled. "I have Sam here. And Cyrus Tiffany. And other able seamen. When we meet up with General Harrison in Ohio, I hope to secure more hands. Perhaps the general can even be persuaded to transfer a certain artillery captain to my command?"

Ichabod swallowed at his friend's sly suggestion. "I'd be honored, sir."

The next morning, the squadron departed on the 150 mile voyage down to Sandusky Bay. Ichabod found life aboard the *Lawrence* fit him like an old shoe—better than that, in fact, because every pair of shoes he'd ever owned had either been long enough but too wide or narrow enough but too short. In addition to spending welcome time with his friend Oliver Perry, Ichabod made a new friend in Sam Hambleton. At thirty-six, Hambleton was quite a bit older than Perry, who was twenty-seven, and Ichabod, twenty-six. But he still had a young man's desire to prove himself.

Dela had boarded the *Lawrence* with Ichabod, but he saw little of her during the four-day cruise. It was only when the squadron approached Cunningham's Island, just north of Sandusky, that the Water Maiden reappeared. Ichabod filled her in on Perry's plans to draw the British squadron out for a decisive battle. Dela, in turn, explained that she'd spent most of the trip with the black seaman they'd met at Perry's headquarters.

"When I sang my concealment spell and came aboard," she related, "Cyrus Tiffany could no more see me than the others could. Later, when I revealed my presence, he acted like it was the first time he'd seen me since Valley Forge."

Ichabod was at a loss. "How's that possible? Doesn't he have the Sight?"

Dela turned away and looked wistfully over the water. "It is best not to consider the matter a yes or no question, Ichabod. Think of the difference between night and day. You and a select few live always in the light, while most humans are mired in darkness unless we choose to hold out a candle to them. Even then, they see more the shadow than what casts it."

"So far, I think I understand," said Ichabod.

"Now, consider a third group. These humans live in neither endless day nor ever night. For them, it is always close to sunset. They see more than most, but less than you. They have flashes of insight. They catch fleeting glimpses, blurred images of things they do not comprehend. Often they recall these images only in daydreams, or in nightmares."

"And this Cyrus Tiffany is one of them, a sunset dreamer?"

The Water Maiden frowned. "I suppose he must be. Sometimes he sees easily through my concealment. Other times, he fails. Even when he succeeds, though, he recalls me only from Valley Forge. It is possible a blow to his head has impaired his memory, as the man himself suggested."

A sudden commotion made both Ichabod and Dela spin around. In response to a barked order from Perry, a sailor was hoisting a signal flag. A few moments later, they saw one of the fast schooners, the *Scorpion*, head north as the rest of the squadron continued west.

Sam Hambleton ran up to the rail. "Mast sighted beyond Cunningham's Island. Could be one of theirs!"

The *Scorpion* soon passed the first island, and for the first time Ichabod could see a line of other islands behind it. Perry directed the rest of the squadron to an anchorage just off the bay. After a while, the *Scorpion* returned, its sheepish commander reporting that its inadequate and inexperienced crew couldn't keep the schooner from getting stuck on a reef. The mysterious ship had escaped.

"It's a safe bet the British know we're here," Perry said when Ichabod and Purser Hambleton arrived in his cabin. "We must be ready."

"Our ships are too short-crewed for battle," Hambleton insisted. "The *Scorpion*'s mishap on the reef makes that clear."

Perry nodded gravely. "I hope our meeting with General Harrison tomorrow morning brings relief. Ichabod, I trust you will add your words to mine as an army officer. Without control of Lake Erie, Harrison's men cannot safely move against Detroit."

Ichabod had almost forgotten—he'd be coming ashore and presenting the order transferring him to General Harrison's army. The order would, naturally, be contained not in his empty envelope but in the spellsong of the Water Maiden.

Which meant she'd be coming, too.

▲▲▲

The meeting on the mainland proved to be no private affair. It was more like a pageant. William Henry Harrison—a slim man with a long, angular face and a hawklike nose—wore a bright-blue uniform, neatly pressed, as did his senior officers. Accompanying them from Harrison's camp upriver were some twenty colorfully attired chiefs representing the Wyandot, the Lenape, the Shawnee, and other Indian nations.

Oliver Hazard Perry and his senior officers made a strong impression, too, in comportment if not in dress. What especially impressed the Indian chiefs, however, was what they heard. Not in the form of soothing words or conciliatory promises but in a blast of raw power—that of the *Lawrence*, the *Niagara*, and the rest of the squadron firing their guns in salute.

"Your squadron appears ready to take the battle to the enemy," General Harrison said. "As August turns to September and then October, our window for operations will narrow."

"My men are eager to proceed," Perry allowed, "provided we can address certain . . . matters I have described in my letters." The master commandant shot a cautious glance at the Indian chiefs huddled several paces away, speaking rapidly in their native tongues and pointing to the American ships.

Harrison followed Perry's gaze and gave a brief, meaningful nod. "I reply now in well wishes, sir. A greater reply will follow."

We will get no reinforcements from Harrison today, Ichabod told himself as he stood, feeling awkward and conspicuous, next to Sam Hambleton. The voyage to Sandusky had revealed the weak condition of Perry's squadron. The problem wasn't just vessels with skeleton crews. It was morale. *The men know they cannot take on the British in their present . . .*

"Crane?"

Perry's voice jolted him out of his ruminations. Ichabod took several steps forward.

"General Harrison, I have the pleasure to present Captain Ichabod Crane of the Third Artillery Regiment," Perry continued. "General Dearborn has transferred him to your command for the remainder of the summer campaign. I had hoped you will allow him to remain on the *Lawrence* for now."

The general turned to his staff and waved a languid hand. "I don't remember approving any requests for additional artillery officers."

Ichabod cleared his throat nervously and hoped Dela was ready with her spellsong. "Would you like to see my orders, sir?"

Harrison's close-set eyes narrowed. "I think not, Captain. The master commandant and I have more pressing matters." Then he and Perry turned and entered a hastily erected tent. The public part of the meeting, the pageant, was over.

His brief interview with William Henry Harrison had at least settled one question. Ichabod was free to stay aboard the *Lawrence*—because no one in the army would even notice his absence.

▲▲▲

It took two weeks for Harrison's "greater reply" to arrive, in the form of dozens of additional volunteers for the squadron. They couldn't have come at a better time. After a short cruise to scout a British base near Detroit, Perry had brought his thinly crewed vessels back to anchor at Put-in-Bay, north of Sandusky. Then Perry's thin ranks promptly got even thinner as lake fever and dysentery swept the squadron, sending half the men to their hammocks in agony. Perry himself was stricken as well.

Ichabod, miraculously, was not. So it was he, along with Purser Hambleton, who greeted the new recruits as they came aboard the *Lawrence*. Dela, magically concealed as always, stood nearby. So did Cyrus Tiffany, who once again appeared not to see the Water Maiden.

Most of Harrison's reinforcements were volunteers from Kentucky and southern Ohio. Some had no nautical experience and would be useful only as marines, but others had spent years sailing or poling boats along frontier rivers. They were rough, brawny men who knew their way around a deck and seemed spoiling for a fight.

And two of the newcomers weren't just brawny. They were veritable giants.

The smaller of the pair wasn't much taller than Ichabod but far, far wider. His long, magnificently muscled legs looked like they'd be more at home on a racehorse than a man. His arms, by contrast, were comparatively short but thick, like those of an alligator. His wide-set eyes, large nose, weak chin, and habit of smacking his lips together made Ichabod think of a snapping turtle. The man wore a flat brown hat, tilted rakishly with a red feather stuck in the brim, along with a brown jacket, red flannel shirt, and pantaloons dyed red and brown in a diagonal pattern. Both the long rifle slung over his back and the long knife hanging from his belt looked well-worn by frequent use.

The other newcomer to the *Lawrence* was so massive that Ichabod could scarcely believe he was human. Close to seven feet tall, the man was dressed in a blue-and-white checked shirt and solid-gray pantaloons. The color of his short-brimmed hat, pulled low over his brow and the tops of his eyes, matched the stiff black whiskers jutting from his cheeks and chin. The man's neck, chest, arms, and legs bulged with cords of muscle resembling skeins of anchor line from some gargantuan ship.

"Who d'I haff ta hit up for a shot of rye?" asked the turtle-faced man as he strutted up to Ichabod and Hambleton. "One 'a you lot?"

The purser looked disdainfully at the new recruit. "I am Mister Hambleton, and this is Mister Crane. First things first—you must be assigned. Do you have any nautical experience?"

"Experience!" snorted the man as he tugged his hat into an even more rakish angle. "Don't you get who you're talkin' to? I'm known up and down the Miami and the Ohio and even the old Mississipp'! I'm a salt-river roarer! I'm a ring-tailed squealer! I can outrun, outjump, outshoot, outbrag, outdrink, and outfight, rough-and-tumble, no-holds-barred, any man on both sides the river from Pittsburgh to N'Orleans and back again to Saint Louis!"

Hambleton was unimpressed. "So, I take it your answer is yes?"

The turtle-faced man hooted in derision, turned, and slapped his companion on the back. The larger man didn't crack a smile, though.

"Cock-a-doodle-doo, son, you still don't get it," said the boastful recruit. "I'm Mike Fink, king of the keelboats! And my pretty-faced, sweet-talkin' buffalo of a friend here is . . ."

"Bull!" Dela suddenly announced at the same time Fink did.

"I met him once, Ichabod, years ago on the Hudson," the Water Maiden whispered quickly. "He knows his way around a sailboat."

Only Ichabod heard her words, of course. So he spoke up.

"You look like you can handle a sheet, Bull. Uh, Bull what?"

The giant looked down at Ichabod—an experience the tall artillery captain wasn't used to—with dark, disdainful eyes that sparkled like polished obsidian.

"Just Bull."

The giant turned away and pushed his hat back, looking with a practiced eye at the masts and rigging of the *Lawrence*. Mike Fink giggled as his companion stomped across the deck, seemingly testing the planks. Then Bull grasped the end of a trailing rope with one hand, ran his other hand up the rope about three feet, and pulled in opposite directions. His biceps bulged so sharply that Ichabod thought they might rip the man's shirt.

The rope held.

"Seen better," Bull muttered. "It'll do."

Now it was Hambleton's turn to snort. "Glad you approve, Mister 'Bull.' Seen better rigging on some river scow, have you?"

Ichabod could see Bull's jawline rippling as he clenched his teeth. But the giant said nothing. He didn't even look in Hambleton's direction.

Fink put his hands on his hips in mock exasperation. "Well, now you done it! Insulted Bull's pride. He's a *seafarer*, Mister Navy Man. A bosun on whaling ships. When the war started, and the Royal Navy shut down the whalers, he came inland to work the river trade. Won't find a fella who hates Brits more than ole Bull."

Hambleton looked dubious. "Well, you're both marines until we figure out what else you can do. Move along, now."

As Ichabod watched the newcomers cross the deck to join the other recruits, Cyrus Tiffany sauntered up to him. Only by comparison with Fink and Bull was the white-haired old sailor anything other than a burly giant of a man himself.

"Don't like the looks of them two," Tiffany whispered. "Don't much like any of 'em, truth be told. Mister Perry needs men he can trust."

"What makes you think you can't trust these men?" Ichabod asked.

A scowl creased Tiffany's face. "Don't rightly know. A feelin'. I get a feelin' sometime, when things ain't quite right."

Ichabod saw Dela standing behind Tiffany, her hands spread wide as a signal. It reminded him of what she'd said about the sailor's faulty memory. Placing a hand on Tiffany's shoulder, Ichabod leaned in conspiratorially. "I'll keep an eye on them, rest assured."

Tiffany shrugged. "Suit yourself. I's keeping an eye on 'em for Mister Perry."

▲▲▲

With the addition of Mike Fink, Bull, and the other reinforcements, the Lake Erie squadron mustered about five hundred men—still short of a full complement for each ship. Even after Perry and most of the others got over their bouts with lake fever and returned to duty, the crews varied widely in capability and motivation. Most, including Perry himself, had never been in a ship-to-ship fight.

On the ninth of September, a patrol schooner returned to report British ships approaching. Perry quickly convened the squadron's officers on his flagship. That included Ichabod, who'd been made an acting lieutenant on the *Lawrence*. He was surprised to find Dela was absent.

Thanks to scouts and defectors, Perry knew much about the British squadron. His foe had an advantage in long guns; the Americans would have to close with the enemy to make effective use of their shorter-range but devastating carronades. Perry also knew his mostly inexperienced crews would not be capable of elaborate maneuvers. So, he urged each commander to stay in line once battle began, assigning each a specific British target. Master Commandant Jesse Elliott's *Niagara*, for example, would attack the British ship *Queen Charlotte*. Perry's own *Lawrence* would take on the British flagship *Detroit*.

Jesse Elliott slouched in his chair, obviously skeptical. "Are our officers to exercise no independent judgment? A hundred factors could render your plan obsolete at the first shot."

Perry's answer was conciliatory. "As you say, Commandant Elliott, battles are no mere stage plays. Each may have to act as character and circumstance warrant. My plan allows for such judgment. Nevertheless, as the inestimable Lord Nelson once said, 'If you lay your enemy alongside, you cannot be out of your place.'"

Elliott still looked dubious. "The fog of battle is thicker than you know."

Ichabod thought such disrespect for a commanding officer merited a stern response. But Perry didn't offer it. Instead, his eyes twinkled as he reached down and pulled a blue object from a locker.

"This shall be the signal for action." Then Perry's eyes meet Ichabod's. "Mister Crane, would you be so kind?"

Ichabod stumbled forward to grasp the proffered end as the master commandant unfolded the flag. "Don't Give Up the Ship" read the white letters on a blue field. "When it appears at the masthead," Perry instructed, "remember your instructions."

The squadron's officers exited the cabin with a mixture of apprehension and inspiration on their faces. All except for Jesse Elliott, that is, who simply looked annoyed.

▲▲▲

Hours later, with most of the crew of the *Lawrence* dozing on deck or below, Ichabod stood at the rail and looked out over the dark water, straining to catch any sign of movement.

Dela hadn't just missed the command briefing; she seemed to have left the ship entirely. Had the Water Maiden decided she had more pressing business elsewhere? With a British attack imminent, surely Dela understood that the inexperienced Americans might need her spellsong to strengthen their morale.

The sun had not yet rose when Ichabod heard a splash of water and saw a small blue figure climb up the side. Dela had her trident in one hand and her net slung over her shoulder. She slipped to the deck and bent over, panting from exhaustion.

"Where have you been?" Ichabod asked with barely contained impatience. "We may go into battle any time!"

Dela looked up at him with wide eyes. "Did you think I abandoned you?"

He gulped. "Well, I, uh—that is to say . . ."

"I would *never* do that, Ichabod. My service to this ship and fleet required a brief absence."

He thought it wise to let her catch her breath and explain in her own time. After a few moments, she continued. "Remember the night we first met, in Norfolk? You told me you had repeatedly spied some great monster in Chesapeake Bay. I said you had not imagined it—that there *was* a Sea Serpent there, that it sometimes swam up the York River, and that Folk allied with the British had once tried to use the monster to defeat the American cause."

Ichabod nodded.

"Well, around sunset last night I saw something similar swim past the ship."

Ichabod gasped.

"I feared our enemies might again be planning to deploy a sea creature in battle," she went on. "We cannot be sure only Indians have received gifts of power. The British may possess them, too. I had to find out. So I dove into the lake and followed the monster."

"Did it lead you to the person controlling it?"

Dela looked dejected. "I found no one. The creature escaped me entirely. While it may not be as massive as the Sea Serpent of the Chesapeake, it moves itself faster through the water. I saw only glimpses of enormous fins and a coppery hide. It was many miles from here, and headed rapidly east, when I turned back."

Ichabod considered her words. "So we've seen the last of it?"

She shrugged. "It is possible the monster will return. Or that it is not the only one in the lake."

Ichabod was about to reply when a loud voice called from the top platform of the mainmast. "Sail ho!"

Another voice answered with the same shouted words. Then another.

Feet pounded the deck. Fists pounded cabin doors. Ichabod exchanged looks with Dela, who dashed to the foremast and began to climb, looking for a good perch. Ichabod's hand brushed the hilt of the curved cutlass he'd substituted for his officer's sword. Battle had come at last. This time, Ichabod Crane wasn't watching from a distance. He'd be right in the thick of it.

Oliver Hazard Perry came on deck, buttoning his coat. "What's it look like?"

"A clump of square rigged, sir, and fore-and-afters!" shouted the top lookout.

Perry quickly gained the quarterdeck and produced a spyglass. After a few moments, he nodded his head and began issuing orders. Catching Ichabod's eye, he beckoned with a jerk of his head.

"Prepare the starboard carronades, Crane," he barked. Then, as the other officers ran off to perform their assigned duties, Perry motioned Ichabod closer to speak in low tones. "Old Cyrus would stay by my side, but I can't have that. So I've given him a disagreeable, if necessary, task. He's stationed on the berth deck. With ball and blade if necessary, he's to keep any shirkers from going below to hide. If something happens to me, see to him, Ichabod. He's not as able as he once was."

Before Ichabod could think of a response, Perry spun and sprinted away, yelling commands to a group of sailors milling around the mainmast.

An hour later, after Ichabod had deployed his gunners and had them pile up ammunition beside each cannonade, he saw Perry standing once again on the quarterdeck, peering through his spyglass. The sun had risen, filling the mostly cloudless sky of early morning with bands of orange and streaks of blue.

"Look there, men!" Perry cried.

Ichabod joined the rest of the crew in lifting their heads. A winged figure soared high over the topmast of the *Lawrence*.

"An eagle!" one of the sailors exclaimed.

"Yes, a bald eagle!" Perry agreed. "Our country is surely with us!"

As the crew cheered, Ichabod felt not exhilaration but foreboding. He knew a bald eagle was not the only possible identity of what flew overhead. He glanced up at Dela, still perched in the riggings of the fore topsail. She nodded grimly and walked to the end of the spar. With a graceful dive, the Water Maiden leapt into Lake Erie and swam in the same northeasterly direction the flier was headed.

Meanwhile, the crew raised the flag signaling "underway to get." The squadron sailed out of Put-in-Bay and headed northwest into the open water of the lake. The breeze blowing from the southwest was a gentle one, leaving Perry visibly frustrated by their slow pace.

It was hours before the full British squadron came into view. Perry and his officers quickly identified the enemy ships and arranged their own battle line accordingly. Two of their schooners led the way, followed by the three brigs—the *Lawrence*, the *Caledonia*, and Elliott's *Niagara*—and the smaller vessels.

Ichabod's cheeks, neck, and hands were all coated with sweat. His knees were knocking. He tried willing them to stop. *You've trained for this moment*, he told himself. *Time to win your reputation. Time to do your duty.*

Perry stood confidently before the mustered crew, holding up his battle standard. "My brave lads," he cried, "this flag bears the last words of Captain Lawrence! Shall I hoist it?"

"Aye, aye, sir!" they all shouted—all but Ichabod, whose dry throat managed only to croak.

Cheers rang out when the white-lettered "Don't Give Up the Ship" became clearly visible. Crewmen dumped sand on the deck to keep it from getting too slippery and strung up their sleeping hammocks to catch flying debris. Cooks ran among the sailors and gunners, distributing rations in case the battle lasted many hours.

Ichabod took comfort from the preparations. He watched for Dela's return. And he prayed.

Boom!

The blast from the first gun screamed over the water like some devilish banshee. The British cannonball fell harmlessly into the placid lake. Ichabod realized he'd been holding his breath. Relieved, he let it out.

The second cannonball didn't miss, however. It smashed into the *Lawrence* and rolled across the deck.

"Steady, lads!" Perry called.

Then the third ball struck, and the fourth, and the fifth. Planks cracked. Splinters flew. Officers barked commands. Sailors and marines cried out defiance and alarm. Some of their cries ended in screams of agony. Others ended abruptly in a silence that would never again be broken.

Before long, across the length of the flagship, there was pandemonium punctuated with panic and death. Lightly wounded men stayed at their posts. Gravely wounded fell to the deck, groaning and hoping for succor. When the slow-moving *Lawrence* finally got to within seven hundred yards, Perry shouted the order to engage the British ship *Detroit*. Their guns fired. But the range was too great—the broadside had no effect.

The *Lawrence* and the two schooners at the front of the line managed a few good shots with their long-range guns, but they had only six among them. The British ships had many times that number, training most of their fire on the *Lawrence*. Meanwhile, the rest of the American squadron had barely fired a shot.

"We must get in closer!" Perry yelled. "Signal *Caledonia* to bear up so *Niagara* can engage!"

As the battered *Lawrence* limped closer and closer to its intended target, Ichabod recalled Perry's special instructions and dashed across the gun deck, dodging ragged holes and wounded men as he made his way to the hatchway that led below.

There stood Cyrus Tiffany, blocking the hatch as he thrust the bayonet of his musket in the face of two marines. Their arms were around a third man, from whose waist dangled only the stump of a single leg. "You skulkers won't get by me!" he roared over booming cannons and desperate cries.

"Stand down, Tiffany!" Ichabod ordered, somehow finding a loud voice of his own. "We must get the wounded below!"

The old sailor glowered stubbornly. Then Ichabod saw the light of understanding in Tiffany's dark eyes. He lowered his weapon and stood aside, allowing the marines to stumble past. Looking lost and addled, Tiffany stared down at the berth deck, now awash with saltwater and blood, and snorted.

It wasn't a quick, explosive snort. It was a long, rattling sound, like a spooked horse would make.

It was an incongruous moment in the midst of indescribable horror. And it made Ichabod realize he couldn't leave the confused old man alone.

"Come on, sailor!" he yelled. "We must go prepare another broadside!"

Tiffany looked up at him with a curiously pensive expression.

Ichabod had an inspiration. "Mister Perry needs you, Cyrus. He needs your strength."

The sailor squared his shoulders and locked his jaw in determination. "Let's go, sir."

As Tiffany climbed to the higher deck, Ichabod turned and surveyed the gun crews. In just a few minutes, the situation had gone from bad to catastrophic. Few of the gunners were unscathed. Many lay motionless in pools of blood.

Then he caught sight of Mike Fink crouching next to a carronade, loading its muzzle with grapeshot. The burly man, his hat tilted so extremely that it covered half his ruddy face, grinned at Ichabod with half a visible mouth. "Ain't nobody better than me with a rifle, so I figured I'd try my hand with this!"

The *Lawrence* shuddered. "We're taking broadsides from both directions!" Ichabod yelled in alarm.

"Right back at ya!" Fink bellowed at the faraway British. Then he fired the carronade.

Tiffany yanked hard on Ichabod's sleeve. "Mister Perry. Gotta find Mister Perry."

Ichabod nodded and headed for the quarterdeck. Fink and Tiffany followed. Only a handful of crewmen remained on their feet. Among them, most conspicuous of all, was Bull, his arms bulging as he shoved a pile of wreckage out of the way to let them pass.

The giant glanced around the ruined ship. "She's lost," he said simply.

Then the four of them looked up simultaneously, past the tottering tangle of wood, canvas, and rope that had once been mast and sail, to see at the battle flag still fluttering in the breeze. *Don't Give Up the Ship.* Ichabod had previously found the motto audacious and stirring. Now it seemed only to mock him.

Another gun fired. But the sound didn't come rumbling over the water from the enemy ships. Astonished, Ichabod turned and saw Oliver Hazard Perry standing defiantly behind a smoking cannon, the only one left on deck that hadn't been knocked askew. Sam Hambleton was standing there, too, albeit more shakily, holding the gun's sponge.

The first lieutenant of the *Lawrence*, John Yarnall, lay propped against a box next to Perry and Hambleton, his face covered in blood from a nasty wound across his scalp.

"What's Mister Elliott doing now?" Perry asked Yarnall.

Ichabod rushed forward and saw the *Niagara* still far off but headed in their direction. The brig was coming in at a right angle, however, not coming up alongside. *What is Jesse Elliott doing?* Ichabod thought. *His maneuver won't draw fire from the* Lawrence.

Anger burned in Perry's narrowed eyes. "I'll fetch him up!" Then he saw Ichabod approaching. "Crane! I have a mind to get over to the *Niagara.* Go see if the small boat's seaworthy. And find me strong backs to row it!"

"Aye, aye, sir," Ichabod said.

"Yarnall, I'm leaving you in command," Perry ordered. "Do what you must to save the wounded. Sam, you're staying, too. As for me, I'm going to get that blasted flag you gave me."

Ichabod sprinted back to Tiffany, Bull, and Mike Fink. "We must lower the gig. Mister Perry is leaving the ship."

"Surrenderin'?!" exclaimed the incredulous Fink. "I figured that young fella had more fight in 'em."

"Mister Perry would *never* give up," Tiffany insisted.

Bull pointed a beefy hand at the mainmast. The others lifted their eyes to see Perry's battle flag coming down. Across the *Lawrence*, other eyes saw the same thing—eyes stinging with sweat, tears, and blood. They cried out in despair and disapproval.

"The men sure *think* he's givin' up," Fink observed.

"The men are mistaken." Ichabod's body was shaking from head to toe. Not from fear—from fury.

He was furious at Mike Fink for questioning Perry's courage. He was furious at the crewmen, even the grievously wounded ones, for doubting their commander. He was furious at the British for pouring their murderous fire into the *Lawrence*. He was furious at Jesse Elliott for holding the *Niagara* back from the fray.

A sliver of his fury was even reserved for Dela, who'd never returned from pursuing the flier at the start of the battle.

"See here, men," Ichabod barked at the others. "There's a job to do. We've got to get the commandant to the *Niagara*."

"In a rowboat?" Fink snickered. "I don't mind shootin' sittin' ducks, but I ain't fixin' to be one."

Ichabod stomped his foot. "The contest isn't over. We can still prevail! Perry's the kind of man who bends but never breaks. What kind of men are you?"

In answer, Cyrus Tiffany issued another snort, this one sounding determined, not nervous. Bull merely ground one massive fist into the palm of his other hand, a fierce smile making his black whiskers stand out stiffly from his grizzled face.

Fink held up his hands. "I reckon we're no worse off on a stinkin' rowboat than a sinkin' sailboat."

▲▲▲

The gig was, indeed, intact. As the four men lowered the boat into the water, a puzzled expression came to Tiffany's face. "No guns. They ain't firing no more."

Ichabod nodded. "The British think Perry's surrendering, too."

"They'll soon see different."

Oliver Hazard Perry swung into the boat, his folded-up battle flag tucked under an arm. The master commandant looked kindly at Tiffany, appraisingly at the beefy Fink, and with evident fascination at the gigantic Bull. Then his eyes meet Ichabod's. "Let's get underway."

Their respite from British fire proved to be brief. After a couple of minutes, the small boat emerged from the shadow of the *Lawrence*. Immediately, a new fusillade began. Round shots whistled over their heads and drew a curtain of splashing water all around the boat. There was canister and small arms fire, too, filling the air with angry swarms of death.

"Put your backs into it, men!" Perry yelled—but he needed haven't bothered.

Tiffany was already grasping his oar with two big hands and heaving. Mike Fink was grasping his oar with two mighty hands and heaving. Bull was grasping his oar with two gargantuan hands and heaving.

Ichabod rowed as well. He felt the boat shoot across the lake like an arrow from a bow, closing the half-mile gap between the *Lawrence* and the *Niagara* at a seemingly impossible speed. But though his heart hoped otherwise, Ichabod's head told him his own puny efforts had little to do with it.

If I stopped rowing altogether, our pace wouldn't slow a mite.

Another cannonball landed so close it sent a wall of water crashing over the boat. The wave struck Ichabod's head like the kick of a mad mule, leaving him dazed and dizzy.

Thinking immediately of his companions, he tried to focus his eyes enough to check on their condition. His glimpse of Perry was sharp enough to see vigor and determination written his friend's face, but Ichabod struggled to see the others as clearly. Their bodies were blurry, as if he were seeing them through a cloudy pane of glass.

The air felt thick enough to choke him. The boom of guns and the crash of water vanished under a smothering blanket of silence. Everything around him seemed to be growing larger. Or perhaps, he thought wildly, he was shrinking. Mike Fink's nose looked oddly elongated. Tiffany's head bulged in unnatural directions. So did Bull's.

Although he couldn't see or hear them, somehow Ichabod knew that British marines had fired another volley. He could make out indistinct streaks in the air that could have been hurtling musket balls. Then he saw something rise from the boat and block several of the streaks.

Shaking his head frantically to dispel the fog enshrouding it, Ichabod regained his grip on the oar and concentrated on rowing. When he looked up a few moments later, he found his senses had recovered—and not just his eyes. His ears were working fine, although it took Ichabod a moment to comprehend what he was hearing.

Fink was laughing. Tiffany was singing some old sea chanty with surprising energy. Perry had joined him. Even Bull was humming along in a low, rumbling voice.

Then Ichabod felt his oar snap. Splinters flew from his side of the boat, where another British shot had found its target. Among other things, the shot confirmed Ichabod's suspicions: His lack of an oar had no effect on the speed of the boat.

The next British shot was more debilitating. It landed in the center of the boat, miraculously missing its passengers but punching a large hole in the hull.

Ichabod whipped off his hat and began bailing water out of the boat. "We won't be afloat much longer!" he cried.

"Nor need we be," Perry announced. "Ahoy, there!"

The *Niagara* loomed above them. Ropes dropped. Fink and Bull released their oars and used the ropes to pull the gig alongside. Soon, they were all climbing aboard the brig, which was still well crewed and showed little damage from the battle.

Master Commandant Jesse Elliott strode forward. "How is the day going?" he asked.

The man's absurd question left Ichabod seething and about to mouth a series of curses. But Perry merely wiped the grimy sweat from his brow and glared. "Badly. We have been cut all to pieces."

Elliott stared at Perry with an expression Ichabod found unreadable. Perry wasn't returning the stare. Instead, he was looking at the distant sails of four American ships that had yet to engage. "Why are the gunboats so far astern?"

Elliott seemed to swallow nervously. "I'll bring them up."

"Do so, sir," Perry snapped.

Elliott paced a few steps, then stopped and turned as if to say something more. Now it was Perry's turn to stare. Obviously flustered, Elliott walked quickly away. A few minutes later, Ichabod saw the man standing, and apparently fuming, in a small boat of his own as crewmen rowed him toward the squadron's straggling ships.

This matter isn't over, Ichabod thought. *Not by a long shot.*

▲▲▲

It was the *Niagara*—under the command of a new and vengeful officer, its eighteen carronades belching canister and grapeshot, Perry's blue banner flying from the masthead—that turned the tide of battle.

And now it was the *British* squadron that seemed to shrivel under murderous fire. The *Queen Charlotte*, trying to maneuver into better position, lost most of its sails, and thus its maneuverability, after a merciless broadside. Then the British flagship, the *Detroit*, was reduced to a twisted wreck after the damaged *Queen Charlotte* careened into it, the latter's bowsprit plunging into the former's rigging. The two ships, entangled and immobilized, became easy targets for blasts of American cannister.

The action was over in fifteen minutes. The British squadron signaled their surrender with desperate cries and white handkerchiefs. With daring and determination, Oliver Hazard Perry had turned abject defeat into absolute victory. But Ichabod knew that what had made it all possible—Perry's rapid journey from the *Lawrence* to the *Niagara*—were the herculean efforts of three men: Cyrus Tiffany, Mike Fink, and Bull.

I played a small part, Ichabod allowed. *But not one likely to earn even a paragraph in the official record.*

"Ho, there, Crane," said Perry, smiling in relief and exultation. "Keen to test your horsemanship again?"

"Sir?"

"I must get word to General Harrison that the British have lost their naval support, that *now* is the time to strike Detroit. Perhaps you and Midshipman Montgomery will act as couriers once more?"

Courier duty was the last thing Ichabod wanted to resume. But, of course, he would do what was required. He nodded.

Perry reached inside his coat, which was covered in streaks of soot and blood. He fumbled in its pockets, coming up empty. "Blast it all!"

"What's wrong, sir?"

"Here I am with the most important dispatch of my career to send, and I have nothing to write it on," Perry complained. Then he looked down at Ichabod's own uniform. It was torn, most of its buttons shorn off. "What's that you've got in your coat?"

Ichabod froze. *The envelope!*

Dela was still missing. Without magical assistance, a reader would see no words on the blank sheet of paper within. "You're a godsend, my friend," said Perry as he held out a hand. Seeing no alternative, Ichabod handed over the envelope.

Perry opened it quickly, pocketed the blank page without even looking at it, and removed his hat to use as a writing surface. Producing a pencil and scratching out a brief message on the back of the envelope, he handed it back to Ichabod. "Montgomery is somewhere here on the *Niagara*. Find him quickly and get ashore. I'm going to draft those three stout oarsmen of ours to take me back to the *Lawrence*. I'll accept the British surrender on my flagship, or what's left of it."

Ichabod saluted and stumbled off to comply. As he reached the hatchway and was about to descend, his curiosity got the better of him. He hurried into a deserted corner and opened the folded envelope to read the hastily penned dispatch.

"U.S.S. Niagara, Sept. 10th — 4 P.M. Dear Gen'l: — We have met the enemy and they are ours; two ships, two brigs, one schooner and one sloop. Yours with great respect and esteem, O.H. Perry."

Chapter 17 – The Forlorn

September 1813

Dela couldn't shake the feeling that something was wrong. Horribly wrong.

The Water Maiden stood at the rail of the *Niagara*, watching apprehensively as sailors lowered the brig's small boats. The breeze was light and welcome in the afternoon heat as the militiamen climbed into their landing craft. Bright sunlight streaming from a cloudless sky gave the eager men a clear view of their destination—a sandy shore near the mouth of the Detroit River.

By the look of it, there was nothing to be worried about. After defeating the British squadron a couple of weeks earlier, Oliver Hazard Perry's ships ferried most of General William Henry Harrison's army over Lake Erie to attack the British stronghold. Detroit's defenders had already fled, however. Harrison's 3,500 men, mostly Kentucky militia along with a few regular soldiers, faced no opposition as they came ashore.

Dela knew the American army, soon to be reinforced by a thousand mounted riflemen riding north from Ohio, would easily outnumber their fleeing enemies, the troops of British General Henry Procter and the Indian warriors led by Tecumseh.

She also knew Perry's naval victory had deprived the British and Indians of crucial supplies. And she knew that, contrary to her initial fears, there'd been no Folk intervention against Perry. No attack on his ships by the enormous monster she'd seen in the lake. No gifts of power to turn the tide of battle. No spellsong to weaken American morale.

But the winged fairy she'd spotted just before the naval battle had escaped—again. Her pursuit had accomplished nothing other than separating her from Ichabod Crane and the American squadron. Fortunately, they hadn't needed her to prevail. Still, she told herself, the flyer must have had a purpose for being there.

It couldn't have been just to draw me away from the battle.

Unconsciously, the Water Maiden fingered the shell necklace at her throat and began to sing, soft and low. She thought of home, her village beneath Long Island-on-the-Holston where her mother and the rest of the Gwragedd Annwn awaited her return. She thought of Har the Tower traveling south to talk with the Elf Prince Veelund and look for enchanted weapons among the Cherokees and Creeks. She thought of Goran, not so far away in Ohio, undertaking a similar mission. The thought that the Sylph might soon find his way north to Harrison's army brought a flush to her cheeks.

And Dela thought of her human friends, new and old. Of Ichabod, so desperate to prove himself. Of Peter Muhlenberg, the former Pennsylvania congressman who died a few years earlier. Of the aged Nanyehi, who still lived with her family on Tennessee's Ocoee River. Of the even more aged Daniel Boone, who now lived somewhere far to the west, in the Missouri Territory.

"That's how I always picture you—standing near the water, singing me a song."

Dela turned. A tall, heavyset human stood before her. He'd removed his hat, revealing a few remaining strands of white hair swept back over a pair of oversized ears. Although more than sixty years old, his ruddy complexion and ready smile marked him as robust.

But as she looked into his big brown eyes, turned down sharply at each corner, Dela saw not the face of the senior statesman he was or even the brash battlefield commander he'd once been. She saw only the face of the kindly young herdsman who'd rescued her on a riverbank and nursed her back to health.

He had something to prove back then, she recalled. *Just as Ichabod Crane does now.*

"I will always have a song for you, Governor. Or should I call you *General?*"

Isaac Shelby laughed and shook his jowly head. "Isaac will do. It'll do just fine."

The Water Maiden turned and saw more boats coming ashore.

"Drove my Kentuckians hard to get to General Harrison's camp, Dela," Isaac said. "Plum wore out our horses, though we had to leave 'em back in Sandusky, anyway. Most of my men are crack shots. They've hunted. They've fought Indians. How they'll fare against General Procter and his British regulars, I don't know. But they're angry enough to try it."

"Angry enough?"

Isaac pulled a handkerchief from his waistcoat and wiped his brow. "Their anger began at the Raisin. Back in January, when General Harrison first moved against Detroit, a column of Kentuckians took Frenchtown, just south of here on the River Raisin. A few days later, the British and Indians counterattacked. The Kentuckians fought bravely. Hundreds lay dead on the field by the time they surrendered. But the killing didn't stop. The Indians massacred and mutilated a hundred more after the battle. Some were wounded men lying on the floor of a house. The Indians burned it to the ground, with everyone inside it."

"Tecumseh did that?" Dela was aghast. "I do not agree with the violent course he has chosen, but I am told he is an honorable man."

"Way I heard it, Tecumseh wasn't there," Isaac replied.

The Water Maiden gritted her teeth. "You said the rage of the Kentuckians *began* at the Raisin."

Isaac nodded. "There was another massacre just four months ago. Procter and Tecumseh tried to take Fort Meigs down in Ohio. A relief force of Kentuckians stormed the British battery and spiked the guns. Then the Indians lured them into the forest. Our men surrendered, only to be murdered. Of some nine hundred Kentuckians, fewer than two hundred made it back."

Dela could see her friend's eyes blazing.

He shares their anger. I cannot blame him. But there is righteous anger on both sides here. Revenge follows revenge, bringing only more death and destruction.

▲▲▲

General Harrison stayed at Detroit for several days, waiting for reinforcements before pushing into Upper Canada. Most of his army consisted of Kentucky militiamen led by General Isaac Shelby, also the state's governor. In addition, Harrison's command included a hundred regulars and twice as many Indian allies from the Miami nation. When reinforcements finally arrived on the first of October—a thousand mounted Kentuckians under Colonel Richard Mentor Johnson—Harrison's force numbered 4,500. While some stayed behind to garrison the forts and river crossings, Harrison's column would still vastly outnumber their foes.

If the Americans could catch up with them.

"There is no probability we will overtake Procter," Harrison said, his tall frame bent as he paced beneath a low tent. "He has a week's start on us."

Colonel Johnson's long face formed a scowl. "You didn't need to wait for us. We bloodied the Indians all the way here. You must press them, always press them."

Now it was Harrison's turn to scowl. Standing near the tent flap, and invisible to all but Isaac Shelby, Dela recalled the camp talk she'd heard about William Henry Harrison and Richard Mentor Johnson. The latter had, until recently, represented Kentucky in Congress. Johnson thought himself at least Harrison's equal, both in political stature and military judgment. His plan to deprive the British of allies by attacking Indian villages during the winter, when they'd be forced to stand and fight, had won favor in Washington. But Harrison refused to approve it.

The two men glowered at each other for a time. *Harrison blames Johnson for delaying the pursuit*, Dela realized. *And Johnson thinks Harrison too timid.*

Oliver Hazard Perry stepped forward. "The British column is poorly supplied and poorly led," said the master commandant, now serving as aide-de-camp to Harrison. "General, their pace is likely slower than you fear."

"I agree," said Isaac Shelby, brows knitted in determination. "While most of my Kentuckians are afoot, they'll close the gap quick. They've got good reason."

"Let's get on with it, then," Johnson snapped. "My men can ride ahead and pick off the stragglers."

Harrison glared at him but replied only with a curt nod.

After the officers left the tent, Isaac led Dela off to the side. "Johnson's men are good scouts, but you'll be an even better one," he said.

Dela smiled. "We know each other too well, Isaac. I had already planned to depart tonight."

Shelby dropped his eyes. "You, uh . . . you want to tell me?"

"Tell you what?"

"What's troubling you, Dela. We *do* know each other too well for you to fool me."

She nodded and took a deep breath. Then she told Isaac about the gifts of power. About Tecumseh's brother Tenskwatawa and the confused battle of Tippecanoe. About the Ojibwe weapon at York and the Mohawk weapon at Beaver Dams. About King Alberich's suspicions and Prince Veelund's denials. About the mission that sent Har, Goran, and her in three different directions.

"Tecumseh's out there, his brother at his side," Isaac said in hushed voice. "If they bear magic weapons . . ."

"Then I will intercept them before they can use those weapons against you and your men," Dela promised her longtime friend.

With far more confidence than she felt.

▲▲▲

The enemy had retreated northwest along the Thames River, upon which the British could float their boats of precious supplies. So Dela followed the same course, welcoming the option to swim up the narrow river rather than risk exposure in the open or weave her way through the woods. It was a forest of towering trees—beech, walnut, basswood, maple, oak, sassafras, tulip—growing so thick and close to the water's edge that long stretches of the Thames looked more like a walled ditch than a river.

For the first two days, Dela stayed only slightly ahead of Richard Mentor Johnson's galloping troopers. On the third day, however, Johnson's men began to encounter lagging elements of the retreating column. Trusting they could best the small bands of Indians and Canadians without her help, Dela raced ahead. By dusk of the fourth day, she found herself looking at the camps of General Procter's British regulars and, a little beyond them, the Indian confederacy.

She'd expected the latter force to be far more numerous, in the thousands rather than the hundreds of Indians she saw gathered around their campfires. Dela guessed that retreating across Canada was not what the Indians had in mind when they joined up. Many must have abandoned Tecumseh.

But if they possess gifts of power, they remain a dangerous foe.

Dela strengthened her concealment spell and slipped into the Indian camp. Presently she saw a campfire on high ground some distance from most of the others, around which three figures sat smoking tomahawk-shaped pipes. Their dress and war paint seemed more elaborate than the others'. Guessing they might be chiefs, Dela crept closer.

"The Americans race after us like lost fawns," grumbled one of the men, his eyes narrowing over black-painted cheeks as he stared into the flickering campfire. He was slender and bare-chested, wearing a red-fringed skirt of blackened buckskin. One side of his head was shaved. From the other, his hair hung long and braided. "They tire. Their lines grow ragged. Yet the British general sees nothing but an approaching enemy. He would keep running forever."

Silently, Dela commended her good judgment in studying the Shawnee language during her last extended visit home.

"Procter is not fit to command," sneered a second man, broader of shoulder and dressed in an entirely different fashion: the red coat of a British officer, complete with yellow epaulettes at the shoulders and a medal medallion around his neck. On his head was a red turban from which a single gray feather stuck out jauntily. "He should be wearing petticoats, not the uniform of a man."

Sitting across from the two chiefs, the third man snickered but said nothing. He was shorter and stockier, his bare limbs adorned with bands of copper and hide. His multicolored bandana encircled short, gray-tinged hair. In addition to breechclout and leggings, he wore a large bronze gorget at his throat and a mantle over his shoulders, its black-and-brown stripes fringed with gold.

Fringed with gold. Dela realized she'd seen the mantle's like before, during the conference with King Alberich. It was one of the gifts of power the Shawnee prophet Tenskwatawa had distributed to his assassins before the battle of Tippecanoe.

If this is that same Tenskwatawa, then the red-coated man must be . . .

"Tecumseh, can we not *demand* Procter turn and fight? While we still have warriors to make a stand?" the slender chief asked.

The turbaned chief nodded. "I will speak to him again tonight, Firm Fellow. Already the Wyandot have dwindled to half their number, while warriors of the Ottawa, the Potawatomi, the Shawnee, and the Kickapoo slip away each night. Brave men will follow a coward for only so long. Soon the rest will scatter like autumn leaves before the wind."

Tenskwatawa raised a shaking hand. "Tell the white general he will have victory if he turns to fight. Tell him the Great Spirit has willed it."

Firm Fellow snorted. "You speak words of prophecy, yet what victory have your words brought? The loss of Prophetstown? Our pointless occupation of Detroit? Our British father's disaster on the great lake? I put more trust in bullets and blades than fine words."

Shaking his head dismissively, Tenskwatawa fingered the mantle draped over his shoulders. "Our Creator has purified me and sent me down to you full of shining power. Our Creator has led me to the door. All you must do is follow me through it. Our wondrous future lies beyond."

"Our brother has brought us gifts, Firm Fellow," Tecumseh said. "Now we must use them well. Procter cannot understand; no white man can. But if the general heeds my counsel and strikes tonight, under cover of night, he will unknowingly bait our trap. Harrison will blunder into it. He will lead his tired thousands to their deaths."

Dela felt the hair rising on the back of her neck.

I was right! There is great danger here!

She moved closer. She was rewarded only with silence as the three men sat staring into the fire, each apparently occupied with his own thoughts.

Dela considered using spellsong to force Tecumseh to reveal his plans but quickly reconsidered; she was entirely alone in a camp of enemies. If Tenskwatawa or other Indians possessed the Sight, they'd be immune to her magic and capable of raising an alarm. There was also the question of Tenskwatawa's "spirits," the Folk supplying him with enchanted weapons. If they were present in the camp in sufficient numbers, they might capture and interrogate her.

Or worse.

Then Dela's eyes fell on an object lying some distance from the campfire. It was another gold-fringed mantle wrapped into a bundle. She recalled the enchanted powder horns Alberich had shown them. Was this bundle another supply of horns? Or some other gifts Tenskwatawa planned to distribute?

The Water Maiden decided she couldn't afford to leave the bundle behind. For more than an hour she hid, suppressing her impatience and waiting for an opportune moment to act. Then it came. Tecumseh rose to his feet. "Time for my conference with Procter. It will strengthen my demand for battle if you are with me, Firm Fellow."

The slender chief nodded and the two walked away, leaving only Tenskwatawa sitting before the fire. Dela kept hoping he would leave as well. However, the human kept staring intensely into the flames, poking them with a stick.

Realizing that her errand would best be accomplished before the night ended, Dela picked up a stick of her own. It was an old trick, she thought, but this Tenskwatawa struck her as more a talker than a hunter. She straightened and threw the stick as far as she could in the opposite direction from where the bundle lay.

When the stick crashed into the leaves of the forest, the Shawnee prophet jerked to his feet. Dela had expected him to run quickly toward the sound. Unfortunately, Tenskwatawa took only a few steps.

That will have to do.

She scampered to the bundle, lifted the unwieldy mass over one shoulder, and ran toward the river. Whether because of the distraction she caused or the spell she sang, Tenskwatawa appeared not to notice her.

Dela reached the north bank of the Thames and peered downriver to select her path back to Harrison's army. Leaning against a massive tulip tree, the Water Maiden breathed a sigh of relief.

Then drew it quickly back with a gasp.

From her right side came the furious bellow of Tenskwatawa, presumably having discovered his bundle missing. And from her left side came a different sound—a whoosh, followed by a whack. Inches from her face, still quivering, was the shaft of a short, thick spear embedded deep in the trunk of the tree.

Dela turned to flee, which was probably why the second spear passed not through her breast but past it, landing a short distance away in the soft mud. As she ran, the Water Maiden's eyes widened in alarm.

For the missile was tipped with copper and covered with intricately carved runes.

The bundle on Dela's back slowed her pace not only by weighing her down but by repeatedly striking overhead branches. Her mind, at least, was racing. *Folk rangers!* A far greater danger than any human pursuers would be, and no doubt intent on recovering the enchanted weapons they'd supplied Tenskwatawa.

It required only two more copper-tipped missiles, each just missing her, to convince Dela her safety was more important than her prize. Dropping the bundle, she dashed toward the river. Then she stopped short. Two shadowy figures loomed before her, blocking her path to the sheltering water of the Thames. Dela gripped her trident tightly with one hand and filled the other with her beaded net.

The rangers strode slowly forward, holding their own weapons at the ready. Passing from cover into a patch of open ground, the two fairies revealed themselves. The moonlight fell on breechclouts and leggings, on heads shaved bald except for Mohawk-style stripes of dark hair. Each had a wooden spear-thrower hanging from his belt. One held a copper-bladed tomahawk, its haft carved with symbols of expert enchantment. The other held a long, curved war club shaped like a raptor's leg with a round, red-tinged ball of metal clutched in its claw.

One of the fairies opened his mouth to speak, but Dela had no interest in a contest of words. She leapt forward, jabbing at the tomahawk-wielding man with the tip of her trident while casting her net at the other. The enchanted beads of gemstone and bronze woven into the net guided it unerringly and made it spin unnaturally fast. Before the club-wielding ranger had a chance to react, his head, arms, and weapon were hopelessly entangled.

"You will not trap me so easily!" snarled the first ranger as he swung the tomahawk at her head.

Dela parried with a sweep of her trident, then used its momentum to her advantage. Planting its blades in the ground, the Water Maiden vaulted into the air, lashing out with her feet and striking the ranger in the chest.

He grunted and dropped his weapon. Yet he also managed to catch one of Dela's heels in his hand and yanked. She landed hard on the ground, knocking the breath out of her.

Rolling to her side and gulping for air, Dela still had the presence of mind to wrench the trident from the ground. Seeing the club-wielding ranger about to free himself from the net, the other recovering his tomahawk from where he'd dropped it, she coughed and braced herself for another round. Then she heard the sounds of approaching feet and voices crying out.

Crying out in Folktongue. More were coming.

Her duty was clear. Spinning on her heels, Dela sprinted to the Thames and dove into the shallow water. Boosted by the favorable current, she shot down the river like a bullet fired from a human's rifle. The shouts of her pursuers faded into silence.

Dela had lost the bundle. She'd lost her net. She'd nearly lost her liberty, if not her life. But she'd found what she was looking for—proof that her suspicions were warranted. The Americans *were* walking into a trap. And their enemies would have magical assistance.

▲▲▲

"How can we stop General Harrison's attack?"

Dela had been surprised to find the Americans only a short distance from the British camp. Looking desperately for Isaac Shelby, she'd nearly run headlong into Ichabod Crane, who'd been spending a sleepless night reading a book and praying for the Water Maiden's safe return. Together they'd roused General Shelby with the news of Dela's discoveries.

"I'm not sure we *can* stop it," Isaac replied groggily, "but first things first. Were you followed? Even a few fairies wielding spellsong could wreak havoc among the men. Sap their courage. Prompt some to desert. I've seen it tried before."

"I know," said Dela, recalling in vivid detail their fateful trek to Kings Mountain during the last war.

General Shelby approached a group of sleeping Kentuckians and barked orders. They grabbed their guns and ran off to comply. Within minutes, there were twice as many sentries ringing the camp. They watched their commander pace the perimeter with a lanky naval officer stumbling awkwardly along behind him.

But there was no sign of movement. No sign of Folk or human scouts.

After a few minutes, General Harrison joined them, still buttoning the buttons of his rumpled jacket. "What is it, Shelby?" he demanded. "Did one of our pickets report in?"

Isaac shook his head. "Just making sure proper vigilance is preserved, General. We've driven the men some eighty miles in less than three days. Our enemy is close. If I were them, I'd consider a sneak attack under cover of night against a tired army."

"Our enemies are tired, too," Harrison observed. "Tired and unsupplied. They won't risk an attack tonight. We'll meet them on our terms tomorrow."

As the general walked away, Isaac and Ichabod exchanged meaningful glances. They were no doubt thinking the same thing Dela was: If events proved Harrison right, it wouldn't be for the reason he stated. It would be because of her timely warning. It would be because Procter and Tecumseh preferred to launch a surprise attack on a sleeping camp, not an *expected* attack against a *roused* army.

Dawn came without further incident. Harrison held another conference with his officers. Scouts had seen the enemy forming up along the road. Procter and Tecumseh had chosen defensible ground between the river on their left and a densely forested marsh on their right.

"Shelby, we'll deploy our regulars and your best volunteers in the center to fix the enemy while Colonel Johnson's riders sweep around their flank," Harrison said.

"If the marsh is as muddy and the trees as thick as scouts report, mounted men won't be able to make much headway there," Isaac observed.

"Then we'll dismount and fight man-to-man," Johnson insisted. "The Indians have run from us many times before."

"But not so often with Tecumseh leading them," Oliver Hazard Perry added.

As it happened, Harrison decided to change his plan anyway.

When she and Ichabod rode out with Commandant Perry to get a look at the enemy, Dela saw the same surprising feature the humans did: a small, narrow swamp bisecting the enemy lines. On one side, stretching from the Thames River across the road to the little swamp, were General Procter's British regulars, standing in two loose ranks in a lightly wooded area. Extending from the other side of the swamp to the large, forested marsh on the left was another patch of relatively open ground. Filling that gap were the warriors of Tecumseh's confederacy.

William Henry Harrison and Richard Mentor Johnson had seen the same thing—and judging from the deployment of the Americans, Harrison had adjusted accordingly. The bulk of the army, Shelby's infantry, were no longer marching forward. Instead, Johnson's mounted troops were forming up in front of the army.

"He's going to ride right into the enemy on both sides of that swamp!" Perry said with enthusiasm. "Johnson's an audacious man, I'll give him that."

"Why is that squad of riders lining up in front of the others?" Ichabod asked.

"That'll be Johnson's forlorn hope, and I'll wager he's among them," Perry replied.

Ichabod frowned. "That 'forlorn hope'—it's the vanguard, you mean, to draw the Indians' fire?"

"Yes. Once the enemy fires, the rest of Johnson's men will move up and attack before the Indians can reload."

But while Dela was listening to the two humans' conversation, she wasn't looking in the same direction. Her eyes were scanning the thick line of ash, oak, and beech that formed the marshy forest to the left. She'd spotted painted foreheads, feathered caps, and the glint of gun barrels among those trees. And she'd also seen a round, determined face framed by a multicolored bandana above and a shiny metal gorget below.

Tenskwatawa was there. Something told Dela she should be there too.

"Ichabod," she whispered. "Find some reason to leave."

The artillery captain looked flustered. Then he swallowed and began to speak.

"Mister Perry, sir, I fear I must leave your side for a short time."

The master commandant was nonplussed. "Crane, now is no time to lose your nerve."

"I, uh—that is to say, no, sir. It's not that. I want to see if Colonel Johnson will let me join him."

Now Perry seemed astounded. "*Join* the forlorn hope, you mean? I admire your courage, but your skills at horsemanship are hardly up to the task."

"Don't you see, sir?" Now Ichabod's words sounded more desperate than addled. "Another chance has come, a chance for me to prove myself. I cannot let it slip by like the others!"

Perry sighed and waved a hand. "As you will, Mister Crane. But might I suggest . . ."

Ichabod never heard his friend's advice. Nor did the Water Maiden, who was perched on the saddle behind him. Ichabod had already spurred his horse to a gallop.

The two raced rapidly toward the American left. They passed within a dozen paces of a startled Isaac Shelby, who managed only to call out, "Wait, you two!" before they were too far away to hear anything more.

Just as their horse had nearly reached the front rank of Johnson's men—twenty mounted Kentuckians, including the colonel himself, wearing hunting shirts dyed dark blue and holding their rifles high—someone within that "forlorn hope" let out a loud whoop. Another answered it.

"Charge!" yelled Colonel Johnson.

"Remember the River Raisin!" yelled someone else.

The twenty Kentuckians shot forward, their horses' hooves drumming a relentless rhythm. Just behind followed a twenty-first rider, but he was no Kentuckian in a dyed hunting shirt. He was an artillery captain in an ill-footing uniform coat, holding on for dear life as his horse tried to catch up with the others.

Over the pounding hoofbeats, and over the sounds of war already audible from other side of the battlefield, Dela heard something else—a sound she immediately recognized. A sound she feared.

Spellsong. A summoning spell, coming from the marshy forest to their left.

Dela looked back at the rest of Johnson's waiting men. Their horses were ambling forward, not yet charging, but they seemed impatient to enter the fray. It was only obedience to Colonel Johnson that kept their impatience in check.

I cannot let these brave men blunder into a trap.

"Turn left toward the forest!" she shouted, tugging Ichabod's sleeve. "Our real enemy is there!"

Reluctantly, the human did as she asked. A second later, as they galloped at an oblique angle away from the others, Dela turned her head and watched with horror as dozens of Tecumseh's defending warriors blasted the forlorn hope at close range. Where seconds before there were twenty saddles filled with whooping Kentuckians, there were now nearly as many empty saddles, their riders have tumbled to the ground, likely dead or grievously wounded.

"Remember the Raisin!" came a call from behind them, from the ranks of Johnson's other Kentuckians, now rushing forward to join the action. Some rode two to a saddle. Some were already dismounted and dashing forward with guns leveled.

"We're coming, colonel!" one shouted.

Ichabod suddenly drew up his mount, returning Dela's attention to the forest ahead.

"Can't ride any closer!" he said. "We must go on foot."

The two dismounted and ran to the edge of the marsh. There was the loud report of a gun. A ball whistled over their heads. Then a warrior holding a smoking rifle stepped into view. He cast it aside and drew his tomahawk. The next blast came from Ichabod's pistol as he fired at the charging Indian, knocking him to the ground with a ball to the shoulder.

Dela could hear the summoning spell grow louder, as if two Folk were singing. "Keep going, Ichabod!" she urged. "Deeper into the forest!"

The two wove their way through thick tree trunks. They jumped over fallen logs and sloshed through water that reached halfway to Ichabod's knees and more than halfway up Dela's entire body. Another warrior confronted them, this one wearing a wooden hat much like the ones the Oneida wore, though it sported two upturned feathers rather than one. Ichabod rushed forward to engage the man, sword to tomahawk. With the help of Dela's deftly wielded trident, the two quickly dispatched their foe and continued forward.

Now there was another voice singing the summoning spell, forming an eerie and unsettling trio. Shortly thereafter, Dela got her first look at what they were summoning.

To be precise, she *felt* its presence before she could see it. The air turned suddenly cold, as if the temperature had dropped thirty degrees and she and Ichabod were trudging through an icy marsh in February rather than a muddy marsh in October. The frigid air seemed to reach inside her, through her nose and mouth, to clamp its frosty fingers around her beating heart.

She felt the monster's terror magic try to freeze her in place. And she felt something else, an urge that consumed the monster itself and over which it had no control.

It was hunger. A limitless, insatiable desire to feed.

The monster towered a dozen feet over her head. Its skin was ashen gray and stretched thin over protruding bones. Its face was long and skeletal, its desiccated mouth failing to obscure rows of pointed yellow teeth. Its large, deeply recessed eyes glowed a sickly yellow. From its skull protruded jagged horns that looked like a pale, rotting facsimile of a buck's antlers.

Dela glanced over at Ichabod Crane, whose face had turned nearly as ashen as the beast's. His eyes were wide with a desperate fear.

"What . . . what is it?" he managed to ask.

"A Wendigo," she said flatly.

"A what?"

"A Wendigo. My friend Skenandoah once spoke of them. This ice giant was meant to charge from the marsh and take your army from the flank."

Her words seemed to lend Ichabod strength. She could see him resisting the grip of its terror magic. Dela began singing her courage song, rattling the shells of her necklace to accentuate the spell's effect. A determined smile came to Ichabod's face. He slumped forward, as if he'd been suspended by a rope that was just cut, then straightened and lifted his sword.

"It will charge no one if it's dead," he muttered.

I wish there was some other way, Dela told herself. *But Ichabod is right.*

The Wendigo spread what lips were left to it and hissed, its yellow eyes staring longingly at its presumed next meal. Then it lumbered forward, bony arms dangling at its sides.

"Watch out—those claws are razor-sharp!" Dela said quickly before resuming her spellsong.

Ichabod yanked the scabbard from his belt, arming himself with something else to parry the monster's attacks.

The Wendigo's terror magic was so powerful that Dela doubted she could confuse or demoralize it. This battle would be one of bone, bronze, and iron. The Wendigo had the advantage in size and reach. They must defeat it with cunning and speed.

Hissing again, the monster swung his right arm at Ichabod, who swatted at it with his scabbard. He'd hoped to bat aside the blow while thrusting his sword at the monster's torso, but the maneuver went wrong from the start. Ichabod's scabbard missed the Wendigo entirely, then flew out of his hand as the human lost his balance. Fortunately, by slipping on the wet ground Ichabod had managed to fall below the Wendigo's swinging arm.

Dela seized the initiative. First she swiped at the monster's leg, smiling with satisfaction as her enchanted blade slashed gray flesh. Then she spun on one heel and thrust her point upward at its sunken abdomen.

For a beast with seemingly atrophied limbs, however, the Wendigo had surprisingly good reflexes. Dela's thrust didn't reach its belly. The blade stopped inches away, held by in place by the monster's bony fingers wrapped around the shaft of the trident.

The Water Maiden tried wrenching her weapon free of the Wendigo's grasp to no avail. She tried again, straining every muscle of her small frame in an attempt to win a tugging match with a fourteen-foot giant. She failed, although her expertly magecrafted weapon had at least channeled enough stored magic keep the match tied. The enchantment wouldn't maintain its potency for long, however.

"Just let go!" shouted Ichabod, who'd gotten unsteadily to his feet.

"I cannot," she spat through gritted teeth. "Run, Ichabod! You are no match for it."

"Neither are you!" the human insisted. "Trust me. Let go!"

Then she understood. Dela released her grip.

Having strained its own muscles against Dela's magically enhanced pull, the Wendigo couldn't halt the inevitable when the counteracting force disappeared. Propelled by the monster's own unnatural might, the weapon plunged into the Wendigo's abdomen.

"Huzzah!" Ichabod shouted, lifting his sword and leaping exuberantly on one foot.

Dela stepped back and watched the Wendigo wobble on two spindly legs, then sink to its knees. While it was unlikely the trident had dealt a mortal blow, the sleep magic stored in its blades began to do its work.

Turning to Ichabod, Dela was about to commend her friend for quick thinking when she heard the clang of wood on stone. Her head whipped around just fast enough to catch a glimpse of the monster's hand before it struck her.

In that split-second, as she watched its claw rake her side, her legs thrust the Water Maiden's body back enough that the talons only sliced a gash across her abdomen rather than gutting her like a fish. Still, the searing pain made her teeth clench and her eyes water. She could feel hot blood gushing from the ragged wound.

She heard another clanging sound—metal on bone this time. Ichabod had rushed forward and struck at the Wendigo's right leg. With a whoop much like the forlorn hope of Kentuckians had made before their charge, Ichabod wrenched his sword from the monster's thigh and swung it again.

Iron disrupts magic, she reminded herself as she stumbled back, pressing on her wound and looking for her trident. It was lying on the rocks where the Wendigo had discarded it. She lifted the weapon with both hands, letting the blood flow freely from her side.

Ichabod's second swing cut clear through the monster's leg, severing it close to the hip. The creature was now balanced awkwardly on two elbows and a knee, though it was still far from defenseless. Dela's voice caught in her throat as she saw the Wendigo jerk its head and catch Ichabod full in the chest with the side of its twisted antler. The force of the blow lifted the human off his feet and threw him nearly a dozen paces to collide with a tree.

With a defiant cry, the Water Maiden charged.

The Wendigo leaned on its right elbow and swung at her with its left hand. Dela parried the blow, then dove into a sideways roll. With a splash of mud and a snarl, she leapt at the monster and drove her trident into its open mouth.

It was over in an instant. Dela made no attempt to hold onto the trident as she fell back on the ground. The Wendigo made no attempt to dislodge the weapon; it made no move at all. It simply died with a bronze point in its brain, its ravenous hunger silenced at last.

She was relieved to see Ichabod on his feet and walking slowly toward her, shaking his head as if to clear it. "Are you wounded, Dela?"

Nodding, she touched the gash on her side and felt blood continuing to ooze from it. Ichabod yanked his cravat from his neck and knelt, wrapping it around her slim waist and tying the ends in a tight knot. Whether he was surprised to see her blood stain his white cravat blue instead of red, Dela could not tell. Only deep concern was written on his gaunt face.

"I've got to get you out of here," Ichabod said, slipping his lanky arms under her knees and shoulders.

"No, I can walk," she insisted. Waving him away, she rose to her feet. Wincing as the effort produced new waves of pain, she strode to the monster's carcass and recovered her trident, its blades now covered in a sticky, translucent liquid.

She forced a smile. "We should return to the battle."

The two retraced their steps. When they reached the edge of the marsh, they came upon a lithe Shawnee wresting his tomahawk from the skull of a fallen Kentuckian. At the sound of footsteps, the warrior looked up and twisted his face into an angry scowl.

His cheeks and forehead marked with streaks of black paint and dried blood, braids of dark hair jutting from his half-shaved head, the Shawnee uttered a war cry and rushed at Ichabod—presumably the only foe he could see.

Dela grimaced and lifted her trident. But to her surprise, Ichabod proved more than ready for the Indian's charge. He caught the tomahawk on the edge of his sword, then shoved with such force that the Shawnee was knocked back, lost his footing, and staggered to one knee.

Before the Water Maiden could intervene, Ichabod pushed forward and aimed a cut at the hairless side of the Indian's head. With a single fluid motion, the kneeling man transferred the axe to his left hand, used it to parry Ichabod's blow, and pulled a knife from his breechclout.

"Beware the knife!" shouted Dela, circling the two and looking for an opportunity to strike.

Ichabod had already seen it. With a dexterity Dela had never before seen him demonstrate, the American captain stepped backward. The Shawnee's knife pierced only air. Careening to his left, balanced precariously on one foot, Ichabod brought his blade down with all the power he could muster.

The blow severed the Shawnee's hair braids—and more beyond that. The Indian sprawled lifeless in the dirt.

Ichabod spun and looked at her with triumph in his eyes. The expression turned quickly to concern as Dela grew dizzy and stumbled. With two big bounds Ichabod was at her side and reaching down to steady her.

Dela took a deep breath. "A passing faint. I can still go on."

Ichabod seemed poised to protest when she forced another smile to her lips. "Walk ahead and I will follow."

He reluctantly complied. They crossed the gap to the fallen Kentuckian. Ichabod bent low, placed his fingers on the trooper's neck, and rose with the man's rifle in his hands, shaking his head sadly.

The two continued only a few steps down a sharp incline before Ichabod abruptly cried out and pointed. Dela's eyes followed his finger and looked down the hill at the tableau before them. There was Richard Mentor Johnson, swaying wildly but still in his saddle. The colonel's left arm hung limp at his side. His left leg had been hastily bandaged at the thigh. Johnson's pistol was thrust forward, over the head of his horse, by his shaking right hand.

The pistol's intended target was a tall, broad-shouldered Indian wearing a red uniform coat and standing some dozen paces in front of Johnson. The man's hair was wet with perspiration and hung in unruly strands from beneath a red turban. He was aiming a rifle back at Johnson while emitting a shrill call for aid from his fellow warriors.

A loud report made Dela gasp. More than one gun had fired.

Smoke trailed from the muzzle of the Indian's rifle.

Smoke trailed from the muzzle of the colonel's pistol.

And smoke trailed from the muzzle of the borrowed rifle Ichabod Crane had rapidly lifted to his shoulder.

Johnson swayed again in his saddle but did not fall. It was the red-coated man who toppled to the ground. Dela heard running feet and shouting men just before two Indians reached the side of their fallen companion and bent over. Seconds later, the wailing began.

Then the Water Maiden realized Ichabod was no longer beside her. He'd clambered up the hill and was searching the dead Kentuckian frantically. With difficulty, Dela trudged back to join him, finding Ichabod with a salvaged horn, pouring powder into the end of the upturned rifle.

This time, she didn't need to force a smile. It came unbidden. "Ichabod, you need not worry. The battle is nearly won."

He cast her a puzzled look. "What are you saying, Dela? There are enemies all around us."

"Enemies who will lose heart when they realize what has happened," she replied. "Do you not yet realize it?"

Ichabod stared back, confused.

"That Shawnee man you slew at the edge of the marsh? That was Chief Firm Fellow. The other, the chief you shot with the rifle—that was Tecumseh."

Ichabod's jaw dropped.

"They have just lost their two strongest leaders. Without them, the Indians will flee. Without them, the entire confederacy may well fall into disarray and despair."

Another wave of dizziness overcame her. When it passed, she realized Ichabod had not again rushed to her assistance. Instead, the man was kneeling, his lips mouthing a silent prayer.

Dela sighed. "You have proved your mettle beyond your wildest dreams, Ichabod. You may have singlehandedly won your war right here, with no one to witness your heroics."

Ichabod Crane met her gaze calmly, although his cheek seemed wet from something other than sweat.

"I had the only three witnesses that matter: My God. My friend. And myself."

Affection and pride washed over Dela like a warm bath. In spite of her exhaustion, in spite of the lancing pain in her side, she felt strength returning to her limbs and color returning to her pale-blue face.

Dela's relief turned to joy when she saw the first ranks of Isaac Shelby's infantry came into view. Surely any Indians not yet demoralized by the loss of their leaders would now retreat in the face of overwhelming numbers.

Then, in an instant, the warm feeling disappeared. It was replaced by icy needles piercing the top of her head and all the way down her spine. Dela's breath turned to cold mist. She doubled over, the pain of her wound now joined by a crippling, all-consuming hunger.

The Wendigo they'd killed *had* been commanded to charge the Americans from the marsh. But not to do so alone.

Dela lifted her head and saw a pair of sunken eyes in the forest. They glowed a sickly yellow. She saw a second pair. A third.

A long, ash-gray leg appeared between two trees. A few paces away, sharp claws sliced through a heavy limb as if it were a rotten stick. The entire tree line were quivering, as if countless Wendigos were pushing massive boughs aside to emerge from the marsh.

Dela was but a single ranger, weakened and bleeding. There was no hope of victory. There was only the promise of noble defeat— fighting for a just cause. Fighting to save lives. Fighting to save her friends.

"Get to Isaac," she murmured to Ichabod. "Tell him to pull back. Tell him . . . save the men."

Without waiting for a response, Dela willed her legs to run. It wasn't so much a run, actually, as a controlled stumble, but it propelled the Water Maiden up the slope and into the face of the hungry horde.

For the last time, each word shaped and caressed by deep emotion, Dela sang her courage song. The spell felt puny in the face of the Wendigos' terror magic, like a stream of water aimed at a raging wind. Still she sang.

The first Wendigo to step entirely out of the forest became Dela's fixation. It towered over her, hissed at her, baited her. She careened in its direction, aiming the blades of her trident upward at its narrow, emaciated chest.

The blades never reached their target. With a mighty sweep of its arm, the Wendigo brushed her trident aside. Dela felt it being jerked unceremoniously from her grasp. Then she felt something else jerk, something inside her. There was, strangely, no new stab of pain. Indeed, she no longer felt the agonizing pain in her side. She no longer felt the fatigue in her aching legs.

As her broken body crumpled painlessly to the ground, Dela no longer felt anything except the icy needles still pricking her ears, cheeks, and neck.

Frozen in position, but not by fear, the Water Maiden looked up at the Wendigo's skeletal face, its twisted horns, its glowing yellow eyes. Then two shots rang out, followed shortly by running feet. Ichabod Crane stepped between her and the Wendigo. A moment later, Isaac Shelby stepped into the gap beside Ichabod.

Dela was tempted to shut her eyes; she didn't want to watch the two humans die at the hands of the Wendigos. Still, she also wanted her last sight on earth to be of her friends.

What her eyes beheld, however, was no massacre. It was crackling sparks, glistening lights. The telltale signs of Shimmer. A burst of wind struck her face.

Still more unexpected images filled her eyes. She saw what appeared to be a Pukwudgie grasp the handle of a spear-thrower with two slim fingers, fit a thick missile in the groove, then hurl it with tremendous force at the face of the nearest Wendigo. She saw more Pukwudgies, armed with stout bows, dip their arrows into troughs of flaming pitch and then loose them at a rampaging ice giant. She saw a tight rank of Folk, bristling with spears and war clubs, advance steadily at two charging monsters.

Most surprising of all, Dela saw a stout, red-skinned ranger confront a Wendigo on her own, turning aside a swat of its claws with a broadsword and crushing its leg with a single blow of her heavy spiked mace.

In just minutes, the battle was over. Nearly a dozen Wendigos lay still, twisted, and charred on the ground. Dela felt Isaac Shelby lift and cradle her in his strong arms. Then a Goblin's face filled Dela's field of vision, regarding her with cold scarlet eyes.

"You have caused a great deal of trouble, Dela of the Gwragedd Annwn."

The Water Maiden wondered if perhaps she were dreaming. The impossibility of what she'd just seen, and the absurdity of Betua's greeting, were equally hard to fathom. Then she felt the corners of her mouth rippling. Such absurdity had only one fit answer. Dela giggled.

Betua arched an eyebrow. Then the Goblin threw her head back, her floppy ears jiggling, and roared with laughter.

Both Isaac's face above her and Ichabod's face, visible beside Betua, wore expressions of utter bewilderment. But Dela didn't care. She joined the Goblin's raucous laughter, though it was odd to laugh while feeling no sensation below her neck.

Betua rapidly explained. It was a war party of Paissa, not Pukwudgies, who'd arrived by magical transport accompanied by Betua, who'd been visiting the Paissa village when reports arrived of a blue-skinned ranger carrying contraband to Tecumseh's army.

"I thought for certain I had finally identified the source of those mysterious weapons," Betua added with a snicker. "We had no idea you were on the side of the Americans until we arrived here and saw you lying here, your back broken, while your American friends rushed forward to defend you."

"The Wendigos," Dela began. "How were they . . . ?"

"Summoned?" Betua finished. She held up a bronze gorget like the one Tenskwatawa had worn at the campfire. At close range, Dela could see spellsong runes inscribed on its shiny surface.

The Goblin beckoned to an approaching Paissa mage.

"The mage can use field magecraft to stabilize your condition, Dela, but you must be taken quickly to a guildhall if your life is to be saved," Betua said.

"To . . . to the Paissa village?" the Water Maiden whispered.

The Goblin shook her head. "The Paissa resent the intrusion of foreign Folk in their territory and the theft of their Wendigo herd. They came here to reassert their authority. But they are no friends of yours—or mine, in truth. They will not reveal the location of their village to you, just as they have made me swear not to reveal its location."

Dela heard Isaac Shelby's low, rumbling voice. "I will take her to her village on the Holston. I can care for her wounds on the way. I've done it before."

Betua gave the heavyset man a long, searching look. "You mean well, human, but you do not understand. There is no time for an overland journey. She requires magic transport. The Paissa will not consume scarce power to send her to some distant river."

"Tell us what must be done!" exclaimed Ichabod Crane.

"There is but one answer," Betua said. "The Paissa will transport her to Detroit. My Folk will care for her."

Dela didn't need to voice her doubt, her suspicion. The Goblin saw it in her eyes.

"You can trust us at least this far. You are not the first foreign ranger I have brought to our mages for healing. In fact, that first patient remains there still, recuperating in their guildhall. Based on what I heard him mumble in his fitful sleep as I bore him across the Blur, you and he are . . . very well acquainted."

Recognition filled the blue-green eyes of the Water Maiden.

Betua chuckled. "Your recovery will not last so long, Dela. Goblins have more experience mending broken backs than broken wings."

Chapter 18 – The Oath

October 1813

In his time, Har the Tower had encountered many different kinds of people. He'd trained with burly, sour-faced Dwarfs and squabbled with skinny, sour-faced Lutki. He'd befriended a philosophical Sylph, an empathic Water Maiden, an Elf prince with the dark-stained hands of a smith, and a brilliant Nunnehi scout as adept at soothing a crying child as she was at taking down a monster with song and blowgun.

Among humans, Har had also met all kinds: fearful farmers and brave soldiers, maids and mothers, masters and slaves, heroes and villains. He'd fished with Peter Muhlenberg, hunted with George Washington, saved the life of Thomas Jefferson, and fought alongside Alexander Hamilton.

But as he lay on a small hill overlooking the Elk River and watched the Tennesseans milling around their militia camp, it occurred to Har that he'd never had a traveling companion quite like the one sprawled next to him in the high grass.

She was curious and cunning, free-spirited and sarcastic. She had proved to be an expert archer, an impressive tracker, and, frequently, loudly bored. Roza said precisely what she thought and did exactly what she pleased.

Har couldn't stand her.

▲▲▲

After Har's last meeting at Grünerberg, where he'd learned of the existence of the gifts of power, he'd journeyed to Spirit Forest to deliver King Alberich's accusation that Elves were behind the plot to supply the enemies of America with enchanted weapons.

Prince Veelund had snorted dismissively. "We have too many problems of our own to concern ourselves with the imperial designs of some human kingdom over the sea. Do your Dwarfs not see that truth plainly?"

Har sighed. "Some do. Our king does not."

Veelund turned away, seemingly lost in thought as he strolled past the colorful tapestries that decorated his audience chamber. Then the prince stopped in front of the water clock in the corner. Har could hear a gentle trickle, the soft whirring of wheels, the metallic clanking of gears.

"This quarrelsome Alberich of yours," the Elf prince began. "Do you think he would consent to a face-to-face meeting?"

It was an intriguing question. On the one hand, Alberich was supremely confident in his ability to size up his opponents and drive hard bargains. On the other hand, Alberich would be loath to allow an Elf lord to visit Grünerberg. Emissaries, the king could tolerate, if carefully monitored. But a visiting lord would inevitably arrive with an entourage. Alberich wouldn't risk allowing Elves to wander his colony, assessing its resources and defenses.

"Prince Veelund," Har began with trepidation, "your idea has merit. I admire the impulse. But I do not think King Alberich will consent to a visit to Grünerberg."

The Elf turned and smiled. "You misunderstand me. I have no intention of going there. Would Alberich consent to visit *me* here at Spirit Forest? He could even march here through the Blur if he wanted to spare the magecraft and stretch his legs. Is he not a ranger like yourself?"

A ranger, yes. But he and I have little in common.

"Your invitation may appeal to Alberich," Har agreed. "But he will want to hear it from me in person, not by message spell."

"Off with you, then," Veelund said with an amused wave of his soot-stained hand.

Har fidgeted. "Prince, I cannot return directly to Grünerberg. My mission requires I first range west, among the Cherokees and Creeks, looking for gifts of power and clues to their supplier."

With a practiced finger, Veelund traced the outline of the craftsman sigil embroidered on his surcoat. "A worthy mission—and I, too, would be interested in any clues you can find. After all, the true conquests, the only ones that cause no regret, are those made over ignorance. Please allow us to offer whatever assistance you may require."

Har gratefully accepted.

"Indeed, our assistance will go beyond provisions, Har. A ranger from Spirit Creek will accompany you on your quest."

This time, Har's response was more hesitant. He preferred to choose his own ranging companions.

"My friend, I really must insist," Veelund said. "After all, four eyes see more than two. And if you run into trouble, four arms are stronger than two."

Diplomatic considerations, not the prince's argument, ultimately convinced Har to accept the offer. He'd regretted it, though, as soon as he saw the ranger Veelund selected: Roza, the very bow-wielding Elf ranger who'd accosted Har on his first visit to Spirit Forest.

▲▲▲

And Har had regretted the choice every day since.

"Tell me again why we journeyed so far," Roza demanded as she turned on her side, basking in the early morning sun and twisting a lock of nut-brown hair around her finger. "What could these humans possibly tell us about enchanted weapons?"

We had to come all the way here because of you! Har wanted to shout. *Because I could not show up at Blood Mountain with an Elf and hope to get anything but icy stares from the Nunnehi.*

Instead, Har forced a smile to his lips. "It is someone else I hope to find, not the Tennesseans, who may be able to help us."

"That is what you say, peddler man," said the Elf, reusing the insult she'd coined during their first encounter at Spirit Forest. "But I think you lengthened our journey because you enjoy my company."

"You are a fine traveling companion," replied Har, meaning not a word of it.

The two crawled closer, peering through the canebrake at the camp. From snatches of human conversation, Har had learned that the general in charge of the Tennesseans gathering at Fayetteville was Andrew Jackson, a native Carolinian who'd crossed the mountains as a young man, settled in Nashville, and later represented Tennessee in Congress.

Har knew the man only by reputation. The Dwarf's friend John Sevier, current congressman and former governor, had repeatedly tangled with Andrew Jackson. The two Tennesseans had even come close to dueling each other. But Har resolved not to prejudge Andrew Jackson as especially hot-tempered.

After all, I do know John Sevier.

The Tennesseans were about to march south against a faction of Creek Indians who'd attacked American settlements in the Mississippi

Territory. Warriors led by Red Eagle and other rebellious chiefs had overrun a settlement called Fort Mims. Hundreds of whites and friendly Creeks had been savagely killed, including women, children, and unarmed men. Because the "Red Sticks," as the Creek faction called themselves, were supplied by British agents, the Americans saw the conflict along the southeastern frontier as yet another theater in the war that began in 1812. Thus, thousands were mobilizing in Georgia and Tennessee to avenge the fallen of Fort Mims.

They were hardly the only ones mobilizing. While Tecumseh, who led the Indian Confederacy on the northwest frontier, had succeeded in persuading the Red Stick faction to go to war, it was opposed by the Creek National Council. Other Indian nations of the region also sided with the Americans. Some of their warriors had already joined up with General Jackson's forces at Fayetteville.

Which is why Har had come here, looking for a friend.

Snap!

At the sound of a stick breaking underfoot. Roza lifted her bitternut-hickory bow and reached for an arrow. Har's hand shot to the handaxe at his hip.

"Hold it, you two!" said a firm voice with a distinctive twang. "Gotcha in my sights."

The Dwarf and the Elf gave the same reply at the same time: They started singing a concealment spell.

"That's right pretty, but I ain't interested in music just now," said the voice. "Put your weapons down and don't move a muscle. I can shoot the whisker off a squirrel at a hundred paces, so don't think I can't shave that beard of yours clean and then some, little man."

Har shot Roza a warning glance. "This is a Sighted human with a firearm trained on us. Best do as he says."

The Elf looked murderous but did not argue the point. She dropped her bow.

The Dwarf saw movement to his left. The muzzle of a hunting rifle emerged slowly from the canebrake, followed a moment later by its owner.

He was tall, stoutly built, and clad in the standard dress of the frontiersman: a hunting shirt, leggings, and moccasins of buckskin. Except for the man's dark eyes and the raccoon-fur cap on his head, his appearance greatly reminded Har of Daniel Boone. Both had the sharp gaze and stealthy gait of an experienced hunter. And both had full faces better suited to bouts of laughter than of anger.

236

This human wasn't laughing. "That's better. No more sneakin' and crawlin'. Best to stand tall when you meet someone new, or what passes for standin' tall among you lot."

"I assure you, sir, that my companion and I—"

"That's mighty formal talkin' for the likes of me," the frontiersman interrupted. "But Betsy does tend to make folks mannerly."

Roza looked around in puzzlement. "Betsy?"

The man waved his rifle. "I always name 'em Betsy. The one I learned to shoot with was my first love. Named her Beautiful Betsy. This one—well, right now I'm callin' her Hungry Betsy. Been keepin' her busy down round Huntsville way, what with Colonel Coffee's men—"

"Make no sudden move, Long Knife," said a new, deep voice from the other side of the small hill. "Put down your gun, slowly."

Har recognized the voice instantly, breathing a sigh of relief. The man in the coonskin cap exhaled a big breath of his own, presumably to steady himself, then placed "Betsy" gently in the tall grass. As for Roza, the still-puzzled Elf's intake of breath looked like the harbinger of something explosively loud. Har decided to head it off by speaking first.

"Gulkalaski!" he exclaimed as the Cherokee man strode into view. "Just the man I came to find."

"It seems I found you, Har the Tower, and just in time."

The frontiersman smiled broadly. "Thought *I* was king of the canebrake, but you've gone and knocked that crown clean off my head!"

It was at this point that Roza's patience ran out. "Will someone tell me what is happening here?! Are we captives? Which one do I need to kill?"

Both humans stared open-mouthed at the Elf ranger as she furiously stamped the ground with her leather turnshoes. Har put up a warning hand.

"We will not be killing anyone, Roza," he said quickly. "This is the human whose farm we visited back in the Carolina mountains. Gulkalaski, your wife revealed under spellsong that you had gone off to fight the Creeks. We guessed you would come to General Jackson's camp, as other Cherokee volunteers have done. We came to ask for your help."

The white human snorted. "Well, we're on the same side, then! I'm used to your sort comin' round to trick people out of their corn and pots and the like. Not used to Wee Folk being helpful."

Gulkalaski looked questioningly as Har. The Dwarf responded with a short nod. The Cherokee lowered his rifle warily.

"Name's Crockett," said the frontiersman. "David Crockett. Got a farm east of here, near Winchester. When I heard about Fort Mims, I joined up with the volunteers. Been down in the Mississippi Territory with John Coffee, huntin' and scoutin'. Then Colonel Coffee sent me with a message for General Jackson. Best go deliver it."

Crockett had accompanied his last line with the same questioning look Gulkalaski had shot at Har. The Dwarf responded the same way, and soon the four were trudging through the high grass toward the tree where Crockett had left his horse tethered.

Har welcomed the opportunity to catch up with Gulkalaski, whom he'd not visited for many Blur years. The Cherokee, his wife, and his sisters-in-law were still farming and raising cattle on Alarka Creek. Gulkalaski spoke of his occasional trips over the mountains to his friend Sequoyah's store in Tuskegee and the talk he'd heard there of a pan-Indian alliance against the United States. When Gulkalaski heard the Red Sticks were on the warpath, he'd set off to offer his services as hunter and scout to whomever would fight the Red Sticks.

"Did the same thing," Crockett chimed in. "My dander was up, and nothing but war would set it right again. But it was whites and Creeks massacred at Fort Mims. You're Cherokee. Why'd you volunteer?"

Gulkalaski looked at Har and raised an eyebrow. The Dwarf shrugged, hoping the Cherokee would take his meaning. *I do not know this Crockett, but he is a Sighted human fighting for the American cause. It likely will do no harm for him to hear.*

So Gulkalaski talked of the Folk ranger who had visited Sequoyah's town in the guise of a Great Wolf, of Gulkalaski's battle with the giant Uktena serpent, and Tecumseh's talk about "gifts of the Great Spirit" and the red war club Tecumseh had pointed at him, seemingly ineffectually, at Soco Gap.

Har halted, his body trembling with excitement. "This is precisely why I came looking for you, Gulkalaski—my mission to track down those gifts of power and trace them to their source. Did Tecumseh describe who gave the weapons to his brother?"

The other three halted as well. Gulkalaski shook his head. "I assumed the messengers visiting Tecumseh's people pretended to be spirit animals, like the one I saw. He said nothing to the contrary."

"You *assume* a great deal, I think," said Roza, looking at the Cherokee through half-lidded eyes. "You assume the ranger you chased has something to do the gifts. And you, Har—you assume the same Folk are supplying both Tecumseh's people and these Red Stick Creeks. There may be no connection. Dwarfs always jump to conclusions and end up flat on your faces."

The frontiersman had watched the exchange with a mixture of disbelief and fascination on his stubbly face. Now he grabbed the coonskin cap off his head and swatted it against his thigh with a delighted whoop.

"You reckoned wrong, little lady," Crockett said, provoking a resentful glare from Roza. "One thing we know for sure is that Tecumseh feller and them Creeks got the same supplier."

Har and Gulkalaski exchanged quick glances. "The Red Sticks!" they exclaimed simultaneously.

Crockett nodded. "Heard in camp that the rebels named themselves 'Red Sticks' after Creek war clubs. Even heard they passed out different-sized bundles of clubs to different towns and had their chiefs toss one out every day so they'd know when to attack. Maybe so. But I figure at least some of them sticks are magic wands or somethin', like you say."

"Like the one Tecumseh pointed at me," Gulkalaski said slowly. "But it did me no harm."

Har the Tower cocked an eyebrow. "It could be that the weapon's enchantment was depleted by frequent use. Or it casts a spell that a human with the Sight can easily resist."

When they reached the camp, Gulkalaski went off to find the other Indian volunteers. The two fairies followed Crockett to the headquarters of Andrew Jackson.

The Tennesseans called the general "Hickory," Har recalled, and at first glance the nickname suited the man. Jackson was tall and thin, his face rough and weathered like tree bark. He looked older than his forty-six years, his reddish hair showing streaks of gray above a pronounced widow's peak. But his dour expression, stiff posture, and steely eyes marked Jackson as tougher and more immovable than his seemingly lean frame suggested.

239

"A message," Crockett told the general. "Red Sticks are on the march. Headed up to the Tennessee River with enough men to threaten Colonel Coffee's position."

Jackson thumped a nearby table. "Coffee won't face 'em alone. How far is his camp?"

"Near on thirty miles," Crocket replied.

The general nodded to his other officers. "We'll get there by midnight."

Har had seen enough to doubt Jackson's confident prediction. Many of the men in camp looked young, nervous, and ill-equipped. Marching them rapidly across wild country, and perhaps right into battle, seemed improbable and risky. The Dwarf could tell Crockett shared his skepticism. While Jackson began issuing orders, the frontiersman leaned on his rifle, a dubious expression on his face.

When Har turned his eyes from Crockett to Roza, he saw a very different expression. She looked delighted. "Finally, something interesting!" she exclaimed. "I want to see some of those 'gifts of power' in action!"

"What?" Har said, horrified. "You want to see magic used against the Americans?"

The Elf's eyes narrowed into slits. After a few moments, however, her face unclenched. "I do not mean *that*, exactly. I am merely curious about the weapons. Surely we can keep them from doing any real harm."

The Dwarf wasn't satisfied. "We do not even know what these enchanted red sticks are or what they can do. I prefer not to find out in the field, with lives at stake."

Roza shrugged and said nothing more.

How could she say such a thing? he thought. *Is she that bored—or that bloodthirsty? Or have she and Prince Veelund been fooling me all along?*

As Crockett turned to leave, Har motioned to Roza and scrambled to follow. *A Red Stick attack might useful after all. It might be just the test to reveal her true intentions.*

▲▲▲

As it turned out, Andrew Jackson knew his Tennesseans well. Within the hour his army had broken camp and begun their rapid march south.

David Crockett rode ahead with the other scouts. To Har's surprise, Roza had asked to go with him—and even more surprisingly,

Crockett had consented. As the two galloped off on Crockett's horse, Har felt a sense of foreboding. If Roza wished the Americans harm, interfering with the army's scouts might advance her ends. She could use spellsong to lead Jackson's men into an ambush. As for Crockett, his Sight might protect him from her magic, but Har had no idea if the man could handle himself in a fight. Roza might put two arrows into the rangy frontiersman before he could even raise his rifle or draw his knife.

Despite Har's worries, he chose not to stop her. Nor did he accompany her. The main column of Tennesseans might need his help. And Gulkalaski, who'd arrived without a mount, hadn't been assigned to ride forward with the other scouts. Har saw the march as an opportunity to learn more about the Cherokee reaction to the war.

"Some of my people agree with Tecumseh, and with Creeks like Red Eagle," Gulkalaski admitted as the two walked a little ahead of the column. "Some were fooled by those Folk messengers I spoke of. Others came to their own conclusions. They believe the time to strike is now. A few have left their farms and towns to join Tecumseh's alliance, or even the Red Sticks."

Har shook his head. "What do they hope to gain?"

"Independence. The freedom to live as they choose on their own lands. For our own reasons, many Cherokee have adopted new ways. We farm. We make our own tools. Our women spin and weave. Even so, will the whites leave us alone? If they do, we will gladly live in peace. If they do not, we must fight for what is ours."

The Dwarf studied his friend. "You sound convinced of the need for war yourself."

The Cherokee's eyes burning with intensity. "No. My people have fought the whites before—fought and lost. I am willing to fight again if need be, but that time has not come. Tecumseh and Red Eagle and the others will bring only death and destruction. Besides, giving chiefs more power is not the answer. Who signs unfair treaties? Who gains by selling hunting grounds they do not hunt and farms they do not farm?"

This man sees through more than spellsong, Har reflected. *And the problem of poor leadership are hardly confined to humans. For every Queen Virginal, there is at least one King Alberich.*

"I do not trust them," Gulkalaski continued. "Tecumseh is a Shawnee. Red Eagle is a Creek. For generations, we have warred with Shawnees and Creeks. These chiefs talk of brotherhood now, but what

241

they truly seek is domination. You can tell by the friends they choose. Their British suppliers care nothing for Indian people. Neither do the Folk who fool them with magic tricks and arm them with magic weapons."

▲▲▲

It took Jackson's army only ten hours to reach the settlement of Huntsville. There, they met up with John Coffee's mounted volunteers—and learned that there were no Red Sticks nearby. The report Crockett had carried to Jackson proved to be wrong.

"It served a good purpose, anyway," Har heard Jackson tell Colonel Coffee, a heavyset man with a disheveled uniform and an amiable face. "We are now gathered in force."

"We can get at the Red Sticks before winter comes," Coffee agreed. "And before our men's enlistments run out."

Har could see Jackson's jaw muscles clench. "The men will defeat their country's enemies, Coffee, and then go home—in that order."

Over the next couple of weeks, Har the Tower saw little of Roza or any of his human friends. While the army started building a base, Fort Strother, on the Coosa River, Coffee's mounted troops foraged for food and chased small bands of Red Sticks. Crockett and Gulkalaski went with them, applying their skills as hunters to the army's overwhelming need for food. Roza went along as well, saying she preferred the privations of the trail to the boredom of camp life.

Much as he longed to accompany them, Har stayed behind to learn more about Andrew Jackson. He found the general to be a stubborn but realistic man who knew his supplies were limited and his men wouldn't remain indefinitely. One afternoon Har witnessed a telling incident. When a hungry man saw Jackson in camp, chewing with his mouth full, the trooper demanded angrily that the general share whatever food he'd been hoarding.

"Certainly," Jackson replied, reaching into his pocket and offering the man a handful of acorns. The trooper walked away, chagrined but still looking desperate.

The army's appetite became even more insatiable when a new group of Cherokee volunteers arrived. One brought word of Red Sticks at Tallushatchee, a Creek town some fifteen miles away. Jackson acted quickly, sending the Cherokee scout on to Coffee with orders to attack the town. This time, Har knew his proper place wasn't in camp. Fortunately, the scout rode from camp with an extra horse in tow. The man never saw the beefy, four-foot-tall Dwarf sitting uncomfortably on its back.

The first person who did was Roza, sitting in a tree when the Cherokee and his magically concealed companion, the latter reeling awkwardly on the horse's back, rode into Colonel Coffee's camp. The Elf's greeting consisted of doubling over in laughter.

"The Tower totters!" she said between giggles. "But will it fall and shake the earth?"

Crockett ran up to slap Har on the back. "What's the news?"

"Not good," said the Dwarf, shaking his head. "The promised supplies never arrived from upriver. Jackson's food is almost gone."

Gulkalaski joined them, a satisfied grin on his face. "The news is not bad at all. I hear we are off to attack the Red Sticks. We will win a great victory."

Roza snorted. "I have seen what passes for victory here. Coffee and his men catch a couple of enemy scouts, they run off with corn from an enemy farm. This is no army. It is a raiding party with an empty stomach—and no stomach for real fighting."

Crockett rubbed his face with a grimy hand. "I'd sooner bring these Red Sticks to heel by raidin' instead of killin'. We're volunteers, little lady—farmers and trappers and shopkeepers doin' their duty. Not soldiers in blue coats and fancy hats."

"*Not* soldiers—that much is clear," Roza agreed. "Have you ever taken a life in battle, Davy?"

Crockett shook his head ruefully. "Should never have told you about that 'Davy' business. Got to keep callin' me that, do you?"

"As long as you keep calling me 'little lady.' "

Gulkalaski thumped the butt of his spear on the ground. "Stalking their forests and taking their corn will not make the Creeks give up. Only fear of death will. That is why I have come. I have sworn an oath to the Maker of All Things never to rest until we have killed the Red Stick chiefs and all who follow them."

There was a long silence. Har was troubled. He knew Gulkalaski to be brave and resourceful, but he hadn't expected such ferocity. Crockett looked taken aback as well. The Tennessean was staring with wide eyes at the long bronze blade at the end of Gulkalaski's spear.

By contrast, Roza looked exuberant. "Finally, a human who understands the true nature of war."

Her comment stabbed Har in a tender spot. *I understand the true nature of war. It may be necessary, but taking pleasure in it is not.* He felt his control disappear. He felt hot anger come to the surface, like blood from a wound.

"How many lives have *you* taken in battle, Elf?" Har snapped. "Too many to count?"

He expected a sharp-tongued insult in response. It didn't come. Instead, Roza shrugged. "I would say thirty, though I may have slain more from afar. As a ranger of the Black Forest, I fought in the wars with your Lord Alberich's Rhineland horde. I spied on Dwarfs. I baited them into ambushes. I sliced my blade across their necks and shot my arrows into their chests. Here in America, I scouted the fortress on Blood Mountain and helped prepare our assault. With my own hands I slew three Nunnehi warriors. I would do it again if my prince commanded it."

With a start, Har realized that it was likely *he*, not the Elf ranger, who'd killed more foes than he'd bothered to count.

"I hear your unspoken question, Dwarf, though you lack the courage to ask it," she continued. "If my prince commanded it, would I battle the Nunnehi again? Or your Dwarfs of Grünerberg? The answer is yes. But Veelund will not give that command. Joining with the Great Alliance during the first American war brought our colony nothing but defeat and ruin. Veelund will not make such an error. He is too wise."

▲▲▲

With Roza at his side, Har the Tower peered through the trees at Tallushatchee and judged it an unlikely site for the grand military victory Gulkalaski envisioned. The town was a small collection of houses built of earth-and-rivercane walls and roofed in thatch. The Creek inhabitants looked no better provisioned than the hungry Tennesseans and Cherokees about to attack them. Colonel Coffee had divided his nine hundred men into two columns, each approaching from a different direction. A third group of riders waited only a few dozen paces from where the two fairies crouched in the tall grass.

"This Coffee is more skilled at war than I thought," Roza said.

Har cocked his head, not catching her meaning.

"You just watch and see," she added with an appreciative chuckle.

A moment later, the riders took off in the direction of Tallushatchee, yelling and firing guns and kicking up a cloud of dirt. Har heard an answering chorus of whoops, gunshots, and whistling arrows from the defenders. Then he looked at the hundreds of Tennesseans who'd who formed a circle around the town.

If the scouts were meant to draw the first volley, the other militiamen should be rushing in behind them to attack before the Creeks can reload, Har thought.

But they were not. Some of Coffee's men were still on their horses. Others were dismounted. All stayed well away from the town. Then Har saw the surviving American scouts emerging from the dirt clouds they'd thrown up during their charge. Behind them, shouting taunts and brandishing weapons, followed dozens of Creek warriors, their hair bound in colored cloth and pierced with feathers, their faces painted for war.

From Har's right, hundreds of American rifles barked their own vengeful taunts at the pursuing Creeks. Nearly as many bullets repainted the Creeks' faces, breasts, arms, and legs in shades of red.

Here and there, a few militiamen pitched forward with holes or arrows in their bodies. But by far the greater losses were among the Creeks who'd been baited out of cover into a deadly circle of crackshot Tennesseans. The warriors fled, running or limping or crawling back into the town. This time, Coffee's army eagerly pursued.

Har saw Gulkalaski among the pursuers, riding with other Indian allies who wore white feathers or deer tails in their hair to distinguish them from the Red Sticks. Har also saw Crockett, smoke trailing from his long rifle, heading into Tallushatchee with an uncharacteristically grim expression on his ruddy face.

Roza stood up. "Come on, Dwarf! We will see nothing more from here!"

Har hesitated. He hadn't just come to watch a battle; he'd come to stop enchanted weapons or spellsong from being used against the Americans. So far, he'd witnessed neither. Would magic-wielding attackers come from the sheltering forest, just as the Tennesseans had used its shelter to encircle the Creeks? Or did the greater threat lie inside Tallushatchee?

The latter, he decided—but by then Roza had already disappeared behind a wall. Sighing, Har the Tower jogged after her.

Within the town, the narrow trails between the houses quickly filled with triumphant militiamen and dead or dying Creeks. A mass of Indian women and children came tumbling out of several small houses and ran toward Colonel Coffee, holding their hands up and asking for succor in both broken English and their native tongue. Several dismounted Tennesseans lowered their guns and stepped forward to conduct the prisoners to the rear—only to be fall to the ground, wounded or seeking cover, as three Creek men leapt from behind the mass of women and children, loosing arrows and drawing their tomahawks.

"Look out!" Har shouted, forgetting that his voice was masked by spellsong.

His mouth stayed open in horror as the Tennesseans responded with deadly fire. The three Creek warriors were torn apart. But several women and children also stumbled and dropped in the rain of bullets, some screaming in agony, others silenced forever.

Roza appeared at Har's side and pointed to a sizable house near the center of town. "There, Dwarf. They will make their final stand there."

Several warriors retreated to the house. A single Creek woman was sitting in front, propped against the wall. As she thrust open the door with her foot to let them inside, Har could see dozens more crammed inside.

"Surrender!" shouted a militia captain.

"Surrender or be destroyed!" yelled a volunteer, his gun held high.

"Surrender, for God's sake," muttered David Crockett as he walked past Har, pushing his powder horn away and raising his freshly loaded rifle.

Two more warriors fled into the house. The Creek woman near its door was moving around in the dirt, bent at an odd angle.

Was she hit? Har wondered. *Or is she trying to get to . . .*

Then he saw more clearly the bent shape between her legs—even as the woman loosed an arrow from her foot bow with a satisfied grunt.

Its force knocked the foremost Tennessean back several feet. He lay doubled over, the arrow sunk deep in his groin.

The blast of a dozen guns made Har cup his ears. The Creek woman lay spread-eagled and lifeless. A few feet away, Crockett stood with his rifle smoking, transfixed by the sight.

Ears still ringing, Har looked around to see how the rest of the battle was going. It wasn't. The Creeks were no longer putting up a struggle; Tennesseans were leading prisoners away and searching houses. A militiaman emerged from a small lean-to, shaking his head. "No corn!"

"Only a few ears over here," said another.

"Bet I know where all the food is," said a third Tennessean, his shirt sleeve ripped off and his arm exhibiting a knife wound. He used his good arm to point at the house in the center of town. "They got it all in there."

"Let's burn the dogs out!" cried the first man, running to an abandoned campfire and thrusting a stick into the embers.

"Burn 'em out!" other Tennesseans chanted.

An officer tried calling into the house, demanding that the remaining Red Sticks surrender. He got no response, and then was bowled aside as nearly a dozen militiamen ran up to the house and tossed burning sticks on its walls and thatched roof. Within minutes, the structure was engulfed in fire.

Har turned away, sickened not just at the sight of the flames but at the sounds and smells they produced from inside the house. He saw Crockett standing in the same place as before, his rifle dropped to the ground, his sooty face streaked with what Har initially assumed was sweat but then realized might be something else.

"Why ain't they givin' up?" he said. "What's the point of this?"

"They expect no quarter," said Gulkalaski, appearing next to the frontiersman. "They will fight or die. It is the way."

"It's a damned fool way," Crockett said.

The four stood there for a time, watching the house burn. Then Crockett turned to Har. "Tell me true. Ain't there Wee Folk around here somewhere, bewitchin' the Creeks so they won't give up?"

Har shook his head. "I have listened for spellsong since the battle began. I hear none."

"Nor do I," said Roza. "Your question is misinformed. You humans need no magical manipulation to kill each other. Anger, greed, desperation—your passions are all the prodding you need."

Gulkalaski cleared his throat. "You speak as though only humans feel these things. I know better. I know of war as your Folk nations wage it. I have seen the scars of its survivors."

Har again felt the pain of something sharp jabbing his heart. *Not all such scars can be seen, even by a human with Sight.*

▲▲▲

On November 7, just two days after Colonel Coffee's riders rejoined Andrew Jackson's army on the Coosa, a Creek youth arrived at Fort Strother, looking desperate and exhausted. Har followed as the boy was brought to the general's tent.

"My father, Chief Chinnabee, declared our loyalty to the National Council," said the tired youth between gasping breaths. "Now Red Sticks have our people surrounded. Red Eagle says all will die unless we swear to wage war on you."

"I won't let that happen," said Jackson, eyes blazing.

Har hurried to where the Cherokee scouts were camped. He found Gulkalaski and Crockett standing off to the side talking to Roza, who was smiling and waving her hands. *The word is already out*, Har realized.

"Jackson will have the numbers and the guns," Gulkalaski said. "Red Eagle will fall. With my own hand, I will make sure he never rises again in this life."

Crockett shook his head. "We ain't creepin' up on em' like at Tallushatchee. Red Eagle knows we're comin'. And he's got a thousand warriors with no women and children to defend. I hope the general knows what he's doin'."

"He knows that if he does not take decisive action now, winter will shrink and scatter your army," Har said. "But he does not know all that he faces. The Creek chief will surely have magical assistance the Creeks of Tallushatchee did not."

Roza shrugged. "And Jackson will have you and me. I tire of sitting and watching. And it has been too long since I have seen a Dwarf in combat. Do you not long to display your skill, Tower?"

"I long only to find one of those enchanted clubs," Har remarked, "and trace it back to its source."

It took two days for the army—1,200 infantry and 800 of Coffee's mounted men—to make it the twenty-five miles down the Coosa to the outskirts of Talladega, where Chief Chinnabee's people were holed up in a small stockade built next to a stream.

Jackson organized his infantry in three lines. Just before dawn on November 9, they advanced slowly through the forest toward Red Eagle's camp. On both wings, mounted volunteers rode forward in long columns, planning to join up on the other side of the fort and close the circle on the Red Sticks besieging the stockade.

Crockett's regiment and the Cherokee scouts rode together on the right flank, allowing the Folk rangers to stay close to their human companions—Roza seated on Crockett's horse, Har on Gulkalaski's. While the column advanced, Har spotted half a dozen Red Stick bowmen, faces painted in streaks of red and black. They loosed not a single arrow. Instead, the stealthy warriors melted into the trees, probably hoping some of the mounted volunteers would dismount and give chase. But the Tennesseans kept to their task, successfully closing their circle and causing the friendly Creeks in the stockade to shout in appreciation.

Then, just as Coffee had done at Tallushatchee, Jackson sent a vanguard of Tennesseans straight at Red Eagle's camp, hoping to provoke a reckless response. "Press in, boys," an officer ordered. The circle began to contract.

Then Har heard a new, unexpected sound. Not rifles firing. Not humans yelling, grunting, or dying. It was a loud cracking noise, followed by a thump of something heavy hitting the leafy floor of the forest.

Had a tree blown over? The wind was calm. Har couldn't imagine how either Jackson's Tennesseans or their Creek foes could fell a tree in the middle of a pitched battle. It *could* be done by a Folk mage, however.

Or a human with a magecrafted weapon.

Before Har could as much as whisper to Gulkalaski, the Cherokee man had already yanked his reins and dug his heels into the flanks of his mount. They raced along the battle line, followed closely by Crockett and Roza.

There was a second cracking sound, like someone breaking a gigantic carrot in half.

"It is what we have feared all along!" Har said.

"Not all of us," Gulkalaski corrected him. "It is what I have *hoped* for all along. Who else would have a magic weapon but a chief? He will find me no easy prey." The Cherokee pulled his gift spear from leather thongs tied to his saddle. Its bronze blade caught a ray of the sunrise and flashed a reddish brown.

When the four friends passed the last mounted trooper, they discovered a rapidly expanding hole in the American line where militiamen were backing away from the fight. Red Stick warriors were streaming into the breech, some charging the panicking Americans, others slipping into the sheltering woods.

"They're gettin' away!" cried Crockett.

"That is the reason!" added Roza, pointing across a small meadow.

There were two swaths of green, orange, yellow, and brown stretched across the ground near the retreating Tennesseans. They were stout oak trees, but they hadn't been uprooted. Two stumps were clearly visible a few feet away. Something had snapped, not chopped, the trees about five feet up from the ground.

Standing next to the fallen oaks, and looking no less stout himself, was a bare-chested Creek dressed in a kilt of multicolored cloth hanging low over buckskin leggings. He wore metallic bands at his wrists and ankles, a tuft of reddish-gray feathers in his dark hair, and a fringed mantle of fur around his neck. In one hand was a rifle; in the other was a two-foot-long war club made from a single piece of hardwood, inlaid with shiny stones and painted crimson except for its knobby tip.

"Red Stick!" Gulkalaski leapt from the horse, spear in hand, and dodged a couple of warriors making a mad dash for the woods. "Face me, chief of the Creeks!"

The kilted man smiled and slipped into a fighting stance, his war club lifted high. "I am called Red Eagle, Cherokee man—or William Waterford by my Scot relations. But I do carry a red stick. You would be wise not to come too close."

"I will come only close enough to take your magic weapon from your dead hand," rejoined Gulkalaski, twirling his gift spear.

The glint of its bronze tip wasn't lost on Red Eagle. His eyes narrowed. Then his mouth puckered in admiration.

"The spirits have favored you with a gift as well, I see. Why do you ride with the Americans? Have you not joined our confederacy? Do you not share Tecumseh's dream?"

Gulkalaski grunted. "I see his dream for what is truly is: a nightmare for the easily fooled. I told Tecumseh this myself and sent him away. To you, I will not be so merciful."

Red Eagle's eyes flashed. "You call me a fool? You, who serve your American masters and dare to challenge me with nothing but arrogant words and a puny spear?"

Har had scrambled from the horse and circled to the left, looking for any other club-wielding chiefs or Folk rangers. The Creek chief paid the Dwarf no mind, either failing to pierce his concealment spell or deeming him the lesser threat. Har glanced behind him and saw Crockett swinging his rifle at a Creek warrior. There was no sign of Roza.

"Do not be rash, Gulkalaski," Har advised. "We do not know what that weapon can do."

But the Cherokee man had already responded to Red Eagle's provocation by leaping at the chief, the tip of his spear aimed squarely at the man's broad chest.

Sweeping his rifle across his body with his left hand, Red Eagle knocked Gulkalaski's spear aside. With his right, the chief swung his war club at the Cherokee's unprotected skull.

At the last possible moment, Gulkalaski's head suddenly jerked down, as if an unseen hand had grabbed the cat-claw necklace at his throat and yanked. The thick, fire-hardened knob of the club missed by inches. The momentum of his swing threw Red Eagle off-balance, his club striking the hard ground near Gulkalaski's right foot.

There was a flash of sparks. The ground trembled as both Red Eagle and Gulkalaski were knocked to the ground. The tremor was so forceful that even Har the Tower, standing many paces away, nearly lost his own footing.

The red club had, indeed, been expertly magecrafted, with enough elemental magic to increase its mass and density many times. "Back away, Gulkalaski," Har warned. "This is a weapon beyond your power to face alone."

"He will not have to," said another voice. The figure of Roza the Elf appeared from behind one of the felled trees, holding a nocked arrow at her chin. Before Har could object, she loosed it.

Although Red Eagle didn't appear to be able to hear the fairies' voices, some sixth sense must have warned him. The Creek chief rolled to one side, Roza's arrow burying itself in the ground. Red Eagle looked down at the quivering arrow and rose quickly to his feet, waving a fist at his fellow Creeks still pouring through the gap in the American line.

"Can you not tell friend from foe?" he bellowed at them. Then he eyed Gulkalaski regaining his own feet. "You will not divert me, Cherokee. I have more fit targets for my red stick than your soft head."

Gulkalaski laughed. "I can think of no better target than yours for my blade."

Har whipped out one of his handaxes. Although he would prefer to take Red Eagle alive to question him, the Dwarf would not let his Cherokee friend fall to a blow from a Folk-crafted weapon. He would stop Red Eagle, one way or the other.

Then the chief did something Har did not expect. He turned and sprinted toward the same forest into which his fellow Creeks were escaping. Har heard Roza swear as another of her arrows flew harmlessly through the space Red Eagle had just occupied.

"Running will not save you!" Gulkalaski yelled.

Flight was not Red Eagle's intent, however. After a few steps, he halted in front of another oak, wider and higher than the first two he'd felled, and swung his red stick.

Again Har heard the impossible sound of a solid trunk snapping like a twig. Red Eagle stepped nimbly aside as the tree's enormous mass of branches and foliage began to fall toward his pursuers.

The Dwarf saw Gulkalaski veer off to avoid the falling tree. Then Har's eyes caught sight of Roza, and his heart skipped a beat.

She wasn't running—she'd bent to pick up a dropped arrow. There was a thick branch falling straight for her back.

"Roza!" Har shouted in warning.

But that's not all he did. Har lurched forward, his speed surprising even himself as he closed the distance. Reaching Roza's side, he drove his hand roughly between her shoulder blades, pounding her to the ground. Then Har the Tower gritted his teeth, braced himself, and took the full force of the branch on his broad back.

Crack!

Was that the branch or my spine?

An explosion of pain made it hard to tell. The force of the blow drove him to his knees. Har opened his eyes and saw Roza slithering out from under him. Wincing, the Dwarf rose slowly to his feet, discovering with relief that no bones were broken.

"Are you injured?" asked Gulkalaski, stepping over several branches to reach his side.

Har shook his head. He was only dazed, and the ache in his back was already starting to recede.

"You . . . you took a blow meant for me," stammered Roza, her eyes wide in astonishment. "You are truly a Tower."

The Dwarf forced himself to grin. "You are a fine traveling companion, as I said. I simply do not wish to continue my journey alone."

The sound of running feet made Har and the others look over their shoulders. Several companies of Coffee's troops, dismounted, were filling the gap in their lines. Some of the retreating militiamen then turned, the arrival of reinforcements stiffening their resolve, and began to advance against some forty Creeks threading their way between the fallen trees.

"The circle's broken no more," said Crockett, now standing beside Gulkalaski. "Maybe now they'll give up."

They watched the Tennesseans press their advantage, several Creek warriors falling to rifle balls and slashes of steel. They watched the rest begin to surrender. Then Gulkalaski's face fell.

"I see too few captives," the Cherokee announced. "Most of the enemy host got through the gap. Many hundreds. Red Eagle escaped. The war goes on."

"He wielded a gift of power," Har said. "There was nothing you or anyone else could have done to catch them all."

Gulkalaski looked at Har for a long while, his face hard as stone. Then he spoke again.

"I vowed to kill the Red Stick chiefs and all who follow them. I swore a sacred oath. I hoped to prove myself, and to remove a grave threat to my people and yours. But I proved only that I am one who tries and fails. It is a new name I have earned, though not one I have wanted. In my tongue, I am now *Tsu-na-la-hun-ski*."

Roza looked just as taken aback as Har felt. Then he heard Crockett clear his throat.

"How do you say that? Ju-na-lun . . ."

"Tsu-na-la-hun-ski," the Cherokee said again.

Crockett tried again. "Ju-na-lusk-a?"

Har could sense his Cherokee friend's frustration and disappointment with the outcome of the battle. But somehow Crockett's butchered pronunciation of his new name managed to make the Indian smile, then laugh. Crockett, Roza, and Har soon joined him, relishing the relief after the stress and exertion of the past few minutes.

The man who had once been Gulkalaski slapped Crockett on the back. "If 'Junaluska' is the best you can manage, so be it."

Chapter 19 – The Bend

Their stomping horses raised a massive cloud of dust before the gate. Junaluska saw the startled faces of sentries and the rapidly retreating forms of messengers within. He smiled in satisfaction, marveling at the difference a month could make.

When he'd left Fort Strother in mid-January, General Jackson's command had dwindled to little more than a hundred men. Most of the Tennessee volunteers and militia, David Crockett among them, had gone home, their commissions ended, their bellies empty. So had most of Jackson's Indian scouts.

Junaluska had been among the last to leave. While anxious to see his wife again, he wasn't abandoning the war for good. Instead, he'd concluded the only way to win it—and to fulfill his oath—was to recruit more allies. Now, as he rode into the newly invigorated Fort Strother a month later, its cramped quarters and adjacent meadow teeming with thousands of men, Junaluska realized he hadn't been only one to recognize the need for new recruits.

After all, the startled sentries at the gate wore blue uniform coats and light-gray trousers, not frontier clothes of homespun cloth and buckskin. And as Junaluska entered the fort, he was accompanied not just by the dozens of Cherokee warriors he'd personally recruited but by hundreds of other riders—Cherokees and Choctaws and friendly Creeks he'd met on the trail, Indians coming to bolster Jackson's army.

"This is not the desolate place you described," observed his friend Sequoyah, riding uncomfortably on Junaluska's right, his lame knee bent at an odd angle. "I have never seen so many warriors."

"This is the place we need to be," said the deep-voiced rider on Junaluska's left, a broad-shouldered man with a pronounced brow and thick, wavy hair tinged with gray. In his youth, as a Chickamauga Cherokee, the man had borne the name Nunnehidihi, or "he who kills the enemy in his path." The Pathkiller had fought John Sevier's

Tennesseans and other white militia. Later, as a successful planter and elected member of the Cherokee Council, his wise counsel had earned him the name Ganundalegi, or "he who walks on the ridge of the mountain."

The Ridge, as he was known among the whites, now rode at the head of five hundred Cherokees joining Andrew Jackson's army. "This is the place we will win honor for ourselves and our people," the Ridge continued. "It is the place we will draw out the last of Tecumseh's poison."

Junaluska had been fascinated to learn of the Ridge's own confrontation with Tecumseh. It happened at the council of Tuckabatchie, where Tecumseh had convinced several Creek chiefs to attack the Americans. The Ridge, attending as a Cherokee representative, approached Tecumseh after the meeting and threatened to kill him if he tried to bring the Cherokees into the confederacy.

Junaluska had himself issued the same threat to Tecumseh only weeks after the Ridge did, at Soco Gap. Now Tecumseh lay dead on some northern battlefield—or so the talk would have it.

Soon Red Eagle will join Tecumseh in the world of the spirits.

After the riders dismounted and the Ridge went looking for General Jackson, Junaluska caught sight of three familiar faces. Two were expected: Har the Tower and Roza the Elf, sitting on a high branch of a pine tree. The other face was, however, entirely unexpected.

"Kolana!" Junaluska exclaimed as a tall white man in a blue coat and a high hat shook his hand. "What brings the Raven to roost this fall south?"

"The same that brings you here—a shot at those Red Sticks," said Sam Houston, rubbing the deep cleft in his chin with one hand, giving Sequoyah a backslap with the other.

Junaluska pointed at the sword hanging from Houston's belt. "You fly high for one who started so low."

Houston slumped, obviously remembering the first time they'd met. Back then, the Raven had been a troubled, intoxicated youth. Then he straightened. "I'm a regular soldier now. A lieutenant in the Thirty-Ninth Infantry, Gulkalaski."

The Cherokee shook his head. "Not Gulkalaski. I no longer lean, my friend. I am Junaluska, the one who tried but failed. I have returned to try again—to try and to win."

"You and every other man at this fort," said Houston. Then the lieutenant glanced up furtively at the nearby pine tree and stepped closer to whisper. "Though not all here are *proper* men."

Junaluska was thankful Sequoyah had never learned English. The Cherokee shopkeeper hadn't understood Houston's reference to the two Folk rangers watching from the branch.

"Kolana, where is the camp of our brothers?" he asked in Cherokee.

Clearly confused by the change of subject, Houston pointed south to a meadow beyond the fort.

"Sequoyah," Junaluska said, "would you take our mounts and gear to the camp? I want to see if any Tennesseans I fought with at Tallushatchee and Talladega are still here."

Sequoyah nodded, although Junaluska could tell he was puzzled by the request. It was only after he rode out of sight that Junaluska motioned to the two rangers in the tree—and forever changed the course of Sam Houston's life.

▲▲▲

"Jackson has had a rough time," Har said about an hour later as he, Roza, and Junaluska watched Lieutenant Houston walk slowly away. Although Houston had seen glimpses of magical creatures all his life, the afternoon's revelation of Folk realms and their involvement in human affairs had left the young soldier dazed and speechless.

"Did Red Sticks attack the fort?" Junaluska asked.

Roza shook her head, flicking the bronze tip of an arrow with her finger. "That human Andrew Jackson prefers to move and strike, not crouch and wait. I like him."

Har frowned. "Right after you left, fresh recruits arrived. The general decided to take the field again. His recruits were not merely fresh, however—they were green. The Tennesseans killed some Red Sticks, but the price was steep."

"Tell it true," the Elf ranger insisted. "Jackson faced an enemy with magic weapons."

"We do not know that," Har insisted, then turned back to Junaluska. "The army fought the Red Sticks southeast of here, at Emuckfaw and Enotachopco Creek. Roza and I were not there to witness it. We had gone west, investigating rumors about a cat-headed giant terrorizing the local humans."

Junaluska's eyes widened. "A monster? Did you find it?"

Roza sighed. "Our summoning spells drew no response."

"When we got back to the fort, we used spellsong to question Jackson's men," Har said. "They reported no crashing sounds, no tremors, no falling trees. The enemy merely came in great numbers and used the terrain to their advantage. Red Sticks appeared to come out of nowhere to attack one flank and then melt into the trees to attack the other. Either Red Eagle was not there, or he choose not to use his enchanted war club."

The Elf ranger snorted. "You place too much credence in the faulty senses and foggy memories of humans."

Har responded with a mocking grin. "You once accused Dwarfs of jumping to conclusions. Has spending so much time with me corrupted you?"

Junaluska was surprised to see a blush come to Roza's cheeks as she stomped away.

▲▲▲

When Andrew Jackson's army, now swollen to 3,500 men, left Fort Strother in March to reenter the heart of Red Stick country, Har stayed close to Junaluska and the other Indians while Roza kept a close eye on the blue-coated regulars of the Thirty-Ninth Infantry, including Lieutenant Sam Houston. After marching south down the Coosa and building a supply depot on the river the army turned toward Tohopeka, where scouts had reported the largest enemy concentration.

Two days later, at a conference of American officers and Indian leaders, Junaluska stood next to the Ridge and looked down at a rough-drawn map of Tohopeka laid out on the ground. It depicted the extreme, horseshoe-shaped bend in the Tallapoosa River where the Red Sticks had built their settlement. Across the top of the "horseshoe," the Creeks had built a wall of logs about four hundred feet long.

General Jackson's narrow face bore an expression of grudging admiration. "It's difficult to conceive a situation more eligible for defense than the one they've chosen."

"It's a strong position, sir, but isn't it also a sort of trap?" Colonel Coffee asked.

"You'll make it a trap, that's certain," Jackson agreed. "I want your mounted brigade and our Indian friends to cross the Tallapoosa here"—he pointed to a point about two miles south of the horseshoe bend—"and encircle their position. When we break that stockade with cannon and drive them back, they'll have nowhere to go."

Major Lemuel Montgomery, commander of the Thirty-Ninth Infantry, inclined his head dubiously. "What are the Red Sticks up to, general? Shouldn't they stay on the move instead of being holed up in a town?"

After whispering a brief translation to the Ridge, whose command of English was limited, Junaluska shot a meaningful look at Har the Tower, sitting nearby under magical concealment. The Dwarf nodded in agreement with the Cherokee's unspoken observation.

This could be a trap, all right—a trap set by the Red Sticks for the Americans, not the other way around.

"The Red Sticks can't run forever," John Coffee was saying. "They'll run out of powder. They'll starve."

"As will we, if we don't bring things to a head," Andrew Jackson said. "I am determined to extinguish them."

Yes—we must extinguish all of them, Junaluska thought. *Including the chiefs who lead the Red Sticks and the Folk who supply them.*

▲▲▲

The distant sound of Jackson's artillery was exhilarating. At every cannon boom, the Cherokees cheered their allies and jeered at the Red Sticks trapped in their hundred-acre peninsula of death. Soon the enemy's wall of logs would crumble. Soon the blue-coated regulars with fixed bayonets and the Tennessee militiamen with knives and tomahawks would slash through their lines.

And when the Red Sticks swarmed the canoes they'd stashed on the north bank of the Tallapoosa and tried to flee, the waiting Cherokee would finish them off.

Or so they thought at first. Then the minutes stretched into hours. The American cannons continued to pound. Attackers and defenders continued to exchange sporadic gunfire. And nothing else happened. The Red Sticks' stockade held.

Junaluska sat impatiently on his horse, watching for movement on the opposite shore. Har sat behind him. To his right, Junaluska's friend Sequoyah was talking with a short, slightly built man dressed in a fine gray suit. John Ross, a friend of the Ridge, owned a trading post near Chattanooga. If Junaluska hadn't known better, he'd have guessed the young man was one of John Coffee's white troopers, not one of the Ridge's Cherokee warriors.

But is *he a warrior, really?* Junaluska wondered. John Ross was a shopkeeper; so was Sequoyah. Other Cherokees along the line had never faced battle before. They were determined but yet untested.

With a grunt of frustration, Junaluska dismounted and walked to the water's edge, his eyes still fixed on the canoes lining the opposite shore.

"Jackson may have cornered his prey, but they have a lot of fight left," whispered Har, who'd gotten off the horse to follow.

Nodding, Junaluska turned away from the river. "We should do something to help."

"You are," Har said. "The general's plan makes sense. The Red Sticks cannot escape."

Junaluska grimaced. "The plan is as good as far as it goes. But that does not—"

The sound stopped him in midsentence. Har heard it, too, which is why his hands shot to the leather thong across his chest. The Dwarf was reaching not for his battleaxe but for the stringed instrument, the *scheitholt*, strapped to his back, for the sound the two friends heard was not the footfalls of running men or the thump of wood on metal. It was spellsong.

"Folk ranger!" said Har, pulling the scheitholt over his head. "I must play a counterspell."

"The tune is a familiar one," Junaluska began, "one that I have heard many—"

Har raised a hand to cut him off. "It is a concealment spell. A ranger seeks to become invisible."

The Dwarf began strengthening his own concealment spell, shielding his and Junaluska's words and actions from the other Cherokees around them. So he didn't see what Junaluska saw on the edge of the forest.

"The spell is *not* to make a Folk scout invisible, Har," he said, clenching his jaw. "It is to make *them* invisible—until they strike."

Har jerked his head up to see what Junaluska saw: a line of Red Stick warriors emerging from the trees, faces and bodies painted for war, guns and bows at the ready.

The two friends hurried forward. Junaluska picked up the loaded rifle he'd left next to his horse, cocked the hammer, and raised it to his shoulder. But Har again raised his hand.

"Wait, Junaluska!" he cried. "The ranger is only repeating the concealment spell over and over. He makes no attempt to confuse or demoralize. Let me try confusing the enemy instead. Drawing you and your warriors away from the river may be their intent."

Junaluska lowered his rifle as Har began to sing and play. While the concealment song coming from the woods was low, soothing, and regular, Har's confusion song featured high, discordant notes and an erratic rhythm. Even Junaluska found it disorienting. The voices of his fellow Cherokees and the snorts of their horses faded to a faint murmur. The shapes of the approaching Red Sticks became indistinct, as if he saw them through the cloudy lens of a spyglass.

Junaluska closed his eyes and struck the top of his foot with his rifle butt, welcoming the jolt of pain as a distraction. He felt the spell's effects dissipate. Then he opened his eyes and saw, to his satisfaction, that the Creeks had stopped their advance and were now looking around in consternation, seemingly puzzled about where they were and how they'd gotten there.

Har changed his song. Now his fingers strummed the larger, lower-pitched strings of his scheitholt. He pitched his voice lower, too—but not to soothe. His words were deep and menacing. The weapons in the Red Sticks' hands began to shake as they backed into the trees, their expressions fearful. Junaluska realized the Dwarf had shifted to another spell, one designed to demoralize.

It was working. The would-be ambushers were fleeing the field.

Then Junaluska's smile froze on his lips. A new figure appeared, a chief exhorting his men to take courage and halt their retreat. As he bellowed and blustered, the reddish-gray feathers in his hair shook. The chief waved his war club furiously—a long, red club inlaid with shiny stones.

For a second time, Junaluska brought his gun to his shoulder. He aimed. He fired. Then he cursed, realizing he'd missed his target.

Red Eagle stared contemptuously at the Cherokee warrior, who'd snatched his bronze-tipped spear from its saddle strap and started running. The enemy chief paused, apparently considering whether to shoot his rifle or take Junaluska on face-to-face. Choosing the latter course, the Creek chief assumed the same fighting stance he had at Talladega, lifting his enchanted club in one hand and preparing to parry with the rifle held in the other.

Remembering his encounter with the Uktena, Junaluska decided on a bold move. When he was within a dozen paces of Red Eagle, the Cherokee drove the point of his spear into the ground, allowing his momentum to vault him over the astonished chief.

As he passed above, Junaluska kicked down at Red Eagle's skull, delivering a hard blow he hoped would stun the chief. Then Junaluska landed on two feet, yanked his spear free of the ground, and spun to deliver a thrust.

But Red Eagle wasn't there. He'd leapt to one side, crouching in the grass and raising his war club to strike the earth.

The tremor knocked Junaluska back, jarring his spear loose from his grip. Red Eagle pounced, aiming the club at the Cherokee's unprotected chest.

Barely in time, Junaluska managed to wriggle to the side, his necklace of Wampus claws jangling as his torso twisted just enough for the club only to graze his left side rather than strike with full force. Even so, the club's magic delivered such force that Junaluska was thrown violently to the ground. Ignoring the stab of pain in his side, he drew his knife from his belt and prepared to dodge or parry Red Eagle's next attack.

He didn't have to. Red Eagle backed away, eyes wide, as Har the Tower stepped in front of Junaluska, wielding his great battleaxe and scowling fiercely. The Dwarf stood only about four feet in height, a child facing a man, yet Har's odd clothes, long yellow beard, and stocky frame seemed to confound Red Eagle.

But only for a few seconds.

"You dropped your spear of power, yet still you conjure a bearded spirit to distract me, Cherokee," spat Red Eagle. "I know not what other gifts you possess. I know only that with my mighty gift, I must prevail."

Red Eagle is not Sighted, Junaluska realized. *By sheer force of will, he withstood the terror spell. So Har revealed himself to help me.*

"I am no conjured spirit, human," said the Dwarf. "You will find my axe is very real."

Red Eagle's answer was to swing at Har. The knobby end of the war club met the sharp blade of the battleaxe. Junaluska heard the blade cut a notch in the club, but the human's blow, propelled by elemental magic, had the greater force. Har was thrown clear off the ground.

The Cherokee warrior hadn't wasted the time Har bought him. He scrambled forward and recovered his spear. He ran at Red Eagle, slashing at his face.

This time the Creek chief swung his rifle instead to knock Junaluska's point aside and came at him with the club. Junaluska backed away, sweeping his spear to slam into Red Eagle's side, although not with its blade. The impact of the spear shaft made Red Eagle groan but inflicted no wound.

Har had regained his feet and was approaching from another direction. Red Eagle's eyes took the measure of his two antagonists. "Now the hunt begins," he said with a mocking smile. Then Red Eagle turned and reentered the forest.

"Does he truly think we are foolish enough to chase after him?" the Dwarf asked.

Junaluska leaned against his spear to catch his breath. "If I judge him correctly, Red Eagle sees himself and his men as the hunters and us as the prey."

Har nodded, also breathing heavily.

Then realization came to Junaluska like a candle in a dark cabin. "The ambush was never meant to smash our line. He meant to draw us away, like you said."

Before Har could reply, Junaluska turned and ran back to the riverbank, where Sequoyah and John Ross had continued their conversation, oblivious to what had just happened thanks to Har's spell. The line of canoes still stretched across the opposite bank. And from beyond the Creek settlement came the sound of American cannons still blasting the log stockade.

In his mind's eye, Junaluska saw the Red Stick plan clearly. "They will hold out as long as they can, bloodying the Americans, then escape across the river."

"Which is why you and your companions are waiting here, to block their way," Har said.

Junaluska shook his head. "I will wait no longer."

With that, he slipped his powder horn over his head, then dropped his spear and other gear. Running along the riverbank, he soon found the Ridge's place in line and shouted for his attention. Junaluska pointed over the river. Without waiting for an answer, trusting that the Ridge understood, he dove into the Tallapoosa.

The water closed over his head with a cold slap and stabbed his skin with needles of ice. Junaluska told himself the fastest way out of the frigid river was across it. He swam, submerged, until his lungs felt as if they would burst. When his head broke the surface to take a breath, he heard shouts and gunshots from both the front and rear. Some Red Sticks must have seen him swimming the river and understood his intention. The Ridge and his warriors must have guessed Junaluska's intention as well and were firing their own guns to keep the Red Sticks occupied.

Junaluska submerged and crossed the remaining distance to the peninsula, emerging near a line of Creek canoes. He grabbed the rope tied to the first boat, then stooped to pick up a second. The action may well have saved his life—an arrow whistled just over his head and skidded along the marshy ground.

The archer was short and thickly built with shiny rings in his nose and earlobes. Dropping his bow, the warrior raised his tomahawk and rushed forward with a savage cry. Drawing his knife, Junaluska dodged the Creek's attempted slash, spun on one heel, and sliced a deep gash across the warrior's thigh. The man fell to the ground, mumbling curses. Junaluska left him where he lay, sheathed his knife, gathered the two tow ropes, then added a third. Wading into the river, he crouched low and tugged at the ropes, trying to dislodge the canoes from the mud.

Again and again he yanked. Finally, his efforts were rewarded. The canoes slid into the water.

Suddenly he found himself in shadow. A tall, thin warrior with long hair bundled in a turban loomed over Junaluska, holding a long knife and leering in triumph. The Cherokee had no time to draw his knife or even dodge the coming blow.

But it never landed. The tall Creek stiffened, his eyes bulging, and dropped his weapon. Then he tumbled backward, blood gushing from a hole in his chest. One of the Cherokee marksmen across the river had scored a timely hit.

The next minute felt like an hour. Junaluska swam as fast as he could with one arm pulling the tow ropes. Half a dozen bullets made small splashes in the Tallapoosa. Nearly as many arrows made larger splashes. Miraculously, none of the Creek missiles struck home.

The next set of splashes all around him were bigger still. Three Cherokees had waded into the water to pull the canoes ashore. Then three more warriors followed Junaluska's example, diving into the river and swimming toward the other side while their fellows kept Tohopeka's defenders pinned.

Soon there were many bodies in the river. Most were Junaluska's allies, gasping and grunting as they swam across or pulled boats back. A few of the bodies, both ally and enemy, floated motionless. Within minutes, nearly all of the Red Stick canoes were on the near riverbank and swarming with Cherokees, Choctaws, and friendly Creeks wearing white feathers or doe tails thrust into their turbans, bandanas, or top knots.

"As men we go!" cried the Ridge, holding his rifle high. "Stain this hostile stream with blood!"

"With blood!" answered the Cherokees, beating tomahawks and gun butts against the sides of their canoes.

With blood, Junaluska agreed silently as he clambered into a boat. *Beginning with any chief who wields a red stick.*

The first wave of canoes to once again cross the Tallapoosa were met by a deadly volley of bullets and arrows. The second wave faced scores of enemy warriors brandishing blades and gun butts. When Junaluska disembarked, twisting his spear in his hands and searching for his first target, he was pleased to see his friend Sequoyah aiming his rifle at a trio of defenders running out of a house. To his left, John Ross was struggling in the grip of a heavyset Red Stick warrior. Ross had lost his own weapon and was using both hands to try to keep his foe's knife from plunging through Ross's fine cravat.

Junaluska rushed to his aid. It was the enemy Creek, not Ross, who found a blade piercing his windpipe.

"Thank you, brother," said the young shopkeeper, staggering backward.

But Junaluska didn't stop to reply. He pressed on, hoping to see a red war club in the hand of his next foe.

▲▲▲

It was only much later that the absence of Har the Tower struck him like a lightning bolt.

The rest of the Indian allies, plus John Coffee's men, had crossed the Tallapoosa and fallen on the Red Sticks. Most of the Creek settlement had been reduced to burning timbers or piles of rubble. Hundreds of enemy Creeks lay died or grievously wounded. Others had surrendered, or were trying to swim away.

With his enemy facing attack from the rear, General Jackson had seized the opportunity and ordered the blue-coated regulars of the Thirty-Ninth Infantry to spearhead the final assault. First over the top of the log wall was the regiment's commander, Major Montgomery. A bullet to the head had killed him instantly. Second over the wall was Lieutenant Sam Houston, waving his men forward with his sword. Houston had taken an arrow to the groin but fought on until he could no longer move. Then he'd asked another officer to yank out the barbed arrow, and even threatened him with his sword until the reluctant officer complied. With blood gushing from his wound, Houston had picked up a musket and, hobbling as best he could, led another assault on another Red Stick position. Again he'd fallen, musket balls smashing his arm and shoulder.

Or so Roza excitedly told the story as Junaluska rested against the side of a burned-out cabin.

"Houston is dead, then?" he asked.

"Or as good as," Roza replied.

"You mean you just *left* him there?"

The Elf gave Junaluska a withering look. "I had my own tasks to perform, human. There was a Folk ranger somewhere behind the log wall using a concealment spell. First I had to counteract it. Then I went looking for the ranger. I was unsuccessful."

"We faced the same threat," Junaluska said. "Then Har used his—"

"Where *is* the Dwarf?" Roza demanded.

Junaluska stopped short. He hadn't thought of Har since diving into the river to steal those first canoes. Had the Dwarf stayed on the far side and used spellsong to help Junaluska and the others win their part of the battle? Or had he crossed in one of the boats and gone looking, as Roza had, for the enemy spellsinger?

With growing unease, Junaluska looked around the smoking ruins of Tohopeka. There was no sign of the Dwarf. Then he ran to the river and began pushing a canoe into the water. Roza ran past him and leapt into the craft. They had gone only halfway across the Tallapoosa when the figure of Har the Tower appeared at the edge of the distant forest, doubled over.

"Har!" shouted Roza in alarm. She seized a paddle with her thin arms and tried, with only modest success, to help Junaluska propel the canoe forward.

By the time the two reached the other side, Har had stumbled closer to the river. Seeing their worried faces, he waved a dismissive hand. "I am unharmed. Merely tired."

"Did you catch the ranger?" Roza asked.

"Never saw one," Har explained. "When Junaluska began to cross the river, it occurred to me Red Eagle might succeed in rallying his men and attacking from the rear. I chased them deep into the woods but never caught them. Dwarfs are not made for running long distances through forests. That is more your style, Elf."

Roza raised an eyebrow and made to reply, then seemed to think better of the idea.

▲▲▲

At the American camp, Junaluska waited outside the general's tent with Sequoyah and John Ross while the Ridge conferred with Andrew Jackson. Sequoyah beamed with pride as he pointed to a jagged wound in his forearm. Ross, shaken but unhurt, seemed grateful merely to have survived the ordeal.

Lying nearby were dozens of Americans and Indian allies who'd been less fortunate. Some would never rise again. Beyond the camp, packed together under guard in a nearby clearing, were hundreds of Creek captives, almost all women and children.

"History furnishes few instances of a more brilliant attack," said General Jackson as he emerged from the tent. "Your men do honor to all your people, Major Ridge."

The Cherokee leader was clearly pleased by both the compliment and the newly bestowed military rank. "Our people fight long," he replied, with difficulty, in English. "We fight to defend. We fight for our future. With my own hands, I fight—first in youth and now by your side."

"You have," Jackson agreed, either not noticing or choosing to overlook the Ridge's allusion to his past life among Dragging Canoe's Chickamauga. Then the general pointed to the prisoners. "Twice we asked the Red Sticks to surrender. Twice they refused quarter. Few of their men survived."

"We question them," the Ridge suggested. "Red Eagle and other chiefs still missing. Must hunt them down."

"We must. Our enemies must be made to know that their prophets are impostors, and that our strength is mighty and will prevail. Then, and not till then, may we expect to make a permanent peace."

The two leaders headed for the clearing. Junaluska followed. The first two Red Stick captives, an old man and a young girl, denied knowing what had happened to their chiefs. But the third, a woman with silver streaks in her long hair, was more cooperative.

"I have not seen Red Eagle," she said, "but I saw Chief Menawa go past my cabin to the river. He was limping and bleeding. He ordered two other men into a canoe with him."

"Did they make it to the other side?" Jackson asked.

Junaluska did not hear the woman's answer. His attention was drawn to a large fringed blanket on the ground next to her. At first he thought it covered a bundle of clothes, perhaps the Creek woman's sole-remaining possessions. Then it moved.

"Look out!" he shouted—but words of warning were not all that Junaluska hurled.

A Red Stick warrior had thrown off the blanket, surged to his feet, and drew back his arm, aiming a long knife at the back of Andrew Jackson's head.

The bronze blade of Junaluska's spear sunk deep into the breast of the would-be assassin, throwing him several feet back and stopping his heart forever.

The Creek woman screamed. The other captives rolled away in fear. But neither General Jackson nor Major Ridge flinched; both were experienced warriors. The American's lean hands had formed bony fists while the Cherokee leader had drawn his tomahawk.

When no others rose to attack, the two leaders relaxed. Junaluska walked past them, placed his foot on the chest of the dead man, and wrenched his spear free.

Jackson reached up to brush a lock of sweat-soaked, reddish hair from his forehead. "What is your name, sir?"

"I am called Junaluska."

"Ah, *that* name," Jackson said. "Are you the same Junaluska that Major Ridge just spoke of, the one who dove into the river to steal the first canoes?"

Junaluska nodded, noticing that Sequoyah and John Ross had hurried over.

"Twice you have served our cause well, Junaluska," the general continued. "As long as the sun shines and the grass grows, there shall be friendship between us, and the feet of the Cherokee shall be toward the east."

"Your words are as straight as the hickory shaft of my spear," said Junaluska. "May your deeds prove as unbending."

Jackson obviously appreciated the first part of Junaluska's response. But the second part caused his steely eyes to narrow. Major Ridge intervened. "You are a man of your word, General. This is known across the land."

"This is known," echoed John Ross and other warriors standing nearby.

Junaluska, however, hadn't bothered to wait for Jackson's response. Instead, he'd crouched next to the dead man, looking closely at his face and the feathers in his hair.

This is no chief. There is no red club here to recover. The battle may be over, but my task remains incomplete.

▲▲▲

Over the next several days, both General Jackson and Major Ridge sent out hunting parties to find Red Eagle and other escaped chiefs. Junaluska rode out with them. They found a few stragglers, but no signs of the quarry they sought.

When those Americans who'd survived their wounds — including, incredibly, Lieutenant Sam Houston—were stable enough to move, the army marched south to the confluence of the Coosa and Tallapoosa rivers, where they picked up more reinforcements and supplies. The day after they arrived, Junaluska and Roza were standing on the riverbank, watching Har cast his fishing line, when they heard several shouts of alarm.

"An attack?" Roza asked incredulously. "Are the Red Sticks mad?"

The three sprinted back to camp. What met Junaluska's eyes there filled him with a combination of alarm and shame. Andrew Jackson stood, aghast and angry, looking up at the tall gray horse standing before his tent. At the general's feet was the carcass of a freshly killed deer, and seated on the horse was Red Eagle.

"How dare you, sir?" the general demanded. "You ride to my tent after having murdered women and children at Fort Mims?"

Red Eagle glared back. "I am not afraid of you. I fear no man, for I am a warrior. I have nothing to request for myself. Kill me if you desire. But I come to beg you to send for *our* women and children, now starving in the woods. Their fields and corn cribs have been destroyed. Conduct them here, that they may be fed."

The chief's words did not mollify Jackson. "We have conducted ourselves with honor, sir, while your savagery is—"

"I exerted myself in vain to prevent the massacre at Fort Mims," Red Eagle insisted. "I am now done fighting. The Red Sticks are nearly all killed. If I could fight you any longer, I would most heartily do so. Send for the women and children. They never did you any harm. But kill me, if the white people want it done."

Jackson remained stone-faced. But other observers did not. "Kill him!" shouted Americans and Indian allies alike. "Kill the traitor! Kill the butcher of Fort Mims!"

Yes, kill him, Junaluska thought. *Unless his kind are exterminated, this will never be over.*

"Silence!" Jackson commanded. The gaunt general walked to the tall horse, patting its flank glistening with sweat. "*Kill him?*" the general repeated. "Any man who would kill as brave a man as this would rob the dead!"

The crowd murmured in perplexity and disapproval. Junaluska simply walked away, feeling his fury rise up like bile and leave a bitter taste.

After a few moments, he heard the two fairies walk up behind him. "Look what I recovered from his horse," Har said.

Junaluska turned. The Dwarf held a long, red-painted war club inlaid with precious stones. But for the first time, the Cherokee noticed a pattern of strange devices carved into the wood.

"These runes contain a concealment song," Har observed. "There were *never* Folk rangers with the Red Sticks. Their gifts were enchanted with more than one power."

"That is how their warriors seemed to disappear from one place and reappear in another," Roza said. "It was not just expert woodcraft."

"And it is how their fugitive leader managed to ride into the American camp, right to the tent of his mortal enemy, without being stopped," added Har.

The three watched as General Jackson invited Red Eagle into his tent.

"This may be the moment peace is finally secured," Har said.

"Or the moment Jackson proves too easily conquered by tender words," Roza said.

Junaluska gazed at the blade of his spear, though his eyes beheld a place far away from where they stood. Then he allowed his exhaustion and disappointment to mingle into a deep sigh. "All I know is that I am going home to Yona. Home at last. Home to stay."

Chapter 20 – The Light

Bell wiped the wet streaks from her cheeks and wished she was at her willow place.

She imagined dipping her feet into the cold water that flowed past the island. She imagined the cool breeze rustling the canopy of willow leaves. She imagined lying under its shade, her Bob resting and smiling by her side.

Then Bell groaned, the cramps bringing another welter of sweat and tears to her face. In her condition, she'd never make it from her master John Dumont's house all the way to her island of willows. And even if she could manage the journey, she'd have to make it alone. Bob hadn't come to see her in weeks.

"Your boy won't be back," Dumont had told her. "Charles Catton will never allow it. He says Bob must marry one of his slaves, not one of mine."

Bell and Bob weren't married, at least not in the way others were. They hadn't spoken the words. But they'd been keeping company for more than a year. Bob had often spoken of Master Catton's ill temper and cruelty. He'd threatened to run off, maybe all the way to Canada. He'd even asked Bell to run off with him.

It was a silly idea, Bell knew, and she'd said so. "You never make it. Maybe I can get my master to buy you. Then we together forever."

Bob had dismissed her with a laugh. But she'd resolved to try. She'd offered prayers of thanksgiving that God had bound her to John Dumont rather than an evil man like Charles Catton. Dumont was pale, fat, and talked too much, but he was a good master. He took care of her. He called her nice names. He praised the wool yarn she'd spun. He complimented the cider she'd made. He savored her honey cakes, raved about her gingerbread, and always ate seconds when she made her prized snip-raapjes out of salt pork and turnips.

When the other slaves ridiculed her as a "white man's pet," Dumont comforted her. When Missus Dumont or the children were unkind, he defended her. He only whipped her sometimes, and only when she deserved it.

When she'd asked her master to buy Bob, though, Dumont had shrugged. "Don't have the coin, Bell. And Catton won't sell. With the war drawing so many volunteers and militia up north, it's hard to get field hands, slave or free."

Now, sick and suffering alone in the sweltering heat, Bell saw her beloved only in her memories. She turned over on her straw palette, laid out in the Dumonts' storeroom, and closed her eyes to visit her memories once more.

"Have you seen Bob?"

Bell's eyelids fluttered opened. John Dumont bent over her, shaking her shoulders. She shook her head and tried to rise to her feet, which dangled far beyond the short palette.

"No use getting up, not in your condition." Dumont placed his hand on her belly and pushed her back onto the straw. "Charles Catton and his son just stopped by. Seems Bob ran off this morning. If you see him, tell him to take care of himself. They're after him."

Had her Bob made his long-promised bid for freedom? Bell hoped not. He'd never make it to Canada. And even if he did, she'd never see him again.

Bell wiped her brow. Then she swallowed and made herself ask her question again. "He's just afeared. Master Catton's beat him again. If you was his master, he'd never—"

"No!" Dumont insisted. "He's Catton's hand. You'll have to forget all about him."

No! Bell shouted, but only in her head.

Presently she opened her mouth and began to pray in a low, raspy voice. She knew Master Dumont was the man God had appointed to be her master. Even so, he was just a man; God would have to take a direct hand. He'd hear her prayer better if she was saying it good and loud, kneeling in her special willow place. But maybe a fervently whispered prayer right here, right now, could still get to God's ears.

Dumont backed away. *He thinks I've gone crazy*, Bell thought. Then she screwed up her face as another wave of pain made her clutch the sides of her pallet with long, strong fingers.

"You'll be fine, Bell, you'll see," Dumont was saying. "We'll find you a husband here on the farm. How about old Tom? He's a fine buck. And he's been lonely since I had to sell his wife."

But Bell wasn't paying attention. She'd resumed her prayers. She asked God to carry her Bob back to Master Catton's, safe and sound. She asked God to soften Catton's heart so Bob could visit her. And she asked God to deliver her from painful sickness.

Bell fell silent. It wasn't the sound of Dumont still talking about Old Tom that prompted Bell to halt her prayers. It was the sound of running feet.

"Bell, you in there?"

She sucked in a breath and sat up straight, her body no longer trembling. Now the chill running up her spine made her feel exhilarated, not exhausted. *My Bob is here! He's come for me!*

"You there, boy, what do you think you're doing?" Dumont was next to her at the window scowling down at the tall man. "Hurry back to the Cattons if you know what's good for you."

"Not much point in that, Bob," said another voice. "We'll take you back, to be sure. But we'll be in no hurry."

Bell gasped as the elegantly dressed figure of Charles Catton emerged from the woods, followed closely by a younger man wearing work clothes. Both carried walking canes. Bob didn't turn around to see the Cattons. He was staring up at her, his close-set eyes wide with panic.

"I only come to see Bell," he explained, his voice cracking. "I was goin' right home after."

Charles Catton cocked his head to one side, looking reproachful. "Now, Bob, I quite clearly forbade you to come here again. You knew it was wrong."

This time Bob did turn around, his hands clenching. "I had to see my Bell! I jus' wanted to—"

"You *dare* raise your voice to me?" Catton snapped. "After I forgave your transgressions? After I offered you pick of the girls to take to wife?"

"Don't want any of 'em," Bob insisted. "I want Bell."

Watching anxiously from the window, Bell couldn't decide whether or not she was glad she'd learned so much English during her time on the Dumont farm. Hearing Bob's words of devotion thrilled her. But Catton's accusations had filled her with dread.

And his next words filled her with terror. "You ungrateful wretch! Charlie, knock down the damned black rascal."

The younger Catton smiled with glee and dashed forward, brandishing his cane.

"No!" Bell cried, thrusting her arms desperately through the window.

The first whack struck Bob's thigh, forcing him to his knees. "Sorry, Master," he muttered between grunts of pain.

Then Charlie's cane struck the side of Bob's head with a sharp crack. "I didn't mean it," begged the field hand. "Didn't mean it."

The next whack came not from young Catton but from his father. He'd swung his cane hard at Bob's face, breaking his nose and splashing his checks with blood.

"Please stop!" Bell sobbed. "Oh God, please, no." No longer able to bear to watch, she shut her eyes and soon lost count of the cane strikes. She felt John Dumont's hands try to pull her away from the window.

"He's had enough, Catton, can't you see?" Dumont asked.

"You manage your *property* however you see fit," said the elderly man, sneering up at Bell and Dumont. "How I manage mine is my own affair."

"Not on my land, it isn't," Dumont said. "I'll have no blacks killed here."

Killed! Not Bob!

Bell forced her eyes open. Whether it was what she beheld that did it, or her sickness, her stomach rippled as if she was about to retch. Bob lay in the dirt, one eye swollen shut, the other glassy and rolled back in his head. He was bleeding from a dozen wounds. From his throat came no more pleas, just low moans.

"Very well," said Charles Catton, stepping back and drawing a handkerchief to wipe the blood from his cane. "Charlie, rope the bull and we'll be off."

The younger Catton tied a short coil of rope around Bob's neck. "Get up!" he ordered.

Bob struggled to his feet, then gagged as Charlie Catton yanked hard.

"Not so tight, man!" Dumont insisted. "You wouldn't put a noose like that on a cow or a horse. You'll only strangle instead of beat him to death."

Looking up at Dumont with a murderous expression, the young Catton loosened the knot at Bob's throat. Then, without another word, he and his father led their slave into the trees.

Fighting first an urge to leap out after them, and then an urge to double over, Bell turned to Dumont. "They just leadin' him off to end it, sir. Can't you, can't you . . ."

Her master shook his head. "Catton won't do that, Bell. Bob's too valuable a field hand. By the time they get home, Catton's temper will leave him. You'll see."

Bell sank to her knees, grabbing Dumont's hand. "Please, sir! I be good. Please go look after my Bob. I be a good girl. I take up with old Tom, like you want. Oh, please, sir!"

After a moment, Dumont withdrew his hand. "Very well. You just lie back down and rest. I'll see young Bob safely home."

▲▲▲

It had been just after noon when the Cattons led Bob away. When Bell awoke, the sun was now low on the horizon. Her master hadn't come back, or he hadn't bothered to wake her if he had. At least she felt a little better after an afternoon's sleep.

"I trust you, God," she said aloud. "You won't let them kill him." Then, with difficulty, she arose and slipped a jacket, petticoat, and skirt over her shift. "But you won't mind, God, if I go see for myself."

Bell walked slowly through the front door and headed around back, to the spot where the Cattons had beaten Bob. Bell could still see drops of blood in the dirt. She drew her leather shoe over the spot, hoping to mark the sole with even a faint reminder of her beloved.

Then, ignoring the need for stealth and the ache in her belly, Bell ran.

She ran into the trees. She ran along the narrow trail, then along the bank of the Hudson, glimpsing a small schooner sailing upriver. What Bell would do when she got to the Catton farm, she couldn't imagine. She knew only that she needed to keep one weary foot leaping in front of the other, to keep running.

The steady beat of her feet striking the ground reminded her of better days, of tavern guests stomping and singing at the Hardenbergh House; of throngs of people, white and brown and black, dancing at Pinkster festivals; of Bell and Bob running together through a moonlit forest, headed for her willow place.

Bell suddenly realized it wasn't just her imagination—she wasn't just hearing her own feet on the trail. There was another set of feet. Running behind her. Running *after* her.

Is it Bob? Or someone coming to fetch me back? Bell turned and spied a surprisingly familiar figure heading toward her. He was a short man, dressed in light-brown pants and a red work shirt. Close-cropped hair, more gray than black, peaked out from below a floppy hat. Before Bell could say a word, the man doffed his hat and bowed low, his mouth broadening into a smile, his eyes dancing.

"John!" said Bell, not quite believing her astonished eyes. "It really you?"

"Me," John agreed, twirling his hat playfully. "You know me, do you, pretty Bell? Long time, it's been. I once met a little girl. Now I see a fine young woman."

Bell returned his smile. "That little girl had only Dutch. Now I talk English, too. I hear what you say."

"Come now," said the laughing man. "Maybe you didn't know the words back then. But you *heard* me."

Feeling suddenly tired, and not only a little queasy, Bell sat on a grassy knoll, spreading her skirt and listening to the sounds of the rushing river. "I s'pose," she agreed. "I's in a bad way back then. Scared. Then you come by, like a cool drink on harvest day. Like a light in the dead of night."

John sat beside her, no longer laughing. "That's the work I do, pretty Bell. The work I's meant to do. My mission."

"Your . . . *mission?*"

Bell glanced toward the river. John followed her eyes, then nodded.

"Down in Georgia, I heard a fine hymn," he said. "Wonder if I recall it?" He hummed a few notes, then grinned as the words came back to him:

> *I stood on the river of Jordan*
> *To see that ship come sailin' over.*
> *Stood on the river of Jordan,*
> *O see that ship sail by.*
> *O sister, you better be ready*
> *To see that ship come sailing over;*
> *Brother, you better be ready*
> *To see that ship sail by.*

O moaner, don't you weep
When you see that ship come sailing over.
Shout: "Glory! Hallelujah!"
When you see that ship sail by.

Bell hadn't heard the hymn before, but by the end she was swinging her toes back and forth. It was the kind of song her Mau-Mau used to sing. The thought made her smile fondly. Her next thought, though, made her sit up straight.

"A ship!" she said. "Saw my first one on a ship."

John scratched his beard. "What'd you see, pretty Bell?"

"A little . . . woman," she replied, now feeling sheepish. "Skin as blue as a berry, and her hair, too."

"Oh, that one." John's hand slipped a hand into his sack. "Seen her some years ago, down Carolina way. With her winged friend."

Bell stared at him in amazement. "A *winged* one?"

"Oh, sure 'nuff," John said, still fumbling around in the sack. "Seen all kinds by now. Why, there was a—"

"I spied the water woman again just last summer," Bell interrupted. "And a little brown one up in a tree."

John guffawed. "You mean *she* was up a tree? Or was *you* up there lookin' down at her."

Bell was about to explain when her belly lurched. She leaned over and fought the urge to vomit.

John had been smiling triumphantly, holding up the twist of red-brown root he'd pulled from the sack. Instantly the smile vanished, replaced by a concerned frown. "Oh, pretty Bell, you should've told me. This ain't what you need. Not t'all."

He stuffed the root back in his bag and he pulled out another, smaller and darker. Drawing a knife, John sliced several slivers off the end of the root, put them in his mouth, and chewed a couple of times. Then he spat out the pulp, rolled it gingerly in his hand, and held it up to her.

"Try this," he suggested. "Put your belly to sleep."

Bell did as he asked. It was sweeter tasting than the other chewing root. Her mouth grew warm, then her throat, then her stomach. The latter began to unclench. Strength returned to her limbs.

After a while, Bell wiped her face. "You . . . you one of 'em, too?" she asked.

"One what?"

"Magic folk. Like the water woman and the tree woman."

John chuckled and shook his head. "No, not like them. You stand tall, pretty Bell, but I could still touch the top of your head if I had a mind."

He sure is slippery. "That's no fit answer, John."

The old man breathed a heavy sigh. "Well, I ain't no ordinary man. That's true 'nuff. But what I am, and where I come from—that, I can't say."

A renewed jab of pain made Bell wince, although it hurt a lot less than before because of the chewing root. John leaned over and rubbed her arm.

"Tell you if I knew," he said, misinterpreting her wince as a reproach. "First memory is coming off a boat down in Jamaica, long ago. Didn't know who I was. An overseer on the plantation named me John. I cut sugar cane 'bout a year, then got shipped up to Charleston and sold to a tobacco planter in Virginia named John Pleasants. He was a good man. A Quaker."

"My master John Dumont's a good man, too," Bell said. "But I never saw him quake."

John chuckled again. "A Quaker is a kind of Christian. They say they's Friends of the Truth, or Children of the Light. The inner light, they mean, the light that glows inside when you know God."

Bell felt a surge of excitement. "I know God, John! I talk to God like my Mau-Mau taught me. When I's in my willow place, I talk to God as loud as I want. Is I a Quaker?"

"No, no," said John, who'd pulled out a chewing root for himself. "But the Friends believe everyone can shine the Light. That everyone *ought* to shine the Light. Just like they believe everyone ought to be free."

"You mean," Bell began uneasily, "they believe masters ought to be kind to slaves?"

John looked at her thoughtfully, head tilted to one side, as he chewed. Then he answered. "Well, sure, they believe in kindness. But the Friends figure if everyone can shine the Light, everyone ought to be free. No more masters. No more slaves. Don't you wanna be free, Bell?"

This time, it wasn't the remaining pain in Bell's side that made her wince. She was remembering her desperate prayers after they took her from Mau-Mau. After Master Neely beat her so bad she passed out. *Oh, my God!* she'd begged. *What a way is this of treating human beings?*

But then her father had gotten her new masters, men who weren't so mean and ornery. That was God's will, wasn't it? He'd answered her prayers by bringing her to John Dumont. When his other slaves grumbled, she'd refused to listen to such ungrateful people. She even went and told Dumont all their bad words. She was a good girl.

"Free?" Bell asked. "What would become of me if I's free?"

"Be up to you to figure out," John replied. "When I was freed, t'was a gift I felt obliged to share."

Bell started. "*You* free?"

The gray-haired man spat a long, red stream of juice. Then he leapt up, drumming a rhythm with his bare feet. "Old John Pleasants made a will. Told his children to free his slaves when he died. Took a few years, but Mister Robert—the old man's son—he went to the courthouse and made it real."

"I walked past the courthouse once, in Kingston. Biggest house I ever saw." Bell recalled its high stone walls and the finely dressed white men standing in the doorway.

"T'was a different courthouse, Bell, down south," John explained. "Anyway, I started goin' around Virginia, meetin' folks and helpin' the slaves. I'd sweat and strain beside 'em under the hot sun, when the work was hardest. I'd laugh and sing and dance beside 'em in the dead of winter, when their lot was the most cruel. I helped 'em endure, gave 'em hope that somethin' better was comin'. Bit by bit, I worked out what that better was. I met other folks, Friends among the whites, Friends who could help find lost fathers and daughters, who could find sold-away mothers and sons. I found Friends in Virginia, in Georgia, in Carolina, and up north, too. Even some Friends right here on the Hudson."

Bell felt her heart skip a beat. He helped slaves find their lost ones? What about all the brothers and sisters she'd never known, the ones sold away from Mau-Mau Bett and James Baumfree?

"Can you help me, John? That why you come here?"

John drew his feet together and clicked his heels. "Didn't come lookin' for you, Bell, though I'm glad I found you. I'm off to see a couple of Quaker families. Got some friends stayin' with 'em, friends I got to take farther on."

It took Bell a while to get his point. "You don't mean white Friends in long coats and high hats. You mean friends who look like *us*."

John nodded. "Friends running from masters. Friends running to freedom."

The realization hit Bell like a blinding lamp. "My Bob run away!" she said, rising to her feet. "His masters came and beat him bad. I's running to see my Bob!"

Even before the wave of nausea hit her, John stepped forward and grabbed her arm. "Bell, you ain't got no business runnin' anywhere. You carryin' a child, right?"

She nodded, a flush coming to her face. It was her second, not her first. Her little baby James hadn't lived long, but she felt certain the new baby would be stronger. She had to make sure the baby had a father as well as a mother. She had to make sure Bob would be around.

"Sit down and rest a while," John suggested, although he didn't wait to see if she'd take the suggestion. He pushed her to the ground, resting her back against a pine tree.

Bell wanted to object. She wanted to shrug off his hand and start running. But once she was seated again, she found her sore arms and tired legs wouldn't mind her. They were happy right where they were. She took a deep breath.

"You ever . . . White folks ever catch you runnin' off with a slave?" she asked. "Ever have to fight to get away?"

John took a deep breath of his own. "I reckon all God's people, all Children of the Light, ought to be free. But we's few and the whites many. I ain't against fightin', no ma'am, but I ain't gonna get folks hurt for no good reason. Heard talk more than once of slaves taking up arms and killing the whites. Some even figured I might lead a revolt. Called me 'John de Conquer,' if they's from the Islands like me. Or 'John the Conqueror' down in Virginia. But that ain't the way, least not mine."

Bell was rubbing her belly, remembering all the tough talk she'd overheard about slave revolts and runaways.

"Like I say, ain't no ordinary man," John continued. "I's good at playing tricks, at making a way out of no way. At hittin' a straight lick with a crooked stick. At winnin' the jackpot with no other stake but a laugh. I'd rather fight a mighty war without force—fight it on the inside, not the outside. That's how we win for sure and forever, Bell— with our souls whole and free. Like the Friends say, what shall it profit a man if he gain the whole world, and lose his own soul? I'd be nothin' but a cruel, vengeful, grasping monster come to power."

"You there!"

Bell gasped as the sound of John Dumont's voice. The man was red-faced and winded, but managed to keep up a trot until he reached them. "Who are you, boy, and what are you doing to my Bell?"

John sprang to his feet, gave Bell a sly wink, and bent low, snatching the floppy hat from his head. "Pardon, sir," he said. "I's just wanderin' by when I seen the girl ill on the ground. Just tendin' to her, sir, and sure relieved her master done come along."

Seemingly placated, Dumont pulled Bell to her feet. "You walk back with me, now, back home before it gets dark."

"But my Bob!" Bell said in alarm. "He safe?"

Dumont nodded. "Once the Cattons got him home, they eased up, like I said. They promised me they wouldn't beat Bob anymore."

"Can I go see him?"

The white man took Bell by both shoulders and met her agonized gaze. "You can never, *ever* see him again. That's what I had to promise so they wouldn't beat Bob anymore. He's a Catton. You're a Dumont. There'll be no more of it."

The tears came, unbidden and uncontrollable. She slumped, and felt each man grab an arm to keep her from falling. As the old man took her right arm, Bell felt him slip several large, bulky items into the pocket of her dress. It didn't stop the tears from flowing. But somewhere, in the back of her mind, she pictured herself lying on the straw palette, looking out the window as she chewed.

It wasn't a pretty picture, exactly. Still, it was something to look forward to. And she'd never tell a white master about it, not even John Dumont. Nobody but her had to know where she got her secret pleasure from.

Well, nobody but God. And John de Conquer.

Chapter 21 – The Fugitive

October 1814

With a graceful twist, Dela rolled over on her back to float on the surface of Lake Ontario. As she looked up at the crescent moon and propelled herself toward the shore with sweeping arms and powerful kicks, she marveled at the healing arts of the Goblin mages.

During the battle on the River Thames, one monstrous Wendigo had torn a deep gash in her side. Another had snapped her back like a twig. But within hours of being transported to Detroit, skilled magecraft had closed the claw wound and mended her broken spine. Scarcely a week later, she was fully healed.

Goran hadn't been so fortunate. During his own monster battle against the Mud Beasts of Ohio, he'd suffered severe lacerations, cracked ribs, and a broken wing. Betua had rescued him from certain death. But she'd already depleted much of the magic in her enchanted horn, limiting the range of her communication spells. She had to carry Goran well over a hundred miles, into the Michigan Territory, to get close enough to request transport.

She'd splinted the fractured radius in the Sylph's wing and bound his ribs, but the journey took its toll on his battered body, and Goblin mages had little experience healing broken wings. When Dela last saw Goran, he was hovering clumsily a few inches off the floor in a Goblin cavern, waving gamely as the Water Maiden followed Betua into a tunnel.

Dela hadn't wanted to leave. But Goran was safe with the Goblins, and duty beckoned her back to the Blur.

Although from her perspective it had been only a couple of weeks since the battle on the Thames, nearly a year had passed in the human world. Finding Detroit no longer in danger and William Henry Harrison's army long since gone, Dela initially crossed Lake Erie to the mouth of the Niagara River, hoping to find Ichabod Crane. During her absence, however, the Americans had largely abandoned the region. So she headed across Lake Ontario to Sackets Harbor, New York. If the Water Maiden could still be of service to the American cause, that was the best place to find out how. And to find Ichabod.

After passing an island just off shore, Dela turned over and swam rapidly toward the hook-shaped peninsula that shielded Sackets Harbor. Tall masts framed against the night sky signaled that most of the American squadron was in port. To the right of the shipyard was a stout blockhouse. To the left, beyond the tip of the peninsula, stood another strong fort with adjoining barracks. Hundreds of men, some wearing uniforms, others dressed as mariners and workmen, were visible along the lakeshore or in small boats in the bay.

Dela bore left, bypassing the garrison, and came ashore at the deserted mouth of a small creek. Giving the barracks a wide berth, she found shelter among some cottonwood trees. Placing her gear on the ground, Dela used both hands to wring the water from her long, dark-blue hair while she studied the small collection of homes, inns, shops, and barns that formed the town. The blaze of many lamps and the bedlam of many voices told her the population of Sackets Harbor had swollen beyond its original size. What was once a modest lakeside village had become one of the largest military bases in North America. Such were the vagaries of war.

Distracted by the bustle in town, she failed to glimpse the tall figure approaching from the fort. When its walk became a run, however, the heavy footfalls seized her attention. A moment later, she broke into a run herself.

"Ichabod!" she cried, holding out a hand.

"Dela!" answered the delighted human, grasping not her offered palm but her entire waist. He spun her around a couple of times, then, suddenly aghast at his burst of enthusiasm, set her down gently. "I'm so sorry! Your back—you were gravely injured the last time I saw you."

The Water Maiden beamed. "No need to worry, my friend. Goblin healers *are* as talented as Betua promised."

"Ah, yes, the one with the red eyes and floppy ears." Ichabod stroked his bony chin. "Ever since that day, I've regretted agreeing to let her take you. I'd only just met her."

Dela shook her head. "No, Ichabod, your instincts proved to be good. Have you not learned to trust them yet?"

The lanky officer bowed in mock supplication. "I continue to learn, my dear Water Maiden. I've had plenty of time to."

"Oh? Are the wartime duties of a captain of artillery so light?"

Ichabod pointed to the epaulettes on his shoulders. "It's Major Crane, actually, though I've spent most of the past year moving mud and stone, not troops in battle."

"Major?" Dela felt a surge of pride. "Your commander must have heard of your heroics."

"He heard no such thing," Ichabod said. "As far as he is concerned, I did nothing more than act as a courier to General Harrison's army—just as Commodore Chauncey, who commands the naval forces here, knows nothing of my presence at the battle on Lake Erie."

"But, then, how did you come to—"

"I was promoted to major for 'meritorious service and general good conduct,'" said the officer with a lighthearted chuckle. "It means that while I haven't proven myself in battle, I am a competent staff officer. You needn't worry about my feelings, Dela. I have learned a great deal since this war began, starting with the most important lesson of all: Do right because it is right, not because it will earn you renown. Besides, even if I were inclined to tell my story, who would listen? I don't believe one half of it myself."

Raucous laughter from the town reclaimed her attention. "Sounds like your fellow soldiers and sailors are having a merry time tonight, Ichabod. Why did you not join them?"

"Not everything has changed for me, Dela. I still prefer a quiet night with a good book to stuffy social affairs. Indeed, I passed on an invitation to dine this evening at Commodore Chauncey's residence. The officers are entertaining a visitor from New York, a colonel sent by the governor to assess our defenses."

"That does not sound like a stuffy social affair at all," she said reproachfully. "It sounds like a conversation you should have joined."

Ichabod cast her a sideways glance. "The truth is, I didn't relish hearing another night of toasts to a certain officer. He commands the *USS General Pike*, one of the ships built here last year. He received a letter from Virginia a few days ago. His sweetheart accepted his proposal of marriage."

"Does his good fortune bother you so much?"

"It isn't his good fortune that bothers me, Dela," replied the uncomfortable officer, "as it is my *ill* fortune. I, too, had feelings for the young lady, Miss Eliza King of Norfolk. Now she will marry another."

Dela patted his arm. "A good man, at least?"

"A great man, by all accounts," said Ichabod. "After the war, Eliza will become Mrs. William Montgomery Crane."

▲▲▲

It took nearly an hour to persuade Ichabod to attend the party. Dela's appeals to duty and brotherly affection failed, as did her request that Ichabod ask the governor's emissary about the war. What finally turned the tide was Dela's offer to attend the party with him, magically disguised.

So it was that Major Ichabod Crane entered Commodore Chauncey's residence arm in arm with a slender woman dressed in a light-blue gown, dark stockings extending to stiff leather shoes, and a white lace cap. The Water Maiden had assumed a more youthful version of her guise as Cordelia Lynn, a prim and proper lady of the Hudson Valley.

"I'm surprised to see you here tonight, brother, and with such a lovely companion." Dashing in the crisply pressed uniform of a master commandant, Will Crane kissed Dela's hand with a dramatic flourish. "Why have we not been blessed with your presence before, Miss Lynn?"

"I only just arrived from Kingston to visit my cousin, sir," Dela replied, wondering if Ichabod could make it through the evening without giggling. "I hear you command the *Pike*. Were you acquainted with the late Zebulon Pike?"

"I did not have that honor, although I have learned much of him from Ichabod," Will said.

"And you can learn even more of him from *The Analectic Magazine*," said a new voice from Dela's right—a high, carefully modulated voice that struck her as vaguely familiar. "My essay about General Pike will be published in the next edition—that is, if the editor can manage to tear himself away from his other duties to complete the task."

"How droll," said Will, arching an eyebrow. "Miss Cordelia Lynn, may I present Washington Irving, the editor of *The Analectic Magazine*."

Washington Irving? That boy who took the voyage up the Hudson with me? Dela looked at the full-grown, well-dressed man before her. No matter how many times she experienced the time difference between Folk realms and the Blur, the effect could still be startling.

"That's *Colonel* Irving to you, sir," he corrected with a sly smile. "I serve as aide-de-camp to the governor. He dispatched me to Sackets Harbor to judge its defenses."

"And have you rendered a verdict?" Dela asked.

"So far, I can judge only that there is no defense for staying in such a desolate, rain-soaked corner of the country," Irving said, "though I suppose there is a certain relief in change, even though it be from bad to worse. When travelling in a stagecoach, it is often a comfort to shift one's position, if only to be bruised in a new place."

"None of us is in Sackets Harbor for the mud, or the company," Will said with a smirk. "We do our duty and make the best of it."

Washington Irving ignored the jibe. He was staring intently at Dela's face—or, more specifically, at the space above her head where Irving imagined he saw the youthful face of Cordelia Lynn. "Have we not met before, ma'am?"

"Not to my recollection," Dela replied, seeing Ichabod's mouth twitch nervously.

Irving seemed dissatisfied but decided not to pursue the matter. "I am inclined to make a toast," he said loudly, attracting the attention of the other guests. "On previous evenings, I have heard others raise a glass to Master Commandant Crane and his newly betrothed. It was not my place to toast an officer whose acquaintance I only recently made. But I've since learned that his betrothed, Eliza King of Norfolk, was the childhood companion of Susan Wheeler Decatur. Susan and her husband, Commodore Stephen Decatur, are among my closest friends. So now, ladies and gentlemen, please join me in toasting another naval officer with the good sense, and good tactics, to capture the heart of a Norfolk girl!"

As the rest of the company raised their glasses in salute, Dela looked up apologetically at Ichabod, who'd managed to don a polite smile. She opted to shift topics. "So, Mister Crane, tell me about this ship of yours. Have you commanded the *General Pike* long?"

"Only a few months," Will replied. "She's what navy men call a corvette, Miss Lynn. Not quite as large as a frigate, like the *Mohawk*, or as light as a schooner, like the *Sylph*."

Dela had been completely unprepared to hear that word come out of Will Crane's mouth. "The . . . *Sylph*?"

He looked nonplussed. "Yes, ma'am, the *USS Sylph*. Built and launched here in Sackets Harbor last year. The schooner's name comes from some obscure Swiss writer, I think. He claimed a Sylph was an air spirit or some such rot."

The name of Paracelsus is not so obscure where I came from, Dela was tempted to say.

"If you're near the shipyard tomorrow, I'll point her out," Will added. "The *Sylph* is nestled right next to another schooner, the *Lady of the Lake*."

Now Dela was even more shocked by the unexpected parallels. Her thoughts turned quickly from the *Sylph* in the harbor to the Sylph she left behind in Detroit. He'd spoken again of his brother, sister, and father. And she'd related her latest conversation with her frustrated mother, still insistent that Dela settle down at Long Island-on-the-Holston and start a family.

A Sylph nestled next to a Lady of the Lake—a ship named after my own grandmother Nimue, companion of King Arthur. Merely a coincidence?

In the Goblins' underground grotto, Dela and Goran often sat together, dangling their feet in the water. She'd waited for Goran to take her in his arms. She'd waited in vain. Something held him back. Did he still believe he had nothing to offer her, as Skenandoah had once suggested? Was it the problem as simple as Goran still being in physical discomfort, having not yet healed?

Or was it something more fundamental? Goran had lost everyone he'd ever loved. First his mother, then the rest of his family. *Is he afraid to love—and lose—again?*

Lost in painful speculation, Dela failed to notice Ichabod's initial signals. It took a subtle shove for him to get her attention. "Miss Lynn," he said, keeping his voice level. "Remember that stroll along the shore you requested? Might we take it now?"

"A 'stroll' at this time of night, with a frigid wind blowing off the lake?" Washington Irving asked. "Are you daft, man, or just bored by your brother's talk of shipbuilding?"

But Dela had finally read the urgency written on Ichabod's gaunt face. "A good stiff breeze may do me good, sir," she said. "I would welcome that stroll."

As quickly as propriety would allow, the two made their exit and walked briskly along a narrow street, then turned north toward the harbor. "Will mentioning the *Sylph* reminded me to tell you something important," Ichabod whispered.

What was that?

Dela held up a hand to silence Ichabod and looked over her shoulder. She thought she'd heard footsteps on the road, but she saw no one behind them. She nodded to him to go on.

"A few weeks ago, I led a small detachment about fifty miles south to Fort Oswego to obtain supplies. The night after I arrived, I spotted a small figure flying over the lake. At first I thought it was a bird. As it got closer, I realized it was a fairy. Thinking it might be Goran, I waved my arms to attract his attention. But the flyer didn't respond."

"It was not Goran," Dela said. "I left him behind in Detroit, not yet fully healed."

"It wasn't my only sighting," Ichabod continued. "The next day I was in the woods and again saw a winged fairy. Whether it was the same one as before, I couldn't say. This time, though, he wasn't flying; he was running along a creek. I chased him for a time, but the trees were too thick. I lost him."

A Sylph who chose to run instead of fly? It was an oddity, but Ichabod's tale offered more than that. It was a clue, one that might finally lead her to the source of the gifts of power—and the reason why she and Goran had been followed during prior rangings.

"Lead me there as soon as possible, Ichabod," Dela requested. "Where two winged Folk range, there may well be others."

▲▲▲

One day and one magically concocted order later, Major Ichabod Crane was perched awkwardly on a light-brown mare, his bony elbows and knobby knees flapping in the breeze as he rode south, seemingly alone, from Sackets Harbor. His concocted mission was to seek out any threats to the supply route up from Oswego. His real mission was to help the Water Maiden seek out any signs of winged fairies.

The trail was rough and muddy. Dela would have made better time by lake. But, of course, her friend could never have kept up with her pace on the water, even by rowing or sailing behind her, and leaving him behind was unthinkable. It had been Ichabod, after all, who knew where to look.

Oh, who do I think to fool? Dela chided herself. She wouldn't have left him behind in any event. Dela enjoyed the company of the gallant, if ungainly, Ichabod Crane.

Along the way, she learned much about the conduct of the war. For all the blood and treasure spent along the Great Lakes, neither the

Americans nor the British had gained a decisive advantage there. The only clear losers in the war thus far had been Tecumseh's confederacy in the northwest and the Red Stick Creeks in the southwest.

The end of the European war against Napoleon in early 1814, however, had allowed Britain to transfer new resources to North America. Thousands of fresh troops landed in Maryland and marched to Washington, where they overwhelmed the defenders and burned much of the capital. According to the last dispatches, the British army was headed for Baltimore.

"The next enemy campaign could be against our own base at Sackets Harbor," Ichabod continued as their horse trotted across a marshy meadow. "That's why we devoted so much time to shoring up our defenses. The Britain squadron on Lake Ontario has forced us to bring supplies by oxcart from—"

Dela held up a warning hand. Just as she had after they'd excused themselves from Commodore Chauncey's dinner party, the Water Maiden thought she heard someone following them. Ichabod caught her meaning and wheeled their mount. The two peered into the dark forest from which they'd just emerged, but not a branch moved. Not a leaf crunched under foot or hoof.

The two resumed their journey. Soon they arrived at the east bank of the Oswego River, which was swollen from heavy rains. Rather than head toward the small settlement at its mouth, Ichabod turned upriver to look for a crossing. As they rode, Dela watched the forest. From somewhere within its murky depths came a loud, throaty croak. From somewhere farther off, perhaps from the town at the mouth of the Oswego, came a shrill, high-pitched howl.

Indeed we have *drawn pursuers*, she thought. *A frog and a puppy. Thank God I still possess such keen skills of woodcraft.*

Suddenly, from across the river, new sounds reached Dela's ears: Hoofbeats. Tree branches bending and breaking. And a voice, grunting, shrieking, praying.

"Look there!" Ichabod exclaimed, pointing to a spot where a dirt path extended from the forest to the river's edge. It was a moonless night, wispy clouds partially blocking out the stars. But the faint light was sufficient to reveal the figure emerging from the trees. It was a small palfrey, panting and snorting. On its back was a human girl, of medium height and somewhat plump, riding sidesaddle with two legs extending well beyond her balled-up dress and petticoat.

The girl leapt off her tired mount, apparently intending to lead the skittish animal across the not-so-shallow ford. Twice she glanced back the way she'd just come, her shoulders rising and falling what appeared to be a combination of terror and exhaustion.

Ichabod guessed her intention too. "Hold on!" he called, prodding their mare into the ford from the opposite side. "I'll come to you!"

The girl shook her head energetically, mouthing words that neither Dela nor Ichabod could hear over the rushing water. Fearing the worst, Dela reinforced her concealment and tightened her grip on her trident. When the mare reached the west bank, Ichabod quickly dismounted and rushed to the girl's side, the Water Maiden close at his heels.

"What chases you, ma'am?" he asked. "A wild beast?"

Eyes wide with fright, the young woman shook her head again. "A big . . . a big horse," she stammered. "Black. Came out of the swamp."

Ichabod took her hand, staring into her small blue eyes with his great green ones. "You're safe now, girl. Pray tell us what has you so frightened. Did the black horse chase you?"

"Came out of the swamp," she repeated. "No warning. A towering, misshaped thing."

Dela tugged at the major's loose-fitting sleeve. "May be more than a horse, Ichabod. Some monster may have sprung on her. We need a description."

He nodded and looked back at the girl. "Can you tell us your name?"

"Charlotte," she replied. "Charlotte Rainger. My uncle lives on a farm south of the village. My mother brought me here from Massachusetts to visit him."

"Pleased to make your acquaintance, young Charlotte. I am Major Ichabod Crane of the United States Army. You are safe in my protection."

Ichabod's comforting words accomplished their task; Charlotte no longer looked terrified. To Dela's surprise, the girl was indignant.

"I am *not* so young, major," she insisted, smoothing back a lock of wavy yellow hair. "I am sixteen—practically a woman."

"My apologies, Miss Rainger," said Ichabod, blushing and obviously uncomfortable. "I meant no offense. I meant only to—"

"And it was *not* just a black horse chasing me," Charlotte said, fear continuing to dissolve from her voice. "There was a rider. Queerest rider I ever saw."

Ichabod tried to smile reassuringly but managed only to twist his mouth into a half grimace. "What made the rider look so queer?"

Charlotte opened her mouth to answer, but no words came. Instead, from behind them came a low, rattling snort. Then a long, black shape emerged from the forest, shaking a matted mane of long, black hair.

Dela scrambled past the two gaping humans and ran toward it. Whatever the black shape was, it wheeled and began galloping away.

"Who are you?" demanded Ichabod Crane as he urged his mare forward and, bending low, scooped up Dela to place her on the saddle back behind him. They dashed after their quarry, Ichabod insisting that the rider halt and identify himself and Dela wracking her brain to remember every sort of equine monster she'd learned about during ranger training.

Although Ichabod spurred his steed to greater speed, the gap wasn't closing. The fleeing horse seemed fully capable of matching their pace. "Can't you do something, Dela?" the major shouted over galloping hooves and rushing wind. "Confuse it? Put it to sleep?"

Of course! Do I not wield more than a spear and a net?

Dela rose to her feet on the bouncing back of the mare, holding the side of Ichabod's head with one hand for balance and drumming on her necklace of enchanted shells with the other. She sang of endless meadows stretching beneath a warm sun of endless summer. She sang of hidden springs of clear, cool water. She sang of tall, tasty grass and soft, springy grass.

Dela's heart sank when she felt their own mare's pace slacken. Being in constant motion with no clear view of the retreating black figure made it impossible to narrow the target of her spellsong. She could only hope both charmed horses would slow in tandem.

"It's working!" Ichabod exclaimed. "Look up there. It's stopped!"

Silhouetted against the night sky, their quarry reared atop a mound of earth. A tall black stallion of powerful frame, kicking its forelegs in the cold night air. And on its back? A rider, yes, but not at all what Dela had expected to see. The rider was short and squat, like a human child of enormous girth. A dark cloak tied around the rider's neck covered most of its oddly shaped body.

Pursuers and pursued sat a dozen paces apart on their respective mounts for a moment, staring soundlessly at each other. Then the dark rider's voice broke the silence, the sounds entirely unexpected. There was no haughty challenge, no stentorian command, not even a conciliatory greeting. What spewed from the rider's mouth was a perplexing stream of sounds. Clicks. Grunts. Screams. Sobs. And, interspersed among them, words that Dela easily recognized even though they formed only a meaningless string of gibberish.

Words not in English but in Folktongue.

"Secrets spied!" the rider muttered between derisive laughter and wails of agony. "Love of hate! Ghost in the glen! Long day of night! Diverse shapes! Tale of tiny men! Goblin horse!"

Ichabod looked questioningly at Dela. "What do we do? That boy seems to have lost his head."

"Lost my head!" the rider repeated. Then he yanked his reins and kicked the flank of his mount. Seeming to slough off the effects of Dela's spellsong, the black horse took off down the trail again, the little rider's cackles quickly fading into inaudibility.

Ichabod prodded his mare into a run as well. They raced along the dirt road, past tall trees on their right and patch of swampy ground on their left. Dela chose not to renew her spell, for this time the mare was outpacing the stallion.

Ahead of them Dela could a clearing and, beyond that, a bridge over a small creek. The dark rider had crossed the rough planks of the bridge and stood on the opposite side, shouting more gibberish.

"If we can but reach that bridge," Ichabod said, urging their horse forward.

Thus distracted, the human failed to see the projectile the dark rider threw at them. But Dela saw—and proved the Goblin mages had successfully restored her reflexes. She sprang onto Ichabod's left shoulder, yanking as hard as she could and allowing her momentum to do the rest. The girths of their saddle gave way, the seat slipping precipitously to one side. Dela fell off the horse entirely and crashed into the ground, which proved to be propitiously muddy. Somehow, Ichabod managed to encircle the mare's neck with two long arms and stayed ahorse.

His head had dipped low enough, however, for the rider's throw to miss. Fearing the worst—a dangerous missile hurled from an enchanted gift of power—Dela sloshed through the mud to find it. The object was solid, round, and bright orange.

It was a pumpkin.

Laughing maniacally, the small rider slipped from his own mount, which was still chomping and snorting. As he did so, his cloak caught on something. Dela heard it rip in two. Then a wave of incongruous sensations left her reeling.

Her ears heard the sound of many voices.

Her skin felt the telltale pricks and pressure of an expanding Shimmer bubble.

And her eyes beheld not a pudgy human child standing next to the black stallion but a fairy—a fairy with a thick neck, well-muscled arms and legs, and the gold-colored tips of two feathered wings extending several inches above his snarling, snapping face.

A Sylph!

Before she could react, before she could even make sense of the revelation, the winged fairy spun on a heel and ran along the creek, disappearing into a thicket. Then Dela felt a hand on her shoulder. Having dropped her trident when she fell off the horse, she instinctively snatched her beaded net off her shoulder as she turned.

Another Sylph stood before her, a female dressed in a dark-green gown cinched at the waist with a buff-colored belt. Her chestnut hair hung in a ponytail halfway down her back. The Sylph's hazel-flecked eyes regarded Dela with cold suspicion.

"Where is he, ranger of the Gwragedd Annwn?" the Sylph demanded. "If you have harmed him, you will pay dearly."

"Harmed him?" Dela assumed the female was referring to the male Sylph who'd been the dark rider. "Why would I—"

"Where is he?" the newcomer repeated. Behind her, two other Sylphs leapt into the air and scanned the surrounding countryside.

"Step back, fairy woman," said a voice, a deep and menacing voice that—Dela realized with a shock—belonged to Ichabod Crane, who'd drawn his sword.

But the Sylphs was uninterested in Dela's would-be human protector. The two rangers hovering in the air continued to search the trees. Two mages stood on each side of the Shimmer bubble, sustaining it with magecraft, and the female Sylph only had eyes for the Water Maiden.

"Do you know them, Dela?" Ichabod asked. "Are they Goran's friends?"

The Sylph's hazel eyes narrowed. "I should have known. *You* are the one he spoke of, the one called Dela. Is Goran here, as well?"

Dela shook her head, unsure how to proceed.

"I am Ailee," said the Sylph. "Goran is my brother, although my escorts would have me say Goran *was* my brother. If they knew what I know of you, their reaction would be . . . unkind."

Dela frowned. "Why would they . . ."

"The man we seek is my brother, too. Kaden, former captain of the Warriors Guild. Now a Blur-struck invalid. A *madman*." Ailee's eyes rolled as she mouthed the last word.

"Kaden!" Dela said quickly. "I have heard Goran speak often of him, of all of you. He feels a great—"

"Now is *not* the time," Ailee interrupted, inclining her head toward the hovering Sylphs. "A few days ago, Kaden escaped from our village on Iris Isle. Somehow he slipped away from his chamber, made his way down the Thunder Falls, and swam to shore. Rangers have been looking for him ever since. This is the third such search party. How many more the grandmasters will authorize, I cannot say."

If my brother were Blur-struck and missing, I would plead as hard as I could for my people to rescue him, whatever the cost. But I am even less fortunate than Ailee. My brother lies dead in his grave, slain by Pukwudgies.

As concisely as she could, Dela related the events of the past few minutes. "Why is your brother riding and running instead of flying?"

"I do not know," Ailee replied. "It may be his madness. He does not remember who he is. So he may not remember *what* he is, what his wings are for."

The two fairies stood for a moment in silence, looking at the ground.

"Is he . . . safe?" Ailee asked hesitantly. Her eyes were no longer cold. They looked wet.

"Other than speaking nonsense, he seemed physically undamaged," Dela said.

"No, I mean, is *Goran* safe?"

Dela nodded. "He was seriously wounded in battle but is now healing among friends." *Calling the Goblins "friends" is a bit generous, but now is not the time for lengthy explanations.*

One of the Sylph rangers alighted next to them on the muddy ground. "Ailee, we see no sign of Kaden and hear no answer to our summoning spells. I will go on from here, but you and the mages must transport back."

Ailee took in a deep breath and gave a brief nod. When the Sylph ranger returned to the air, Ailee looked at Dela. "Will you pass along a message to Goran?"

"Of course."

"Tell him I miss him," the Sylph said in a trembling voice. "Tell him our father misses him, too, despite everything. Tell him we love him."

That much, we have in common, Dela thought as the Shimmer bubble rippled, shrank, and disappeared, transporting four of the Sylphs back to their village. The remaining Sylph ranger flew off in the direction Dela had indicated.

During the conversation with Ailee, Ichabod Crane had stood at Dela's side in rapt fascination. After the last flashes of Shimmer disappeared, however, he shouted in alarm and pointed to the trail.

The girl, Charlotte Rainger, had apparently decided to ride after them. She was standing next to her palfrey, both panting with exhaustion. But they weren't alone. There was another horse standing there, too, equally exhausted. Its dismounted rider didn't look tired at all. He looked amazed—and triumphant.

"I knew it!" said Washington Irving as Dela and Ichabod approached. "I *knew* there was more going on than met my jaundiced eye. You, Cordelia Lynn, you lied to me at the dinner party. I recognized you from before, from that voyage so many years ago up the Hudson. But then, you were a middle-aged matron of the valley. Only by some form of goblin sorcery could you have gotten younger while I got older."

Dela opened her mouth to reply but Irving raised a finger to silence her.

"I followed you and Major Crane from the party the other night," he continued. "I overheard you two speak of flying fairies. So, when you rode out the next day, I followed again."

"Across many miles of forest and marsh and stream," said Dela, not bothering to hide her admiration. "Without being discovered. And resisting my spellsong all the way—at least in part."

Irving flashed knowing smile. "I don't understand all this, not yet, and I can only guess the meaning of 'spellsong.' But we will have plenty of time on the way back to Sackets Harbor for you to explain it to me. And I thought my days at the magazine had run their course! Once I share my new tales with my readers, the mysteries of Diedrich Knickerbocker will seem little but a trifle. My sketches of James

Lawrence and Oliver Hazard Perry will be tame by comparison. *The Analectic* will be the talk of New York! With so profitable an enterprise, perhaps I can, while still young, arrive at that happy age when a man can be idle with impunity."

Dela tried not to respond to the earnest young writer with laughter. "We *will* have plenty of time together on the way back to Sackets Harbor, Mister Irving. That much is true."

▲▲▲

Much later, Dela tore herself reluctantly from Ichabod's embrace and climbed onto Washington Irving's horse. "A difficult work of spellsong is putting it mildly," she told Ichabod. "Irving is not fully Sighted. But his powers of perception are strong, if intermittent. I really have no choice but to accompany him back to Sackets Harbor and ensure that my spell fully takes root, that his memories remain safely clouded."

As if on cue, Irving shook his head. "The . . . horseman," he said to no one in particular. "The horseman had lost his head. He . . . he threw something, threw it across the bridge."

"He did," Ichabod agreed, managing to look both sympathetic and mischievous. Then he pointed at Charlotte Rainger, who was rubbing the flanks of her palfrey and whistling a merry tune. "Your memory spell has worked on her, it seems."

"She will remember only meeting you on the banks of the Oswego," Dela said.

"But just in case, shouldn't I escort her back to the farm? Perhaps pay her mother and uncle a short visit? That will fix her new memory more securely. To meet an officer in the wilderness, and then not have him see her home—that may strike them as odd."

Dela nodded, though not in agreement. Charlotte wasn't even partially Sighted; the spell was already in effect. But Dela knew why Ichabod wanted to tarry here for a time. And she wholeheartedly approved.

Besides, Dela was anxious to be on her way. After reaching Sackets Harbor, she would immediately travel by lake back to Detroit. Back to Goran. She had so much to tell him, so much to say in his sister's words and in her own. And a new plan to share with him—a new plan for both of them.

For Dela now knew the location of the Sylph village.

"So, Charlotte," she heard Ichabod say as the two humans rode away. "You said your home is in Massachusetts?"

"Yes," said the girl, "from a county on the border with Rhode Island. It's called Norfolk."

Chapter 22 – The Gears

Har the Tower sat up and pushed the human-woven blanket to the edge of the pallet. Then he got to his feet and walked to a small window. He couldn't sleep, so he figured he might as well watch the sun hurtle across the sky.

When Har accompanied Roza back to Spirit Forest after the last Red Stick chiefs surrendered, he'd planned only a brief audience with Prince Veelund before continuing on to Grünerberg. Har knew King Alberich would want an in-person report, and to add Red Eagle's enchanted war club to the Dwarfs' collection of magecrafted weapons.

At Roza's insistence, however, Har had showed the red stick to Veelund, who'd asked for time to study it. Given a private room in the ranger guildhall while he waited for Veelund to return the item, Har passed the time by delving into the guild's extensive library, looking up every reference he could find to winged Folk. In addition to the Sylphs of Cornwall, and to the indigenous Mialuka his friends had previously sought out in North Carolina, there were entries on the Greenies of England, the Pillywiggins of Wales, the Aziza of West Africa, the Peris of Persia, and several others. Identifying the rangers who trailed Goran and Dela could be the key to tracking the gifts of power to their source.

Whether his friends had already found that source, however, Har couldn't say. On his very first day at Spirit Forest, he'd asked to use the Elves' message chamber. To send messages from the field, rangers used personal instruments, such as Har's scheitholt and Goran's flute. But most Folk nations had more massive iterations—huge horns, enormous harps, or gigantic drums fashioned of monster bone and sinew—arranged in special chambers and kept continuously infused with elemental magic to send brief messages over long distances.

While Veelund had forbidden Har from entering the chamber itself, he was permitted to write messages for delivery. So far, however, Har had received no response from Goran or Dela. That fact, combined with his duty to report to King Alberich, made him increasingly impatient.

Today's audience with Veelund must be my last.

▲▲▲

As Har followed his escorts through the Elf village, past shabby buildings and even shabbier inhabitants, he felt his resolution soften. As much as Veelund had delayed his departure, Har could understand the prince's own determination to solve the riddle of the gifts of power. Unless the prince could clear his name, and that of his Folk, the future of Elfkind in America was very much in doubt.

They passed a line of ramshackle dwellings, reminding Har of his first visit to Spirit Forest. But this time, none of the hovels on the winding street was filled with desperate Ellyllon children. The hovels were empty. It was the street *itself* that was filled with the Elfish Folk of Wales. Ellyllon of all ages and walks of life. Ellyllon with bundles slung over their backs or in little wheeled carts. They looked thin, haggard, and tired, but none looked desperate. They were smiling.

Momentarily blocked by the crowd, Har and his escorts stood for a few minutes and watched a trio of Elf rangers lead the Ellyllon to an intersection and then leftward. "Where are they going?" Har asked the escort at his side.

"Home," said the warrior, and nothing more.

To a newly constructed district of the village, perhaps? Or to another encampment of tents beyond its walls? Har could only speculate and knew that voicing his speculations would produce no more details from the tight-lipped warriors.

Hearing the word "home" did, however, restore Har's determination. When he arrived at the Royal Hall and found Roza waiting to usher him in, the Dwarf began rehearsing what he would say. *I appreciate your gracious hospitality, Veelund, but with or without the war club, I must be off. Duty requires it. And I must discover the fate of my friends.*

"The prince has been held up," Roza said as they walked into the great room. "He asks that you wait while he attends to an important matter."

Har shrugged, hoping his impatience wouldn't show. "Do you know if he is returning Red Eagle's club today? I really should take it to Grünerberg with me."

Roza's long hair rippled like a veil as she shook her head. "I have heard nothing of it since you first presented it to him."

Trying to act nonchalant, he cast another admiring look on Veelund's elaborate water clock. Brought in by a small pipe, a stream of water filled a top chamber. Through a series of paddles, gears, and cams mostly obscured from view, the falling water drove two notched wheels that showed the passing time in Blur days and Shimmer days.

Har listened to the water trickling in and out of the clock. He listened to the steady ticking of its gears. Then Har drew closer, trying to see around its front panel into its inner workings, only to be startled by the high-pitched trill that signaled the end of another Blur day.

"Trying to compute how long I made you wait?" Veelund bustled into the great room, his surcoat swirling. "I apologize for the delay."

"Not at all," Har said. "I only just arrived."

Veelund drew his lips into a wry smile. "I do not refer to our meeting today, Har. I have kept you in our village, away from your duties, far longer than you intended, have I not?"

Har bowed low. "My primary duty is to serve as emissary to the Elves of Spirit Forest. To foster better relations."

The prince laughed. "When courtly words blow as wind, the tall Tower sways? Is that the way of it?"

"Something like that," Har agreed, then recognized the moment of levity as an opportunity. "But now that you mention it, sir, and though I appreciate—"

"Have you thought more about my invitation?" Veelund interrupted.

"Your *invitation*?"

"For your King Alberich to journey here to Spirit Forest. To continue our negotiations personally."

"Yes, of course." Actually, the idea had slipped Har's mind entirely. He shot a quick glance at Roza, still standing awkwardly in the corner. "Though if I am to convey your gracious hospitality properly, I fear I must be—"

Veelund interrupted yet again. "You know, Har, that water clock is more than just a tool for devising schedules and making astronomical observations. It is a tool of instruction. I often study it, as you were, to remind me that the passage of time is inexorable. Of our desires, it pays no heed. Its lesson is that we should endeavor to *do* something, that we may say that we have not lived in vain, that we may leave some impression of ourselves on the flow of time."

"Never took you for a philosopher, Your Majesty," Har said. *What are his fancy words meant to tell me?*

"About that invitation, Har," Veelund went on. "I wonder if you might reconsider its delivery. We could send it at once by message spell. That way you can remain here and help us prepare for Alberich's arrival."

"As I said before," began the Dwarf, trying not to sound irritated, "King Alberich is more likely to make the trip if I deliver your invitation personally, as protocol requires."

"Protocol!" Veelund chuckled. "Protocol and ceremony and such things may be necessary in order to dazzle the people. But surely those of us who rule need not bother with such formalities. All who have gained such rank should be brothers, whatever may be their nation of birth."

As promising as the Elf's talk of brotherhood sounded, Har willed himself not to be distracted. "Prince Veelund, I sent a message to Grünerberg days ago but have yet to receive a reply. Perhaps there is a problem with your spellsong chamber. Or perhaps my Folk do not yet trust Elves enough to respond. I truly think I should be—"

"Your prior message concerned only a personal matter. Surely a request from one ruler to another would be treated with greater immediacy."

Har racked his brain, trying to come up with a diplomatic way to describe Alberich's prejudices. He shot a quick glance at Roza and saw an expression of alarm on her freckled face. Veelund saw it, too. He sighed, arching an eyebrow and inclining his head slightly.

It was then that Har felt his stomach lurch.

"Your Majesty, how did you know my message was a personal one?" the Dwarf asked.

Veelund was looking at Roza. "An invitation in the ranger's own words would be better, of course," he said, ignoring the Dwarf's question. "But we have his earlier one, and your close association with him. That should be enough to devise an authentic message."

The tightness that had begun in Har's stomach now extended far beyond it. His hands formed tight fists. His leg muscles clenched tightly. His eyes narrowed into slits. The tightness in his throat nearly kept him from speaking.

Nearly.

"What is your real purpose in inviting Alberich to Spirit Forest?" Har demanded, his voice sounding unnaturally husky.

Neither Elf answered him.

"I shall do as you ask, my prince," Roza said. She walked to the door, keeping her eyes fixed on the floor.

Har watched her go and felt the tightness suddenly leave his body. Now his legs were shaking in anticipation. His clenched fists were trembling in anger, his lips fluttering from indecision, forming and then discarding unspoken a series of words, demands, and insults.

Veelund turned his attention to Har, regarding him with a sly smile. "Must I spell it all out for you? I had always seen you as reasonably astute—for a Dwarf."

Har considered his options. He and Veelund were alone. While the prince was well-built and strong-willed, his muscles had developed from pounding a forge, not fighting in battle. He'd allowed Har to enter the room fully armed. Veelund appeared to be unarmed.

How quickly would the armored guards outside be able to reach Veelund's side? What would it gain Har to attack if escape were impossible? And if he tried it, what critical information would he never obtain?

"You wonder if you would rather have my life or the truth," said the prince. "Your thoughts might as well be chiseled on your face."

Har gritted his teeth.

"I am no military man," Veelund continued. "Still, even I know that the moment of greatest peril is the moment of victory. I know that at this moment, in the righteous fury of your defeat, you want to yank one of those axes from your belt and strike. I have no defense. Yet I also have no fear. I feel positively gleeful! Is there joy in danger, then?"

"I have never felt joy in killing, Veelund. Or in betrayal."

"So you do begin to understand what has happened," the Elf prince replied.

"I understand you mean to bait Alberich here under false pretenses, so you can kill him."

Veelund shook his head in mock disgust. "Oh, no, I would not bring your impetuous king here to kill him. I would keep him in Spirit Forest for a time. For however long it takes to negotiate appropriate . . . consideration. We are greatly in need of aid, as you have seen."

Har erupted in frustration. "You can seek aid without subterfuge or violence. You spoke of trade, of peaceful coexistence!"

"So I did. And a trade is precisely what I have in mind."

"No," Har growled. "What you have in mind is seizing a king for ransom."

Veelund shrugged. "Ransom. Consideration. Exchange of value. Call it what you will."

The Dwarf scowled. "I call it a crime."

"Has the emissary now become a judge?" Veelund asked, turning to look at his bookshelf. "In truth, a prince is sometimes obliged to commit crimes. But they are the crimes of his position, not his personal preference. And as for the supposed victim of this 'crime,' who is a greater threat to peace between our two nations than Alberich himself?"

Har chose to treat the question as rhetorical.

Veelund wheeled around and pointed a finger. "You are not my only source of information. I know your king schemes with other Folk against us. I know he desires war, war without end, war until all Elfkind grovels beneath his feet. That will *never* happen. A great people may be killed, but they cannot be intimidated."

Taking a couple of steps toward Veelund, Har tried softening his approach. "There are always alternatives to war. If you will only—"

The prince held up a hand. "Keep a respectful distance, unless you mean to provoke them."

Har froze and cast a quick glance over his shoulder. While his attention had been fixed on Veelund, he'd failed to notice four Elf warriors enter the room and spread out behind him. Though shorter and slighter than Har, they were clad in suits of magecrafted chain mail with hard bronze helms on their heads and sharp bronze swords at their belts. In their gloved hands were bows of bitternut hickory, arrows nocked.

"Again, I admit I am no soldier," said the prince. "Nevertheless, I know there is only one favorable moment in war. Talent consists in knowing how to seize it. If your intent was to settle our differences with brawn, Har, you have missed your moment—though I have always thought your real talents lie elsewhere."

Veelund stared at Har, as if daring the Dwarf to make the next move. The warriors stood motionless along the back wall. But the room was far from silent.

Tick-tock. Whirl-whirl. Tick-tock. Whirl-whirl.

From behind him, from the water clock, came the sound of the gears. Of metal teeth clicking together. Of wheels turning. Relentlessly, unerringly turning.

Without his conscious direction, Har's own teeth began clicking together in concert with the gears. The rhythm proved to be surprisingly calming. He felt his body relax. His arms and legs no longer trembled. His disjointed fears and speculations seemed now to mesh as closely as the gears did. They found clarity. They formed a single conclusion in Har's mind—a confident conclusion, though hardly a reassuring one.

"You lie," the Dwarf said. It was neither an accusation nor a complaint. It was a statement of fact.

"Do I, now?" replied the prince, looking mildly curious.

"Whatever else you may be, you are no fool. You *know* luring Alberich here and taking him hostage will earn you no ransom. It will only bring the very war you claim not to want."

Veelund's eyebrows shot up. But he said nothing.

"You claim to know Alberich's mind. You think if you suggest he journey from Grünerberg to Spirit Forest on foot, he will not be able to resist such a grand adventure."

"Do you not agree?"

Har nodded curtly. "Alberich will enter the Blur. And he will never leave it. Your rangers, your *assassins*, will see to that."

Veelund inclined his head, as if offering a grudging respect. "It is a clever plan, Har, surely you must give me that. When you have an enemy in your power, should you not deprive him of the means of ever injuring you? Alberich's death will leave a rival Folk leaderless at a critical time. And few will suspect our hand in it. After all, would he not be journeying here at our invitation, to negotiate a pact from which Elfkind would richly benefit?"

The Dwarf turned his head and rubbed his nose, chancing a look over his shoulder at the mailed archers. They still held their bows, arrows nocked, but had not yet raised them.

Tick-tock. Whirl-whirl. Tick-tock. Whirl-whirl.

In his mind's eye, Har saw two sets of carefully crafted bronze teeth coming together. He saw one wheeled shaft turning another, relentlessly, unerringly turning.

Another realization came to Har's mind. At first it trilled, like the little clock bell that signaled the passage of a Blur day. Then it tolled—deeper, louder, ominously, like a large brass bell he'd once seen in front of a human church.

"I saw a large troop of Ellyllon today," said Har, allowing his hands to drift ever so slowly to his sides. "They were setting off on a journey of their own. A journey 'home,' I was told."

"A joyous day, indeed, for many in need," the prince said. "It was my duty to wish them a happy homecoming that kept you waiting. Sorry for the inconvenience."

Har disregarded the attempt at misdirection. "And might this home of the Ellyllon lie north and west of here? In the Carolina mountains?"

Veelund grinned. "I am no ranger, Har. The geography of the Blur is not my expertise. I prefer to direct my gaze to the heavens."

The Dwarf followed the Elf's eyes upward, looking through the small window in the ceiling at the darkening sky—and hoping the Elf wouldn't see Har move his hands closer to his belt.

"I heard a tale once," Har said, "from a human friend named Junaluska."

"You rangers make such odd friends."

"It was an old Cherokee tale about a nation of white-skinned Folk called the 'Moon-Eyed People,' a nation the Cherokee supposedly drove away," Har continued. "Junaluska also spoke of a war between the Yunwi Tsunsdi and a foreign Folk that I now believe to be those same Moon-Eyed People. I now believe it was the Yunwi Tsunsdi, not the humans, who drove them off—who drove off the Ellyllon host from the hilltop mounds they had originally seized by force from the Yunwi Tsunsdi. The defeated Ellyllon fled here to Spirit Forest, as refugees of war."

Veelund groaned. "Leave it to a human to ruin a rollicking tale with moralistic nonsense."

Har's hands now rested on the handles of his two handaxes, a development he hoped the Elf prince wouldn't notice. "This is a familiar tale to you, I think, and you disliked it even without the 'moralistic nonsense.' You decided it needed a different ending."

"Can you truly blame me?" Veelund said, holding up his hands in mock surrender.

"I can and I do," Har replied, trying to calculate how quickly he could drop to the floor after launching his missiles. "Again you lie. You spoke of peace, yet you have secretly renewed a war of conquest against the Yunwi Tsunsdi."

The prince dropped his hands. "I always knew your talents extended beyond brute strength, Har. You reason well—for a Dwarf. Alas, not well enough."

Perhaps I should hurl one axe, drop and roll, then target one of the warriors with the other.

"I have renewed no war," Veelund proclaimed, sounding just as earnest as when Har had first met him. "I have ordered no Elf into battle. These Yunwi Tsunsdi you speak of? They left their village of their own accord. So, why should the Ellyllon remain here in torment and poverty? Why should they not return to the abandoned village they once called home?"

Har stared at the Elf prince, trapped in a moment of unexpected indecision. *Veelund is a master of lies. And I never suspected a thing. Big, brawny, blundering Har the Tower . . . I never had a clue. He lied to me for years. He is doing it again.*

But Veelund *looked* sincere. *What reason does he have to lie now?*

"You claim the Yunwi Tsunsdi abandoned their village?" Har asked. "Why would they surrender what they had once paid so dearly to recover from the Ellyllon?"

The expression on Veelund's face suggested neither triumph nor deceit but merely exasperation. "*Do* use your brain, Dwarf. Why did your people leave your homes in Germany to immigrate to America? Were you forced out by Elf armies?"

Har frowned. "There were shortages. Not enough humanwares, not enough game. And many humans had already left our lands to go to America, so we—"

"There is your answer!" Veelund exclaimed. "Many of those Cherokee you speak of have signed treaties with the whites and found new homes in the west, in what the humans call the Arkansas Territory. As they leave, so do sources of humanwares for the local Folk. So do game animals. It should come as no surprise that the Yunwi Tsunsdi decided to follow them westward."

Try as he might, Har couldn't fault Veelund's logic. Ever since the Arrival, Folk nations had relocated repeatedly to stay near the human communities with which they had the closest ties. The migration from Europe to America by Dwarfs, Elves, Goblins, and other Folk was simply a continuation of that process. Indeed, by comparison, Yunwi Tsunsdi migration to Arkansas was a much shorter journey, a less wrenching change in their way of life.

Nevertheless, something about the explanation didn't ring true. During the past few minutes, Har had learned an excruciating lesson. Behind Veelund's logical words crouched a paranoia just as monstrous as Alberich's. Underneath Veelund's soft touch was a hard fist.

Har was no diplomat—that much was now clear. He was no master of clever banter or discerning glances. He was no scholar, no philosopher, no conjurer of grand ideas or intricate plans.

But he did have two hard fists.

And as Har the Tower fell, raining those hard fists down on three Elf warriors, with one handaxe buried in the stopped heart of the fourth and the other axe quivering in the oaken wall behind Veelund's head, the Dwarf's mind was consumed with a single thought. It wasn't about the Elf arrows now buried deep in his back and thigh. It wasn't about the seriousness of his wounds, or whether one of his sword-wielding assailants was about to deliver a final mortal blow. It wasn't about the Elf prince watching the melee with a satisfied sneer.

No. Har's only thought was of his own willful blindness, his foolish arrogance.

Alberich was right. Alberich was right all along.

Chapter 23 – The Rose

Lightning flashed across the midnight sky once. Twice. No doubt thunder rumbled across the river after each strike, but Goran never heard it. The continuous thunder of falling water drowned it out.

"It was not your sister's mention of 'Iris Isle' that jogged my memory," said Dela, who lay next to Goran in a patch of tall grass. "When Ailee said your brother had 'made his way down the Thunder Falls,' during his escape from the Sylph village, my mind went immediately to this place. I remembered hearing the noise from many miles upstream. And I remembered seeing the winged ranger framed against the sky, flying from the island to the mainland. It all fit."

Not for the first time, Goran wondered if she'd let her eagerness overwhelm her good judgment. When he had first glimpsed these rocky cliffs, soaring nearly two hundred feet above the lower surface of the Niagara River, his heart skipped a beat. The cliffs were, at least, a high spot in an otherwise low-lying landscape. But after many days of exploring the site, Goran and Dela had neither found any Shimmer walls nor provoked the Sylphs to make their presence known.

There had been little chance to continue their explorations this day. Heavy rains began just after dawn. It was well after dark before the storm let up, with a final crescendo of lightning and parting shower of cold rain. As the clouds dissipated, the moon made its first appearance. He gazed up at it, the lustrous nighttime visitor that had so thoroughly charmed him during his journeyman rangings across the Carolina countryside.

Then Goran closed his eyes and whispered the words of the prayer he'd said every day since Dela had returned to Detroit after her encounter with Ailee. *Maker of All Things, please bring strength to my sister and hope to my father. Please bring peace to my brother's ravaged mind. And please show me the path to bring us all back together.*

As he finished his prayer, he heard the Water Maiden rise to her feet. He felt her touch his arm. He opened his eyes. Then he drew in a quick breath and held onto it desperately, as if it were a lifeline to a drowning child.

Stretched across the sky, glistening in the moonglow like the edge of a Shimmer bubble, was the faint but unmistakable arc of a rainbow. Dela squeezed his arm, sending a jolt of excitement through his mostly healed body. Of course, the touch of her hand always gave Goran a thrill, but his excitement had another cause. He'd interpreted Dela's unspoken message.

Iris Isle, Ailee had said. It must have been named after the ancient Greek goddess of the rainbow, Iris, the messenger goddess who flew down to earth on wings of gold-tipped feathers.

The Sylphs *were* here. Somewhere.

▲▲▲

It wasn't until a day later that Goran and Dela finally discovered the entrance—and not by their own doing. They had been sitting in a tree, finishing their dinner, when they heard voices from the other side of the Niagara River. Immediately on alert, Goran pulled his bow over his head. Dela set down the picked-clean spine of a trout and grabbed the trident she'd set against the bole of the tree.

Three Folk rangers were walking along the river. One bent over and dragged away some cedar boughs, revealing a small canoe. They climbed in, carefully placing several leather-wrapped bundles in the floor of the boat, and began paddling.

After struggling for a time against the swift current, the trio reached Iris Isle. They disembarked and removed their bundles. When they passed almost directly below the tree from which Goran and Dela watched, the Sylph nocked an arrow as a precaution—but Dela waved a finger.

Then she mouthed a single silent word: *Dryads*.

One of the newcomers produced a coil of rope and walked to the tip of the island. When she unrolled it, Goran could see it was not a single line but a rope ladder, the ends of which the Dryad tied to a tree. The other two slung their leather bundles on their backs and, without hesitation, began climbing down the ladder.

"Where are they going?" Dela whispered as the two Dryads climbed out of sight.

Goran found he didn't need to reply with words. He simply pointed. There were two winged figures now hovering above the gorge, waving at the third Dryad as she began her climb.

Before Dela could respond, before Goran could think of what to do next, the two winged figures then flew straight at them. Loaded bows in hand, they nodded meaningfully in the direction of the island's tip, toward the rope ladder.

Goran realized the two Sylph rangers, whose faces looked familiar but whose names he didn't know, were ordering them to follow the Dryads. But he didn't feel like walking across the forested island. He also didn't feel like fumbling his way down the ladder.

"Do you trust me?" he asked. The Water Maiden smiled and nodded.

Goran reached around her back and lifted her into his arms. Then he jumped from the tree branch, relishing the feeling of wind rustling his feathers, of rejuvenated muscle and reknitted bone propelling him into the air, and of Dela's arms wrapped firmly around his neck. With several powerful sweeps he flew toward the Sylphs, who'd headed back to the cliff. He followed them, his face wet from the mist, though perhaps not only from that.

Soaring over the gorge, then banking to his left, Goran could see where the Dryads had gone. Directly underneath the waterfall was a cavern shielded by a massive ledge. The two Sylph rangers approached it at an angle, gliding into the space between the falling water and the cliffside. Again Goran followed their lead, fighting his way through a surprisingly strong headwind into the cave.

He found himself confronted by two arrows pointed at his chest.

"We come as friends," Dela started quickly, slipping to the ground and holding her hands out. "I am Dela, ranger of the Gwragedd Annwn, and my companion is—"

"We know who you are," the taller Sylph said gruffly. "And we know *what* you are."

I was a fool to think I could ever be welcome here.

"We have come to volunteer our services to Ailee," Dela continued, "a greenweaver of your village who has been—"

"We know that, too," the Sylph ranger interrupted. "When you were first spotted on Iris Isle, Ailee came forward to admit she might have inadvertently disclosed our location. You, Dela, have been granted permission to see her. The other, who calls himself Lonefeather, will remain here."

Dela exchanged a look with Goran. "Surely he could be allowed to—"

"He will stay here in the cave—*alone*, as is only fitting," said the Sylph with finality.

One of the Dryads, thin and standing nearly four feet tall, flashed her enormous green eyes. "This man is of your own Folk. Why may he not enter?"

"He *was* of our Folk, Hespera," the Sylph snapped. "Now he flies alone. Made Lonefeather by his own mouth. Made traitor by his own hand."

The Water Maiden reached down and gave Goran's arm a squeeze, as if to say, *Do not worry. You will not be alone for long.*

I wish I had her confidence, he thought as he watched Dela follow the rest through the Shimmer wall at the back of the cavern. *But I fear my vigil will be a lengthy one.*

▲▲▲

To one kept outside in the Blur, it was, indeed, a lengthy wait. After the first night in the cave, Goran ventured out to shoot a trout for breakfast. By the fourth night, he no longer bothered to keep a constant watch on the Shimmer. He spent hours exploring the islands above the waterfall, the gorge below, and the surrounding countryside.

Although constant activity kept him from wallowing in gloom, his enforced solitude still took a mental toll. Goran thought of his lost brother, of his sister and father on the other side of the Shimmer, of Dela, whose affection and loyalty felt entirely unearned. And of Har, whose aid and companionship would have been most welcome. Before Goran and Dela had left Detroit, the Goblins had allowed them to send a message to Grünerberg, seeking information about their friend. *Har safe*, the reply message had stated. *Expected home soon.*

Goran thought about that message as he flew out of a pounding rain into the windy cave. *Perhaps the Sylphs will allow Dela to send another message to Grünerberg.*

As fate would have it, at just the moment Goran took refuge from the rainstorm, a single Sylph emerged from the Shimmer. Unlike the first two rangers, whose identities Goran did not recall, this Sylph was more than just a vaguely familiar face.

"You look wet but otherwise well," Ceredan noted. The impassivity written on the guildmaster's owlish face wasn't the sort of greeting Goran used to receive from his teacher. At least it wasn't a scowl. "This Dela of yours is an impressive young woman, full of intelligence and grace. She has also proved to be most persuasive, despite the fact that she and her Folk have Sylph blood on their hands."

Goran could think of no apt response to that.

"You will be permitted entrance, but with limitations," Ceredan continued. "You will not set foot in any guildhall, or anywhere near the monster pens. In fact, you and Dela would be well advised to remain in your father's house for your entire stay, which I imagine will be brief."

"Did she explain why we have come? To aid in the search for Kaden?"

Ceredan looked down. "Yes. But it was not her most persuasive argument. In truth, the Council of Elders entertains little hope of recovering your brother."

The news felt like a slap to Goran's face. Though in truth, it was only one of many. "So, then, why was I permitted entry?"

Ceredan kept his eyes averted. "Dela pointed out that if we distrusted your motives as much as we say, leaving you outside was too great a risk. You might decide to fly off and betray our location."

▲▲▲

Having spent much time in underground domains such as Grünerberg and Detroit, Goran was surprised by how much the Sylphs had managed to make their new home within Iris Isle look like their prior open-air villages. The main cavern was improbably vast, its ceiling so high above the tops of the guildhalls, storehouses, dwellings, and other buildings that Sylphs had plenty of room to stretch their wings. They'd even carved numerous narrow tunnels through the ceiling into rock formations and tree trunks on the surface, letting in natural light to form something like a sky of intermittently shining stars. That Goran and Dela had spotted none of the small holes during their exploration of the island was a testament to the skill of the mages and craftsmen involved.

"Magecrafting a cavern this large must have consumed much elemental magic," Goran remarked as Ceredan and two warriors ushered him quickly past groups of gaping, whispering, and fuming Sylphs.

"Relocating is always a costly endeavor," Ceredan said.

"A cost our Folk had to pay because of your treachery," one of the warriors added with an icy stare.

Well, so much for small talk.

After a few minutes they reached a path lined with small, wood-framed houses. Standing in front of one were Dela and Ailee. As the

311

former watched with satisfaction, the latter rushed forward to throw her slender arms around Goran's waist.

"I have waited so long for this day," Ailee said. "I have imagined it so many times. What I would do. What I would say. Now it has all fled my mind."

"Your arms around me is all the greeting I need, Little Curlew," Goran replied.

Behind him, Ceredan cleared his throat. "Mind the conditions of your visit, Goran. If you or Dela have any questions, you may send your sister to the guild with a message for me."

"For you . . . personally?" Goran asked.

Ceredan's eyes met his. Goran saw something like regret in them. "I am the only guildmaster you will see or speak to. The only guildmaster who was willing."

Much smaller than their family home on the Knob, this house was little more than a common room and two bedchambers. "I will share Father's room during your stay," said Ailee, hurrying to remove a plate of crumbs from the table. "And you can share—"

"Dela will take your room," Goran cut in. "I am sure I will find one of the chairs out here most comfortable."

His sister had clearly assumed he and Dela were mated. Surprisingly, Goran found that he wasn't embarrassed by her assumption. Neither was Dela. The corners of the Water Maiden's mouth were wiggling, as if she were suppressing a giggle. Only Ailee looked horrified.

"Is that . . . is that my son?" came a raspy voice from one of the bedchambers. "My son, finally come back to me?"

Brae lumbered into the common room, twisting slightly to allow his wide girth and not-fully-retracted wings to pass the doorway. Ailee rushed forward to take the old ranger's arm and help him into a chair.

"I have come back, Father," Goran said, trying not to wince at Brae's frail appearance.

"I always knew you would make your way home," Brae said with a hint of his characteristic boastfulness. "I always knew I would see you again."

"You words come as a great relief. I admit that I was not—"

"Why should you be relieved?" Brae asked, sounding puzzled. "Why would any father not dream of seeing a son like you again? One of our Folk's greatest heroes?"

He thinks I am Kaden. The loss of both his sons has taken much from him.

The realization felt like yet another punch. But Goran took it without flinching. "I mean only that hearing you speak to me is like finding shade on a hot day."

"It *is* hot," Brae agreed. "Ailee, would you be a good girl and bring me a glass of that fine elderberry wine your mother made?"

"Perhaps a glass of water would be best, Father," she said, casting Goran a meaningful look.

With Brae smiling amiably and looking out the window, Dela took Goran's arm and pulled him aside. "I have news about the search."

"Ceredan already told me—the council has given up."

"Not entirely," Dela countered. "They have forbidden Sylph rangers from doing anything to interfere with their other duties in the Blur. But I was successful in convincing them to allow us to continue the search ourselves, from here."

"They will let us stay?" Goran asked dubiously. "A feared enemy and a hated traitor?"

"For a time, yes." Dela glanced at Ailee, who was helping Brae take a sip of water. "Your Folk truly do see Kaden as a great hero. They would be pleased to see him live out his days in as much comfort as they can provide. Still, their new colony is in great need. Their larders and monster pens are depleted. They need their rangers out hunting and gathering resources. Not hunting for a fugitive, no matter how well respected."

Well, at least that's something. "What of the Dryads? Their visit appeared to be expected. Have their Folk established trade with the Sylphs?"

"Of a kind," Dela said, "but from what I have overheard, the Dryads are themselves beset by shortages. Those bundles they carried here? I caught sight of one being unwrapped. They are not filled with food or humanwares. The Dryads bring books. Scrolls. And sacred relics, unless I missed my guess."

▲▲▲

As days became weeks, the mystery of the Dryads proved to be the only one Goran and Dela made any progress in understanding. During one of Ceredan's occasional visits, Goran brought up the winged rangers who'd trailed him in the Blur and the gifts of power used by British-allied Indians against the Americans during the recent war. Goran's meaning was about a subtle as a roaring Catawampyrie.

Clearly offended by the implicit accusation, Ceredan left. His visits got rarer.

As for Kaden, Goran and Dela drew a search grid onto a map. Then they made rangings in multiple directions, focusing on mountains, hills, bluffs, and other places a deranged Sylph might find familiar. Using spellsong, they questioned numerous humans. There was no sign of Kaden. Indeed, Goran and Dela were struck by how few humans in western New York, western Pennsylvania, or southern Ontario reported seeing magical creatures of any kind, even after the fairies used spellsong to recover magically suppressed memories.

It was Hespera the Dryad, during a subsequent visit to Iris Isle, who provided a partial explanation. While almost all Sylphs were forbidden to talk to Goran and Dela, the rule didn't apply to visitors. And when the three fairies discovered one day that they had a good human friend in common, the late President George Washington, Hespera became still more talkative.

"I knew George best when he was a mischievous boy," the Dryad beamed. "Our visits grew sparse as he grew into manhood, and then into the leader of a nation. His duties consumed too much of his time. As my duties did mine."

"Your duties as a trader of books and relics?" Dela pressed.

The Dryad cocked her head to one side of her long, slender neck. "I am warden of the Ranger Sisterhood, Dela. I command all who range for what is left of the Dryad domains of North America."

"What is *left* of your domains?" Goran repeated. "Have your Folk been at war?"

"In a sense, Goran, but not in the way you mean. We have not taken the field of battle for a long time."

"If it is not from battle, then," Dela asked, "what has brought your Folk to—"

"Our war is an *inner* struggle, a war against our worst instincts," Hespera interrupted. "It is a war from which, I am gratified to say, we have emerged victorious. At the same time, it is a war we were always fated to lose."

Now it was Goran's turn to cock his head. "I do not understand. How can you win and lose at the same time?"

Hespera raised an eyebrow. "You should understand better than most, ranger of the Sylph. Though from what I have heard, perhaps that title no longer suits you."

Goran sighed. "I have . . . paid dearly for doing what was right."

"As have we." Hespera turned and took a few steps. "You know the awful truth of the monster pens, I take it?"

Dela and Goran exchanged quick glances.

"Our mages kept their secret secure for generations. But after the Crossing, as we established Dryad troops across America's inland forests, the truth proved harder to disguise. I figured it out, as did other rangers. We refused to keep the secret. The more Dryads learned of it, the greater the resistance to the old ways became."

Goran cleared his throat. "We, too, were disgusted by what we learned, and have been trying to discover some means of producing magic without resorting to monster pens. Please tell us more of your 'resistance to the old ways.' "

Hespera looked at the Sylph with something like pity. "There are matters about which I cannot speak to outsiders. I will say only this: Monsters may be more plentiful here than in the Old World, but no resource is inexhaustible. With more and more Folk migrating here, such game is increasingly hard to find, even for those still inclined to hunt it. Soon there will be a reckoning. After much debate, we Dryads have chosen how we will face it. Your Folk will soon face the same decision. I pray you will seek God's wisdom when that time comes."

I have heard such words before, Goran realized. "You speak much like a human I know, a man called John Chapman."

Hespera smiled. "Johnny is our great friend. It does not surprise me to learn of your acquaintance. Remember that God, the Maker of All Things, constantly talks to us. He uses different words for different people, however. Listen, and you will hear the words meant for you."

After the Dryad departed, Dela turned to Goran. "If her Folk have devised a way to break the link between magic and monster pens, why would she keep it from us? And why are they bringing their books, scrolls, and relics here? When the Dryads leave Iris Isle, they carry no trade goods back with them."

Goran thought of Ceredan and other Sylph scholars. Of course they would be thrilled at the prospect of adding another Folk's artifacts to their own library. But did the Dryads hope their gifts would somehow influence Sylph policy? If so, their strategy was ill-conceived. It had been Goran's experience that scholarly Folk tended to be the most dogmatic, the least open to any new ideas that challenged their long-held ones.

"I will ask Ailee to take a message to Ceredan," Goran said. "Let us see if we can get a look at one of those Dryad books."

▲▲▲

It took three requests for the guild to let one of their newly acquired prizes pass into the hands of "the traitor and his accomplice." Tellingly, it was a book about mere plants and trees, no doubt used by the Dryad equivalent of the Greenweavers Guild to train apprentices. In its pages, Goran and Dela found no secret knowledge about the production of elemental magic or the intentions of the Dryads. But Goran did find one chapter fascinating.

"Listen to this," he said, sitting at the table where Dela was poring over the search map. "*To weave green is to bring together yellow and blue, fire and ice, in strong and subtle combination.*"

"Is this a schoolbook or an album of verse?" the Water Maiden said with a giggle.

"No, really, listen—this is interesting."

Pretending to be duly chastened, Dela crossed her hands in her lap, though the corners of her mouth continued to twitch. "You have my full attention. Do instruct me, teacher."

"*Mages think in terms of raw power, of magic channeled into bright beams that force the elements of nature to conform to their will,*" Goran read. "*Water churns and turns. Air becomes gentle breeze or merciless gale. Heat takes form as spark of flame or bolt of lightning. Solids harden or soften, grow lighter or heavier, ripple into whatever shape the mage wills. And all four elements, woven together in proper sequence and proportion, form the Shimmer.*"

Dela rolled her eyes. "Poetic, to be sure, but hardly a revelation."

"There is more," Goran insisted, then kept reading. "*Crafters manipulate objects. Spellsingers manipulate moods. Only we weave together animate and inanimate. Living and dead. Cultivators and inhibitors. Magic and antimagic.*"

The Water Maiden blinked in surprise. "Antimagic? That does sound important."

"It goes on to give examples," Goran added, flipping to the next page. "*Among the most potent inhibitors on dry land are members of the cypress and pine families.* When I visited Veelund at Spirit Forest, he said their walls held up against Nunnehi attack because they were made of cypress and pine. I assumed he meant their wood could be readily enchanted to form a magical shield."

"But what those trees really do is disrupt elemental magic somehow," Dela said, knitting her brows in concentration. "The book referred to dry land. Does it list any aquatic inhibitors?"

Goran turned another page and ran a finger down the margin. "Here it is: *Naiad sources report best results with arrowhead, water primrose, water cabbage, and especially water lilies.*"

Dela stood up excitedly. "Our greenweavers grow such plants at the edge of our village, along the Shimmer! As an apprentice, I was trained to scout suitable sites by looking for concentrations of water lilies. Now I can guess the reason: Water lilies make it harder for monsters or Folk to spot our home, or to gain entrance to it. Does the book say how such plants inhibit magic?"

Goran shook his head. "Perhaps greenweavers have some feel for the magic properties of growing things. They see no need to spell it out in their schoolbooks. As spellsingers who cannot absorb elemental magic, we lack a context that even their youngest apprentices already possess when they read this book."

Dela sat on the edge of her chair, hunching forward and resting her elbows on her knees. "What about that word 'cultivators'? What does the book say about those?"

"There is a long list here," Goran replied, turning another page, "and I don't recognize many of the names of . . ."

Then his finger stopped about halfway down. He began reading again. "*Over the generations, Dryad greenweavers have formed several schools of thought. Some champion the laurels. Others, the olive and ash. Perhaps the greatest capacity can be found among the fruit-bearers, such as plum, cherry, apple, pear, and strawberry. Still, do not neglect their cousins, the thorn-bearers. Their stems may repel the touch. But their flowers wield great power.*"

Goran glanced down at the Water Maiden, whose head now rested on her laced fingers. "I have always loved roses," she mused. "When I was a young apprentice, a teacher spoke of meeting a human writer named Edmund Spenser. She had us read one of his sonnets. It began with something like: '*Sweet is the rose, but grows upon a briar.*' "

Edmund Spenser! Goran knew his works well. He even remembered the concluding lines of the sonnet Dela had begun:

So every sweet with sour is tempered still,
that maketh it be coveted the more:
for easy things that may be got at will,
most sorts of men do set but little store.
Why then should I account of little pain
that endless pleasure shall unto me gain.

Dela was still hunched over on the edge of her chair, chin in hand, her heart-shaped face tilted so she could gaze at him with inquiring eyes. The loose neck of her gown had shifted, revealing a sharply defined collarbone and an artfully rounded shoulder.

Goran felt a rush of wind, though the air of the room they shared was perfectly still. He felt a rush of water, though his skin was perfectly dry. He heard something rushing at him, then through him, though the two fairies were motionless and alone in the perfectly quiet house.

I have made complex what should be simple. I have made difficult what should be easy. I saw only the thorn, not the bloom.

Goran felt his pulse quicken. Then he smiled. "Your teacher who met Edmund Spenser surely cast a memory spell after their encounter, but it did not fully succeed. The human must have been partially Sighted. He recalled some of what he saw and heard, however hazily, and later wrote an epic called *The Faerie Queene*. Have you read it?"

Dela shook her head—then drew in a quick breath when Goran knelt and took her hands in his.

"You should." He lifted the back of a pale-blue hand to his lips, then stared deeply into blue-green eyes that turned up at each corner.

" '*Gather the rose of love whilst yet is time,*' " Goran quoted as he pulled Dela close. Her lips were soft as rose petals.

▲▲▲

It couldn't last.

Goran had known it from the start. He'd known it all along. Nevertheless, he let himself think otherwise. He let himself hope.

Many weeks had passed. He and Dela no longer felt confined to the house of Brae and Ailee. That didn't mean they were allowed outside it, though, except for forays into the Blur. Still, Goran and Dela no longer *felt* confined in the house. Within its walls, they felt free. Free to study and learn. Free to launch ever more elaborate searches for Kaden, and free to weep after each proved fruitless. But also free to laugh. Free to love.

Goran had never known such happiness, even though it came with two painful disappointments. One was their failure to find his Blur-struck brother. The other was the Sylphs' dogged refusal to allow Goran to send a message to Har. Three searchers would have been better than two. And, more to the point, Goran and Dela missed their friend.

It was just after breakfast when someone knocked on the door. Guessing it must be Ceredan, Goran rehearsed in his mind the new arguments he'd devised to convince the Sylph Council to permit a spellsong message to Grünerberg.

Ceredan was, indeed, at the door, a grave expression on his round face. But he wasn't alone. Four armed warriors stood behind the guildmaster.

"What . . . what has happened?" asked Goran, alarmed. *Has someone found Kaden at last? Or, perhaps, just his body?*

"A Council meeting," Ceredan replied. "A meeting I had sought to delay—for a time."

Then Goran understood. *The news isn't truly about Kaden.*

"The elders no longer believe the recovery of your brother is possible," the guildmaster explained. "They insist the Rangers Guild focus on other priorities. And they insist you and Dela leave Iris Isle immediately."

At least they have no worse sanction in mind. Bren once called for my execution.

"They trust us so much?" Dela asked with a smirk. "They would accept as honest our vow to keep Iris Isle a secret?"

"It is not your honesty they trust," Ceredan said. "It is your sentiments. Your affection for your father and sister, Goran, most of all."

Goran felt alarm turn to rage. "They would threaten my own family with—"

"Control yourself!" the guildmaster snapped, as if the stern teacher and impetuous student were back on the Knob. "The elders have issued no threat. They reason only that, however misguided you may be, you will not endanger your family by revealing our location to our enemies."

"To the Dwarfs of Grünerberg, they mean," said Goran bitterly. "Or Dela's Folk. Or Sighted humans in the government of the United States. If the elders truly see these groups as enemies, how can we not interpret that as an admission of guilt?"

Ceredan stiffened. "Must you seize every opportunity to attack? To accuse our rangers of stalking you? To accuse our Folk of supplying enchanted weapons to the Indians? Your conspiracies grow more and more outlandish."

"You make no denial," Goran observed.

"You make no accusation worthy of my time or respect," Ceredan replied.

Goran pointed a finger. "I have heard such talk before. From guildmasters who refused to face the truth. From Sylphs who led our Folk to disaster. From Sylphs who stood aside and let that disaster come."

The guildmaster's head jerked, as if Goran's words had slapped him in the face. When Ceredan looked up, there was no sympathy in those owlish eyes. "You will leave at once. We allow a few minutes to gather your belongings and say your farewells."

From behind Goran came his sister's anguished plea. "Please, sir. May I not come argue on his behalf? May I not plea for mercy? Or just for a final evening meal, as a family?"

"You may not." Ceredan stepped back and nodded to the warriors. "You may request only a few minutes of privacy. That, we may grant, but only that."

▲▲▲

It had taken all of Goran's fortitude, and a firm tug from Dela, to leave his sobbing sister and bewildered father behind. Then, as they passed through the Shimmer into the windy cave beyond, Goran felt a powerful impulse to turn and fight his way back to his Little Curlew, to fight his way through the entire Sylph army if need be.

But he resisted. To challenge the injustice of his banishment, his second and presumably final such sentence, would do no good. He had been Goran Lonefeather before. Lonefeather he would remain.

Or so his thoughts wandered, until he felt the Water Maiden's warm breath on his cheek and her warm arms encircle his neck. "I am waiting," she urged. "Or would you rather have me leave the cave with a dive instead of a flight?"

Goran took her in his arms and headed for the massive curtain of falling water at the mouth of the cave, managing a wan smile. "Where do we go now?"

"I should think that was obvious," Dela said, returning the smile. "To Long Island-on-the-Holston. To see my mother."

Chapter 24 – The Crossing

March 1822

Junaluska had taken the trip before.

On previous occasions he'd ridden southwest from his home on Alarka Creek, passing through mountain gaps to reach the headwaters of the Coosawattee River. He'd followed its winding path all the way to its junction with the Conasauga, where the Cherokee had built their new Council House. From there, on those previous trips, Junaluska had traveled west another sixty miles, past Lookout Mountain, to visit his friend Sequoyah in Willstown.

This time would be different. Junaluska wouldn't go all the way to Lookout Mountain and Willstown. He wouldn't have to; the Council House was where he would find Sequoyah.

Furthermore, this time Junaluska would be in no hurry to get back home, for even if Junaluska *did* hurry back, there would be no pair of young women waving from the cornfield. No joyous greeting from their older sister, Yona, standing on the porch. No arms pulling Junaluska from his saddle into a tight embrace.

There was no one to welcome him home at all, except for cattle, chickens, and an old dog. Over the harsh winter, a mysterious fever had taken first his beautiful Yona and then each of her sisters, even as it left Junaluska unscathed. After each death, he'd boiled willow root to wash the body, rubbed it with lavender, and buried it in a hill overlooking the creek. After the last sister passed and Junaluska completed his seven days of ritual mourning, he'd begun his trek over the mountains. He could not bear to stay in his home alone.

Is it truly my home anymore?

Junaluska had started off with the vague notion of visiting Sequoyah in Willstown. Then, during stops along the way, he learned that his friend had been on an extended stay out west, in the Arkansas Territory, and was only now returning east with Chief Oolooteka to meet with the Cherokee National Council.

321

What business Sequoyah and his uncle—also called John Jolly—might have with the Council, Junaluska had no idea. He knew only that his friend would be there. Junaluska hoped there'd be other familiar faces there, too, faces of men he'd known in his younger days. Days of peril, to be sure, but also days of adventure and comradeship.

Days when he'd never felt alone.

▲▲▲

It was near midday when Junaluska urged his horse into a shallow ford across the Coosawattee and spied the small settlement. It was bustling. Horses thronged the riverbank, drinking and resting. Some were surrounded by young Cherokee boys and girls rubbing their flanks and offering them feed. Other horses, larger ones for pulling carriages, were being tended by black slaves.

The latter signified wealth that only a few Cherokees possessed. *Familiar faces, indeed*, thought Junaluska, frowning at the sight of the slaves.

The Council House formed the center of the settlement. Strictly speaking, it wasn't a single structure. Across a dirt courtyard was a modest log house with a thatched roof and covered porch. To either side and facing each other were two large shelters, roofed but otherwise open to the air. The shelters featured three long benches, stair-stepped to allow four rows of spectators to witness what transpired in the courtyard.

The Cherokees filling the benches were a mixed company, some dressed in buckskins, some in farm clothes, and a few in the finer clothes of planters and merchants. Among the latter group were two friends Junaluska had made during his time with Andrew Jackson's army.

Major Ridge, as he'd been called since Horseshoe Bend, was one of the nation's most prosperous men. His large plantation, located only twenty miles from the Council House, employed dozens of slaves and other laborers to grow corn, cotton, and tobacco. Major Ridge was whispering to his young protégé, John Ross, another successful businessman who owned a trading post and plantation on Chattanooga Creek.

Both served on the thirteen-member National Council. Both men wore dark tailored coats, brightly colored waistcoats and trousers, and white shirts with cravats tied tightly at the neck. But Major Ridge's shock of unruly gray hair contrasted sharply with the younger man's dark, carefully combed hair.

Two men stood in the courtyard addressing the assembled Cherokees. As Junaluska approached, the voice of one brought a smile to his parched lips.

"Some of you witnessed my demonstration last year with my daughter Ahyokah," said Sequoyah, slipping a finger underneath his red-and-white striped turban to scratch his head. "You saw me use my syllabary to send her a message from another room. Now you have heard me read you a message from far away, from your brothers in Arkansas."

"You needed no talking leaves to bring that message!" shouted an old man. "Just your tongue, or the tongue of your uncle next to you!"

"Ah," John Jolly said. "I could speak the words, yes. But how would you know they are truly the words of your brothers unless they are written down?"

"Are you not their principal chief?" the old man demanded.

"I am," Jolly said, smiling broadly, "and pleased to hear that you *always* take a chief's words to be the whole truth."

Laughter swept the audience, but Junaluska was in no such mood. Sequoyah's mention of his daughter Ahyokah was a painful reminder of Junaluska's recent loss. *And the children Yona and I will never have together.*

"There are many uses," Sequoyah said. "You who have fought in battle. Would it not be useful to send written commands rather than rely on the memories of young scouts?"

Several men nodded in agreement.

"And what of the affairs of our nation?" Sequoyah added. "Why should anyone have to learn English to know the words of our leaders, or the words of the Americans? We can print our *own* books, our *own* newspapers. We can print treaties in our *own* tongue, for all to read."

The murmur grew louder as many Cherokees discussed Sequoyah's argument. John Ross caught Junaluska's eye and motioned him to the bench, yielding his seat and striding into the courtyard.

"Sequoyah has the right of it," Ross said. "At an early age, I learned to read and write in English. As president of your National Committee, I negotiate with the Americans. I could not do that without speaking their tongue. But when I send a report home, I would rather write it in our own language."

Another old man stood and pointed an accusing finger. "You, John Jolly. You say this paper bring greetings from our brothers in the west. I care not whether I hear them in our tongue. They are *not* Cherokee words. They are American words. They are words to trick us into selling our land and leaving our homes."

"Each must make his own choice," Jolly said, glancing nervously at John Ross. "My people chose to find a safer home in Arkansas."

"While most of our people have chosen to remain *here*, on the lands of our ancestors," Ross said. "Some have even marked down land claims under the treaties of 1817 and 1819 to earn citizenship in the United States."

Junaluska had done that himself, listing his farm and hundreds of surrounding acres of ridge and forest as his treaty claim.

"Tennessee has refused to recognize them," Jolly pointed out. "North Carolina and Georgia say they have bought the claims out. They will *never* treat you as full citizens."

"I came here to offer my syllabary, not to debate politics," Sequoyah said. "Yet I believe that the more of us read and write our own language, the more powerful and independent our nation will be. The more we will preserve our way of life."

The crowd grew still. Then a man rose from the bench behind Junaluska. He was tall and thin, his haggard face framed by plaits of long gray hair.

"I am Fivekiller," he said in a reedy voice. "Many of you know me. My mother, the Beloved Woman Nanyehi, is known to all. If she were here, she would tell you of her pride in our people, in the progress we have made. She would urge us to continue expanding our farms and perfecting our trades. To learn to write and read our own language, as Sequoyah has done. But she would also urge us to part with no more of our lands."

"Your mother's counsel is always welcome," Sequoyah replied.

"Have *you* not sold land to the Americans yourself, Sequoyah?" Fivekiller demanded. "Have *you* not signed treaties, the kind that pushed my mother off her land?"

Sequoyah's face reddened. Then he limped slowly to the shelter to meet Fivekiller's defiant gaze.

"I left Tuskegee because I no longer saw a way to live there as a Cherokee, not with so many whites settling nearby," Sequoyah answered. "I moved my family south to Willstown. Perhaps one day I will move again, but not because I wish our nation to be weak. I wish it strong. And not because I trust the whites more. I trust them less."

"This is no time for such talk."

The deep voice of Major Ridge quieted the crowd. "You all know my heart. Long have I been a voice on the council for resistance against American schemes to swindle our people. I have traveled with John Ross to Washington to plead our case, though I am no master of the white man's tongue. And you all know the fate of Chief Doublehead."

The audience was now deathly silent. Fifteen years earlier, Doublehead had taken a bribe to sell Cherokee land without approval of the council. It was Major Ridge who had gunned Doublehead down. *And finished the job with his own tomahawk*, Junaluska recalled.

"While my English is poor," Major Ridge continued, "many in the next generation, including my own son John, have learned to speak, read, and write it. That was wise. We have learned many useful things from whites. Now we will learn a useful thing—but *not* from whites. Sequoyah has done us a great favor. I accept it gladly."

The barrel-chested speaker of the council clasped arms with a grateful Sequoyah. "Your kind words honor me," said the latter. Then he addressed to the crowd. "You have witnessed what the syllabary can do. It is no magic trick, no work of evil spirits. Spread the word. I will teach all who wish to learn. And if any of our people still think I am making a fool of myself, you may tell them that what I am doing will *not* make fools of them."

Later, after the crowd dispersed, Junaluska found Sequoyah talking to John Jolly and, to Junaluska's surprise, a visibly less belligerent Fivekiller.

"My friend!" Sequoyah's eyes shone with delight. "It has been far too long. Gentlemen, I have the honor of presenting Junaluska, hero of Horseshoe Bend."

Jolly inclined his head. "My friend Kolana, also called Sam Houston, speaks well of you."

"And he, of you," Junaluska replied. "As for you, Fivekiller, I once had the great fortune of seeing your mother Nanyehi. Is she well?"

Fivekiller shrugged. "For a woman who had seen more than ninety years, she is remarkably spry and alert. When I left her home at Womankiller Ford she was out gathering healing herbs for a—"

"You, there!" shouted a youth, leaping from an exhausted horse. "I seek the man Fivekiller!"

"You have found him. What has happened?"

The young man answered between panting breaths. "Just rode from Ocoee . . . from the crossing . . . Beloved Woman . . . your mother . . . death stalks her."

▲▲▲

Nanyehi's house on the Ocoee River was larger than other homes in the area. It was more than a house, in fact—it was in inn, built with four extra rooms to accommodate guests.

Three were now filled with relations: grandchildren, cousins, nieces, nephews, and Nanyehi's brother Long Fellow. Fivekiller reserved the fourth for Junaluska alone. He said it was a great honor to house such a hero. Junaluska spent much of the first two days at Nanyehi's bedside, holding the great woman's withered hand and speaking in low, soothing tones. Sometimes she seemed to have recognized his words. Other times, she simply slept or stared up wordlessly.

Why he'd insisted on accompanying Fivekiller to the Ocoee was a mystery even to Junaluska. After all, he had seen Nanyehi only once, and from a distance. Perhaps it was an attempt to recapture that thrilling moment from his youth. Perhaps it was because of what he and Nanyehi shared, their special connection to the magical world. Or perhaps it was because he found rushing to Nanyehi's deathbed a convenient excuse for declining Sequoyah's invitation of a lengthy stay in Willstown.

Junaluska liked Sequoyah's wife, Sally, and their children, but the invitation had made him cringe. He had no desire to see a happy family up close.

It hadn't taken long, however, for Junaluska to tire of seeing a *sad* family up close. Nanyehi's relations were fine people coping with an impending loss of the woman they called "Granny Ward." His heart went out to them. Still, he couldn't help wincing whenever they cried and embraced and prayed together.

He felt grief as well, and he had no family to share it with.

Or so Junaluska was thinking as he knelt to dig up passionflower roots. Much of the sun-drenched hill was covered with the purple passionflower, a plant much revered among his people. The river itself had been named after their word for it, *ocoee*. Cherokees made medicinal use of its roots, stems, and flowers. During the summer months they enjoyed its luscious fruit, the maypop.

326

"You will never be a greenweaver, human, even if you spend a lifetime on your hands and knees," said a familiar voice.

Junaluska rose and spun around, expecting to see only the lithe form of Tana Song Snake, come to pay respects to her dear friend Nanyehi, but was pleasantly surprised to find two Folk rangers with her. Goran the Sylph wore his usual forest-green cloak and stockings, his lone kingfisher feather rising high above his felt cap. The third ranger's blue skin and long trident marked her as Dela, the Water Maiden he'd heard so much about from Goran and Har.

Speaking of which. "Where is the fourth of your company?" Junaluska asked. "Where is the Tower?"

The fairies exchanged puzzled looks. "Har is not already here?" Tana asked. "When he did not meet us at Blood Mountain, we assumed he had come straight here."

"I have not seen him," Junaluska replied.

Dela looked thoughtful. "We sent a message to Har from my village. But there was no response. We concluded Har must have already gotten Tana's earlier message about Nanyehi's condition and left Grünerberg to meet us."

"He may yet arrive at any time," Goran pointed out. Then his face clouded. "I take it you have seen Nanyehi? How is she?"

"She may well *depart* at any time," Junaluska said, averting his eyes and thinking of another beloved woman lying close to death, though in the shivering cold of winter rather than the fragrant warmth of spring.

Tana reached out a hand. "Nanyehi has touched many souls. I had no idea you were among them."

Junaluska struggled to frame a proper reply. Now was not the time to speak of his own losses, nor would he claim a friendship he didn't really have.

▲▲▲

Dela used illusion spells to draw the other Cherokees out of the house. Soon Junaluska and the fairies were looking down at the frail form quivering beneath a frayed blanket. Then Tana cast her own spell, singing in dulcet tones as she shook the turtle shell shackles on her ankles. Nanyehi's body stopped shaking. Her almond-shaped eyes, no longer squeezed shut or thrust open in confusion, regarded the visitors with something like the sharpness of youth. Her full lips formed a peaceful smile, creasing her face with deep lines that suggested not the desecration of age but the accumulation of wisdom.

"T-T-Tana, my f-friend," she managed, then cleared her throat. "I am glad you are here. Though I doubt this final journey of mine will require armed escort."

"Do not speak like that," Tana said. "We have come to visit and heal, not say goodbye."

The old woman's chuckle became a wheezy cough. "I am not the confused girl you once met. Death comes to my door not as an enemy but as a friend. I have had a full life in this world. Now, I turn my feet to the sky. I follow the Path of Souls to the world beyond."

Tana took Nanyehi's hand. The old woman squeezed it. "How is your family?"

"Huli and the twins are fine," said the Nunnehi scout, wiping a tear from her cheek.

Nanyehi looked past Tana and spied the Sylph. "You honor me with your presence and the token you wear in your cap. Where is Har? Surely where Goran Lonefeather goes, the Tower cannot be far."

"We expected him to . . . Har has not yet arrived," Goran said hesitantly. Then he affected a sly grin. "Sometimes he dawdles. He may be fishing some stream as we speak. You must be patient, like the rest of us."

"I will do my best." Nanyehi coughed again. Then she looked down and saw Dela's hand clasped tightly in Goran's. The sight produced a satisfied sigh. "Even without Har, I see you do not lack for companionship."

Goran looked embarrassed. "Well, you see, I reunited with my sister and father, and, well, Dela and I began to—"

"I need no details," Nanyehi interrupted with a smile. "It took you long enough."

"That is what I said," Tana agreed. They all shared a laugh.

All except Junaluska. It was then Nanyehi seemed to notice him for the first time. "You—I have seen your face before, as if in a dream."

He stepped forward and knelt. "I am Junaluska."

"And you have the Sight, I take it?"

He nodded.

"I know your name," she said. "Fivekiller spoke often of Junaluska. The man whose heroics helped defeat the Creeks at Horseshoe Bend. The man who saved the life of General Jackson. Why have you come? Are you distant kin? Did we meet in some long-ago time?"

"No, though as a child I did see you once from afar—talking to *her*, I think." Junaluska pointed to Tana.

With evident effort, Nanyehi suppressed a cough. "Then . . . what has brought you here?"

Junaluska answered without thinking. "I have suffered a great loss."

The other fairies looked surprised. Nanyehi merely lifted a finger and wagged it. "Tell me of it, son."

And then, as if the old woman had removed a stopper from a bottle, Junaluska's story poured out. He spoke of years of happiness on Alarka Creek, in the deep gap of the mountains, marred only by the fact that he and Yona had no children. Then he spoke of the harsh winter, and the fever that took Yona and her sisters from him. He spoke of grief so broad and deep it seemed destined to drown him, no matter how hard he might try to swim for shore.

"Your face tells a tale I have read many times, on many faces," Nanyehi said. "A tale written on my own face after my first husband died at the hands of the Creeks. A tale I read on the face of my friend John Sevier whenever he spoke of his first wife, Sarah."

"Your . . . *friend* John Sevier?" Junaluska asked. "Did he not lead men against our warriors and raids against our towns?"

"Yes, but there were also occasions when he made peace." Nanyehi rubbed the side of her nose. "John was my friend, though we often did not see eye to eye. There was good and bad in him, as there is in his rival Andrew Jackson. As there is in us all."

Another fit of coughing overtook the old woman, prompting Junaluska to take her hand.

"John loved his Sarah dearly," said Nanyehi in a softer, shakier voice. "They built a life together. Her death shattered that life. But it did not shatter John. He rose from its ruins and built a new life, with a new wife. Bonny Kate, they called her. A formidable woman. A woman who . . ."

Her voice trailed off, her eyes losing the sharpness Tana's spellsong had restored.

"He grew to love Kate dearly, too," Nanyehi added, her voice now only a whisper. "As I loved my Kingfisher. As I loved my Bryant . . ."

Nanyehi continued to mouth words, but no more sound came from her lips. Her hand grew limp in Junaluska's grasp. She curled up on her side, her body beginning to shake again.

"The power of the spell is broken, and I dare not cast another so soon," Tana said. "We should allow her to rest. Perhaps when we see her next, Har the Tower will be among us."

▲▲▲

But that reunion was not to be.

Over the next several days Tana twice attempted a mood spell to bring Nanyehi around enough to converse, as she had on the first day. But the old woman's faculties proved beyond the power of spellsong to restore. And their missing friend never arrived.

"Could something have happened to Har on the trail?" Tana asked as the four stood on the hill of passionflowers. "The frontier is not so wild as before, but many dangers remain."

"Har may not have received the news at all," Goran pointed out. "We have been out of communication for so long."

Dela looked crestfallen. "Are you suggesting that—"

Junaluska never heard the rest of her question. It was interrupted by shouts. As he and the fairies watched with growing alarm, the women who'd been washing pots next to the inn dropped them and rushed inside.

This may be the end, Junaluska thought. The three fairies sang concealment spells and headed down the hill, Junaluska close behind.

The room was crowded when he stepped inside. Nanyehi's brother Long Fellow stood against the opposite wall. Children of varying ages knelt around the bed of their Granny Ward, while Fivekiller and the other adults formed an outer circle, weeping and praying. Realizing his friends were too small to see over the mourners, Junaluska held out a hand to each of the women. Tana and Dela understood instantly and nodded. He lifted them effortlessly to his shoulders.

Then the Cherokee women took deep breaths and began to sing. "*Nanyehi. Nanyehi. Nanyehi,*" they sang, over and over, for as long as they could without taking a new breath. Tana, intimately familiar with their funeral customs, joined the chorus. Dela followed her lead.

Junaluska closed his eyes in respect for a woman he'd barely known and yet had seemed to know his heart. Fate had knocked her to the ground more than once. She'd risen every time. Determined to live. Determined to love. And now, at the end, Nanyehi was far from alone. A crowd of family and friends mourned their beloved woman.

Who will mourn me?

As Junaluska continued to pray, keeping his eyes tightly shut, he heard a flutter of wings. Goran had no doubt found a suitable perch on some shelf or high table from which he could take his last look at his longtime friend.

A little later, when they all stepped outside for fresh air, Junaluska overheard a conversation between Fivekiller and one of the little boys.

"I saw it, Uncle—I did!" the boy insisted.

"Tell me again what you saw, Jack," Fivekiller humored the boy.

"A light over Granny's head. Something shiny. It flew like a bird."

Fivekiller smiled. "And did the bird just disappear?"

The boy shook his head. "It flew out the door."

"Well, I hope it found its way home," said Fivekiller, tousling Jack's hair.

Rather than participating in the burial rites, Junaluska decided to leave the inn. He would head back home—or, at least, to the new home he was now determined to make for himself.

As he filled his pack with provisions, Junaluska said his farewells to Tana, Goran, and Dela and wished them good fortune in their search for Har. He also told the fairies what Nanyehi's great-grandson Jack had witnessed.

"The boy must be at least partially Sighted," Dela concluded. "He saw Goran fly through the room."

Perhaps, Junaluska thought. *Or perhaps Nanyehi has risen yet again.*

Chapter 25 – The Survivor

As the rowers propelled the boat up the Elizabeth River, Ichabod recalled many a quiet night walking past the docks of Norfolk and relishing his solitude.

But that had been many years ago, and a different Ichabod Crane—or Ben Crane, as he was then called. Thin, gangly Ben Crane, trapped an ill-fitting naval uniform. The "other" Crane, the tall lieutenant standing in the shadow of his shorter but more illustrious brother, the war hero Will Crane.

Now, as commander of the United States Army's largest stronghold—Fort Monroe, at the tip of the Virginia peninsula—Ichabod Crane wore his major's uniform with grace, although his coat had lately grown tight around his midsection. *No one calls me thin any more*, Ichabod mused, running a finger along a whiskered cheek that had become downright jowly. Many men gain weight under similar circumstances, or so he'd been told.

Ichabod groaned softly, not wanting the rowboat's crew to hear. That was another difference between the man he'd been and the man he'd become: Solitude was the last thing Ichabod desired at the moment. He longed to be with his wife, Charlotte, and their newborn son, Charles. But he'd left them behind in Rhode Island when he assumed his new post. Charlotte needed a few months to recuperate before joining him in Norfolk, as their doctor had advised.

"We're headed there, Major Crane," said the bosun, pointing to a small floating dock. "Will you be needing a ferry back to Fort Monroe this evening, sir?"

"No, I'm staying in town." Ichabod had been pleasantly surprised upon his return to Norfolk to recognize many sailors from the nearby naval station. Some, he'd known during his own naval service under Stephen Decatur; others, he'd met during his brief service with Oliver Hazard Perry.

Ichabod's thoughts turned to his two former commanding officers, Decatur and Perry. Both had helped to shape the officer he'd become. And both were dead. In 1819, yellow fever had taken Oliver Hazard Perry's life while he stationed in the Caribbean. A year later, a bullet had taken Stephen Decatur's life—a bullet fired by a fellow officer, James Barron.

Their senseless and ill-fated duel would come up during dinner, Ichabod knew. Though more than five years had passed, the duel remained a frequent topic of discussion in political, military, and diplomatic circles. Its presence in tonight's dinner conversation would have a different explanation, however. As the newly arrived commander of Fort Monroe, it was Ichabod's responsibility to pay his respects to one of Norfolk's most prominent couples, Luke Wheeler and his wife, Ginny. He'd first met them and their daughter Susan, Stephen Decatur's widow, just before the start of the War of 1812.

Although their acquaintance had been brief, Ginny Wheeler had also played a key role in making Ichabod the man he was today. After all, she was the first Sighted person he'd met.

▲▲▲

"It was murder, pure and simple."

Luke Wheeler's hand shook as he stabbed the roast, and not just because the former mayor of Norfolk had just passed his seventy-first birthday. Wheeler brought up the Decatur-Barron duel shortly after dinner began, just as Ichabod had expected. While his wife, Ginny, talked of Stephen with fondness and regret, her husband couldn't contain his rage.

"Stephen knew he faced more than a ritual to satisfy honor!" Wheeler fumed. "He faced a man who truly wished him dead."

Ichabod had heard the story many times. Barron had nursed a grudge against Decatur since 1808. That was the year of Barron's court-martial on charges of "unpreparedness" as commander of the USS *Chesapeake*, which had been defeated and boarded the previous year. Barron's surrender to a British ship had greatly embarrassed America, widening the rift between the two countries. Convicted and suspended from service without pay, Barron blamed not his own conduct but political pressure and the petty jealousies of the officers who'd judged him, including his former friend Stephen Decatur.

After many years abroad, Barron returned to America in 1819, hoping to restore his reputation. Decatur spoke out forcefully against reinstating him, provoking the embittered Barron to challenge him to a duel. While Barron was badly wounded, Decatur's wound had proved fatal. He'd died within hours.

"My dear, we should talk of happier times," Ginny suggested, her half smile proving insufficient to hide her embarrassment. "Our guest needn't bear our tragedy with us. Major Crane, I understand you have recently become a father. How soon may we meet your—"

"Make no mistake," Luke Wheeler interrupted, seeming not to notice his wife's attempt to change the subject. "I do not call Commodore Barron the murderer, at least not on his own. That scoundrel Jesse Elliott is equally guilty."

"*Captain* Jesse Elliott, you mean?" Ichabod recalled with disgust the haughty officer's conduct during the 1813 battle of Lake Erie.

"The very same," Wheeler said. "Elliott and Barron were longtime friends. When Barron sought reinstatement, Elliott was one of the few officers to champion his cause. I think it was more his hatred of our Stephen than his love of Barron that motivated Jesse Elliott."

Seeing Ichabod's puzzled expression, Ginny sighed and shrugged. "Susan is convinced of it, Major Crane. After Stephen died, she found a packet of letters his friend Oliver Hazard Perry had entrusted to him before sailing to the Caribbean. Perry had originally planned to file formal charges against Jesse Elliott for his misconduct on Lake Erie. To avoid the national spectacle of a court-martial, President Monroe persuaded Perry to withdraw the charges in exchange for sending him to Venezuela with newly bestowed rank of commodore."

"But Oliver never came back," Ichabod observed.

"Correct—and Jesse Elliott became convinced that Stephen, now in possession of the evidence, would pursue the court-martial on his own," continued Wheeler. "Susan believes it was Elliott who stoked Barron's anger at Stephen and blocked all attempts at reconciliation. When Barron finally demanded satisfaction by duel, Elliott served as his second. Susan is convinced Elliott conspired with Stephen's second William Bainbridge, another officer who secretly nursed a deep resentment of our son-in-law. Elliott and Bainbridge set up the duel in such a way that both men's shots would likely find their targets. *They* were Stephen's murderers, too."

Ichabod glanced at his largely untouched plate of roast beef and vegetables, frowning as he considered the Wheelers' words. Theirs was a wild story, rife with speculation, yet there were reasons to credit it.

Ichabod knew both Stephen Decatur and Oliver Hazard Perry held personal honor and the reputation of the navy in high regard. With his friend dead, Stephen might well have felt a duty to take up Perry's cause. And from what Ichabod knew of Jesse Elliott, hatching such an underhanded conspiracy would not have been out of character.

"I fear our loose talk has spoiled Major Crane's dinner," Ginny said.

Luke Wheeler cleared his throat nervously. "My apologies, sir. I should have offered our courtesies, not our controversies."

"Not at all, Mister Wheeler," Ichabod said. "While you know that your son-in-law was once my commanding officer, you may not know that I also became acquainted with Oliver Hazard Perry and Jesse Elliott during the war. To learn more about Commodore Decatur's death is disconcerting, I admit, but not unwelcome."

Ginny surprised Ichabod by laughing merrily. "Well said, sir, particularly for one who once struggled to finish his sentences. Where is that insecure young lieutenant I once met?"

Ichabod took the compliment in stride. "I have learned much, ma'am. Including the need to accept the truth as it is, rather than as I might fancy it to be. I'm grateful to you and Mister Wheeler for having shared such truth tonight."

She nodded graciously, then quickly averted her eyes.

"Yes, well, as it happens," Luke Wheeler stammered, "I fear I must face another truth. Those bank records, dear. I must finishing reviewing them. Will you excuse me, sir?"

Rising to his feet with his host and hostess, Ichabod lifted a glass. "By all means. And here's to your success. On a dark night like this, I myself would rather face a headless horseman than a stack of bank receipts."

They all laughed at Ichabod's joke. Ever since the publication of Washington Irving's story "The Legend of Sleepy Hollow" five years earlier, Ichabod had endured countless questions and jests. At first, the tale of schoolmaster Ichabod Crane's ill-fated ride had greatly annoyed him. He could not, of course, tell anyone the real story of the "headless" horseman, and the hapless Ichabod Crane of Irving's tale bore no resemblance to the army major in charge of Rhode Island's Fort Wolcott, and now of Fort Monroe.

Or so Ichabod assured himself.

"Major Crane, if you be willing, may we end our evening with a stroll?" Ginny asked. "The river can be charming on a night like this, as you may recall."

▲▲▲

The noisy bustle of a thriving port had receded to a faint harmony of chirping crickets and lapping waves by the time Ichabod and Ginny reached the low bluff overlooking Chesapeake Bay. Only then did he realize the import of their location. This was the spot he'd visited often while first stationed at Norfolk, the place from which he'd looked out over the water, both hoping and fearing to catch another sight of the great Sea Serpent.

It was also the place where Ichabod had first met Goran and Dela. Where he discovered that seeing magical creatures was a gift, not a sign of madness. Where Ginny Wheeler had revealed her own Sight to him, the night he made his fateful decision to leave the navy for the army.

Ichabod turned to the richly dressed woman, her shawl drawn tightly over her shoulders. "I think, Mrs. Wheeler, we did not find our way here by accident."

She smiled, forming small wrinkles around her mouth. "Call me Ginny, Major Crane."

"Ichabod," he suggested. "That is, if saying my given name does not make me ridiculous to your eyes."

Ginny shook her head. "It would never do that, Ichabod. After all, I can guess what other readers could not. That some truth lurks hidden in Irving's fanciful tale."

"It does, indeed, Ginny, although I am sworn to reveal no details."

"You must do as honor demands, Ichabod. You share that trait with my dear Stephen. It is why I brought you here. You deserve the whole truth. I break no vow by sharing it. It is my truth to share, though I had never thought to do so."

"But . . . I thought you and her husband had already—"

"What Luke told you is true as far as it goes. There is, however, more to the story, or so Susan has confided in me. Though even she doesn't know it all."

The breeze blowing off the bay grew suddenly stronger, chillier. "Are you still comfortable here, Ginny? Should we retreat back to town?"

The woman shook her head. "I am perfectly comfortable, sir. The salty smell reminds me of home."

"Of the Carolina seashore?"

"Yes." Ginny took a deep breath. "I'll get to that in a moment. But first, you should know that Stephen's falling out with his former friend James Barron did not start with the *Chesapeake* affair. It began years earlier, with two other incidents. One involved our daughter Susan. The other involved, well, a monster."

Ichabod felt like he'd been slapped across the face. *A monster?*

"I should explain the latter first," Ginny said. "I heard this from Stephen himself. While inspecting a cannonball works in New Jersey, he saw something impossibly large fly over the firing range. Stephen swore it had the face of a horse, horns, leathery wings, and a long body ending in a forked tail. He ordered the gun crew to fire, but the shot did not bring the monster down."

"Did the gunners see it, too?"

Ginny shrugged. "When Stephen told his story to his fellow officers, they discounted it as a daydream or trick of the light. James Barron, in particular, wouldn't let the matter go. He repeatedly ridiculed Stephen about his 'Devil of New Jersey.' "

"Surely wardroom jests would not make two friends into enemies," Ichabod commented.

"Not by themselves, no," she said. "It was Stephen's infatuation with Susan that did it. In those days Luke spent much time up in Washington conducting his political and business affairs. Susan often went with him. She was young, sharp minded, beautiful, and, I must admit, rather flirtatious. She became the belle of the capital. Among her suitors were Vice President Aaron Burr and Jerome Bonaparte, the brother of the French emperor."

"And Stephen Decatur, I take it?"

"Yes. Theirs was a whirlwind romance. After only four months, they were wed."

"*That* was what drove the two men apart?" Ichabod marveled. "Was Barron yet another of Susan's suitors?"

"That wasn't it." Ginny cast her eyes downward. "You see, Susan's romances hadn't always been discreet. You know how people talk, envious women more than most. Because of Susan's reputation, some of Stephen's fellow officers cautioned him about the propriety of the match."

"Including Barron?"

"*Especially* Barron," Ginny affirmed, still looking at the ground. "Shortly after Stephen met Susan, he encountered Barron here in Norfolk, not far from where we now stand. I can only guess the words they exchanged, but Stephen left greatly offended."

"Why would he care so much about Barron's opinion?" Ichabod wondered. "Were they so close?"

Ginny Wheeler lifted her head. "I suspect Barron didn't just object to Susan's reputation, Ichabod. He objected to mine."

"To . . . *your* reputation?"

"James Barron was born in Norfolk," she continued. "He grew up hearing certain stories about Luke and Susan and me. If you will forgive the indelicacy, the widely held view was that Susan was Luke's illegitimate daughter. Some said it was only *after* I'd given birth that Luke married me, out of guilt. Others said Susan had been born to some other woman while Luke was up in Maryland, and that he'd married me after returning to Norfolk in an attempt to cover up his indiscretion."

Struggling to reconcile the reputation of the Wheelers of Norfolk with such sordid tales, Ichabod could think of nothing to say. Ginny seemed to guess his predicament.

"You needn't worry about offending me," she said, patting his arm. "It was a long time ago. And, after all, it's not as though the rumors were without foundation. Although I raised Susan from infancy and love her dearly, I did not give birth to her. I have no natural children."

Ichabod slipped his hands in his pockets, a nervous gesture that had the unintended effect of withdrawing his arm from her hand.

"Oh, so it is *you* who are offended?" With a rueful grin, Ginny turned to gaze once more over the water.

"Why, no, Mrs. Wheeler . . . that is to say, Ginny . . . I had no intention to . . ."

"So, the stammering Ichabod returns. Well, I cannot blame you for being startled. I have startled myself by admitting the truth to you. Even Susan does not know—only Luke. And even he does not fully understand."

Realizing he'd hurt her feelings, Ichabod held out his hands. "You need not tell all, Ginny. But if you wish to, I will listen without judgment."

She took his hands and gave them a playful squeeze. "I appreciate the gesture, although it was never a fear of judgment that kept me from telling my tale. It was the conviction that no one would believe me. Not even my husband, whom I have grown to love deeply."

It took Ichabod a moment to catch her meaning. "So there *is* magic involved, then. Or Folk. Or monsters."

"All three, in truth. When I met first Luke Wheeler, I was wandering the streets in a daze. Truly and painfully alone. You see, Ichabod, I'd never seen anything like Norfolk before. Anything so large, so spacious, with so many people."

"Oh." Ichabod tried to work out the dates in his head. He knew Stephen had died in 1820 at the age of forty-one, and that Susan had been a couple of years older than her husband. So Ginny must have met and married Luke Wheeler around 1777. "Were there no towns in North Carolina back then? I seem to recall a few names: Edenton, New Bern, Wilmington . . ."

Ginny gave his hands another squeeze. "Arithmetic cannot give you the answer. Only I can. When I was born, my parents lived with a few other families on an island. We were beset by a host of calamities. Disease. Foul weather. Crop failure. We would have died had local natives not taken pity and invited us to live in their village."

Ichabod nodded gravely. "Friendly relations between our peoples have been all too rare. Although I have fought Indians in battle, I nevertheless believe that if we could only—"

"You don't understand. It was *not* an Indian village. We were given refuge by a magical Folk. They called themselves Pukwudgies."

"Pukwudgies!" Ichabod couldn't have been more surprised. "From what I know of them, they are a cruel and warlike Folk."

"The Pukwudgies I knew weren't like that at all. They'd foresworn violence of any kind. They were kind and generous, sharing what little they had and offering us sanctuary in their village by the sea."

Ichabod had more questions than he could put into words.

After a while, Ginny spoke again. "You know about monsters, Ichabod? About their connection to Folk magic?"

He nodded. "My friend Dela explained it to me. Fairies catch monsters and hold them in pens, draining their power so fairies can wield magic and sustain the Shimmer."

"So, then," she said, "I suppose you can guess what would happen if a Folk decided they could no longer, in good conscience, hunt and imprison monsters."

Ichabod considered the implications. "They would lose their magic. Their Shimmer walls would fail. Except for the rangers, the Blur would either kill the fairies or leave them permanently insane." He thought of Goran's brother Kaden and shuddered.

Ginny bowed her head. "Imagine, if you can, watching that happen to fairies you'd come to know as family. It was the worst horror I've ever known. Worse than the constant hunger I suffered during my nine years in the Pukwudgie village. Worse even than witnessing the death of my own parents from starvation, since I was only a small child when that happened. But when the Shimmer failed, when I watched the remaining Pukwudgies die, I was ten years old. And, suddenly, lost in an unfamiliar world."

This time, Ichabod grasped the implications more quickly. "If you lived nine years in a fairy village, then . . ."

"Then in reality some one hundred and eighty years had passed in the Blur," she confirmed. "When Luke found me on the streets of Norfolk, I was a newly arrived girl who'd been born nearly two centuries earlier. He didn't know that, of course. He knew only that I was a confused and desperate child who needed a home. He found me one, with a Missus Morgan who lived in a place called Currituck. That was, oh, the summer of 1769. Luke came to visit me a few times, just to make sure I was being taken care of. A kindly man, my husband, though he sometimes likes to pretend otherwise."

"But then how did you come to marry him?"

"It was about eight years later. That rumor about Luke fathering a daughter in Maryland was true. He never told me about the mother, and I never asked. He'd come back to town with no wife to take care of the baby or to present to Norfolk society as her mother. He turned to me in desperation. Because no one in Norfolk knew who I was, he figured, no one would be the wiser. His plan didn't wholly avert scandal, but it worked well enough for us. It didn't take long for us to fall in love, and for me to fall just as hard for little Susan. I've had a happy life here for the most part—happier than I'd ever dreamed as a starving little girl in the Pukwudgie village or scratching out a living in the woods with the widow Morgan."

"I see why you kept your secret so long," Ichabod said. "Someone without the Sight would have deemed you a madwoman."

They stood together for a long while, listening to the waves lap the shore. Then she took his arm. "The evening chill grows colder. Let's head back."

"As you wish, Ginny," he replied.

After they'd walked a few steps, however, he abruptly stopped and looked down at her. "Ginny is a nickname, I take it?"

"Of course," she said. "My parents named me after the ruler of England at the time I was born. Elizabeth, the Virgin Queen. My parents named me Virginia Dare."

Chapter 26 – The Thicket

October 1826

"Hush, child," Bell whispered. She dared only a whisper, though she knew little Sophia, sniffing and struggling in her arms, would respond better to a song. She dared only a whisper, for anything more might wake others in the house. Bell dared only a whisper, for it was not yet dawn.

The timing was God's idea, not hers. She'd talked it out the last time she visited her willow place. "I'm scared to go at night," she admitted to God, who would have known if she was lying anyway. "But if I go in the day, they'll all see me." After the two conferred for a while, God supplied the answer. If Bell left just before dawn, she'd make it out of the immediate area before anyone she knew spotted her. Later, in the daylight, any strangers she met would figure she was on an errand.

"Yes," she agreed eagerly. "That's a good thought! Thank you, God, for that thought!"

Bell hadn't always heeded God's wisdom; that much, too, she had to admit. She'd prayed like Mau-Mau Bett taught her. But sometimes Bell heard back only what she wanted to hear. She'd *wanted* to believe John Dumont was a good master, that God had sent him to guide and protect Bell and her four children: Diana, Peter, Elizabeth, and Sophia. Dumont had certainly been kinder than the Nealys, and kinder than the Cattons had been to her beloved Bob, whom she'd never seen again after that day they beat him so viciously.

His lack of cruelty didn't make John Dumont an honest man, though. *He's a liar!* It didn't make him a good man. *He sold my Peter away from me!* And it didn't make him a fit master. *He whips us for thieving—but what's he done all his life but steal from us?*

Little Sophia stirred again, filling her lungs as if about to wail. "Hush, hush," Bell whispered, pulling the blanket tighter around her three-month-old. She couldn't stop to feed Sophia now. Snuggling her would have to be enough.

Then Bell raised her hand to scratch her nose—and felt nothing.

Will I ever get used to this? Using her thumb to push the stub of her index finger out of the way, Bell used her intact middle finger to scratch her itch.

Dumont had made her a promise. After New York passed a law to free all slaves by the year 1827, he promised to liberate Bell a year early if she worked hard and didn't cause any trouble. Unfortunately, she later mangled her hand while threshing oats, losing most of her index finger and weakening the others. She couldn't work or spin thread as fast as before.

Still, Bell did what she could, rising early and spinning late into the night, even to the neglect of her children. Just after Sophia was born, she'd asked him to fulfill his promise.

He refused. "You'll have to wait, Bell."

"You promised me free papers. I done all the work I could do!"

"Not enough, not with that bad hand." he'd said sternly. "You got to *earn* those papers."

I did earn 'em! Bell had shouted in her head. *I earned 'em my whole life!*

But she knew better than to keep arguing with Dumont. He'd already sold her five-year-old, Peter, to his wife's nephew, Solomon Gidney. Now Dumont was threatening to sell her daughters, too, to cover what he claimed was her "unearned keep." As a girl, Bell had watched a master sell away her Mau-Mau's children. She was determined *not* to let the same thing happen to her.

So she resolved to stay long enough at Dumont's farm to spin the rest of the season's wool. Whatever Dumont might do, he couldn't rightly say she left any debt unpaid. When the spinning was done, she'd leave her master forever. Her man Tom was too old and weak to travel, and she couldn't take all three girls on the road with her. So she'd take little Sophia and leave Elizabeth in the care of the eldest, Diana.

We'll all be together again, Bell told herself. *Peter, too. God will show me how.*

"Ku-ke-le-ku!" crowed the rooster. Dawn was nigh. *Time to go.*

Bell piled clothes and food on a handkerchief and tied it up into a makeshift knapsack. Slinging it over her shoulder and drawing Sophia close, Bell crept across the floor, placing each foot carefully to avoid the creakiest planks. She lifted the latch and opened the door, pausing to listen. No one stirred. Not too surprising on a Sunday morning.

How many times had she fled a master's house, desperate, in tears? As a little girl, she'd run away from the Hardenbergh House after spilling molasses on a big-eared officer. A few years later, she'd run away after Mister Nealy beat her senseless. And as a young woman, pregnant with Diana, she'd run away after the Cattons beat her Bob.

Now Bell was leaving again. But not in shame or in terror. She was heading confidently toward a better future. She was reclaiming what should always have been hers. And when she came back, it would be only to reclaim the same for her children.

She entered the woods, following a northerly road that would take her along the Hudson. Though she hoped to be miles away from the Dumont house before the sun came up, she refused to let her hope turn to desperation.

Bell would *walk* away. She would never run away again.

▲▲▲

Some time later, as Bell reached the crest of a hill, she held her breath and looked back the way she came. There was no one else on or near the road. So far, she was safe.

"They's all still asleep, pretty Bell," said the voice behind her. The sound startled little Sophia, who immediately began to cry. But Bell had a different reaction entirely. She laughed and spun around.

"John de Conquer!"

The small man bent low, removing his hat to reveal a head now mostly bald. "John'll do. We's old friends, you and me. Though the little one is a new face."

Then he reached into his floppy hat and pulled out a dried flower, its shrunken pink-white petals surrounded by a whorl of three narrow green leaves.

Bell took it gratefully and put it in the pocket of her apron, but by then Sophia was bawling up a storm. "She's hungry," Bell explained. "Don't mind, do ya?"

"Naw." John sat down beside her as Bell drew a shawl over her dress and fumbled a moment until Sophia was drinking instead of crying. "Where ya headed, pretty Bell?"

Her eyes widened at that, for Bell had no fit answer. She'd started out going northwest because that seemed like the freest direction. If she walked far enough that way, she'd reach Canada. That was impossible, though. Then, without her having to mouth the question, God up and dropped the answer into her head.

"The Quakers," Bell said. "Headin' toward them Quakers you told me 'bout."

"Good people up Marbletown way," said John as he fished into his pocket and pulled out a chewing root. "How long you reckon on visitin'?"

Bell accepted a piece gratefully and brought it close to her mouth. Then she stared into the old man's twinkling eyes. "Long as it take."

John smiled as he chewed. "Ever met Levi Roe?"

Bell spat out a reddish stream. "Saw him once at market. He help me?"

"If he can."

When Sophia was full and drowsy, Bell got up. "Why ain't you come to see me in so long?"

John tossed his hat in the air and caught it on his head. "Been south, Bell. Lots of work there."

"Your mission?"

"Yep," he said, following her back to the road. "Many sufferin' down south. I ain't about to forsake 'em, the weak and the helpless. Gotta teach 'em freedom is comin.'"

Bell felt a tingle on the back of her neck. "Is it? For sure?"

"For *sure*. Freedom jus' has to come, in its time."

She pulled the blanket tight over little Sophia and glanced back the way she'd come. "Mighty nice to see you, John, but I best be off."

"I know," said the old man. "Freedom's time come for you. That's why I's here. Why I's walkin' wit' you."

"*Wit*' me?" Bell couldn't deny she'd welcome the company.

"Why not?" John said. "I knows the way."

They went down the hill, then took another road toward Levi Roe's place. It was a rougher, narrower path, taking them past stands of black oak, silver maple, and red cedar as well as patches of thorny shrubs covered in twisting vines of morning glory. The two walked for many miles, walking and talking of many things—of Bell's family and work, her dispute with Mister Dumont, and John's travels across the country.

"There's a mess of sorrow all over," sighed John, whose gait struck Bell as more of a dance than a walk, as if his every step was a beat on some singing drum. "But our people ain't worn down. They's pulled the covers up over their hurtin' souls, pretty Bell. They's fought the hurt with a laugh and a song."

"Sound worse off than me," she said, feeling a little guilty.

" 'Bout a month ago, got a certain feelin'," John explained, "like I's supposed to come see ya. So I did."

Bell cast an apprehensive look over her shoulder, as she had every mile or so. As before, she saw no one. Also as before, John chuckled and shook his head.

What they heard next didn't come from behind them. The sound came from ahead, where an animal track crossed the road. It was a low, gruff voice: "What cause you got to laugh?"

Bell knew that voice. Her heart sank as Charlie Catton came lumbering out of the trees, his nearly two-hundred-pound frame crammed into a fitted blue coat, blue pants, and a white work shirt open at the collar. The sight of his walking cane made Bell gulp. A step behind Catton was a shorter, slimmer man in a faded green shirt and darker green pants and waistcoat. Where Catton's face was round and rough, the other's face was round and oddly delicate, with widely spaced eyes, a long nose, and a narrow chin. The man carried no cane, but there was a long, wicked-looking knife thrust into his belt.

"Come now, Charlie, no need to be unfriendly," said the smaller man with a sneer. "Might be they're out doing the Lord's work."

"You ain't too far wrong, mister," said John good-naturedly. "Sunday morning's the best time to be about my—"

"That's *Mister* Vos, boy, and he wasn't speaking to you," Catton said, glaring at John. Then he turned to his companion. "See what friendly talk gets you, Herman? Uppity folk. Folk that don't know their place anymore."

The one called Herman Vos nodded toward John. "That what you are? Too uppity to know your place? Too uppity for field work?"

"Oh, I ain't done field work in many a year, Mister Vos," said the old man, brushing the air with a dismissive hand. "Been on the road. Peddlin', you might say. And fishin' every pond I see, 'bout as much."

"I haven't seen you at market," Vos said. "What have you been peddling? Is your master a cobbler? A blacksmith?"

Bell shot John a wary look, but he just chuckled. "Ain't had a master in many a year neither, Mister Vos."

Vos slapped his companion on the arm. "You see, Charlie? Being friendly isn't the problem. The busybodies in town and the politicians up in Albany are. Soon there won't be more than a handful of slaves left in the valley."

Little Sophia, who'd been quiet for a long while, picked this moment to let out a long, satisfied yawn. It made Charlie Catton scowl more fiercely. Then he locked eyes with Bell and cocked his head. "Don't I know you, girl?"

She felt her pulse quicken. "Don't think I's had the pleasure, sir."

"You're a queer filly, tall and black as night," he replied. "The kind I'd remember, though I might not want to. You ever visited our farm with your master?"

If only I could have, she silently fumed. *Just to see my Bob one last time before he died—before he died from the beating you gave him!* But all she dared to speak was a simple truth. "No, sir."

Somehow, Catton knew Bell was holding back. Maybe he read it in her angry eyes. He took a step closer. "Where you headed? You're no free one, like this old buck. I can tell. Who's your master?"

"She's my niece," John de Conquer said, putting a protective arm around her. "We's headed up the road for services."

"You wouldn't be lying to us, would you—*Uncle?*" Vos asked as his finger traced a pattern along the bone hilt of his knife. "After I greeted you so friendly-like? I wouldn't call that uppity. It's downright rude."

"Meant no offense, Mister Vos," answered John, who wasn't nearly as alarmed as Bell thought he ought to be. "Never know who you'll meet on the road. Real friendly of you to ask after us."

Herman Vos stopped smiling. "That's no fit answer. I've worked blacks my own life. I can tell when one's lying to me."

After her whispers quieted Sophia again, Bell found herself looking not at John or the farmers but up the road, anxious to be on their way. Catton noticed, growing more suspicious. "Why are you in such a hurry, girl?"

"I was only . . . I was—"

John interrupted her with a big belly laugh, as if someone just told a funny joke. "Oh, we's in no hurry, sir. Only, my niece here got her mouth waterin' for some of Auntie's honey cakes. What, you think we out so early in the mornin' jus' to sing and pray?"

"You keep getting ruder and ruder, boy," Catton snarled, brandishing his cane. "Maybe we should teach you some manners."

The old man shook his head amiably. "Never too good at small talk. Didn't figure on bein' rude, sir. Can I make it up to ya? Do somethin' for ya? You ain't never seen a zigzag dance till you seen mine." Then he glanced at Bell and jerked his head. "Honey, you get your little one over to Auntie's place, over toward Popletown, while I finish talkin' to these fine gentlemen."

Catton, his attention still fixed on Bell, made to object. "I don't care about some zigzag dance. What I want to know is—"

"Hold on, now, Charlie," Vos said with a sly grin. "A little entertainment might be a good way to start our morning. And a good way to teach this old buck his lesson. But we best keep our audience small, don't you reckon?"

It took Catton a few seconds—and the sight of Vos fingering the hilt of his knife—to comprehend his friend's meaning. A grim smile coming to his own lips, Catton waved a hand. "Get out of here, girl, you and your little brat. We got business with your uncle."

Panic welled up inside Bell. She figured she could find Levi Roe's house by herself, but she couldn't bear to leave her old friend. She'd seen Charlie Catton in action before.

John de Conquer seemed to hear her thoughts as though she'd shouted them. "I be fine, honey. Go on, now, and I catch up."

"Yes, go on, now," Vos jeered, "but tell your folks not to hold up dinner for your uncle. He may be a while."

Something in John's twinkling eyes made Bell feel oddly reassured though he ought not to be safe in the clutches of such beasts. Still, as she took a few tentative steps, then began a steady stride up the road, her fear faded. And when she heard the voices of the three men, ever fainter as she walked, other feelings rose up to take the place of her anxiety.

Contempt.

"Got to be punished, boy, there's no doubting that," Catton said. "A few touches of my cane will leave that loud mouth of yours bloody and your ears burning."

Pride.

"Sounds rather crude, Charlie," Herman Vos said. "I had a more refined instruction in mind. I laid my knife on the whetstone just yesterday. Could slice off a few strips of his skin to teach him a lesson, and give us a prize to recall the day."

And a bit of mischief.

"I don't care what you do with me, sirs," whimpered John, letting his normally resonant voice crack and whine in apparent fear. "Burn my ears. Skin me live. Tear out my hair by the roots. But please, sirs, please don't drag me into that thicket!"

"Into . . . *what*? Those thorny bushes over there with all the vines?"

Bell was already so far away she barely heard John's reply. "Jus' so, sirs. Please don't fling me into that briar patch!"

▲▲▲

It wasn't hard to find the Roe place. The family gave her food and encouraged her to feed Sophia again, but they couldn't offer sanctuary. Levi Roe was seriously ill, perhaps close to death.

"Best go on to Esopus," breathed the sickly man. "Friends up there can help."

"I grow'd up thereabouts," Bell said. "Someone might spot me."

"Then I will go with you," his wife said. "No one will molest us on the road."

Though she'd already walked a dozen miles, Bell knew she couldn't impose on the hospitality of the Roes. Nodding, she nestled Sophia snugly in the crook of her arm and followed Missus Roe.

As the women approached the first refuge Levi suggested, Bell had a flash of recognition. "It's the Van Wagenen house! They knew the Hardenberghs, my former masters. Used to play with the two Van Wagenen boys, Isaac and Benjamin."

"They aren't Friends, Isabella," Missus Rose said, using Bell's full name as such folk were wont to do. "Think they'd remember you?"

Thank you, God, Bell thought. "That's the place for me. I shall stop there."

A frail woman greeted them the door. It was the widow Van Wagenen, Isaac's mother, who explained her son and his wife were away. "But you can rest until they get back," she said, exchanging a knowing smile with Missus Roe, who squeezed Bell's shoulder and left.

When Isaac and Maria Van Wagenen returned, Bell found a long explanation wasn't necessary. It wasn't the first time the couple heard stories of mistreated slaves in Ulster County, they assured her. "Stay here as long as you need," said Isaac as Maria helped Bell and Sophia into a rocking chair.

There was a knock on the door. *Did Missus Roe have second thoughts about leaving me here?* Bell wondered.

It wasn't the Quaker woman standing at the door, however—it was John Dumont. "Well, Bell, so you've run away from me."

"Didn't run away," she replied. "I *walked* away."

"Which is why you didn't get far before I caught up."

Bell snorted. "Never meant to get far. Left 'cause you promised me a year of my time."

He shook his head, pointing to her mangled hand. "You know better than that, Bell. You must come back."

"No, I *ain't* goin' back."

Dumont frowned in disapproval. "Well, then, I shall take the child. She's mine by law."

She's mine by right! Bell wanted to shout. But shouting would not keep her or her baby safe. She hugged Sophia close and glared up at him.

"I can have you sitting in jail for this," Dumont threatened.

"I can do that," she said, "but I won't go back."

It was Isaac who spoke next. "Look here, Mister Dumont, you say Bell's injury kept her from earning her freedom as promised, right?"

Dumont nodded, his eyes trained on Bell's defiant face.

"How much work do you figure she's short?" Isaac pressed.

"About twenty dollars' worth of spun wool and another ten dollars of field work, plus another five dollars for the child."

Isaac pointed out the open window. "Bit late in the season for field work. Don't you think twenty-five dollars would cover it?"

Dumont shrugged. "I suppose so, but Bell hasn't got a penny."

"I will pay it," said Isaac, glancing at Maria Van Wagenen's face and smiling at what he saw there. "That will settle her debt, and she'll stay with us."

Although he protested for a while, Dumont found he couldn't rebut the logic of Isaac's proposal. And, after all, it meant twenty-five dollars in hard money right now, not a slave's promise of future work. But Dumont still looked cross.

Bell had eyes only for Isaac, though. "Thank you, Master!" she exclaimed. "Thank you, Mistress! Thank you kindly!"

Isaac shook his head firmly. "I didn't buy a slave, Bell. I settled a debt."

"I work for it, Master, you'll see. I promise."

"You can pay your debt with honest work, yes," Isaac agreed, "though you cannot call me 'Master.' There is but one master, and He who is your master is my master."

"But, then, what do I call you?"

"Why, call me Isaac Van Wagenen, and my wife Maria Van Wagenen."

Greatly annoyed at that, Dumont stormed out the door. Bell hardly noticed. She knew only that though she still sat in the rocker with Sophia on her lap, she felt like she was standing ten feet tall.

▲▲▲

It was just a few weeks later that Bell learned the full extent of her former master's annoyance. As she was drawing water from the well, Isaac came hurrying up. "I heard troubling news at the market about your son Peter. He's gone."

Fear clenched her heart. "You mean he run off? When they catch him they whip him awful bad."

"That's not the talk, Bell. His owner Solomon Gidney's gone, too. They say he went south to Alabama to visit his sister."

"He take my Peter south?" She felt her insides squeeze tighter. "That ain't right!"

"It's not legal either, Bell. Under New York law, children can still be slaves for a time after their parents are freed. But they can't be taken out of the state."

Bell balled up her hands and simultaneously felt the inner fist unclench. *This is the work of the Dumonts.*

The following day, Isabella Van Wagenen, as she'd proudly renamed herself, took to the road. This time she headed south, retracing steps she'd taken during her walk to freedom. She walked this time, too, but made stops along the way, asking after Peter. Asking folks to let her know if they heard any news about Solomon Gidney returning from Alabama.

When she reached her final stop, Bell hesitated briefly in the familiar path, eyeing the assorted herbs she'd planted in the nearby garden and the stones she'd laid in the wall. The twisty vines covering the wall made her think of John de Conquer. She hadn't seen him since their encounter with Catton and Vos. She was certain he'd escaped. She'd have welcomed his help, but she knew others needed him more. And, after all, the kind of help John offered didn't just disappear when he did. She felt inside her apron and carefully pinched the dried trillium flower she kept there.

Bell sighed and strode confidently to the door.

It was Elizabeth Dumont who opened it. The woman made no attempt to be civil to her former slave. "Ugh, a fine fuss to make about a little black. Why, haven't you as many of them left as you take care of?"

Bell crossed her arms. "He take my Peter to Alabamy. Law says he can't."

Elizabeth Dumont snorted. "A pity you aren't all back in Guinea! Making such a hullaballoo about the neighborhood, and all for a paltry black boy!"

Bell knew the bitter woman wanted her to cower, to beg, or perhaps even to respond with violence so she'd get dragged off to jail. Bell would do none of those things; she didn't have to. Instead, she drew herself up to her full towering height and looked down at the hateful woman.

"I'll have my child again."

Missus Dumont snorted for a second time. "*Have your child again?*" she repeated mockingly. "How can you get him? And how will you support him? Have you any money?"

"No," Bell said, and felt neither shame nor misery at the admission. If anything, she felt herself grow even taller—as tall as the tallest tree in the forest.

A free tree. A Baumfree.

"I have no money, but God has enough—or what's better. And I'll have my child again."

▲▲▲

Wearing her finest dress, Isabella Van Wagenen stood on Kingston's Wall Street and looked up at the six-sided steeple that topped the Ulster County Courthouse. She'd admired the steeple every time she'd visited the courthouse. Now, God willing, she was admiring it for the last time.

Her first visit, months earlier, had started poorly. "I come to get my boy Peter back," she'd announced to a room full of lawyers, clerks, and jurors. Encouraged by her Quaker friends to pursue her legal rights, Bell was greeted not with judicious respect but with jeers. *Imagine that*, they obviously thought. *A poor black woman demanding her rights in our courthouse!*

Well, not *all* thought that. The justice of the peace had shown Bell into a private room and asked for the details. Then he'd explained her situation. John Dumont's nephew was the district attorney who'd be responsible for prosecuting Solomon Gidney (another of Dumont's nephews). The clerk of court was Dumont's brother-in-law. "But

Kingston is a civilized town," the justice assured her. "We respect the law."

Ushering her back into the courtroom, he'd handed her a Bible and asked her to swear Peter was her son. Having never seen a legal proceeding before, she'd held up the book and spoken her vow directly to it, provoking a round of raucous laughter. Still, she persevered—and acquired an order for Gidney to appear at court.

Only to see the constable fail to deliver it. Only to see Gidney sail safely away.

Bell had waited and prayed for justice. That's not all she did, though. She traveled up and down Ulster County, telling her story to anyone who'd listen. One stranger directed her to prominent lawyer Herman Romeyn, a kinsman of the Hardenberghs, who said he'd take her case for five dollars. To cover the cost, he found her work in Kingston.

It took many frustrating, heartbreaking months. Finally, though, the day of judgment was here. Fearing a large fine, Gidney had brought Peter back from Alabama. Bell glanced at the steeple one more time, noticing the bright sunlight glinting off the windows, and smiled.

Bell's first glimpse of Peter standing next to Gidney in the courtroom didn't bring her joy, however. Always a rambunctious boy, Peter now cowered like a frightened animal. There were horrible scars on his face, scars so red and jagged that even the justice of the peace gaped in shock. When Romeyn stated the facts of the claim, Gidney responded by denying Peter was Bell's son.

"Is this woman your mother, Peter?" the justice asked.

The boy looked up at Gidney in terror, then cast his eyes to the floor. "Don't know her," he answered with a sob. "Please let me go."

The justice was taken aback. "How did you get those scars, boy?"

Peter fell to his knees. "Got hit by a horse hoof. Got run up against a carriage. Please, sir, let me go home. Back with my dear master."

It was like Herman Vos, that awful man Bell had met on the road, had plunged his sharp knife into her side. *How could my own boy not know me?* Her eyes darted around the courtroom, full of Gidney's relatives, and saw not a friendly face among them. *How could I ever hope for justice here?*

Then her eyes fell on the one Gidney relative whose face *didn't* look triumphant. Like Peter, John Dumont was staring at the floor.

Her former master's lips were moving but made no sound, like he was talking to someone who wasn't there.

Or to someone who *was* there, but not in the flesh.

Seems we got something in common after all, John Dumont.

Bell whispered her own silent message to God. She asked for forgiveness. She asked for mercy. She asked for aid, and not just for her and her boy. Whether Dumont noticed, or had already made his decision, his next words were an answer to her prayer. "Your honor, the boy's just confused."

"What's that, Mister Dumont?" asked the justice.

"The boy doesn't know what he's saying," Dumont continued. "Peter *is* the son of Isabella Van Wagener. Everyone in this courtroom knows that. He ought never to have been taken out of state."

The arguments continued for some time, leaving Bell bewildered. The justice talked of fining Gidney, the prospect of which didn't interest her at all. She just kept watching Peter as he whimpered on the floor. Then she winced when Peter bent his head low and revealed welts on the base of his neck that suggested more scars down his back—the kind Bell had suffered when she was young, the kind that never fully heal.

Finally, the justice spoke his verdict: Gidney wouldn't be sent home with his slave boy and would pay a simple fine. "I hereby order that Peter Van Wagener be delivered into the hands of the mother, having no other master, no other controller, no other conductor but his mother."

They were the words Bell had waited so long to hear. The words that would salve a mother's wound, and maybe save a boy's life. Words that, she knew, would taste bitter in the mouths of her enemies. When she looked over at John Dumont, though, his lips weren't puckered in distaste or scorn. They'd broadened into a smile, though his eyes were still downcast.

Bell returned the smile, not caring if he saw it, and for some reason thought of that dried trillium flower she kept in the pocket of her apron.

Then Isabella Van Wagener rushed forward to embrace her child.

Chapter 27 – The Breeder

Goran looked at the trickling creek and thought of Har.

It was too shallow to provide much of a catch. The Dwarf would have enjoyed the attempt anyway. Goran could imagine Har's huge bulk stretched out next to the creek, a fishing pole in hand. The image brought a grudging smile to lips that hadn't formed one in a while.

"I cannot believe they will keep ignoring us," Dela huffed. "Their treaty with the Nunnehi requires they admit any emissary carrying an Irminsul."

She was pointing to the distinctive device in Goran's hands, the sourwood statuette of a miniature longsword thrust through a tree trunk. Its dull glow, copper and green, was barely visible in the forest shade.

The pair's visit to Spirit Forest was not quite their last hope, but it was close. Surprised that Har hadn't come to pay his last respects to Nanyehi, Dela and Goran had accompanied Tana back to Blood Mountain to coordinate a search. They'd also sent messages to Long Island-on-the-Holston, Spirit Forest, and Grünerberg seeking news of their friend.

The Gwragedd Annwn colony had none to offer. The Elf colony only confirmed Har had left Spirit Forest, headed for Grünerberg. And the Dwarf colony confirmed Har had never arrived.

So, Dela and Goran had headed to Grünerberg, recruiting Dwarf rangers to assist in their search. King Alberich had been helpful at first, but then grew impatient—and impassioned—as the chances of finding Har alive faded. After all, while Har had been missing from Grünerberg for only a few months, many Blur years had passed. If he were alive, Alberich pointed out, surely he would have made contact.

"We must face facts. Har is dead," the king insisted. "He has met his end either in battle with some monstrous foe or at the hands of those to whom he was our emissary. The only one who may have answers to such questions is Prince Veelund. He repeatedly invites me to visit Spirit Forest. Perhaps I should accept—and demand the truth with my sword at his throat!"

Goran, Dela, and Grandmaster Sudri of the Rangers Guild finally convinced the king not to pursue such a reckless course. If the Elves were truly withholding information about Har, the last thing Alberich should do was walk into Veelund's clutches. Better to let Goran, who already had a relationship with the prince, go to Spirit Forest accompanied not by a company of armed Dwarfs but by only a single companion: Dela.

The journey south to Augusta, and then into Spirit Forest, hadn't been particularly onerous. Dela and Goran encountered only a single monster, a Hellhound, and they'd simply given the beast a wide berth. Still, neither arrived in Spirit Forest in good shape. Goran was physically and mentally exhausted from their lengthy and fruitless searches, first for Kaden and now for Har. Dela's constant companionship should have made it easier to bear. But their affection had become mixed with awkwardness.

It wasn't that his love for the Water Maiden had dimmed, nor had Dela's for him, as far as he knew. She was just worn out, too, as well as frustrated by what had happened when she took Goran home to tell her mother, Tesni, about their relationship. The old woman had been shocked. No doubt she'd hoped her daughter would take one of their own people as husband. So, when the message arrived about Nanyehi's failing health, Dela had seized the excuse to leave home again.

Now Dela's anxiety seemed, if anything, greater than Goran's. Perhaps she felt guilty about pursuing their relationship while their friend was missing.

Or perhaps her relationship with Har is closer than I knew.

Goran shook his head, as if to dispel the silly idea. "I wish I had a clearer memory of where I first met the Elves. It may be further east."

Dela shook her own head. "They range across the forest. They must know we are here."

The Elves have something to hide. Why else would they refuse contact? "We may have more success if we . . ."

Familiar sensations stopped Goran in midsentence. A sudden breeze. A faint sound of distant voices. And sparks that marked the passage of elemental magic. Someone had just departed or arrived in Spirit Forest by transport spell.

"Follow the trail!" Goran urged, but Dela was already in motion, springing out of the creek and running after the rapidly dissipating trail of sparks. The Sylph left the ground and flew in the same direction.

Both saw the seam at the same time: a thin line stretching between two trees. Although it disappeared before they got within ten feet of it, the two rangers now had something to go on.

Dela stepped between the two trees and, not bothering to disguise her impatience, struck first one trunk and then other with her trident as if swinging the clapper of some giant bell. The bronze blades of her trident did produce a ringing sound of a sort, though the loudest noise was a continuous whacking of wood on wood.

"We seek audience with the Prince of Elves!" Goran demanded, holding up the Irminsul. "We must see Veelund!"

They kept it up for several minutes, Goran shouting and Dela rattling the trees. They stopped only when a squad of Elf archers stepped out of the brush, bows drawn.

"Stop that infernal racket!" ordered the only one Goran recognized, the ranger named Roza. "Did you truly think your presence was unknown to us?"

Dela glared back. "And did you think *yours* was unknown to *us*?"

"You are required to—" Goran began.

"Enough," Roza said, eyeing the Irminsul with a wary expression. "We are aware of our obligations. But you presume too much. Do you think we have nothing better to do than entertain wayward rangers?"

"You are here now," Goran observed. "You have decided to admit us. There is no need for further delay."

Roza lowered her bow. "Bring them," she ordered, then sang a few words in a low voice, disappearing through the now visible Shimmer wall.

▲▲▲

During Goran's prior visit, he and Har were taken directly to the stockade, ushered through the massive oaken doors of the gatehouse, and conducted to the Royal Hall.

That was not what happened this time.

After they arrived at the gatehouse, only Roza was allowed inside. She returned a few minutes later, her face a mask of indifference that didn't fully hide her confusion. "You will come with me," she stated, then began walking quickly along the log wall rather than back inside the gate.

Goran shrugged at Dela and followed. Only one other Elf, a male, came along. As before, Goran saw clusters of tents and huts dotting the hills around the village, but they weren't the overcrowded camps he'd expected. He saw no throngs of refugees, just lone sentries and small groups of workers. He saw more fence posts than campfires. The camps reminded him more of frontier farms in the Blur than Folk residences behind the Shimmer.

As they got closer to the place Roza was leading them, however, Goran realized his mistake. The camps weren't residences at all. There were only two structures here, ramshackle huts containing equipment and stored corn. Beyond them lay a large, fenced pen from which three Elves were emerging.

Two wore studded-leather garments resembling aprons. The garments extended below the Elves' knees and had sleeves extending to the wrists. The two wore helmets, too, with hanging guards that protected their noses and cheeks. In one hand, each Elf carried a polearm with a bronze head shaped like a glaive—a long, thin point next to a curved piece like a shepherd's crook. In the other hand, each carried a coil of rope.

Monster pens require monster tenders, Goran reflected, though all the pens he'd previously seen were structures enclosing individual stalls, not fenced-in pastures.

The third Elf emerging from the pen was the prince, but he wore no trappings of office. Veelund's bare arms were covered with sweat, while his worn trousers bore reddish-brown stains. Whether they were mud stains or blood stains, Goran couldn't tell.

"I am told you bear the Irminsul," said Veelund, wiping his arms with a cloth. "Do you bring a message from Blood Mountain?"

"No, your highness," Goran replied. "We have come from Grünerberg on an urgent matter."

"Ah." Veelund tossed the dirty cloth aside. "I should have known. You seek news of our mutual friend, Har the Tower. Alas, I have none to share."

Goran glanced up at the rapidly darkening sky. Since they'd been admitted, the sun had traveled from directly overhead to just below the horizon. "Perhaps if we could talk to those who knew Har best, it might reveal some clue to—"

"*I* am the Elf who knew Har best," Veelund said. "I have sent multiple messages to Grünerberg on this matter. He left us to return home. It seems he never arrived. What more can be said? This was months ago in Folk time, years ago in the Blur. You chase forlorn hopes and phantom dreams."

The prince said no more than others had before. Yet the words retained their bite. The Sylph looked at the Water Maiden; she looked back with eyes neither shrouded by forlorn hope nor clouded by phantom dreams. They burned solely with ferocity.

"We will *not* give up," Dela insisted. "If you will not help, we will seek it elsewhere."

"Do your rulers truly endorse your endless search?" Veelund asked. "Rangers are a precious commodity. Are there no monsters to track? Humanwares to procure? I mourn Har's loss, but we must move on. We must do our duty, as he did."

Now Veelund's words felt like the swat of some giant paw. Still, Goran wasn't ready to give up. He glanced over his shoulder at the Elf rangers. "We understand Roza spent much time with Har. Will you permit us to question her, at least? He may have mentioned something that could aid us."

The Elf prince said nothing. Instead, from inside the pen came a strange, bestial cry, something like a combination of a moo and a roar. Veelund nodded to the tenders. They walked back to the pen, the rising moon casting their long shadows on the ground.

"Your loyalty does you credit," Veelund acknowledged, "but it is misplaced. Others deserve your loyalty, too. The life of a single individual is the property of his Folk. And the Folk of America face many challenges. They are more acute for Elfkind, given our numbers. But all Folk grapple with the same enemies: Scarcity. Privation. Dwindling stores of magic."

Dela trembled slightly, a gesture Veelund noticed and seemed to interpret as agreement. Goran knew better. She was furious.

"As Prince of Spirit Forest, I could no more part with one of my rangers for a personal mission than I could allow one of my greenweavers to fiddle with ornamental flowers or a mage to bury his head in some arcane book," Veelund continued. "Nor can I afford to indulge my own passions. I have many such projects in my head, but I am not free to carry out any of them. Instead, I play midwife to Bahkauvs."

Goran's eyes darted to the fenced pasture. Veelund beckoned him forward. Goran couldn't see over the rail, so he rose into the air. The beast curled up in a corner of the pen was large and mostly bovine in appearance, except for catlike fangs and claws, scaly skin, and a long reptilian tail. Nestled next to the monster was a smaller version, though its skin was smooth, its fangs not yet visible.

"The calf is healthy, as is the mother," Veelund said. "This new breed will grow to enormous size in the Blur, yet be easier to subdue when the time comes. Its thicker legs will slow its run. Its blunter fangs, horns, and claws will render the Bahkauv less dangerous."

"You are . . . *breeding* them?"

"Of course." Veelund arched an eyebrow. "Consider the example of humans, who sustain their burgeoning towns and cities by breeding livestock, not hunting wild game. We Elves have studied the human practice. We refuse to be shackled by convention or blinded by arrogance."

"Or guided by prudence, it seems," Goran retorted. "Previous generations of Folk feared the possible consequences of breeding monsters. Of unleashing powers they could not control."

"Do not lecture me, boy," Veelund snapped. "I have heard such words before, from one more qualified to offer them. Yet I rejected Hespera's argument."

"Hespera?" Dela asked in surprise. "Warden of the Dryads?"

"The very same," he said. "Our woodland cousins are a worthy Folk. But they have allowed sentiment to cloud their judgment. In the face of dire peril, they choose sentiment—and surrender. I choose audacity and survival. Many seemingly impossible things have been accomplished by resolute Folk because they *had* to do, or die."

Goran's stomach lurched. "When we met Hespera, she was transferring books and relics to the . . . to another Folk village for safekeeping. You speak of Dryads surrendering. Do you mean they are surrendering their entire storehouse of knowledge?"

"Well, not all of it," Veelund said. "They will keep some items for personal use. How else will they pass the time?"

Dela cocked her head. "I do not understand what . . ."

The Elf prince laughed. "You two have much in common with your late friend Har. He, too, struggled to see what was before his eyes."

"Our *late* friend?" Dela sputtered in rage. "You cannot know that!"

"More sentiment, deployed just as uselessly as the Dryads do," said Veelund, shaking his head. "I have little time and less patience, so I will spell it out. Hespera and her Folk have concluded they can no longer, in good conscience, capture and pen monsters, especially since they say some monsters exhibit a semblance of intelligence."

"It is more than a semblance," Goran said. "We ourselves have met an intelligent monster."

"My mages have as well, or so they claim," Veelund replied. "It would, of course, be wrong to subject a thinking creature to such suffering. Whenever I get such a report, I always err on the side of mercy. I have the monster destroyed."

Dela and Goran looked at each other in horror. Veelund merely looked past them. "Roza, we are fortunate that you and your fellow rangers are not as childish as these two."

"Your confidence honors us, my prince," Roza replied.

"The Dryads recognize that without monsters to power their magecraft, their Shimmer walls will fall," Veelund continued. "So they have decided to abandon their villages entirely, to withdraw in small groups to new homes designed to conserve their remaining magic. Though their thaumaturgical knowledge is impressive and their mastery of greenweaving unparalleled, the Dryads only prolong their inevitable destruction. I told Hespera as much. She did not deny it. Indeed, it seems the Dryad wardens have decided to withdraw into their respective trees alone. They prefer to maintain their final vigils, and then to perish, in solitude."

"Withdraw into . . . *trees?*"

"Yes, into magecrafted dwellings within certain trees that possess great capacity for storing magic," the Elf prince explained. "Hawthorn. Ash. Laurel. Hazel. Cherry. Apple."

Goran saw Dela's eyes widen in realization. No doubt she saw the same thing in his. "Apple trees, did you say?"

"*Especially* apple trees," Veelund agreed with a sneer. "It seems Hespera met a Sighted human named Chapman. His horticultural talents supposedly rival that of Dryad greenweavers. He is assisting them in their plan, out of some sort of misguided religious fervor, I take it. Now, truly, I must return to my hall."

"I restate my request for time to interview Roza," Goran said, "in the hope that—"

"You may spend with Roza whatever time it takes her to escort you from our colony," Veelund commanded as he walked quickly away, "but there is nothing more to say. Your friend is lost."

Groaning softly, the Sylph reached out a hand. After a moment's hesitation, Dela took it. The male Elf ranger led them back the way they'd come, Roza bringing up the rear. Goran thought of several questions to ask Roza, but every time he looked over his shoulder and opened his mouth, she looked back with hard eyes and shook her head.

When their path took them into the shadow of a blockhouse, Dela's hand suddenly jerked in Goran's. But it wasn't the Water Maiden who'd initiated the movement. Roza hurtled past them, holding the trident she'd snatched from Dela's other hand. She struck the back of the other Elf's head with its butt. The ranger crumpled to the ground, unconscious.

Then Roza whirled around "Stay back!" she demanded, her voice barely more than a whisper. "And make no sound!"

Dela glared. "I knew your prince was lying! Are you to be our assassin?"

"Make no sound!" Roza repeated. "We have only a few minutes of nighttime left."

Goran felt a surge of hope. "Only a few minutes left for what?"

"For you to rescue Har the Tower before your cloak of darkness is gone."

▲▲▲

It took several of those minutes for the three rangers to run along the log wall to the spot Roza indicated. "On the other side and about thirty paces up the alley is a small hut with a sloped roof of cedar planks. That is where your Dwarf is held."

"Why not show us yourself?" Goran asked.

"I will play no further part," Roza said. "I owe Har a debt. Though I will pay it, I will shed no Elf blood. But you must. He is guarded at all times."

Dela looked defiant. "*Why* is Har being held? What debt do you—"

"No time for explanations," Roza snapped, pointing to the first rays of the sunrise shooting across the shimmering sky.

Without another word, Goran swept Dela into his arms and flew over the wall. They passed two large buildings with thatched roofs. The third roof was planked and sloped. The Water Maiden pointed to a stack of baskets near the door of the hut. A moment later, she was crouching behind them. Then Goran flew up and let himself land with a thud on the cedar planks.

"What was that?" shouted a voice from the hut.

"Go find out!" shouted another.

When the first warrior ran out the door, he had no chance to raise his shield or use the longsword in his hand. Two of Dela's three trident blades instantly found his throat. The second warrior had more warning. Grinning with anticipation, the Elf filled each hand with a shortsword and aimed a vicious cut at Dela's own neck.

It struck only the spinning shaft of her trident, and before the warrior could bring the other blade into play, Goran's arrow—shot from behind at close range—punched clear through the warrior's mail shirt and drove the Elf into the dirt. Dela dashed into the hut, sweeping her enchanted net into her other hand, and Goran was close behind, another arrow nocked.

They should have been facing three more Elf warriors, each wielding wicked blades and stout shields, but only two were still standing. The third was bucking and kicking atop the long body of Har the Tower, whose shackled hands had looped a chain over the Elf's head and were now choking him with it.

Goran's arrow flew swiftly, burying itself in the oaken shield of an Elf swordsman. Then it was all the Sylph could do to keep the Elf's blade at bay. Twice he parried a sword thrust with his bow, all the while struggling to draw his knife. He couldn't spare even a glance at Dela, but could tell from grunts and repeated clanks of metal on wood that the Water Maiden and her foe remained locked in combat.

Coming at Goran a third time, the Elf swordsman tried a slice. Rather than blocking it, Goran ducked below the blade, swinging his bow with his left hand at the Elf's lower leg. He felt the bow crack as it struck the bronze greaves protecting the Elf's shin. Still, the blow accomplished its purpose, knocking the swordsman off balance. Having finally succeeding in drawing his knife, Goran fell upon the stumbling foe and aimed for the face. Goran's first strike bounced harmlessly off the nasal guard of the Elf's bronze helmet.

His second strike, aimed slightly to the right, did not bounce.

Goran jumped up and whirled to face Dela, but she'd needed no help. Her antagonist's sword lay twisted within Dela's net. The Elf lay beside it, his helmet crushed inward by the edge of the shield Dela has wrested from his grasp.

"That one has the key," croaked Har, who let the third guard fall lifeless to the straw-strewn floor. Dela was soon unlocking the shackles around the Dwarf's wrists and ankles. Har rose to his feet, swayed a moment like a tree in a gale, then groaned.

"I can travel," he insisted.

The top of the sun had just passed the horizon as they hurried down the alleyway. Knowing he'd never have been able to carry the Tower over the wall, Goran was delighted to discover a ladder leaning against a nearby hut. Soon they were scrambling over the wall—or, more accurately in Har's case, rolling over it with great difficulty—and then drawing up the ladder to use on the other side.

Roza waited at the bottom, holding a flask. Not bothering to ask permission, she held it to Har's mouth and pushed his head back. He choked at first but then managed to down its entire contents.

"A healing potion," Roza said. "It will restore your vitality for an hour or so. Perhaps enough to make your escape in the Blur."

Har wiped his mouth and looked at Roza with half-lidded eyes. "Why . . . why did you . . ."

"You *know* why. Now we are even."

"Come with us," Goran suggested. "We must still pass the Shimmer gate, and surely after what you have done you cannot stay here."

Roza shook her head. "I am a ranger of Spirit Forest. I serve my Folk and my prince. As for your exit, there is another less used passage." She pointed to a spot some two hundred paces away. "You will be able to pass the Shimmer with a spellsong I once taught your friend during the war. Remember, Har? The night before Horseshoe Bend?"

He nodded.

"My personal debt is paid, Dwarf," Roza said, detachment audible in her voice. "When next we meet, it will be as enemies."

This time Har stared at her but did not nod.

"And now," said the Elf, turning back to Goran. "One small favor from you. A blow to my head. You must leave enough of a bruise to make my claim of unconsciousness believable."

"Of course," Goran replied. But he never got to keep his promise.

The punch to the back of Roza's head was so hard that she wouldn't have to lie about being knocked unconscious. Her healing potion had taken effect with surprising speed.

▲▲▲

Nearly an hour later, the three friends finally felt it safe enough to stop running. After leaving Spirit Forest, they'd headed not north but east, hoping to outwit their pursuers while staying beneath the canopy of trees along the Savannah River.

Har's magically restored vigor had begun to dissipate. He slumped to the ground, breathing heavily, and for the first time Goran got a really good look at his friend.

The Dwarf had grown no shorter during his ordeal, of course, but he'd lost much weight. His tattered tunic hung loosely over his chest and stomach. His cheeks were sunken and sallow. One eyelid was red and swollen, no doubt from a blow delivered during the recent struggle. But the other drooped low and uneven, a jagged white scar along its length. Another scar stretched from below Har's left ear along his neck to his collarbone, as if someone had pressed a sharp knife against his throat. He hadn't just been held captive. He'd been tortured.

"Oh, Har," Dela cried. She drew him into a warm embrace. "Oh, my dear Har."

Goran averted his eyes. He knew Dela's actions were those of a loving friend, nothing more, but the sight still made him uncomfortable.

After a while, Har gently pushed Dela away. "We cannot stay here for long. We must get back to Grünerberg. Alberich and the colony are in great danger. We all are."

"All in good time," Goran said soothingly. "I think it best we take a roundabout way home, staying east to evade pursuers."

"Alberich must be told," Har urged frantically. "And messages sent to the other Folk."

Dela tried placating him. "Yes, many will be glad to hear of your rescue. Tana has been beside herself with—"

"No, no, not about me," he interrupted. "Do you not understand? It was Veelund all along! *He* was the instigator. *He* sent Elf rangers out among the Indians in disguise. *He* supplied the gifts of power."

A series of raspy coughs kept him from continuing. Dela touched his arm tenderly while Goran tried to make sense of what the Dwarf was saying. "You mean the Elves resumed their alliance with the British?"

Har shook his head. "Veelund wants to spread Elfkind colonies across America. The Ellyllon have already retaken the Yunwi Tsunsdi mound in the Carolina mountains. Other Elves are leaving as well. They journey to lands Indian nations have abandoned or been pushed out of. They occupy other ready-made, Shimmer-shrouded villages of

Folk who have followed their humans westward. They harvest the monsters those Folk left behind."

"If Veelund wanted to drive the indigenous Folk away to take their homes and hunt their prey," Goran asked, "why supply enchanted weapons to the Indians? Why encourage them to attack the Americans?"

"It took me a while to figure that out. Veelund and his craftsmen designed their gifts to be just powerful enough to impress the Indians and make them confident of victory, but *not* powerful enough to bring that victory about. The enchantments were purposefully flawed, the stored magic purposefully inadequate."

It was a wild and unexpected theory. And it offered no explanation for the winged rangers who'd repeatedly followed Goran and Dela. But somehow, the Sylph *knew* it to be true.

"It cannot stand," Har went on. "We must do something to stop . . ."

But now his strength truly failed him. Dela moved closer, taking Har's hand and singing in low, sweet tones as the Dwarf alternately coughed, whispered, and—although Goran could scarcely believe his ears—sobbed.

This time the Sylph did not avert his eyes. This time he watched carefully as the Water Maiden comforted the broken man, running her fingers up his scarred neck, along his sunken cheeks, across his pallid forehead as she continue to sing.

This time Goran watched, his hands clammy, his stomach wrenched in a knot, as his sympathy for Har struggled for supremacy with a darker feeling.

Chapter 28 – The Vote

May 1830

Junaluska kept his back rigid as he rode. The long frock coat he wore—his sole concession to the prevailing fashion—was stretched so tightly over his chest that he feared it might tear if he happened to bounce forward in his saddle. John Ross, principal chief of the Cherokee nation, had loaned it to him. It belonged to another man, of course, not to Ross himself. Junaluska wouldn't have been able to don one of the diminutive chief's own coats.

The other men riding horses or carriages on the dusty avenue wore not just coats but entire outfits of finely tailored clothes: full-length trousers, high-collared shirts, wide cravats tied in loose bows, and waistcoats pulled as tight as ladies' girdles (and for the same reason).

Most took no note of the Cherokee rider in the frock coat. Junaluska guessed they were politicians or diplomats used to seeing a variety of visitors in the nation's capital. The few Washingtonians who did shoot glances at Junaluska's buckskin leggings or his long black hair, which he'd braided high on his head into the shape of horns, quickly averted their eyes when he turned to regard them.

Do I make them feel uneasy? he wondered, stopping to take his bearings. *Or guilty?*

Junaluska first looked east along the route he'd been following, Pennsylvania Avenue. Several hundred paces ahead, the great dome of the Capitol was visible over a line of lush green trees. Then Junaluska looked west, the way he'd come. About same distance away, but obscured from his view, was the residence of the American president, Andrew Jackson.

Junaluska once fought under his command. He'd even saved Jackson's life. Now the president was taking the side of Junaluska's enemies, those who sought to drive him, his young wife, Galilahi, and their two young sons from their farm. Jackson was taking the side of brutal, greedy men who sought to drive all Cherokee off their lands.

Chief Ross and Major Ridge had spent years resisting their enemies' designs. They'd recruited allies among the whites, allies in state capitals and in Congress. Now, at Ross's urging, Junaluska had made the long trek to Washington to add his voice to the chorus.

I cannot sing spells as Har and Goran do. But I can speak truth. And truth has its own power.

Only a few structures stood on Pennsylvania Avenue, which was mostly lined with trees and grassy fields. Junaluska guessed the two-story house on the left was the one he sought. Dismounting, he tied up his horse and walked up the small staircase to knock on the door.

"What is it?" asked the short woman who answered, looking at his braided hair through squinted eyes. "You ain't looking for room and board, are you?"

Junaluska shook his head. "I was asked here to meet a Colonel—"

"Welcome, friend!" said a tall, dark-eyed man in a rumpled suit. "This fella's my guest, Mrs. Ball."

"*Another* one?" The woman harrumphed. "He best pay for whatever he eats or drinks."

The tall man smirked, brushing a long strand of hair off his forehead and resting it precariously behind his ear. "Your hospitality is legend, Mrs. Ball. I remain in your debt."

"That's just the problem!" the landlady snorted before stamping away.

Junaluska followed his former comrade in arms down the narrow hallway, marveling at how little the man had changed. David Crockett now wore the clothes of a politician rather than the buckskins of a frontiersman, but he still had the stalking gait of a hunter and the vigorous look of a man of action. His middle-parted hair extending beyond his shirt collar contained no touch of gray.

"Here we are," Crockett announced. Two other guests stood as they entered the small room. One was a slender, narrow-faced man with close-set eyes and a high forehead beneath a line of thin, wavy hair. He was dressed in a crisply pressed suit. The other guest presented a stark contrast; he was tall and broad-shouldered with hair even longer than Crockett's and a pronounced cleft in his square chin. This man wore not the attire of a Washington gentleman but of an Indian, a dark feather protruding from a weather-beaten hat.

"Kolana!" Junaluska exclaimed as Sam Houston clapped him enthusiastically on the shoulder. "I did not expect to see you. I heard you . . . went west."

Houston's eyes flicked briefly to Crockett, then to the floor. Junaluska instantly regretted his comment. He'd heard the story just before leaving for Washington. After serving in Congress a few years, Houston had been elected governor of Tennessee. A little over a year later, he'd taken a wife—only to see the marriage dissolve within a few weeks. Heartbroken and embarrassed, Houston had resigned from office and gone off to live with the Cherokees of Arkansas.

His heart was broken, much as mine was when my Yona died. Only meeting and marrying Galilahi made me whole again. What may bring this man such peace?

As if in answer, Sam Houston sucked in a breath, looked up, and forced a smile to his lips. "John Jolly sent me here to negotiate with the federal government, much like the job I hear John Ross gave you."

"I am no diplomat," Junaluska replied. "Just a man serving my people for a short time."

The other stranger cleared his throat. "Far more than that, as I understand it, sir. You're another hero of Horseshoe Bend, like Houston here. It is an honor to make your acquaintance. I am Henry Muhlenberg of Pennsylvania."

"He came to Congress a couple of years after I did," Crockett interjected. "But Henry managed to get elected the first time out. Took my district two tries to get it right."

The congressmen shared a laugh, but Junaluska was too distracted to join them. *Muhlenberg. Muhlenberg of Pennsylvania.* He couldn't place the name, though it sounded familiar.

"It surely helped that many Pennsylvanians were used to voting for one of my uncles," Muhlenberg said.

Of course! Now Junaluska remembered Har's tales of General Peter Muhlenberg. Both Peter and his brother Frederick had served in Congress. *This Henry is their nephew, then.*

"There's another member you oughta meet, Junaluska," Crockett said. "Has a room here, too."

While Houston and Muhlenberg stayed behind to finish their conversation, Junaluska followed Crockett back into the hall. They soon found a finely dressed man sitting at a small table with two uniformed officers. "Davy!" exclaimed the civilian, prompting Crocket to roll his eyes. "You're just in time. They're about to leave."

When the three strangers stood, Junaluska noticed that the civilian was significantly shorter than the two officers, whose blue uniforms differed from each other in both shade and style.

"I take it you are the Chief Junaluska that Davy told us about," the civilian said.

"I am no chief, sir," Junaluska replied. "Just a farmer. And, once, a warrior."

"My apologies. I meant no offense. I'm afraid I lack the experience with Indians and with war that my brothers possess. I am Joe Crane, congressman from Ohio."

Junaluska nodded at the man.

"Commodore William Montgomery Crane," said one of the officers, extending his hand. "I command the United States Navy's Mediterranean Squadron. I'm in Washington for consultation."

The taller officer shrugged his narrow shoulders. "And I couldn't very well pass up the chance to see my brothers. I'm Major Ichabod Crane, in command of Fort Monroe down in Norfolk."

"Let me guess, Junaluska," Commodore Crane ventured. "You've come to talk to my brother Joe and his companions about that Indian Removal Bill. A messy business, to be sure."

"More than messy, sir," said Crockett, a serious expression on his normally jovial face. "It's a wicked, unjust measure. We're obliged to drop it in its tracks with a shot between the eyes, like the vicious creature it is."

The commodore opened his mouth to respond, then left it agape, eyes wide, as his brother Ichabod cut him off with a disapproving shake of the head. Then the major turned to Crockett. "That you have the right of it, sir, I have no doubt. But Will and I are in military service. It's not our place to engage in political intrigue, which we leave in the capable hands of you gentlemen."

"Intrigue ain't exactly my strong suit," Crockett replied. "If a member speechifies against me, I'd just as soon sic an alligator on him."

During the ensuing laughter, the two officers seized the opportunity to take their leave. It was clearly what Ichabod Crane had intended, knowing Crockett couldn't resist making a joke. Junaluska found himself admiring the tactics behind the major's graceful exit. *I am skilled with gun, spear, and knife,* he thought. *But I lack John Ross's skill with words, or this man's skill with manners. So why am I here?*

▲▲▲

Over the next few days, Junaluska figured out the answer. Chief Ross hadn't picked him because of some imagined gift of persuasion. As Crockett, Muhlenberg, Crane, and other opponents of the Indian Removal Act took Junaluska around to meet with undecided congressmen, they introduced him as the "famous hero of Horseshoe Bend." For many politicians, it seemed, supporting the Indian Removal Act was as much about supporting their war-hero president as it was about Indian relations. By emphasizing that other veterans such as Colonel Crockett were opposed to the measure—and that some heroes of the late war, such as Junaluska, were themselves Indians—opponents hoped to shift sentiment in their direction.

Time was running short, though. The United States Senate had already passed the Indian Removal Act by a vote of twenty-eight to nineteen. Debate in the House was about to begin, and Crockett and the others expected a closer vote there.

Junaluska wasn't surprised to learn most Southern congressmen favored President Jackson's measure. "I'm the misfit in Tennessee," Crockett explained as they entered another boarding house. "Henry Muhlenberg's trying to recruit other votes from Pennsylvania. We got friends in Virginia, too, and North Carolina. Might add another today."

The congressman waiting in the parlor was a large, jowly man with a receding hairline and curly whiskers. "Daniel Barringer, you rascal, got you cornered!" Crockett teased, lifting his arms as if aiming a rifle.

"Figured I'd let you just this once," Barringer said, turning to Junaluska with a sly grin. "Your friend's hunted my vote more than once on his Tennessee land bill. Never caught me."

Shaking his offered hand, Junaluska decided to play along. "The bear does not fear the raccoon. But even the greatest bear will someday meet his match. Today is the day you meet yours."

The North Carolinian laughed heartily and invited them to sit. David Barringer proved to be not just a quick wit but a sharp mind. His questions ranged widely. Junaluska replied as best he could, Crockett chiming in on certain details. Barringer's biggest concern, however, was not so easily answered.

"I'm a Jackson man," the Carolinian said. "While the president may be misguided, I don't think he hates Indians. He fought alongside Indians. Even adopted a Creek boy as a son! Jackson says the Cherokee will never have a future as a free people east of the Mississippi, because my people will never treat justly with them."

"I do not know the president's heart," Junaluska said. "I know only that he calls us wandering hunters, though we have lived on farms for generations. I know he calls us uncivilized savages, though we have our own constitution and laws, our own seat of government at New Echota, and now our own written tongue. I also know when your states fail to treat us justly, the president does nothing to stop it."

"Presidents aren't kings," Barringer countered. "The power of the government in Washington is limited."

"The president goes after the states when he wants to," Crockett observed. "This ain't about principle. It's about greed—greed for land, and for the gold in the Georgia hills."

Barringer looked dubious. "Are you saying Jackson's just out to make a buck?"

Crockett shook his head impatiently. "But he defends those who are. Look, Daniel, I was a supporter of this administration after it came into power. I am still a Jackson man in principles, but not in name. When he quit those principles, I quit him."

"That may be," Barringer allowed, "but the president didn't concoct the conflict. How can we expect two separate peoples to live within the same state but not under the same laws? If the Indians want to live apart, why shouldn't they go do that across the Mississippi? If we pay Indians willing to move, buy their land and send them west at our expense, that sounds generous to me, not cruel."

"Some of my people made that choice in the past, to take the long, hard journey west," Junaluska said. "They were not paid what was promised. Why should we expect any new promises to be kept?"

Barringer's eyes flashed. "Congress should keep our word, naturally, but you admit some of your people freely chose removal. I am told others are willing to move. Should they not have the right to, as long as Americans keeps our end of the bargain?"

Junaluska knew he must choose his words carefully if he was to win the congressman over. "It is now against our law for any Cherokee to sell land without the approval of the council. Speaking for myself, I do not believe any chief should be able to sell my land without my consent. I also do not believe any chief should be able to tell me I *cannot* sell my land. But you speak of *our* choices and *our* rights as if whites truly respect them. They do not. They will not permit us to live apart under own government. If, instead, we agree to submit to their laws, they deny us the laws' protection."

"That's not so," Barringer said as he squinted and lowered his head, reminding Junaluska of his favorite bull back home. "North Carolina respects the rights of Cherokees who submitted to state authority under the treaties of 1817 and 1819. We honored their title to thousands of acres of land."

"Only some of those titles were honored, and only after Cherokees forced the issue in court," Junaluska pointed out. "Other states refused to honor the land titles at all."

Barringer waved his hand. "There are other avenues to pursue before—"

"No!" Junaluska interrupted. "I have traveled all the way to your capital to tell you all other avenues are closed. Georgia has broken your federal law. It has ordered the Cherokee government dissolved. It has decreed Cherokees will pay taxes and serve in the militia. At the same time, Georgia has decreed Cherokees will *not* be allowed to vote, to bring lawsuits or testify in court, or to make any contracts with whites."

"Georgia's actions are indefensible, I agree. But—"

"Where it goes, other states will follow," Junaluska insisted. "We are to live as slaves in our own land or refugees in a foreign land. Or not to live at all."

Barringer sat back in his chair, fingers laced behind his neck, looking both irritated and confused.

"Daniel, the Indians are just askin' for what they deserve: justice," Crockett chimed in. "Maybe the best thing is for the Indians to find new homes out west. No man's more willin' to see 'em move than I am. But only if they want to. Only if in a manner agreeable to them."

"Surrendering my land will *never* be agreeable to me," Junaluska said. "I am willing to die. I am not willing to move."

▲▲▲

Wandering around a city in a borrowed coat talking to gentlemen in fancy suits wasn't something Junaluska ever dreamed he'd do. Nor was it something he enjoyed. It took some convincing by Crockett and the others to watch the floor debate. Junaluska found himself sitting next to Sam Houston in the House gallery as Wilson Lumpkin, congressman from Georgia, made his case for the Indian Removal Act—and defended his state's policy.

"A large portion of the full-blooded Cherokees still remain a poor degraded race of human beings," Lumpkin stated in mock sympathy. "The inhumanity of Georgia, so much complained of, is nothing more nor less than the extension of her laws and jurisdiction over this mingled and misguided population who are found within her acknowledged limits."

Junaluska was pleased to see so many members shaking their heads or glaring at the Georgian with disdain. Still, Lumpkin talked on and on, alleging it was *Georgia* that suffered decades of injuries at the hands of both Indians and the federal government, and that only wealthy elites were against removal. "They divide the spoil with the Cherokee rulers," he said, "and leave the common Indians to struggle with want and misery, without hope of bettering their condition by any change but that of joining their brethren west of the Mississippi."

For nearly two hours Lumpkin spun his web of slanders. Finally, he brought his speech to a belligerent end. "Georgia will not beg. We deny your right of jurisdiction! Upon the subject of our sovereignty, we fear nothing from your sentence. Our right of sovereignty will not be yielded."

The loud applause Lumpkin received made Junaluska wince. Then the Cherokee caught the eye of David Crockett, who winked as if to say the debate has only begun.

A Connecticut congressman named William Ellsworth spoke next. One reason so many Cherokees opposed removal, Ellsworth said, was that they deemed the western lands unsuitable for settlement. "They cannot be happy and secure there. And may they not judge for themselves? The eyes of the world, as well as of this nation, are upon us. I conjure this house not to stain the pages of our history with national shame, cruelty, and perfidy."

For days the debate continued, speakers in opposition greatly outnumbering those willing to defend the Indian Removal Act. Three allies, in particular, spoke so powerfully that Junaluska resolved to burn their words in his heart.

"There is one plain path to honor," said Henry Storrs of New York. "Retrace your steps. Acknowledge your treaties. Confess your obligations. Redeem your faith. Execute your laws. It is never too late to be just."

"The Indian here makes his last appeal," said George Evans of Maine. "All other sources of protection have failed. It remains with us whether he shall return in joy and hope, or in sorrow and despair. Will we listen to his appeal? If we do not, then is their sun about to set, it may be in blood—and in tears."

Then Crockett stood up. He talked of many things. Duties and treaties. Friendship and brotherhood. The right of Indians to make decisions for themselves. "If I be the only member of the House to vote against this bill, and the only man in the United States who disapproved of it, I'd still vote against it," Crockett proclaimed, "and rejoice in my vote till the day I die."

There were many more speeches. Junaluska gave up trying to follow the confusing arguments and found himself gazing across the chamber at a statue. It depicted a robed woman in a headdress. To her right stood an eagle with wings outstretched. To her left was a snake coiled around a column. Sam Houston said the eagle symbolized vigilance; the snake, wisdom; and the woman, liberty. But when Junaluska viewed the statue, it just made him think of Goran Lonefeather, Tana Song Snake, and his wife, Galilahi. It just made him anxious to return home.

While the final debate was confusing, the outcome was but a matter of counting. Ninety-seven members of the House voted against the Indian Removal Act—including Daniel Barringer of North Carolina. It was a strong showing for the opposition.

Alas, it wasn't strong enough. One hundred and two congressmen voted yes. The bill passed.

Drinking and scheming late into the night, Crockett and the others assured Junaluska the fight wasn't over. There would be legal challenges. There would be other bills. It would take years for the ponderous federal government to act.

But these were political battles for others to fight. Junaluska was no politician. Soon he would leave Washington, expecting never to return. *Only one battle remains for me. I must fight it now, and I must fight it alone.*

▲▲▲

For much of the next day, Junaluska watched visitors and servants enter and exit the great house from its newly constructed north portico. He pulled a servant aside and asked for an appointment but received no reply. So he waited outside for hours, nibbling on scraps he'd pocketed from the previous night's late dinner and whittling sticks with his hunting knife.

It wasn't until late afternoon that a footman conducted Junaluska into the house. When they reached the cracked door of a round room, a short man in a high collar accosted them. "What is your business, sir? The president has endured a long day of meetings."

"Andrew," said a soft but authoritative voice. "Show him in. I will have no more need of your services today."

Scowling, the short man pushed open the door to let Junaluska pass, then closed it behind him. Waiting inside was a much thinner, much grayer version of the man Junaluska had met so many years before. But the man's eyes still bored with a powerful intensity. His face still looked as if it were carved in hickory.

"Pardon his manners," said President Jackson, taking a seat and inviting Junaluska to do the same. "Andrew Jackson Donelson is not only my secretary but my nephew. He thinks me ancient and frail. He would protect me."

The implication was obvious. "I have come to *talk*, General."

"Of course you have. I explained to Andrew that you and I are old companions, comrades in arms. Besides, age has not exactly left me defenseless."

Several possible replies raced to Junaluska's lips but none seemed likely to accomplish his task. Instead, he took a deep breath.

"You and I *have* fought together," Junaluska began. "We fought Creeks who threatened the peace, who conspired with your enemies and mine. Together, we tasted victory. Now I taste only ashes and blood. Your Removal Act lights a fire that will consume my people. It is a tomahawk held over our heads."

Jackson sighed. "It is the only answer at hand for a grave question. My policy will separate your people from immediate contact with the settlements of whites. It will free you from the power of the states, and enable you to pursue happiness in your own way."

"My way is to work my farm and live in my mountains, where my children were born and where they will one day marry and have their own. Do whites pursue happiness so differently?"

"Most Indians aren't like you," the president said. "Their game has disappeared. A large portion have acquired little or no property that can be useful to them. They find themselves surrounded by whites practicing the arts of civilization. Their numbers lessen. Their morals decay. Perhaps beyond the Mississippi, under the protection of the government and through the influence of good counsel—"

Junaluska snorted. "When did you last visit our nation? Things are changing. Almost all Cherokee farm corn. Many herd cattle and horses. Our women spin and weave. More and more are learning to read and write in our own tongue. For those without land of their own, there are common fields to work. For those who cannot work, the rest share what we have."

"You see only what you wish to see, not what is," Jackson protested.

"I might say the same of you."

Junaluska rose to his feet, fingering his necklace. It had always seemed to bring him good fortune just when he needed it. But what magic had once flowed through the Wampus claws had surely faded. He had hoped his presence alone would be enough, that it would remind the president of the service the Cherokees had done the American cause.

And the service Junaluska had done Andrew Jackson himself.

"Do you remember my gift spear?" he asked. "I still keep in close. It is outside your White House now, thrust through my saddle."

President Jackson caught Junaluska's meaning. He stood up as well, straight as a ramrod. A broad smile cracked the hard wood. "I am pleased to see you again, Junaluska. I look upon you with eyes of gratitude. But the only relief for your people is to abandon your lands and move west."

"That, we will never do willingly. Your soldiers will have to force us at the point of a gun."

Jackson's smile disappeared. "Sir, your audience has ended. There is nothing I can do for you."

There was nothing more to say.

When Junaluska reached the fence where he'd tethered his horse, he touched the bronze tip of his spear with a quivering finger and cast a final look back at the White House.

If I had known at the Battle of the Horseshoe what I know now, American history would have been differently written. If I had known that Jackson would drive us from our homes, I would have killed him myself.

Chapter 29 – The Fortress

Goran watched the Dwarf army materialize in the clearing. Most were warriors in scale armor holding hook-bladed swords, double-bladed battleaxes, long-shafted poleaxes, or massive warhammers. Others were hunters, lightly armored in boiled leather and carrying bows or javelins with practiced grace. Several dozen rangers and mages completed the complement from Grünerberg. As was the colony's custom, each Dwarf wore colors denoting one of the six nations: the dark red of the Harz, the royal blue of the Tyrol, the crimson and silver of the Rhineland, the black and gold of the Ruhr, the dull gray of Rügen Isle, and the black and tan of the Lutki.

When enough Dwarfs had moved to the side, making sufficient room in the clearing, Goran lifted his flute and played the prearranged signal. Crackling sparks and snatches of Folktongue voices signaled the arrival of the next contingent. Its sheer size amazed Goran. Nearly the entire fighting strength of Blood Mountain now stood in the clearing next to their Dwarf allies. Nunnehi warriors wearing deerskin clothes and snakeskin bands on their wrists and ankles, drumming the long hafts of spears against the short hafts of clubs and tomahawks. Nunnehi archers wearing mantles fringed with fur and topped with fox-head hoods. Nunnehi shamans smoking intricately carved pipes as they added their magic to the Shimmer bubble over the clearing. Nunnehi scouts wearing azalea garlands and singing lush harmonies, accompanied by rattles, shackles, and gem-studded flutes.

Once again, recent arrivals bunched together to free up space. Once again, Goran played his signal song. This time, though, the transport spell brought only a handful of additional fairies, shorter and stockier than the others. While the faces of the Dwarf army were a ruddy pink and those of the Nunnehi a warm copper, the faces of the newcomers were a cold, metallic red.

"Birdman!" Betua exclaimed. "I see you no longer wobble through the air like a buzzard."

Goran smirked. "No thanks to your Goblin healers, though you need not have spared my feelings by bringing so few."

Betua sighed deeply, which made her large ears wiggle. "We *are* few. While our elders are as outraged as any at Veelund's crimes, they are wary of depopulating our defenses. There have been Elf sightings along the lakeshores."

"There may already be Elfkind occupying former Paissa villages, you mean? Veelund has wasted no time bringing his conspiracy to its intended end."

The Goblin touched the hilt of her broadsword. "It is time to bring Veelund himself to an end. Is there still an enemy here to smite?"

Goran nodded. "Dela, Har, and I have kept a constant watch. Elf rangers continue to roam these woods. And since the first party of Dwarf and Nunnehi mages arrived to cast Shimmer over the forest, they have twice blocked large-scale Elf transports. Veelund's scarcity of magecraft has again proved to be his fatal weakness. He is trapped here. He knows it."

"So there will be heavy resistance." Betua cast an appraising eye over the crowded clearing. "This is an impressive horde, to be sure, but do we have the numbers to prevail?"

"We are not yet fully assembled," Goran pointed out. "When the final contingent arrives, we can—"

"This is no time for a friendly chat," Alberich snapped as he approached with several aides. "It is time to act, to retain the initiative. Betua, attach your warriors and skirmishers to our left wing! Goran, I need your eyes on the trees as we advance."

The Dwarf king's talk of retaining the "initiative" reminded the Sylph of his first taste of battle many years ago and hundreds of miles away. Back then, an impetuous commander led his troops into the wilds of Pennsylvania, only to be surrounded and slaughtered. Goran had helped his friends George Washington and Daniel Boone survive General Braddock's mistake.

I must help us all survive this one.

"Should we not wait and attack at full strength?" Goran asked. "Veelund is not a man to be underestimated."

The Dwarf king snorted. "Neither am I."

Betua raised a hand. "Perhaps if we—"

"When you deploy your *forces* as instructed, we can proceed," Alberich interrupted, casting his eyes meaningfully across her small band of Goblins as if to underline their comparative unimportance. Then he looked at Goran. "There is no need to wait, Sylph. Our siege engines cannot be wheeled into place until we have secured a path through the forest. And our remaining allies are unlikely to prove decisive in a melee."

That is not my experience, Goran thought, but knew that saying so was unwise. He nodded to Betua and flew toward the trees.

With Dwarf warriors in the center, Goblins and Dwarf hunters forming the left wing, and the Nunnehi the right, the army marched into the forest. At first their pace was brisk. The flat ground and widely spaced trees posed little obstacle. As the army approached the creek, however, the forest thickened. The allies had to weave their way through stands of hardwood, clumps of cane and berry, and thickets of hempweed and creeper. By the time the vanguard reached the creek their ranks were ragged, their units disorganized.

Although he caught only fleeting glimpses of bodies moving through the foliage, Goran was certain Elf rangers were shadowing the column. Veelund would soon know the allies' strength and intentions.

Unfortunately, their first inkling of Veelund's intentions came in the form of a volley of arrows and slingstones raining down on their right flank. "Ambush!" Goran cried.

Nearly a dozen Nunnehi fell. Then came another chorus of bowstrings twanging and slings whistling from the left. Another chorus of death. Several Dwarf hunters sprouted fletched arrows from their sides or splashes of blood from their heads as Elf missiles struck home.

If Veelund had thought to provoke Alberich into rashness, however, he had indeed underestimated the canny Dwarf lord. The light troops on the allied flanks quickly dispersed, taking cover and seeking targets for their own missiles. Meanwhile, the heavy infantry in the center neither bolted in panic nor lumbered after their companions to be picked off one by one by fleeter-footed Elves. Instead, Dwarf warriors formed a series of solid squares between the trees while those equipped with shields formed protective canopies above.

After more enemy volleys managed only to cover the Dwarf warriors' shields with quivering arrows and slingstone-sized dents, the volleys stopped altogether. Nunnehi and Goblin rangers returned from the far woods, shaking their heads in frustration.

Goran frowned. *The "spirits" of this forest are not so easily cornered.*

An unexpected sound interrupted his thoughts: a sharp crack, as if someone had snapped a giant twig. The Sylph propelled himself forward to investigate. Another sound came from the same direction. But it wasn't a crack. It was a bestial cry, the roar of some great cat. When Goran next heard pounding hooves and the dull thud of enchanted bone on wood, the images formed into a sickening revelation.

"Look out!" he shouted as an enormous sycamore that seconds ago had stood on the opposite bank of the creek now soared over the water. Its wide bole landed directly on a Dwarfish square, crushing skulls, ribs, spines, and legs with merciless efficiency. The lower, thicker branches wrought similar havoc among the Dwarfs to either side of the trunk, while the higher branches pinned other warriors under such weight that they couldn't budge.

A second tree soared over the creek, then a third, then a fourth, each landing on and toppling over a separate square of Dwarfs, whose armor proved an inadequate defense against the brute force of the Elves' attack. Behind each jagged stump stood a massive, snarling Bahkauv and an Elf wearing the leather apron of a monster tender. Further back, other duos of Bahkauvs and tenders were moving up to convert other trees into destructive weapons.

Over the bedlam of groans and curses, Goran heard Alberich issuing a stream of commands. Officers relayed the king's orders across the army, shouting "Break!" and "Scatter!" and "Mages to fore!"

Goran sped forward, drawing an arrow. His first shot struck the nearest Bahkauv in the head, just under one of its horns, but was unable to penetrate the monstrous bovine's magic-infused hide. Switching targets for his second arrow, Goran put it through the chest of the beast's Elf tender, killing him instantly.

Hoping another shot at close range would enjoy similar success against the Bahkauv, Goran banked left and nocked his third arrow. But he'd misjudged the length of the monster's paws. The Sylph yanked back just in time as the Bahkauv's lionlike claws raked the empty space where Goran's throat would have been.

Soaring above the fuming monster, Goran scanned the emerging battlefield. While a line of Dwarf and Nunnehi hunters rushed forward to confront the Bahkauvs, their mages were already engaged in a desperate struggle with the Elf tenders, who were of course mages themselves. Some of the Elves swirled the intervening air into gusts of wind to sweep the Dwarfs off their feet. Others hurled balls of fire or bolts of lightning, or formed the loose stones of the creek and the broken branches of the forest floor into great floating fists. Still others cast their magic underneath the forest floor to soften the earth, hoping to trip or immobilize their advancing foes.

But Dwarf mages were just as adept, crafting magical defenses for each attack. And they weren't alone. Nunnehi shamans cast their own magecraft attacks at both the monsters and their tenders, knocking them back with great sheets of driving rain and knocking them over with small twisters of wind and dust. Two Goblin mages joined the fray as well, magecrafting water from the creek into long, sharp scythes of sparkling ice.

Shouts of "Refuse Flank!" jolted Goran out of his distraction. Armored Elves were advancing from the trees, hoping to defeat the allies' lighter troops while the Dwarf heavy infantry was pinned in the center. On the right, Nunnehi of the Rattlesnake Clan had formed a solid rank and were putting up a fierce fight with spear and club. On the left flank, however, the battle line had devolved into a confusing and jumbled melee.

Goran opted to fly left. His first shot felled a green-faced warrior of the Moss Folk as he was about to thrust a spear into a Dwarf's back. Then, even as the Sylph nocked his next arrow, he glided over a duel of flashing blades and ended it with a kick into the sallow face of a Psotniki swordsman who was knocked off-balance long enough for Betua to open her foe's throat.

"I need no assistance with such rabble," the Goblin ranger growled as she spun to find another foe.

Goran returned her growl with a smile, then cried out as a slingstone struck his temple. Instantly disoriented, the Sylph plunged to the earth. Only at the last second did he flutter his wings enough to lessen the impact, though his landing still knocked the wind out of him.

Gasping, Goran rose and found himself covered in mud. He stood in the shallows of the creek. All around him, the battle raged. The Dwarfs and Goblins weren't outnumbered, he realized. But they were retreating anyway, for they faced not just Elf warriors on the ground but unseen archers and slingers in the trees.

Then Goran felt the water surge. The level reached his knee, his waist. Above him came a strangled cry, followed by a rustling of branches. An enemy slinger tumbled into the creek with a splash. No arrow, axe, or javelin protruded from the Elf's motionless body; it was motionless because it was enmeshed, neck to knees, in a net.

With savage shouts, the leading edge of the Gwragedd Annwn warband splashed past Goran and dove at their foes. Enchanted nets soared into the air to yank Elves from the high branches. Tridents flew through the air or stabbed forward from expert hands, blades glinting in the speckled light of the forest as they pierced hearts, heads, or limbs.

There were also Gwragedd Annwn mages creating great walls of water to smash against the enemy ranks. There were still other figures among the newly arrived warband, too, warriors who looked as comfortable in the water as the Gwragedd Annwn but who more closely resembled the Nunnehi in their builds, coloring, and gear, though Goran could see small flaps of skin stretching between their fingers and toes, as if they possessed the hands and feet of frogs.

The Sylph watched three other newcomers fighting nearby in three distinctive styles. Tana Song Snake blew a dart into the neck of one Elf, then spun on one heel to drive her blowgun into the belly of a second before finishing him with a tomahawk. Har the Tower bellowed as he swept one Moss Folk spearman off his feet with his battleaxe, then kicked another with a broad, hard boot, shattering the enemy's ribs.

And Dela, who'd stooped to recover her net from the unconscious slinger, dropped full into the water to dodge an Elfish spearpoint, then leapt to the bank of the creek with her trident thrust before her, impaling her foe. The periwinkle eyes of the Sanziene warrior went wide with shock, then closed in eternal sleep.

Within minutes, the melee was over. Elves who hadn't succumbed to the fury of the initial Gwragedd Annwn assault had melted away into the deep forest. Ahead of them, Goran could see the rest of the battle coming to an abrupt halt as well. The Bahkauvs and their tenders were dead or fled, the Nunnehi faced no more foes, and the Dwarf heavy infantry—or at least those who'd survived the falling trees intact—were reforming into columns.

After greeting his friends enthusiastically—his long embrace of Dela prompting Tana to smirk and Har to roll his eyes—Goran hurried to the side of the Dwarf king, who was receiving casualty reports and giving rangers tersely worded orders.

Alberich glanced at the newcomers resting in the creek. "Not as many reinforcements as I had been led to expect," he observed dryly.

Dela leaned on her trident, breathing heavily. "Two companies were all the Gwragedd Annwn could spare. Our elders feared that weakening our garrison might invite an Elf attack on Long Island while we besieged Spirit Forest."

The Dwarf king considered her words. "That *would* be a clever strategy, and this Prince Veelund is nothing if not clever. Is that why your efforts produced so few warriors as well, Nunnehi?"

Tana gave a quick nod. "Partly. We Nunnehi and the Water-Dwellers, the Yunwi Amayine Hi, have often warred in the past. They do not fully trust us, though I was the one who negotiated the current treaty and so enjoy some respect. They finally consented to join our alliance but also insisted on holding enough warriors back to defend their village."

Goran braced himself for the answer, then asked his question. "What were our casualties?"

The king brushed a weary hand along his whiskered cheek. "Not as great as initially feared. Many warriors were only stunned or pinned by those trees, not critically injured. Whatever Veelund intended, he did us one favor: His forces felled a number of trees we would otherwise have had to clear ourselves. Our siege engines will soon be here."

▲▲▲

Har the Tower had expected his return to action to produce a decisive result. Either he'd find he relished the sights, sounds, and perils of battle, proving he was fully recovered, or, alternatively, coming back to Spirit Forest would shatter his confidence and tear away the curtain he'd erected in his mind, the curtain blocking out months of confinement, loneliness, and suffering in this accursed place.

But as Har sat on a log and watched the Dwarf craftsmen and warriors wheeling their siege engines into position next to the upward-sloping Shimmer wall, he felt neither exhilaration nor fear. He felt nothing. He felt hollow.

"Are you well, Har?"

Dela placed a gentle hand on his shoulder and followed his gaze to the top of the closest siege tower, where Dwarf and Goblin archers were already congregating. Several hundred feet to the left, a line of Nunnehi and Yunwi Amayine Hi archers, eyeing each other warily, waited to ascend the ladder of the other siege tower.

"Though your nickname might suggest otherwise, Har, I think your efforts are best deployed elsewhere," said Dela playfully, pointing to the five engines that lay between the two towers. In the center was the battering ram, a massive cypress trunk suspended on three ropes beneath a planked roof. To the left of the ram were two ballistae, giant crossbows operated by means of winch and trigger. To the right were two mangonels, their long arms pulled back against skeins of twisted rope. When released, each arm would fly up against a crossbeam, launching missiles from its bucket.

Har had never witnessed war machines in action. The Dwarfs of the Harz had last conducted a siege years before he was even born. A motley band of bandits—mostly unscrupulous Elves and Town Folk, along with a few wayward Dwarfs—had been poaching monsters and humanwares along the northwest corner of King Hibich's realm. After one of the renegades used spellsong to lure a large contingent of human children into slavery, Hibich had decided to assault the bandits' base in a mountain called the Koppenberg. Har's father, Daric, had served on a ballista crew. Although they were victorious, Daric had always described the siege as one of the most miserable experiences of his life. Of course, Daric was a craftsman. Being killed or rendered insane by Shimmer failure was an ever-present danger in the Blur.

But not for a ranger. Not for me.

Har looked again at the hunters filling the platforms of the siege tower. They looked excited, yes, but also anxious, as did the craftsmen and warriors crewing the ram and artillery. The longer it took to wear down the magecrafted walls of Spirit Forest, the longer they'd have to brave the perils of the Blur.

Covering Dela's hand with his for a moment, Har stood up and slipped his battleaxe into his belt. The prospect of reentering the Elf colony provoked neither dread nor vengeance. But Hara found he did feel *something*: duty to his allies. He'd do his part to get them home as soon as possible.

▲▲▲

Crash! Creak. Crash! Creak. Crash! Creak.

Many hours into the bombardment, Dela began to think they'd been misled about the Elves' lack of magical resources. Opting to serve in a recovery detail, she'd long since lost count of her sorties along the base of the Shimmer, picking up spent arrows and shot to replenish the attackers' supplies. So far, the Elves' glistening wall had survived the allied barrage intact.

Crash! Creak. Crash! Creak. Crash! Creak.

Not that Dela thought she could do any better. It was difficult enough for experienced hunters and artillery crews to carve a dent in the Shimmer. Her inexperienced hands would surely produce no better results. After all, trying to shoot an iron-tipped arrow will always spoil a Folk archer's aim. And loading the bucket of the mangonel with iron-rich stones, especially the crossed-crystal stones that had proved so effective at disrupting magecraft, tended to unravel the enchantment woven into the catapult's wood frame. Shooting such missiles required frequent, expert repairs.

Crash! Creak. Crash! Creak. Crash! Creak.

Dela glanced across the clearing at the battering ram where Har and a team of Dwarfs, Goblins, and Nunnehi were swinging the giant cypress trunk back and forth, pounding its iron head into the base of the Shimmer with a relentless rhythm.

"You, there, blue-skin!" shouted a ranger of the Yunwi Amayine Hi, waving a webbed hand. "Can you help with this?"

The Water-Dweller and two companions were trying to lift a heavy, iron-tipped bolt that had fallen to earth after striking the Shimmer. Dela shoved a handful of stone crosses into the basket over her shoulder and hurried over to help. They half carried, half dragged the bolt back to the ballista, where three burly craftsmen gratefully added it to their diminished pile.

"Got any for me in that basket?" asked Goran as he alighted next to her, pointing to his empty quiver.

Dela slipped three unbroken arrows into it and gave him a quick peck on the cheek. "Perhaps a rest is wise. You have been at it for hours."

Goran blew out a breath. "You heard the same explanation I did, Dela. The Elves have made their Shimmer thickest at its base, to resist ram and ballista. Our best chance for a breakthrough is higher up. The archers on the siege towers are doing their best, but only I can fly close enough to strike the same spot repeatedly. The longer this takes, the greater the risk our store of elemental magic will be exhausted before Veelund's."

"Would difference will it make if . . ." Dela began.

But the Sylph was already soaring into the air, his bowstring pulled back to his chin. He paused for a moment as a new volley flew from the siege tower and struck the curved Shimmer wall within a few feet of each other, producing a shower of sparks. Then Goran darted forward and loosed his shaft just inches from the same spot.

This time, there was no shower of sparks. Dela saw something more like a plume of flame suddenly erupt from the Shimmer. A hole!

She wasn't the only attacker to notice. With cries of exultation, the archers on the tower dropped their bows and shoved a long, iron-banded plank from its sheath beneath the high platform.

"Hurry!" Goran shouted as he shot another iron-tipped arrow at a spot about three feet to the left of the hole, widening it considerably. "And remember the rope—I cannot get you all to the ground by myself!"

Dela sprinted for the ladder, trident in hand, now wishing she'd posted herself to the tower despite her lack of archery prowess. At that moment, she longed to charge over the gangplank with the others to face whatever may await inside.

To face her enemy, with Goran at her side.

She climbed the rungs as fast as she could. Folk were yelling from above and below. Then a single voice pierced the bedlam. *His* voice. An exasperated voice.

"It's closing!" Goran cried. "I can't stop it!"

"Move away!" answered one of the Dwarfs. "We will shoot another volley!"

Dela pushed herself to her limits, dropping her trident to speed her assent.

"No time," Goran said. This time his voice didn't sound exasperated; it sounded determined.

Oh, no . . .

As Dela's head rose above the level of the platform, she looked along the gangplank to the rapidly shrinking hole. Her eyes met Goran's. He winked, nocked an arrow, and, with a great sweep of his wings, launched himself at the Shimmer.

"Goran!"

Dela jumped onto the gangplank and dashed across the bouncing board, reaching out in desperation. If she reached his ankle, could she draw him back before he entered the fortress alone? Or would he draw her inside with him? Either way, they'd be together.

But Dela's hand grabbed only empty air. Goran had disappeared. And so had the hole.

▲ ▲ ▲

Crash!

The cypress ram threw off yet another drizzle of sparks as it slammed into the Shimmer, its iron spike chipping relentlessly away at the intricate lattice of Elfish enchantments.

387

"Rest!" shouted a red-bearded officer. Brawny Dwarfs, stout Goblins, and sinewy Nunnehi stepped away the ram, all sweating profusely. Har the Tower, who'd stationed himself at the rear, would have kept going, but he couldn't begrudge the others a short break.

When two craftsmen hurried over to talk to the officer, pointing anxiously at the crossbeams from which the ram was suspended, Har realized the break might not be so short. He looked up at the beams. There were visible cracks in all three. Cypress was unfriendly to elemental magic. Iron actively disrupted it. A ram offered the best chance to break the Shimmer, but connecting it to an enchanted machine made the latter wear out faster.

It was Veelund himself who'd given Har and his friends their first useful instruction in thaumaturgy. *Well, he taught it to Goran, anyway. All I ever learned from Veelund was how great a fool I am.*

"Help! I must get to his side!"

Dela's panic-stricken voice prodded Har out of his funk. He saw the Water Maiden trying to reach King Alberich but being blocked by a throng of curious fairies.

"Dela!" Har cried. "What is the matter?"

"Goran slipped through a crack in the Shimmer, but then it closed. He is alone!"

Or, worse, not so alone. "Rest time is over!" Har shouted to the ram crew. "This wall must fall!"

The red-bearded Dwarf scowled. "*I* give the orders here, ranger."

"My friend Goran is on the other side," Har replied, though he was looking at the others, not at the officer. "If not for him, I would still be a captive of the Elves."

The officer pointed to the craftsmen currently working on the crossbeams. "We must wait until they repair the damage. For the sake of a single man, I will not risk—"

"Goran Lonefeather, you say?" said one of the Nunnehi. "I have heard tales of the winged one."

"As have I," said a broad-shouldered Goblin. "This is no way for that hero's tale to end."

Others grunted in assent, including many Dwarfs. Ignoring the officer's protestations, they scrambled underneath the planked roof and took their places. "Heave!" Har yelled as they pulled the ram back as far as its suspending ropes would allow.

"Drive!" he yelled as they pushed the ram forward with the full strength of their muscles.

The iron head crashed into the Shimmer, sending sparks flying. At and around the point of impact, what had looked like a soap bubble turned briefly into an opaque lattice of brightly colored beams. Again and again, Har and the other drove the ram into the same spot, and again and again, the Shimmer flashed and flared.

The resulting sparks weren't the only objects filling the air as other allies attacked the wall with redoubled ferocity. The mangonel crews hurled bucket after bucket of missiles, lighting up large sections of the wall as the iron-alloy crosses did their work. Archers fired from elevated platforms as well as the ground. Every so often, a ballista added a thick bolt to the rain of slender arrows.

After an especially forceful swing of the ram, Har looked up and felt a surge of excitement. Around the point of impact, the wall hadn't dissolved back into translucence. Several dints in the magical fabric were clearly visible. "Keep it at!" he exclaimed. "It is nearly—"

Then he heard something snap.

Before Har had a chance to sound a warning, both the rear and middle crossbeams shattered. The pieces fell on the ram and the crew operating it, followed an instant later by a rain of roof planks. Fairies cried out in pain, tumbling to the ground or stumbling away from the pile of wood and rope that had once been a siege engine.

"No!" Har wailed. *We were so close!*

Spitting dust and swearing with equal fervor, he rolled the ram out from under the debris and tried to lift it on his own. Even for Har the Tower, the task proved too great. He sagged, groaning in exasperation. The wall's solid face began to fade back into blurry soap bubble.

Then another Dwarf, shaking splinters from his head and shoulders, grabbed a handhold close to the ram's head, followed by a Nunnehi warrior with a bloody smear across his forehead and a Goblin who'd discarded a mangled helmet. Together they lifted the ram and shoved it into the weakened Shimmer, albeit not with much force. Four more determined fairies joined in for the second shove, then two more for the third.

It was the eighth shove that did it.

The Shimmer did not crack like the crossbeams had. There was instead a rending sound, like a giant set of hands had torn a giant burlap sack in two. Beyond the now-yawning gap in the wall was a clearing— and the enemy.

His muscles burning, Har sank to the ground, momentarily spent. Amid the cacophony of exuberant cheers, barked orders, and clanking armor, he thought he heard Dela's voice from the breach. He thought he heard her singing.

▲▲▲

As the Shimmer hole closed behind him, Goran found himself hovering above a deserted clearing. To the right was the fenced pasture where he'd gotten his first glimpse of Veelund's carefully bred Bahkauvs. To the left was the gatehouse of the Elf village. Goran could make out only a handful of faces peering over the walls.

Hovering, he glanced over his shoulder and saw distorted images of the allied army, but he couldn't gauge its progress against the Shimmer. After considering the problem for a few minutes, he decided to get a closer look at the stockade's defenses. Flying close to the ground, watchful for any movement in the tall grass, Goran never expected that the greater threat would come from another direction.

His first sign of danger was the arrow that brushed past the gold-tipped feathers of his right wing and sank into his bicep. His second sign consisted of hands grabbing him roughly and driving him into the ground, knocking him senseless.

▲▲▲

Springing through the ragged tear in the Shimmer, her trident in hand and her courage song on her lips, Dela didn't see the fenced pasture on the right, nor the sparsely garrisoned walls of the Elf village on the left. She saw only the scene that confirmed her worst fears. Several dozen paces ahead, Goran was sprawled motionless on the ground. She saw two Folk standing over him with spears pressed to his back and a third hovering overhead, bow in hand.

All three Folk had wings.

Without hesitation, her limbs filled with a force more powerful than fairy magic, Dela dashed forward and hurled her trident. It took the archer full in the chest. It took his life.

The first of three lives they owe me.

Grasping her net, the Water Maiden slowed to a halt within a few feet of the remaining fliers and prepared to fend off their spears, but it proved unnecessary. First the ground trembled. Then came the sound of running feet. The two spearmen exchanged looks and soared upward. By the time Dela reached the side of her beloved, the fliers were speeding toward the stockade.

"Goran," she whispered, turning him onto his back. "Oh, please, Goran."

Dela sighed with relief as his eyelids fluttered. For the first time, she noticed the broken shaft of an arrow piercing his arm. No other wounds were visible, but she couldn't be sure a fall to the earth hadn't inflicted serious injury.

"Healer!" she shouted. "We need a healer here!"

A Nunnehi shaman wearing a headdress of dried tobacco leaves knelt beside them and gently pushed the sputtering Goran down when he tried to rise. After a quick examination found no broken bones, the shaman produced a long, ornately carved pipe, emptied the contents of a small bag into its bowl, and lit it with a twirl of her finger. After sucking in a couple of breaths, making the pipe smoke and spark, the shaman filled her lungs with a third and blew the oddly colored smoke all over Goran's body, from head to foot. With practiced fingers, the healer removed the broken arrow and bandaged the wound. Then she bade Goran to sit up and handed him the burning pipe.

"Draw in a dozen deep breaths," the mage commanded, "and let the magic do its work. I must rejoin my Folk."

Dela touched her arm. "I will find you later and return your pipe."

Looking amused, the shaman pointed to the five other pipes dangling from her belt before joining the stream of passing fairies. By the time the healing smoke took full effect, allowing Goran and Dela to reach the stockade, the allies had begun to reestablish their siege lines around it. Along the northern wall, Nunnehi archers formed front ranks while warriors with spears and clubs waited for craftsmen to finish enchanting their scaling ladders. The Gwragedd Annwn took up position along the shorter eastern walls, the Goblins and Yunwi Amayine Hi along the western ones.

The largest contingent, the Dwarfs of Grünerberg, readied their assault on the gatehouse. Dela was pleased to see Har the Tower, his hair and forehead drenched with sweat, helping wheel one of the siege towers into place.

"Should have known Veelund would have allies of his own," Goran groaned. "Winged ones."

"They are not of Iris Isle, though," Dela said. "Could they be rogue Sylphs?"

"Rogues like I am, you mean, but aligned differently?" Goran shrugged his shoulders and then winced. "I suppose anything is possible."

"Where are they?" King Alberich demanded. "First there were surprisingly few defenders on the walls. Now there are none."

Dela followed his gaze and saw he was right. *What game is Veelund playing?*

"Har, you know this place best," the king said. "Where are the teeming masses you spoke of? Have the Elves retreated to some inner keep?"

The Dwarf ranger shook his head. "The Royal Hall is tall but hardly a fortified keep. As for their numbers, I can only guess many evacuated before our mages could block their escape."

"Let us reduce this place to rubble, then, and their pitiful rabble to dust," said the king, turning to a Dwarf ranger who held a thin flute to his lips. "Signal the assault!"

What came next, however, was not the dulcet tones of an enchanted instrument. It was a sound that only rangers with experience on human battlefields would recognize.

The booming belch of a gunpowder cannon.

An instant later, the central platform of the Dwarfs' siege tower exploded into a cloud of fragments and splinters. Then another cannon fired. The ball landed within a formation of Dwarf warriors, knocking several to the ground.

Dela, Goran, and Har looked at each other in horror. Alberich shook his fist. "This Elf prince uses human contraptions against us."

"Not humanwares, I think," said Goran. "Veelund has likely constructed his own artillery of bronze and brass that can be properly enchanted for Folk use."

Har pointed to smoking muzzles on either side of the gatehouse. "They shoot from raised platforms. We should direct our fire there."

Issuing rapid commands as he fumed, Alberich soon had his archers filling the sky with volleys. A short time later, one of the mangonels slammed a basket of large, jagged rocks against the wall just beneath one of the guns, forcing the Elves reloading it to scramble for cover.

The other cannon fired again, however, prompting a Dwarf crew to dive for cover themselves. From further away came other explosions, other signs that the artillery of Spirit Forest was putting up a destructive resistance.

"Scaling ladders!" a Dwarf shouted. Soon squads of warriors were running toward the stockade, each holding a long ladder.

"It is time we made ourselves useful," Goran said, pointing to one of the ladders placed against the log wall and already half full of armored scalers.

"Yes!" Har bellowed with some of his usual swagger. "It is long past time."

The king held up a gloved hand. "Hold! That is a job for warriors. I need you three here, for tasks only rangers can perform."

"Message and courier duty." Har grumbled.

"*Essential* command and control," Alberich replied icily. "Do you never tire of playing the fool?"

Har's dark expression sent a chill up Dela's spine. *He is dangerously close to losing control.*

Most Dwarfs either rushed forward to join the scaling parties or ran off to render assistance to the siege crews taking the brunt of the cannon fire. Two heavily armored warriors remained at Alberich's side, though, along with Dela, Goran, Har, and two other Dwarf rangers.

The king turned to one of the latter. "Send a message to Tana. I would know the progress against the far wall."

"Yes, Sire," said the ranger—but then his eyes grew wide with astonishment.

Goran gasped. Har cursed. Alberich merely stared, disbelief written on his angular face.

Clouds of smoke filled the air above the gatehouse. Issuing from the smoke was a line of figures. Each held either a spear or a bow. Each had wings.

It took Dela but an instant to discern the direction the fliers were headed, and but an instant more to discern their intent.

"To me!" shouted Alberich, who'd evidently drawn the same conclusion.

The fliers' first two arrows struck the king's two burly guards. Both fell. Other arrows flew past Goran, Har, and Dela—none targeted Alberich. Killing the enemy commander was apparently not their design.

Taking to the air himself, Goran shot an arrow at one of the fliers and then drew his knife. Har grabbed a circular shield dropped by one of the guards and stepped in front of his king. Dela opted for net over trident and grinned appreciatively as it closed around the head and neck of the closest flier. As he fumbled to remove it, he failed to notice Dela's couched trident until it took him full in the chest.

Har slammed the shield into the face of one descending flier. Behind him, Alberich had drawn his sword and parried the initial thrust of a flying spearman, using the momentum to spin his body and kick his leg up at the torso of his adversary, knocking him roughly to the ground. "To me!" the king shouted again as he finished his attacker.

Boots stamped all around them. Reinforcements were coming. Dela jerked her trident free and took a moment to examine her assailant. He was no Sylph. The wings on his back were thin and translucent, more resembling the gossamer wings of a butterfly than the gold-tipped feathers forming Goran's wings.

The Water Maiden felt something hard strike the back of her head. Then she felt nothing at all.

▲▲▲

"Of all my creations, they are my most impressive. Do you not agree, ranger of the Sylph?"

The blurry shape of Veelund loomed over him. Glancing sideways, Goran drew in a quick breath as he spotted Dela lying in the courtyard a few feet away, seemingly unconscious.

Or worse.

His heart skipped a beat. Goran returned his eyes to Veelund. Although the courtyard was full of enemy warriors, the Elf prince was unarmed and unarmored.

This man is no warrior, Goran told himself.

Or perhaps the Sylph spoke the words out loud, for Veelund swept his robe aside to point at the craftsman's sigil embroidered on his surcoat. "My hands were made to hold tools, not weapons. But who is to say the smith cannot defeat the general? From the very first lesson, an apprentice learns to make the most of what he has, to forge disparate elements into strong alloys, to convert seemingly opposing forces into useful work. If the secret of great battles consists in knowing how to deploy and concentrate at the right time, why should a smith not win more than his share?"

Goran tried to piece together what had happened. He recalled struggling with a flying foe, then other hands grabbing him from behind. He sat up, feeling groggy. "D-Dela," he stammered. "What have you—"

"She yet lives," Veelund interrupted with a sneer. "What use have I for a dead hostage? Though I *had* hoped to seize that pig-headed fool Alberich, you two will have to do."

"Creations," Goran repeated, still trying to recover his senses. "One of your most impressive creations . . ."

Veelund glanced over Goran's shoulder. The Sylph turned and recognized the gray eyes, narrow face, and nut-brown hair of the ranger behind him. Crisscrossing Roza's tunic from shoulder to waist were two diagonal straps attached to a backpack. From it protruded wings. They looked far too insubstantial to bear her weight, yet at Veelund's nodded command, Roza touched several gems sewn into the straps in rapid succession. Instantly she shot into the air, as if swept upward by a blast of wind. As she leaned to one side and began a banking turn, Goran noticed for the first time that the ends of her artificial wings were attached to her arms by thin ropes that glistened with evident enchantments.

"The fliers I saw in the Blur," Goran began. "All this time, they were—"

"Rangers in my service, of course," Veelund chimed in. "They performed their task magnificently."

"Manipulating the humans into useless war, you mean."

"Useless?" the prince arched an eyebrow. "Hardly. And you overstate the task. The Americans needed little prompting to feed their hunger for land and treasure. Among the Indians, all we needed to instill was overconfidence. Like your friend Har, you have many admirable qualities, but insight is not among them. You lack the imagination, I think, to turn observation into insight. That is a fatal flaw, for imagination governs the world."

The longer he talks, the longer we live—and the more we learn.

"This creation of yours, this gift of flight," Goran began. "For so great an aid to hunting and gathering, many Folk would pay dearly. Why use it for deceit and conquest? Spirit Forest could amass great wealth in trade."

Veelund rolled his eyes. "Some Elves thought as you do. A party of dissident rangers once stole some of my wings, as well as"—the prince shot Goran a sly look—"*another* conveyance of my design, and fled northward. Their plan, I suspect, was to offer my creations to an enemy Folk in exchange for sanctuary. Of course, I am only speculating. When I sent my fliers in pursuit, their orders were to retrieve my stolen property and leave none of the thieves alive."

"The foolish rebels met their conspirators at a place we knew well: our training field in the mountains," Roza said, her eyes avoiding Goran's. "Their leader knelt atop the great chimney rock and begged me to join their cause. Those were the final words the traitor spoke."

A ranger with the dark features and pale skin of an Alven landed in the courtyard and saluted Veelund. "Shot and powder run short. Soon the walls will fall."

"Then the final stanza has come," Veelund said. "Elves of Spirit Forest, you know what to do. Let us give the poets an end truly worthy of epic verse. Let them sing of golden heroes and ravenous hordes, of a valiant few facing impossible odds. Let them sing of victory!"

As Elf rangers scattered to deliver their monarch's commands, Goran crawled over to Dela, thankful to see her stir from unconsciousness. "Your saga ends in shameful defeat, Veelund, not in victory," he seethed. "You admit you face impossible odds."

The Prince of Elves chuckled. "Are you still so blind, Sylph? I do not *hope* for victory. It is already won! Most of my Folk are long gone. They inhabit well-crafted villages scattered across a vast continent, or will soon reach them. Only a small garrison remained here to hold the attention of your pitiful army."

Dela sat up. Goran threw a protective arm around her. "This ends in defeat for you, then, Veelund, and the Elves unlucky enough to remain with you."

Veelund's smile dissolved. "You best hope you are mistaken, Goran Lonefeather. For if I fall, you and your Water Maiden will fall with me. And such a landing, you will not survive."

▲▲▲

When Har reached the top of the ladder he was confronted by two spearmen, though they didn't confront him for long. His battleaxe painted with their blood, Har looked in vain for other foes to attack. He saw only other Dwarfs standing on the platform or clambering down into the village.

Spotting an Elf dueling a Dwarf in a nearby street, Har leapt from the platform and landed with a grunt. Soon he was bowling aside the Dwarf swordsman and pressing the blade of his axe against the throat of the Elf. "Where are they?" he demanded.

"Where . . . are *they*?" the confused Elf gasped.

"Dela and Goran!" Har snarled. "The Water Maiden and the Sylph. Where did your fliers take them?"

"The hostages." The Elf swallowed. "They would have been taken to the Royal Hall. They . . ."

But Har had learned what he needed. A single punch to the face silenced the Elf. Then Har was running, heedless of the battle raging around him. Running toward the place he'd often visited as emissary, the place of his humiliation. The place where his friends now lay in the clutches of a dangerous enemy.

Veelund has already earned death at my hands. But if they come to harm, his death will be painful and slow.

When Har reached his destination, however, he realized he'd be no lone avenger. The allies had overcome Spirit Forest's defenses on every side. The Royal Hall and its courtyard were encircled—by sure-footed Nunnehi, web-footed Yunwi Amayine Hi, slender-footed Gwragedd Annwn, and broad-footed Goblins. Har added his own booted feet to the circle, soon joined by other Dwarfs trudging up the street from the south.

Then Veelund emerged on the hall's roof, no doubt from some hidden staircase, followed by Elf rangers wearing thin, translucent wings. "Where is Alberich?" the prince shouted. "Does your Dwarf king hide in some far-off tent?"

"Only Elves sneak and hide!" Alberich replied, trotting up to stand next to Har. "Dwarf lords prefer to meet our adversaries on the field of battle, to spit in their faces as we dispatch them to the next world."

"Oh, there you are," Veelund called, sounding more like a scolding teacher than a cornered foe. "Have you finished preening? Or must you issue more adolescent threats?"

Alberich pointed to the streams of advancing warriors thickening the circle. "*You* are the one prattling on to no effect, Veelund. It is done. You are finished. Surrender or die. I care not which fate you choose."

"Neither suits me." The prince motioned behind him. Har gritted his teeth as Roza shoved Dela and Goran into sight. His friends' hands were tied behind their backs. "My fliers seized two of your 'heroes,' Alberich," Veelund continued, "though I admit to be disappointed at having them rather than yourself as my guests."

"If you harm them," Har bellowed, "you will regret it for the rest of your days—which will be few!"

Veelund stared down at Har with indulgent eyes. "You have oft entertained me, oh great oak of Grünerberg. Now, though, you should be silent. The men are talking."

"Make your point!" Alberich snapped.

"It is simple. If you part your ranks and allow us to leave, we will release your two rangers when we are safely away. No more blood need be shed. We will surrender Spirit Forest, never to return. You may do what you wish with it. You may even keep my cannons and replicate my designs, though I fail to understand why your craftsmen have not already produced suitable weapons of your own."

"Our weapons were sufficient to defeat you, Elf," Alberich pointed out.

"Oh, *do* be sensible, Dwarf," Veelund sneered. "Surely you recognize by now there was no true battle here. Most of my army, and most Elfkind, were evacuated before you arrived. The garrison's delaying action merely ensured our Folk's safe arrival in new homes so numerous and well hidden as to remain safely out of your clutches."

Alberich glowered up at the prince.

"Now I offer you a means of recovering these two," Veelund said, "and of losing no more lives this day. Are we agreed?"

Har turned to study his king. The man's face had hardened, as if chiseled in stone.

"We are *not* agreed," Alberich said. "Those two were taken while defending their commander. They proved their mettle and earned the esteem of all Dwarfkind. They are, however, but two captives. You and your garrison represent many more captives—or many more corpses. Those remain the only possible consequences of your crimes. Not freedom."

"Crimes?" Veelund repeated incredulously. "You speak like your lumbering *Tower* there. Leaders cannot afford to be bound by convention or sentiment. For us, necessity dominates inclination, will, and right. Posterity alone rightly judges our actions. I have no doubt how future generations of Elfkind will judge me."

Veelund's insults no longer had any power to wound Har. But Alberich's words had cut him to the bone. *Is the king bluffing? Or does he really intend to abandon my friends?*

"Very well," said the Elf prince. "You have chosen more pointless deaths. Rangers, prepare to—"

"If I may, my prince."

Not even Veelund looked as shocked at Roza's interruption as the Elf ranger herself did. She glanced away for a moment, then reached down to the straps crossing her chest. She undid the fastenings and let bow and quiver slip off her back, followed by her wing pack.

"What is the meaning of this, Roza?" Veelund demanded. "You question my decision?"

Har clenched his hands more tightly around his axe. *Did she mean to rescue Dela and Goran, as she once rescued me?*

The Elf ranger shook her head. "My place is with the garrison. Pray let another ranger wear my wings." She reattached her quiver and picked up her bow, albeit slowly, as if in resignation. Veelund nodded, also looking resigned to an outcome he didn't savor, and waved another Elf over to don the discarded apparatus.

The doors of the Royal Hall flew open. Elves emerged into the courtyard, some with bows and slings, others with melee weapons. They kept streaming out, a surprising number from such a confined area, creating a second rank of defenders, then a third. But when compared with the vastly larger army, their numbers remained pitifully few.

Har watched Roza emerge and take her place in the defense line.

Alberich drew his sword and thrust it over his head. "Take them! Let no one escape!"

In an instant, the air was thick with deadly missiles. Several Dwarfs and their allies stumbled and fell, pierced or struck. Even more Elves did the same. Some of the allies' arrows were directed upward, at Veelund and the growing crowd of Elves around him. But the low parapet around the top of the building proved adequate cover.

Har knew the only way to save his friends was to reach the roof. Climbing up the outside of the building was feasible in theory, but not in full view of Elvish archers and slingers. Better to fight his way through the defenders and ascend the inner staircase.

"For honor and victory!" he shouted, recalling his beloved Queen Virginal's rallying cry.

"For honor and victory!" repeated many of the Dwarfs surging forward with him.

Though the first rank of Elves fought bravely with spears and swords and knives and closed fists, it was less a battle than a slaughter. The odds were too great. Still, every second of it bought the winged Elf rangers another second to make their escape.

But Veelund cannot join them. He cannot survive the Blur. Is he, too, sacrificing himself for his Folk?

Har brushed an Elf aside and made for the open door. Then another stepped into his path. It was Roza. Her bow either discarded or broken, she'd picked up a sword and buckler from a fallen comrade.

"I cannot let you pass, Har."

He gaped. "What is the point of this, Roza? Why defend this evil man to the end?"

"I do not defend Veelund the man. I defend my prince and my Folk. We have the right to survive."

"By any means you deem necessary? At the cost of honor? Of friendship?"

Har saw Roza's sword arm waver, but her eyes stared back, hard and unyielding. "When it comes to our future, yes. As the prince has taught us, inclination, will, and right must yield to—"

"I already heard the wicked words of your wicked prince," Har said. "Now hear my words. Lay down your arms. Stand aside. You know what I must do."

"Just as you know what I must do." She raised her shield higher.

Dela and Goran were in mortal danger; Har could afford no more delay. Nor could he afford mercy. There was no graceful duel, no sparring to size up the foe, no clever attacks and artful parries. Roza the Elf ranger, his former friend and comrade in arms, caught the swing of Har's axe in the center of her shield. That powerful swing, powered by heavy bronze and bulging muscle and grim determination, shattered her shield into pieces. Its irresistible momentum smashed Roza against the ground, driving the blade into her chest. Its irresistible momentum stopped her heart forever.

▲▲▲

"Let us go, Veelund!" Goran cried, pointing to the attackers rapidly overcoming the Elves in the courtyard. "Dozens of your people are crowded onto this roof—not just rangers but warriors, hunters, craftsmen, greenweavers. They wear no wings. They cannot survive the Blur even if they manage to reach it. *You* will not survive it. End this!"

Veelund walked to the Sylph and cuffed him hard across the mouth. "Be silent, captive. That you may yet prove a valuable hostage is the only reason you and your blue Nixie remain alive. But do not test my patience."

Goran spat and wiped his mouth. "You throw away lives for the sake of your pride."

The Elf prince used a flat hand to shield his eyes from the rapidly rising sun and looked east. "One fitted for authority never considers individuals. He considers only things and their consequences." Then he blew out a breath. "Ah, there they are. There must have been some delay at the pens."

Goran heard a great flapping and fluttering of wings, as if an entire squad of Sylph rangers were headed for the Royal Hall. But his Folk were far away, and Veelund's wing packs had no feathers to flutter. Those wings did not flap at all.

Veelund is not just a craftsman. He is a breeder.

The approaching horses had supple bodies and enormous wings. As each landed gracefully on the roof, several Elves climbed up behind its driver, spreading out over the creature's long back. Then the passengers secured themselves with thick leather thongs. When the final two winged horses arrived, warriors seized Dela and tossed her, kicking and bucking, over the back of one of the mounts, tying her to the saddle. Then warriors grabbed Goran and tied him onto the final horse.

"There is nowhere within the Shimmer for you to flee," Dela warned the Elf prince as he climbed up behind her.

"You only prolong the inevitable!" Goran yelled from the other horse.

Veelund threw his head back to laugh. "Such children you are. If this is the best the other Folk of America have to offer, you are all destined to become subjects of Elfkind. Do not worry; our rule may be harsh at times, but it will be for your own good."

At that moment, the staircase door burst open. Har the Tower stomped out onto the roof, other Dwarfs fast on his heels.

"Har!" Dela shouted, wiggling against her bonds. But Veelund wrapped a strong arm around her, leering at Goran, and reached down with his other hand to touch a series of gems and studs embroidered in his belt.

All the other Elf passengers did the same. Then the driver of Goran's horse kicked its flanks, prodding the beast into a run. Flapping its wings, the horse rose into the air. Goran craned his neck to watch the next horse, the one carrying Veelund and Dela, begin its run across the roof.

Then Har leaped into its path. His hands reached for Veelund's mount, but it was already airborne. As it soared overhead, the horse kicked down with a hoof hard as stone. It struck Har in the head. He staggered back, reeling and disoriented—and then, to Goran's horror, Har the Tower tumbled over the side of the parapet.

The Sylph, borne rapidly away by the winged horse, couldn't see over the building to the far side. He didn't see his friend fall dozens of feet to the ground below. For that, and that only, Goran was relieved.

Besides, his attention was soon riveted to the Elves mounted to his front and rear. They looked perfectly motionless, as if frozen in ice. Indeed, it looked as though they were actually covered in a nearly transparent coat of ice, although Goran was close enough to discover the coating was slightly warm to the touch, not cold.

"What is wrong with them?" he called to the still-moving driver.

The Elf ranger snickered. "Another of the prince's creations. Shimmer Belts, he calls them. All who are not rangers will wear them until we reach our destination."

Great Maker. Veelund has conquered the Blur itself!

With a gasp, Goran realized that once the Elves reached their destination, he and Dela would be vastly outnumbered. *And doomed.*

Goran looked around. The party was now flying over forested hills. He also saw that half a dozen rangers in wing packs were escorting the horses. The Shimmer Belts had at least one obvious disadvantage: Of all the mounted Elves, only the driver was free to act. Careful not to attract the attention of the rangers flying alongside, Goran slowly raised a leg and brushed it against the knot of the leather thong binding him to the saddle. Tied by an Elf who likely had little experience with riding, the knot wasn't particularly tight. After several tries, Goran was able to trap one of its loops against the saddle, then enlarge it with his knee. Casting another sideways glance, he twisted again. The knot gave way.

Goran slipped off the horse and plummeted toward the forested hills. But only his arms were bound. Spreading his wings, the Sylph arrested his momentum and banked into a turn. Three of the escorts spotted their escaped prisoner. Drawing their blades, they headed right for him. Goran hovered for a moment, allowing the first two fliers to come within a few feet, then drew his wings and dropped like a stone. The rangers were unprepared for the tactic and ran into each other, cursing as they struggled to regain their equilibrium.

It was the opportunity Goran needed—and proof of another Elfish disadvantage. While the rangers had no doubt been trained in the use of their wing packs, they could never match a Sylph's natural talent in the air. Before they could renew their attack runs, Goran twisted to the side, spread his wings, and flapped furiously to accelerate. Suspecting the Sylph was trying to get above them, the two rangers turned their bodies upward to gain altitude. But Goran abruptly leveled off and barreled toward one of the fliers. With his hands tied behind his back, he could neither attack nor parry with his arms. Instead, the Sylph lowered his head, gambling the Elf would opt to dodge rather than stab.

Goran's gamble paid off. The ranger attempted to rise above the headbutt but succeeded only in taking it on the end of one of his artificial wings. Goran felt his head punch through the thin, rigid surface of the wing. Shrieking, the ranger waved his arm in a futile attempt to regain his balance. While the enchanted pack kept him airborne, the Elf careened wildly through the air and slammed into a high branch of a passing oak tree with a sickening crunch.

Recognizing his good fortune would surely run out if his arms stayed bound, Goran took another gamble. He twisted again and resolved his fall into a swoop along the tree line. A quick glance over his shoulder revealed the two rangers diving toward him, as expected.

Goran turned back to the forested hills and soon spotted his mark. After striking the oak branch, the first ranger had tumbled unceremoniously to the forest floor. Whether it was the branch or the ground that did it, the lifeless Elf's back was twisted at an odd angle. A glint of light drew Goran to the shortsword lying a few paces away from its previous wielder. He dove for it. Soon, Goran's arms were free—and he was armed.

"Surrender, Sylph!" said one of the two remaining rangers, who'd landed nearby and drawn their own swords. "Aground, you are no match for us."

"I agree," Goran replied. He flapped his wings and shot upward.

Groaning in frustration, the two Elves rose in pursuit. Goran had counted on their frustration. Before they quite knew what was happening, the Sylph retracted his wings and began to fall. As the two rangers shot past him, the blade in Goran's hand flashed. It drew no blood but killed its victim nonetheless. Twisting and screaming, the Elf fell twenty feet to the earth even as his wing pack, now freed from its wearer by a slash across its leather straps, continued its inexorable rise into the sky.

The remaining Elf ranger tried to use brute force to accomplish what his companions' awkward flying had not—and nearly succeeded. He slammed into the Sylph, wrapping one hand around Goran's throat while driving the point of his shortsword into Goran's leg with the other. Ignoring the searing pain, Goran tried a cut of his own only to discover that the impact had knocked the sword out of his hand. Thinking quickly, Goran used both hands not to grip the arm that was throttling him but instead the arm attempting to jerk the sword free from the Sylph's leg.

Goran yanked too.

With the Sylph's unexpected help the Elf's sword did jerk free, delivering another lance of blinding pain. Blotting it out and using the momentum of the Elf's retracting sword arm against him, Goran managed to steer the edge of the blade across his foe's abdomen. A stripe of blood appeared. The hand around Goran's throat slackened. With a final effort, Goran hurled the wounded Elf toward the hillside below.

There was no time to lose; Dela and the others were getting away. Goran returned to the ground next to his first victim, tore off a piece of the Elf's tunic to tie around his bleeding calf, then appropriated the ranger's bow and quiver. Now fully armed, and willing himself back into the air despite his fatigue and loss of blood, Goran looked frantically for his quarry. The squadron of winged horses and escorts formed little more than specks above the northern horizon. Mouthing a fervent prayer, Goran followed.

Little of the resulting chase remained long in his memory. Goran flew faster than he'd ever flown before. By all rights, he should have fallen from the sky in utter exhaustion. But he couldn't let Veelund escape justice. He couldn't leave Dela in the clutches of the Elves.

He had to save her. *Just as she had saved me, more than once, in more than one way.*

Slowly but surely, the pursuer gained on the pursued. How he would overcome three fresh rangers, as well as the half dozen drivers with their own mounts and weapons, Goran could scarcely imagine. Still, he had already achieved the improbable. The impossible lay just beyond.

When his reserve of energy was nearly spent, something else improbable happened, something wonderful. The winged horses now several hundred feet ahead of him began to angle themselves toward the ground. One by one, they landed on a narrow outcropping of light-colored rock. The three Elf fliers halted their own flight to hover just above the ledge.

The chimney rock! Goran pulled up to study the situation. What was the best away to effect Dela's rescue? He needed time to think.

The Elf rangers didn't give it to him. They spotted Goran. Two produced bows. The other, a javelin. Then the fliers launched themselves at him.

With Dela tantalizingly close, no doubt struggling against her bonds atop one of those winged horses, Goran felt a surge of renewed strength. He fitted an arrow to his own bow. Hovering in place, and more practiced at airborne archery, the Sylph's missile found its target even as the two enemy arrows flew harmlessly above and below his body. Before he could reload, however, the Elves were upon him.

Against the archers, who'd whipped out knives, Goran was outnumbered but hardly outclassed. He blocked one's thrust with a sweep of his bow, then kicked the side of the other Elf as she flew past, her slash missing Goran's neck by a good foot or more. Knocked off balance, the Elf ranger failed to parry the thrust of Goran's hastily drawn blade. Even as he yanked it free of her suddenly lifeless body, Goran ducked beneath another knife attack.

Unfortunately, the third Elf ranger had an advantage the other two did not—reach. Goran felt a new jolt of pain as the flier's javelin pierced his shoulder. His bow fell from his grasp, followed a second later by his knife. With a final, desperate beat of wings, Goran pulled himself free of the javelin and turned to flee. Then strong hands grabbed both of his ankles.

Goran's newfound energy left him. His hope turned to despair, as if a great wind had snuffed out every candle in the world. Here, he would meet his end, unable to avenge his fallen friend Har, leaving Dela in the clutches of a vicious tyrant.

Rather than drawing him in for a killing blow, the two Elf fliers seemed intent on dragging Goran down to the chimney rock, to where Veelund was no doubt waiting to gloat. The Sylph tried to resist but lacked the strength.

Whoosh!

His senses reeling, Goran struggled to interpret the unexpected rush of wind he heard and felt below him.

Crunch!

Then came the sound of something very hard striking something not quite hard enough.

"To the devil with you!"

Goran couldn't understand why an Elf would curse him so, and in so booming a voice. Then he realized his feet were free. Before Goran could react, however, he felt hands once again grasp his ankles and yank him down with tremendous force. A moment later the Sylph felt his body contact the rocky surface of the ledge, although not with much force. His eyelids fluttered, then cracked open.

There were two Elves lying nearby, one with a crushed skull and the other with the hilt of his knife protruding from his chest. Beyond the edge of the chimney rock, perhaps a hundred feet away and moving swiftly away, was the party of winged horses bearing Dela, Veelund, and the other refugees from Spirit Forest. Indeed, Veelund's party looked much larger than before, as if they'd been reinforced by many more mounts.

And there was one more steed, riderless and snorting in frustration, stroking its wings furiously in an attempt to catch up with the others.

"I lost control of it when I killed the second Elf," the booming voice said dejectedly. "I was fortunate the ledge was only a few feet below when I tumbled off the flying horse, grabbed your ankles, and managed to guide us to a landing."

Goran rolled painfully to his back and looked up at the grim face of Har the Tower. "You . . . have saved me," croaked the Sylph, his leg and shoulder burning.

"And let *them* get away," Har muttered. Then both turned their heads to the northwest.

When the Elves were no longer even tiny specks in the sky, Goran Lonefeather let his head fall to the surface of the great chimney rock and soon added a puddle of tears to the puddle of blood beneath him.

Epilogue – The Travelers

Junaluska slowed his pace and closed his eyes, letting his other senses take over. He heard rushing water and warbling birds. He smelled the fragrance of late spring blossoms. He felt the mountain breeze against his weathered cheeks. At every step, he felt his moccasin sink comfortably into the soft bank of the Tuckasegee River and then resist being lifted out again to take another forward step.

It wasn't just that the mud was sticky; his feet seemed to assert a will of their own. After all, they were on familiar ground. They had, at last, brought Junaluska to the land of his ancestors after months of hard traveling, after years of hard living. His feet demanded a rest.

Yielding to their will, Junaluska halted altogether. He felt his heart lurch as he gazed up at the mountains that framed the river valley. Painted across the green palette of forested peaks were splashes and stripes of pale yellows, fiery oranges, and brilliant reds. Junaluska's first wife, Yona, had loved the lighter azalea hues. His second wife, Galilahi, had preferred the darker reds. His boys had used the orange blossoms to make presents for their mother.

All had loved the mountainside azaleas in their own ways, just as Junaluska had loved each member of his family with a special attention. He'd spent his life—his two lives, really, the first one with Yona and the second with Galilahi and their sons—trying to give them a home, to make them happy, and to keep them safe.

Twice he tried. Twice he failed.

The previous day, Junaluska had visited the site of Fort Montgomery, the place where he and his family were taken five years earlier by American soldiers. They'd been confined there for weeks with little food or water, waiting for removal to the west. It was in the squalid conditions of Fort Montgomery that whooping cough had run rampant, where so many Cherokees succumbed to the deadly disease before their arduous journey even began. It was at Fort Montgomery

407

where his own personal disaster struck, where Junaluska had been forced to go on alone.

He let his eyes fall to the surface of the river. Just ahead lay the mouth of Alarka Creek as it fed its cool, clean water into the Tuckasegee. He'd already visited the rude graves of Galilahi and his boys, dug hastily on a hill near Fort Montgomery. Now, if he turned southeast and followed Alarka Creek, he could visit the hillside grave of Yona, taken from him by another merciless disease another lifetime ago.

Visiting his old farm had been Junaluska's original intention. After that, for the days, weeks, and months that might follow—for however many more years might be added to the six decades he'd already spent in this world—Junaluska had no plan at all. He'd only known he had no desire to live his remaining years west of the Mississippi. He would live them in the land of his birth . . . or die trying.

What would one more death matter, anyway? His wife and children were dead. Countless relatives and friends were dead. His former commander at Horseshoe Bend, Major Ridge, was dead, too—assassinated because he'd signed the 1835 Treaty of New Echota, which traded the Cherokee homeland for federal payments and land grants in the Indian Territory. The Ridge said he had no choice but to strike the best bargain possible, since the passage of the Indian Removal Act had doomed their efforts to stay. Junaluska disagreed, but he hadn't wanted his friend killed. Now there would be retaliation. More death to follow death.

Junaluska looked up again at patches of flame azaleas blazing across the mountains and thought of Tana Song Snake. Most of her Folk chose to follow the removed Cherokee to the Indian Territory, building their new Nunnehi village on a high bluff overlooking the Grand River. It was during Junaluska's final visit there, as they strolled among the locust trees, that Tana urged her longtime friend not to attempt his eastward journey.

"The injustice inflicted on the Cherokee is unconscionable," she had said. "I understand your anger and grieve your loss. But your people live here now, and seek to make it truly their home. Will you not stay and lend your strength and experience to their cause? If you go back east, you will become little more than a ghost, your tale little more than a whisper on the wind."

"I am already more ghost than man," Junaluska replied. "I would rather haunt those lonely mountains than stay here and simply fade away."

She hadn't pressed her point. After all, it had also been Tana who, along with his wife Galilahi, begged Junaluska five years ago not to fight the American soldiers. Neither woman knew the other had made the same argument: that armed resistance would be doomed. It was the fact that both his human wife and his fairy friend agreed that had proved most persuasive.

The thought made Junaluska groan. They *had* been persuasive. Perhaps they even spoke wisdom. But now their words felt like a fragile sort of wisdom—mere words, thin and hollow as reeds, swept away by a current of tears.

"Are you lost, Grandfather?"

Startled that he'd heard no one approach, Junaluska spun around, spear in hand, to confront the newcomer.

Who stood four feet tall but was no fairy.

"I have never seen you before," said the boy, who looked to be about five years old. He had sharp eyes, a lithe build little concealed by his breechclout, and long hair swept back over his ears.

His confident bearing and pleasantly curious expression reminded Junaluska of happier days. The memories made the old man wince as if he'd been stung by some giant bee.

"I have been . . . away," Junaluska answered, averting his eyes. "But these lands were once my home. I once roamed them freely when I was a little boy like you."

"I am not so little," the youth insisted. "None of my cousins stands so tall. None can beat me at ball. When Pa takes me to town, the white boys my age only come up to my chin."

Junaluska shot the other a questioning look. "Your father is a white man?"

"Only part," the boy said. "Three of my grandparents are Cherokee."

"And you live here?" Junaluska asked.

The boy nodded. "Near Valley Town, with the others."

"The others? You mean your mother and father, sisters, and brothers?"

"Yes, and more," the boy explained. "Though most of the others live up on Soco Creek."

Junaluska sucked in a breath. "How many others?"

The boy shrugged. "Pa said a number once. Seven . . . no, eight."

"Eight families, you mean? Eight houses?"

"That does not sound right." The boy's face twisted in concentration. "Eight hundred, I think."

Junaluska gasped. Eight *hundred*! He knew a few Cherokees had escaped the Removal by hiding in the hills or staying on land owned by William Holland Thomas, a white man who'd been adopted into the tribe but retained his property rights under American law. Still, Junaluska had guessed only a few dozen evaded the soldiers.

Eight hundred! If I am to be a ghost, it seems I will haunt more than just white squatters and wilderness.

"My name is Tsaladihi," said the boy. "What is yours?"

"I am called Junaluska."

Tsaladihi's eyes widened. "*The* Junaluska? The great hero?" The boy stared in wonder at the gift spear. "Is this what you used to kill a hundred Creeks at the Horseshoe?"

It seems my tale is more than a whisper on the wind.

"I am just a man," Junaluska said, his leathery face relaxing into a grin as he reached over to tousle the boy's hair. "And my spear is just a spear. Do not believe everything you hear."

Shrugging out from under Junaluska's playful hand, Tsaladihi stomped away a few paces, then whipped around. "I am no little baby! When my mother tells me stories, I know some are not real."

"If she told you I killed a hundred Creeks singlehandedly at Horseshoe Bend, I promise that story is not real."

The boy looked dubious. "So you say, Junaluska."

"So at least you agree I am who I say I am."

"Who else but a hero would carry a magic spear?" Tsaladihi said matter-of-factly.

Startled once again, Junaluska glanced from the bronze tip of the spear to the still-wide eyes of the boy. "What makes you think my spear is magic?"

Tsaladihi open his mouth to answer, then seemed to catch himself and turned away defiantly to face the river. Junaluska followed his gaze and saw something dive suddenly into the water from the opposite bank. An otter? Judging by the splash, it must have been particularly large one. Then he caught a glimpse of webbed feet propelling the diver rapidly down the river. They weren't the furry, pudgy feet of an otter. The toes were too long, the legs too slender.

Junaluska looked down and discovered Tsaladihi casting him a sideways glance. The two stood there for some time, listening to the water. Watching the ripples. Feeling the breeze. Junaluska felt forces welling up inside him, powerful emotions he had never expected to feel again. Pride. Determination. Hope.

"Take me to the house of your mother," Junaluska requested. "We have much to discuss on the way."

There is much more than I ever dreamed of finding here, he thought. *More of our people. More of our lands, our ways, our beliefs. We have built before. Who says it cannot be done again, on such a sturdy foundation? I will live among my people again. I will be no ghost, no mere shadow haunted by the past. I will be a man, perhaps even once again a father. I will be a builder, a counselor, a leader if need be.*

Together we will be the people who tried, and learned, and tried again, and did not *fail.*

▲▲▲

As the ferry pulled away from the dock, belching a dark trail from its smokestack, Bell was careful not to join her fellow passengers in looking back at the receding island of Manhattan. Instead, she stood at the prow and peered out over the East River.

Manhattan was my Sodom. I will not look back, like Lot's wife, to such a wicked place. I will look ahead.

Bell lived some fourteen years in or near Manhattan. She found work as a housekeeper. She found a renewed and deeper faith in Jesus Christ, as well as a just cause in the liberation of her people. And for much of that time, her only son, Peter, lived with her.

Alas, her years in Manhattan also brought much disappointment and suffering. She'd devoted herself to a spiritual leader, calling himself "the Prophet Matthias," who turned out to be a charlatan. When his patron turned up dead, Matthias and Bell herself went on trial for murder. She was exonerated, but the experience greatly pained and shamed her.

As for Peter, he'd fallen in with a rough crowd and was arrested multiple times. Bell repeatedly forgave him and tried to help him find a profession, only to have her gifts squandered and her advice ignored. Finally, while in prison for theft, Peter was promised early release if he'd join a whaling crew heading out to sea.

In his first letter home, sent from his post on the *Zone* of Nantucket, Peter asked her forgiveness for all his transgressions.

"Mother, I hope you do not forget me, your dear and only son," he wrote. Bell asked literate friends to read the passage to her over and over again.

When she boarded the ferry that morning, bound for Long Island, Bell carried most of her meager possessions in a pillowcase slung over her shoulder. But Peter's final letter, mailed two years ago, was too precious to be stowed away. Reaching into an inner pocket, Bell pulled out the tattered envelope and held it against her heart, recalling her son's surprisingly poetic words:

> Get me to my home, that's in the far-distant west,
> To the scenes of my childhood, that I like the best.
> There the tall cedars grow, and the bright waters flow,
> Where my parents will greet me—white man, let me go!
> Let me go to the spot where the cataract plays,
> Where oft I have sported in my boyish days.
> And there is my poor mother, whose heart ever flows
> At the sight of her poor child. To her, let me go. Let me go!

Bell began to hum a little tune she'd made up to fit Peter's words. Then she sang, low and sweet, "Get me to my home / Let me go / Where tall cedars grow / Let me go."

Why shouldn't I sing? she asked God, keeping her eyes firmly closed. *If your people laugh and sing a little as we fight your good fight of freedom, it makes it all go easier. I won't allow my life's light to be determined by the darkness around me. You taught me that, Lord.*

Hearing footsteps behind her, Bell opened her eyes and chanced a quick peek over her shoulder. She didn't become a pillar of salt. The familiar sight of Manhattan was now obscured by blueish smoke. Her new companion at the rail was an aged black man, tall and thin, stooped and scrawny, dressed like a mariner, a narrow leather strap holding a tattered patch against one eye. Beyond him Bell saw other sailors standing together beside a tower of hay bales.

"Been praying, ma'am?" asked the old man, a crooked smile creasing his scarred face. "A fine mornin' for it."

"Why, yes," she said, quickly slipping the letter back into her pocket.

The old man must have spotted the gesture but said nothing of it. "You live 'cross the river, or just visitin'?"

"I go where the Spirit calls me."

"And the Spirit's callin' ya east." The sailor chuckled and turned his eyes toward the dockyards that dotted the western tip of Long Island. "My mates and me answerin' a call east, too. Was stayin' at the Colored Sailors' Home over on Pearl Street. Now we's about to take service, again."

"On a whaling ship?" Bell blurted out.

The old man nodded. "I's a river man, but the others just as soon go to sea."

Before Bell should reply, another set of footsteps grabbed her attention. While the old man had shuffled forward, this one stomped across the deck with heavy boots. He was a white man in gray trousers, a striped shirt, a dark-blue coat, and a round black hat.

The old black sailor was tall. Bell was taller. Her father, James Baumfree, had been taller still. But the newcomer was the biggest person Bell had ever seen—not just impossibly tall but impossibly wide, his massive shoulders threatening to erupt from his threadbare coat, his neck nestled between muscles thick as ropes. Long, gray-tipped whiskers stuck out like pins in a cushion from his full cheeks and square chin.

The black sailor gave a low, wheezy whistle. Then, offering Bell an incongruous wink, the old man rejoined his fellows.

Bell directed her attention back to the giant. He didn't return it. Instead, the man drew in a deep breath of briny air, savored it for a long moment, then blew it out so forcefully that Bell half expected the banner at the ship's bow to be ripped off.

"You a seaman, too, sir?" she asked.

The giant seemed to notice her for the first time. He inclined his huge head into a slight nod. "High seas man, ma'am. Least I used to be."

Bell thought again of Peter. Since his last letter two years ago, she'd heard nothing more. But she refused to believe that signified anything other than her son being otherwise occupied in some faraway land, or his subsequent letters being lost by the uncertain postal service of mariners.

Unable to contain her curiosity, Bell looked into the giant's sea-blue eyes and posed her question. "In your travels, sir, ever hear of a ship called the *Zone* of Nantucket?"

The man started as if someone had struck him hard across the face. He wiped three thick fingers along on his cheek, as if to brush off any mark from the blow, and glared down at Bell. "Why d'you ask?"

"My son . . . he sailed away on that ship. Ain't heard from him in a long while."

His glare softened into a stare. "What's his name?"

"Peter. Peter Van Wagener."

The giant's eyes dropped quickly. "I, uh . . . the fate of the *Zone* is unknown to me."

Bell felt her pulse quicken. "You hear of it?"

Shrugging his massive shoulders, the man kept his eyes averted. "She was my boat, for a time. No more. I'm a lubber now."

Bell scrutinized him. *A ship captain!* Over the years, she'd learned to read faces and postures as deftly as others read printed words. She could tell the giant was holding something back. But she could also tell he was loathe to surrender it to a woman he'd just met.

It was then that the black mariners behind them began a song. Bell had often heard chanties around the docks. But she couldn't recall this particular one:

> *An able sailor, bold and true,*
> *To my way hay, storm along, John!*
> *A good old bosun to his crew,*
> *To my aye, aye, aye, Mister Stormalong!*
>
> *He's moored at last, and furled his sail,*
> *To my way hay, storm along, John!*
> *No danger now from wreck or gale,*
> *To my aye, aye, aye, Mister Stormalong!*

Bell turned to watch the old man and his friends singing in deep, resonant voices. Out of the corner of her eye, though, she could see the giant grinding one meaty fist into the other. And from somewhere within the man's unruly beard came a series of raspy snorts. Meanwhile, the sailors continued their chanty:

> *I wish I was old Stormie's son,*
> *To my way hay, storm along, John!*
> *I'd build me a ship of a thousand ton,*
> *To my aye, aye, aye, Mister Stormalong!*

Now the sound from the giant was a low, continuous muttering, rough and guttural. Still the sailors sang:

Old Stormie's dead and gone to rest,
To my way hay, storm along, John!
Of all the sailors he was the best,
To my aye, aye, aye, Mister Stormalong!

"Enough!" the giant roared. "Know you no other song?"

Bell wasn't watching him; she'd been drawn to the old one-eyed sailor leading the chanty. At the giant's outburst, the other man's eyebrows arched high. Then he grinned triumphantly.

"My—my apologies, ma'am," stammered the white man with evident embarrassment. "Never learned to mind my temper."

"Ain't too good at that either, mister," Bell replied. "That is, uh, Mister . . ."

The giant didn't answer at first. They looked at each other for a while. Then he sighed in resignation. "Alfred."

"Mister Alfred," Bell began, "no cause to be sorry. We ain't all got the same taste for music."

Then a ferry crewman rang the bell. The boat was nearing the dock. Within minutes, most of Bell's fellow passengers had disembarked. Some were merchants headed briskly onto the streets of Brooklyn. Others were workmen, not in as much a hurry, or out-of-towners, who were in no hurry at all, at least not until they figured out where they were supposed to go.

As for the one-eyed sailor and his friends, they were among the first to leave, no doubt to find their ocean-bound whaler. The white giant, Alfred, watched the mariners go with a wistful look. Then he walked slowly into the village. Although Bell originally planned to stop at a store in the ferry district to spend a few of her precious coins on food, her heart led her elsewhere. Hoping to learn more about Peter's fate, Bell followed Alfred at a discrete distance as he ambled onto the main road and turned eastward.

On and on they walked under the blazing sun. Past Brooklyn the houses thinned out, replaced by clumps of trees. The way grew rougher, the road's surface turning from stony to sandy. Every time Alfred slowed or stopped, Bell considered rushing forward to ask more questions about Peter. Every time, though, something held her back. Instead, she stopped when he stopped and walked when he walked, matching his pace to stay far enough behind that he wouldn't hear her following him.

That's why Bell was so surprised when Alfred suddenly spun around and pointed back the way he'd come.

"Why you followin' me?" he asked.

His question wasn't aimed at Bell, however, for another figure had emerged from the trees: the one-eyed sailor. With surprising quickness, the old man shuffled across the ground to stand between Alfred and Bell.

"Ain't gonna hurt you, Cap'n," said the black sailor. "Just makin' sure I's right."

Alfred snorted derisively. "*You* ain't gonna hurt *me*? You figure you ever could, runt?"

The one-eyed sailor looked undaunted. "Ain't much of a readin' man, Cap'n, but even I knows not to judge a book by its cover."

"Don't test me!" Alfred warned. "Be on your way!"

But the other didn't move a muscle, even after Alfred began stomping toward him, bending low at the waist and bellowing as if he were about to rush at the old man. The giant seemed to grow higher and wider with each stride. *Is this Alfred nine feet tall now?* Bell wondered. *Ten?*

There was a tearing sound. The two halves of Alfred's blue coat slipped off a set of impossibly broad and now-hairy shoulders, then the round hat fell off of the giant's head—or, to be more precise, was pushed off his head by two narrow shapes rising from the top of his now-hairy skull.

"I's right!" the one-eyed man exclaimed, pointing to the horns protruding above the other's head. "You're one of 'em!"

"One of *what*?" demanded the creature who'd previously been a man named Alfred. "One of the monsters you fear in the dark?"

The one-eyed man didn't flinch. "Oh, I ain't afeared, Cap'n. Just curious."

The monster looked stupefied for a second. Then with a single bound he reached the old man, grabbed his shirt collar, and lifted him high into the air, the giant's shaggy bovine face now just inches from the other's dark face. Through a flared, light-red nostril, the beast blew short, hot breaths on the old man's scarred cheek.

Bell's own face burned as if *she* were the one struggling in the monster's grasp, getting blasted by steaming breaths. Indeed, her entire body felt flushed and drenched with sweat. But, oddly enough, it wasn't from fear.

Nothing in her experience—not the little fairy women she'd seen as a child, nor even the carcass of the great dog monster she'd once stumbled over in the forest—could have prepared her for the sight of a half-human giant bellowing in rage. And yet she found her initial horror had faded, leaving only an excited fascination.

Then the strange tableau grew stranger still, because the old man was no longer dangling from the shirt in the monster's hands. In fact, he was no longer an old man, or any kind of man at all. What dropped to the ground was a furry creature with oddly mismatched features—the wiry forelegs of a badger; thick hind legs that resembled those of a bear cub; a long, weasel-like body so emaciated its ribs threatened to poke through the skin; a narrow, ratlike tail; and the head and ears of . . . a rabbit.

Bell rushed forward, feeling giddy as if she were a little girl again running through the forest to her willow place. The Lord had sent her an answer to a question she hadn't thought to ask. Something to fill a hole in her heart she hadn't realized was there. For even before the smaller creature began to transform again, Bell knew what shape it would assume.

"John de Conquer!" she exclaimed as she reached his side.

"Very same, pretty Bell," said her longtime friend, who now looked like an older but still spry version of the jolly man she remembered—except, of course, for his tiny, wide-spaced eyes, his moist, diamond-shaped nose, and the long, furry ears that flopped down beside his long whiskers and puffed-out cheeks. John hurriedly yanked up the trousers he'd shed during his initial transformation.

"Well, nah, not the *very* same," he admitted, pulling the suspenders over his shoulders. "Somethin' odd's been happenin'. Havin' dreams lately, night and day. And just now 'nother one."

"Dreams 'bout what?" Bell asked.

"Who I is. Or was, in the before time. Before I got off that boat in Jamaica."

"You recall your home now?"

"Bits and flashes," John answered. "T'was a land across the sea. Sometimes I's a man. Sometimes I's somethin' else."

"Your monster shape," said Bell, still awed by the revelation.

John nodded. Then his eyes went wide, and his rabbit ears shot straight up. "Now I *do* recall somethin' else. A name, for when I's a beast. *Rompo*, other folks called me. Creature of the night. Man-eater."

417

Bell waved dismissively. "*You*, a man-eater? Never heard nothin' so foolish. Don't you know? I already seen your Rompo shape. Walkin' to freedom that day on the Popletown Road. You tricked them white men into tossin' you in that briar patch. You didn't eat 'em; you just put on your Rompo shape and wriggled away."

During their conversation, the two long-lost friends had paid no attention to the horned giant. Now Bell and John seemed simultaneously to remember they weren't alone. As they turned their eyes in its direction, Bell braced herself for a confrontation. But the sight that greeted her made her smile. It drew a hearty laugh out of John.

The fearsome, half-human monster was standing awkwardly in the road, watching them and inclining its great horned head to one side as it chewed its cud.

"One of the greatest captains ever sailed the seas, or so the tales go," John told Bell between giggles. "Always figured him more than a man."

"There's a monster word for me—a Minotaur," said the giant. "Years ago a shapechanger friend of mine named Mike Fink said I must be from a place called Greece. Don't remember. My first childhood memory is bein' washed up on the shore of Cape Cod, and an old sea captain takin' me in."

John de Conquer clicked his teeth excitedly. "Bell, meet Alfred Bulltop Stormalong."

The Minotaur snorted, this time in jest rather than in anger. "No need for all that. The captain who adopted me named me Alfred. His wife, my mother, always called me Bulltop. I didn't know why until much later, when I finally learned what I was. Must've changed sometimes as a child without realizing it, while I slept maybe. When I got my own ship, my crew dreamed up that 'A.B. Stormalong' nonsense."

Bell and John exchanged amused glances. "How 'bout us?" the Rompo asked. "Whatcha want us to call ya?"

The Minotaur stood in silence, its jaws resuming their circular chewing motion, its great bovine eyes fixed on them. Then its broad mouth formed a grin.

"My friends call me Bull."

Much later, after Bell had heard both "monsters" tell each other their stories, or at least as much of their stories as their clouded memories could reveal, she offered her heartfelt farewells and started back along the road, hoping to find shelter before the bright sunshine of late afternoon became the dwindling rays of twilight.

There was a lot to ponder. The two miraculous transformations she'd witnessed that day reminded Bell that the things of this world were not always what they seemed. She recalled the fanciful creatures from Mau-Mau Bett's bedtime stories. She thought about the monstrous beasts from the Bible she'd heard preachers talk about: Giants, Dragons, Behemoths, Leviathans. She remembered one sermon in particular about a prophet called Daniel and the four beasts he saw rising from the sea. A lion with the wings of an eagle. A great, deformed bear. A flying leopard with four heads. A terrible horned beast with iron teeth.

Never thought I'd see the like.

The stories she'd just heard—John de Conquer's tales of his mission to comfort, inspire, and liberate the enslaved, and Alfred Bulltop Stormalong's adventures on land and sea as he sought clues about his mysterious past—reminded Bell that she had her own mission to carry out. She hadn't departed Manhattan just to leave painful memories behind. She had traveled east to fulfill God's plan. To bring freedom to all human beings, and to save their souls.

But only human *souls?*

A verse from the book of Mark sprang to mind: "And he said unto them, 'Go ye into all the world, and preach the gospel to every creature.' "

To every *creature. A great big mission the Lord gave you, Bell. Best get to it.*

She closed her eyes and held up her hands to Heaven as she continued to walk.

No, she corrected herself. *Not Bell anymore. Got a new name to go with my mission.*

Eyes still closed, she would have barreled into the woman who was walking in the opposite direction if the latter hadn't dodged at the last moment.

"Where goest thou in such a hurry?" asked the woman, who wore a shawl and a long dress buttoned tightly at the collar despite the June heat.

"I go east, in service of the Lord."

The Quaker woman, for so her archaic speech revealed her to be, nodded in satisfaction. "What is thy name?"

"Sojourner," came the reply.

"Where does thee get such a name as that?"

"The Lord has given it to me."

"What was thy name before?"

"Bell."

The Quaker woman cocked her head to one side. "Bell what?"

"Whatever my master's name was."

A slight chuckle came from the prim woman. "Well, thee says thy name is Sojourner."

"Yes."

"Sojourner what?"

The woman who'd once been Bell saw much more than just the questioning eyes of the Quaker. She saw the deeper meaning that lay beneath the woman's seemingly simple query. *The things of this world aren't always what they seem*, Sojourner repeated to herself. In her mind's eye she saw John de Conquer, in his all forms. She saw Bull, too, first as a giant man and then as a gigantic monster.

Whether John wears the shape of a one-eyed sailor, a round-faced field hand, or a monster with a rabbit head, isn't he always my friend? Doesn't Stormalong belong on water, with or without his bull head? And though my Peter may thieve and lie and do me wrong over and over again, isn't he always my darling boy?

Another image sprang to mind: a visit to New York's Zion Church. Bishop Christopher Bush was giving a sermon about slavery and quoting the First Book of Samuel: "The Lord seeth not as man seeth, for man looketh on the outward appearance, but the Lord looketh on the heart."

You see through everything, don't you, God? You see what's really there. What really matters.

"Thou art my master, and Thy name is Truth," she said aloud, speaking not to the kindly Quaker woman but to the Lord they both served.

"Sojourner Truth shall be my abiding name till I die."

-END-

Made in the USA
Monee, IL
15 May 2022

96484435R00233